FOR EVER

A Willowhaven Romance

Jenny Hickman

Published by Jennifer Fyfe

www.jennyhickman.com

For Ever / Jenny Hickman - 1st ed.

Paperback ISBN: 9781962278164

Hardcover ISBN: 9781962278171

Paperback Design by: Hani Mashkoor @wavyhues

Character Art (Paperback): Kseniya Bocharova @romannaboch

Dust Jacket Design by: Kseniya Bocharova @romannaboch

Custom Chapter Headers: Coralie Renards @coralie.renards

Case Artwork by: Giulia Soeima @wizzylee

Dust Jacket Typography: Carmen Di Mauro @carmen.dmdesign

Illustrated Maps by: Andrés Aguirre Jurado @aaguirreart

For anyone worried you're not good enough.
You are.

THE KINGDOM OF
WILLOWHAVEN
KINGDOM OF LAUREL
Wrenwich
Swan Mea
Applewood
Frost Ridge
Thistletop
Glassmarsh
Rosehill

Gravale
Pleasant Valley
Crescent Peak
Two Rivers
Ferndon
Briardale
The Divide

Castle Rose
Madame E
Salon
The Black Rose
Ronan's Summer House
Well of Life
Cafe Row
Library
Quill Cottage

Rosehill City
Trevor's Cottage
the divide
Cathedral

Foreword

Although the summer loved the winter,
the two could never meet.
For the autumn and the spring divide them
Ensuring they'll never greet.

Although the day loved the night,
she must do so from afar.
For dawn and dusk always interrupt
keeping them apart.

The same fate befalls all Unseelie fae
who fall for Seelie charms.
If you see one, let her pass,
lest you come to harm.

— *An Unseelie Fable, Author
Unknown*

1

I n the kingdom of Willowhaven, fae are not permitted to marry before the age of twenty-five. Having grown up with an older brother, I'm not certain that twenty-five years is long enough for the men of our kind to mature.

My brother Theo vehemently agreed, downright refusing to leave our tiny mountain village of Gravale until our father forced him out of the house at twenty-eight.

I, on the other hand, have been waiting for this day ever since I was a little girl. With my twenty-fifth birthday on the horizon, it's finally my chance to find a love of my own.

A few weeks ago, Father gave me two options: I could either stay on the freezing mountain and hope a man near my own age would happen upon our village, or I could spend the next six months in the capital city of Rosehill with my cousin Nia.

Needless to say, I chose the latter.

Which brings me to this moment, nestled inside a plush carriage with crushed velvet pillows and damask curtains that sway each time we hit a bump in the road, staring out at a city even more beautiful than I imagined.

Don't get me wrong, Gravale was picturesque, with its sweeping vistas and snow-capped peaks, but this part of the kingdom is more refined. More *alive.* Cattle and sheep dot the endless emerald fields. The perfume of roses and lilacs drifts with the gentle breeze, sweeter than any dessert I've ever tasted.

Outside the carriage's lattice windows, thatch-roofed cottages wait in perfect rows, their gardens overflowing with the first blooms of spring. Birdsong and excited chatter fill the air, the world rousing from a solitary winter slumber.

There are people *everywhere*, more than I've ever seen in once place.

Families share tables outside pastel teahouses that line either side of the street; a crowd gathers on the steps of a temple; a couple embraces beneath an ivy-covered archway near the fountain.

I cannot believe I'm finally here.

My reflection wobbles in the wavy glass as I shift on the cushion. *Drats.* The daisies I tucked into the braid at my crown have wilted. Not exactly the look I was going for. If I pick them out now, there's no guarantee I'll get them all. I'd rather a bevy of sad flowers in my hair than have it look as if I rolled around in a field and accidentally picked up some floral hitchhikers.

The driver rolls to a stop in front of a sandstone cottage with fern-green sills and shutters. Blooming vines climb the corners, stretching green and purple fingers toward the thatched roof.

My mother always promised to bring us here, but Father wasn't quite as keen. Although he attended university in Rosehill, his heart has always belonged to the mountains.

I rub at the familiar pinching sensation in my chest. If only she could have made it back, just this once.

The carriage door swings wide, and I step down onto a slab of stone curving toward my aunt and uncle's arched doorway.

When I thank the driver, his lips tip into a smile beneath his bushy gray mustache before he rounds the carriage to collect my trunk.

This is it. The moment I've been waiting for. The beginning of the rest of my life.

Not everyone gets to reinvent themselves at twenty-five, but I do.

And I don't plan on squandering the opportunity.

The cottage door bursts open, startling me out of my reverie. A woman flies through the gap, the colorful ribbons adorning her stark-white curls trailing behind her like a rainbow. It might have been ten years since I last saw Nia Quill, but I'd recognize that crazy, cackling laugh anywhere.

I open my arms and plant my feet, bracing for the collision. She hits me so hard that we nearly end up in the ferns lining the path. She smells of jasmine and laughter and that mystical sweetness that clings to childhood memories.

"I cannot believe you're really here!" she squeals, drawing back, her shapely brows lifting and her gaze sweeping from my slippers to my gown. "And look at you. Your hair is so long!"

"I know." I had planned on cutting it before coming, but we only have one salon in Gravale and it's only open once a month.

Nia's snowy curls bounce as she shakes her head. "It's stunning, Kerris. Truly. And the color. I would kill for this shade."

The lilac hue washes me out in the winter, but a few days in this glaring sun should remedy that.

Nia's smile widens, showing off the smallest gap in her front teeth. "The men of Rosehill will be falling over themselves to court you."

"Please. With women like you around, I can't see them paying me the least bit of attention." Where did she get such a beautiful dress? The floral corset makes her waist look so tiny.

I press a hand to my own stomach, soft from too many desserts. Old Bonnie always told me that I could be slimmer if I tried. But I refuse to let my desire for trimmer hips and a smaller waist hinder my happiness. And sweets make me happy.

Any man worth his salt will love me either way.

Nia takes me by the shoulders. "When I turn twenty-five this August, we can celebrate me. Until then, it's your time to shine."

The cottage door opens once more, revealing a wafer-thin woman with short-cropped white hair that curls beneath her sharp jaw. "Good heavens!" She tumbles back, barely catching herself on the doorframe.

Nia rolls her eyes. "Calm down, Mother. It's only Kerris."

Aunt Cordelia blinks, then shakes her head as the color slowly returns to her cheeks. "Right. Of course it is. I'm sorry, but for a moment, I thought you were my sister."

My chest starts to tighten all over again.

"You are very welcome, dear," my aunt goes on. "It's been far too long."

Swallowing past the growing lump in my throat, I offer a warm smile. "Thank you so much for having me." I never would've been able to afford rent in the city without her generosity.

"Sure, what else could we do? Leave you to choose one of those mountain heathens? I think not!"

My father may be a "mountain heathen," but he is a good man. *That* is my only condition for a partner, someone who can love me the way my father loved my mother.

Just don't ask me how I'm supposed to do that in only six weeks. It's not a requirement to find a mate by one's twenty-fifth birthday, but for women, every year after twenty-five seems to make her less desirable, whereas men only become more sought-after.

It's asinine and makes no sense whatsoever, but I don't make the rules.

I'm merely governed by them.

My aunt disappears back into the house with a shout for my uncle to bring my trunk inside.

Looping her arm through mine, Nia tugs me toward the cottage. "Tell me all your news." Under her breath, she adds, "And by news, I mean, your requirements for a mate. Are you interested in men or women? Would you rather they have light or dark hair? How tall should they be? Do you prefer someone who works with their hands or an office sort? Personally, I'd go for the first. There's something about a man with calloused hands that makes my blood sing."

Coming from a place where my only options for a mate were older than the hills themselves, I hadn't considered anything beyond finding one with a good heart. Nia speaks about partners as if creating a shopping list for the market. "I prefer men, but beyond that, I honestly don't know."

"Fear not. You can have your pick of any man in this city." She comes to an abrupt halt on the stoop, the hem of her robin's-egg blue skirts sweeping against my ruffles. "Anyone except Nolan Graham. He's mine." A blush blooms across her freckled cheeks as she peers at me through honey-colored eyes. "If that's all right with you?"

As if I would ever set my sights on someone who is already spoken for. "This is your home, Nia. It's only right that you should have first pick."

"If you find a husband in Rosehill, then it will be your home too."

My stomach flutters at the thought. Imagine living in this splendid city, with all this activity right on your doorstep. Back home, the most exciting thing that happened was the yearly Festival of Goats.

It's just as uninteresting as it sounds.

Nia's gaze darts to something at my back. "*Oh, bollocks.*"

The unexpected exclamation makes me snort.

A woman with canary tresses coiled in perfect ringlets saunters up the lane, a peony-pink parasol draped over her equally pink shoulder.

"Who is that?" I whisper.

"Quite possibly the worst fae to have ever been born: Ivee Lynch." Nia spits the woman's name like a curse.

The young woman drifts past the gate with two others babbling behind her in matching celery-green chiffon.

The trio are almost to the lilacs when Ivee's head swings toward the house. Her footsteps slow, a frown marring her brow as she comes to a stop by the forsythia. "Nia Quill? Is that you lurking on the stoop?"

Nia stiffens. "*Shit.*"

I throw my hand over my mouth to muffle my laughter, but it's too late.

Ivee's narrowed gaze slithers over to me. "Who is that with you? I haven't seen her face before."

"Nosey bitch," Nia mutters under her breath as she tugs me back into the warm sunlight. Her tight smile reminds me of those creepy porcelain dolls I've seen in shop windows. "Ivee, *so* good to see you. This is my cousin Kerris Dawn. She's turning twenty-five on the fourteenth of May and has come down from Gravale for a husband."

The women in green trade wide-eyed glances while Ivee tugs the lace on her white kid gloves, her painted lips curling back in a sneer. "Welcome to Rosehill, Kerris. A word of advice: If you wish to find a husband in *this* city, you should purchase a gown from this century."

With a flick of her skirts, Ivee and her friends continue sauntering down the lane.

My cheeks feel like they've been set ablaze, and it has nothing to do with the sunlight dancing through the maple leaves.

Ruffles tickle my palms when I smooth a hand down my skirts. "What's wrong with my dress?" This is the nicest one I packed. The nicest one I *own*.

Nia pulls me back toward the house. "Don't listen to that jealous cow. She's just angry because she doesn't turn twenty-five until the end of June and all the men will be chasing after you instead."

Rosehill is the largest city in the kingdom; surely there are more than enough eligible partners to go around without having to fight over them.

Men are hardly worth such fuss.

Nia and I hurry up the stairs, through a cramped foyer, and into the heart of my aunt and uncle's home. To the right sits the living area with a floral sofa and a patterned rug. Bookshelves extend toward the plaster ceiling on either side of a barren stone fireplace.

If I follow the delicious scent of apples and cinnamon through the low door to my left, I bet I'll find the kitchen.

Nia pauses at the base of a whitewashed staircase, assessing me once more while her fingers tap against her lips. "Although, we should probably find you something else to wear. Do you have anything without ruffles?"

"I'm not sure I do." Apparently, ruffles were in fashion before my mother left Rosehill.

"Never mind. I have plenty of dresses you can borrow."

Is she mad? "I would never fit into one of your dresses." Not only is my chest three times the size of hers, but she's also a head taller than me.

"Of course you will. We just have to find one that covers those." She nods at my chest, then waggles her eyebrows. "I'm telling you,

Kerris, by the time I'm finished with you, the whole city will know your name."

*"You'd be surprised by the number of life's problems
that can be solved with dessert and a new frock."*

— A Seelie Guide to Happiness

Nia's silk skirt clings to my hips and catches beneath my feet every time I try to step forward. Although, it's not nearly as unappealing as her corset mashing my breasts together. "I cannot go out in public like this." If the entire city is to know my name, I'd rather it be for my ruffles than for having my nipples on display.

Nia purses her lips, stacks of gowns and skirts and corsets piled on either side of where she sits on the bed. "If we hemmed it—"

"The length is the least of my worries. My nipples are about to pop out."

"I've been told men are quite fond of nipples."

"Nia!"

She flops back onto her mattress, her cackle echoing around the room. The dresses tumble on top of her, burying my cousin beneath a mound of silk and lace.

I try to stomp over to the bed, but on my way, I trip on the skirt and collapse right on top of her with an unceremonious *oof*. I pluck a pinstriped corset from atop her face, finding her grinning beneath. "May I please have my own dress back?"

"Fine. But we are going straight to Market Street to buy you something without ruffles."

She says it as if I'm bound to protest when I'm as anxious to go shopping as she is.

By the time we find my dress, the entire room is a disaster. I offer to help Nia clean up, but she insists on leaving for town straightaway, saying she would simply share the guest room with me tonight and deal with the mess in the morning.

I change out of the too-small corset and back into my mother's favorite dress. The mauve satin might not be in the height of fashion with its high neckline and flouncy skirts, but at least my nipples are well hidden.

Together, we stroll down the cobbled streets while Nia points out all the best cafés, the library, a handful of greenhouses, and the apothecary that sells creams to make one's skin as smooth as butter.

The sloped-roof homes blend seamlessly with one another like a tiny mountain range. Then there are the houses built in trees that look as if they sprouted roots of their own. Imagine living in a tree house, with birds roosting outside your window, singing you awake every morning.

Sounds heavenly.

Friendly smiles abound, with most people either bobbing their heads or waving at Nia as we pass. The men sport fancy, multi-colored cravats and bow ties. Some even wear top hats. The women twirl lacy parasols over their shoulders, shielding their milky skin from the blazing sun.

And the *fashion.*

I've never seen so many different patterns of fabric.

Nia nods her chin toward two women strolling arm-in-arm across the street. "See that pink dress? Not the light one, the dark one. That's a Madame Ella." She inclines her head toward the burbling fountain in the square. "And the tangerine-colored one over there? That's a Madame Ella as well. She only uses the highest quality fabrics, and no two are alike. Other dresses wear you, but in a Madame Ella, *you* wear the dress."

"And you think this woman will be willing to make a dress for me?" By the sounds of it, the designer must be in high demand. What if she's too busy to take a commission? What if she costs a fortune? I brought a decent amount of money, but I'll need to pay for other things while I'm here too.

Nia comes to a stop outside a building with a cherry-red door. Colorful pansies spill from the low window boxes, a splash of color against gray stone and glass. "There's only one way to find out," she says, swinging the door aside.

Madame Ella's salon is as bright and colorful as the marbles I used to play with as a child. Fabrics of all colors and patterns drape from the walls, swathe dress forms, and hang like banners from the ceiling.

High-quality, indeed. The prints are some of the most intricate I've ever seen.

Where did she find such beautiful cloth? And would you look at all that lace? There must be over a hundred spools.

The unmistakable *click clack* of heels on stones drifts from the back of the establishment, followed by a sultry voice. "I'm afraid we have no more appointments today. You'll have to come back another time." A woman emerges from between two dress forms, gold bangles stacked on her wrists and colorful gemstones sparkling on her fingers.

When she sees us, she sucks in a breath, and her hand flies to her ruby lips.

Nia curtsys like the woman is the queen herself. "Good afternoon, Madame Ella. I'm not sure if you remember me. My name is Nia Quill. You made the dress I wore for my fifteenth birthday."

Madame Ella's gaze flicks to my cousin. "Emerald chiffon with a velvet trim, correct?"

Nia beams. "That's right." She grabs my hand. "I was telling my cousin what a brilliant designer you are. She just arrived from Gravale this afternoon, and—"

"Gravale, you say?" Madame Ella steps closer, squinting at me as if searching for the hole at the top of a very small needle. "You aren't by chance related to Celeste Hanson, are you?"

I force a smile even as my eyes start to burn. "Celeste was my mother."

"Remarkable," she murmurs with a shake of her head, sending her auburn hair tumbling over her shoulders. "The two of you could have been twins."

Everyone in our village said the same thing, and I loved and hated it in equal measure. To look in the mirror and see the person you miss most in the world staring back is a special kind of torture.

"What brings you down from the mountains?" she asks.

"Husbands."

Her eyes widen. "Surely, you're not already twenty-five."

"I will be in a few weeks."

Nia squeezes my fingers. "I know that you don't usually take walk-ins, but given your connection, I thought perhaps you might be willing to make an exception? All she has are her mother's ruffled dresses from thirty years ago." She gestures to my current ensemble, and the unease that had evaporated returns full force.

"Yes, well, ruffles were in fashion back when I made those gowns," Madame Ella says with the smallest smile.

"*You* made this dress?" I don't believe it.

"Of course. Your mother and I grew up together. Thick as thieves, we were. I designed and sewed all the dresses in her trousseau. If you have them with you, I could make some alterations and bring them into this century if you'd like."

"That sounds incredible." While I wouldn't mind a new dress or two, the thought of getting rid of my mother's gowns makes my heart ache anew. Especially since everything else that belonged to her was destroyed. "Thank you so much."

"It's my pleasure. Now, let's see what we can find for you in the meantime." She breezes past us in a jingle of bracelets and starts grabbing bolts of fabric.

This is going to be fun.

In the soft peach wash of sunset, the city looks downright magical.

Bells chime in the distance, marking the end of another hour. Birds soar through the pink clouds, searching for someplace to lay their heads for the night.

Nia takes both my hands, spinning me around so that my skirts billow like a daffodil's trumpet. "I told you that Madame Ella was a sorceress, didn't I?"

I'm not even sure sorceress accurately describes what Madame Ella managed to do in just a few hours. Not only did she tailor this teal silk and lace masterpiece, but she also promised four more dresses in the next few weeks. After seeing her behind a sewing machine, there's no doubt in my mind that she will be able to revive my mother's gowns.

The price she charged for it all feels scandalously low, even by Gravale standards—not that I'm complaining.

"Thank you, Nia. I couldn't have done any of this without you." I yawn into my fist. I'm going to sleep like the dead tonight.

"You act as if the day is over when it's only begun."

"You have more plans?" From the gleam in her eye, I'm not sure whether to be nervous or excited.

"Of course I do. You're not only here to shop for dresses, Kerris." She tugs me back toward the city center. "You're here to shop for a husband, and it just so happens that I know where to find the perfect one."

"Small talk is overrated. Find someone with whom you can share the silence."

— *Kerris Dawn, an observation*

When Nia said we were going to a pub, I assumed she meant a snug little room with a turf fire, low stools crowded with men in wool caps, and an unhealthy dose of cigar smoke thickening the air.

Instead, The Black Rose is a spacious warehouse-turned-brewery, with twinkling fae lights stretching across the exposed-beam ceiling. Tables extend from within the space, spilling onto the streets so patrons can enjoy the balmy spring air over a frosty pint.

The best part is, there are men *everywhere*, each one more handsome than the one before.

As Nia and I slowly pick our way through the crowd, we're met by no less than ten who offer to purchase our drinks. Nia says yes to two of them, and we end up taking a table at the back with two half-pints of amber cider a piece.

Nia gracefully settles herself on the stool like a queen taking her throne, spreading and smoothing her skirts so they lay just right. I, on the other hand, must use the bar at the bottom to climb up like a child.

Not only did I inherit my mother's lavender tresses, but I also got her height as well—or lack thereof.

The liquid in Nia's glass sloshes as she extends it toward me. "To finding a husband."

I tap my glass against hers. "To finding a *good* husband." By the looks of it, neither of us would have any trouble finding a man willing to accept our proposals. The issue will be finding the *right* man.

The icy cider tickles my throat, tasting faintly of the apple juice I used to drink as a child.

Two men share the table next to us, oblivious to the world as they smile and stare into each other's eyes, their hands laced as one.

What must it be like to be so taken with another that you notice nothing else?

I cannot wait to find out.

Will I meet my future husband tonight? Only time will tell.

Nia sips slowly, scanning the crowd as if searching for someone.

Setting down my drink, I lean an elbow on the table. "Is your man here?"

The ribbons in her curls flutter when she shakes her head. "Not yet. But he will be soon."

"How did the two of you meet?"

"We met here, actually. He was the only one in his group who didn't offer to buy me a drink."

"And that made you want him?" Seems a bit odd to me.

"No, his beautiful eyes and pouty lips did that. I decided to give him a chance because of his response when I asked why he didn't offer."

I find myself leaning closer, the condensation on my glass slipping down my fingers.

She mirrors my position, resting her forearms on the glossy tabletop. "He told me that he wouldn't catch my attention by being like all the rest. So, naturally, I asked why he wanted to catch my attention when there were so many other women in the pub. Do you know what he said? He said, 'I haven't noticed any of the others since the moment you walked through the door.' When I tell you I swooned, I mean I damn near fainted."

The nicest thing a man has said to me was that I looked like I had strong teeth. That was about four years ago, when Father and I took a trip to one of the villages off the mountain.

"He sounds amazing." Perhaps her fellow has a single brother.

Fae light sparkles in Nia's eyes as she tilts her head toward the entrance. "I do hope you think so, because Nolan and his friends just walked in."

Sure enough, three newcomers traverse the maze of people and tables. The golden-haired one at the front must be Nolan. Although he appears to be a few inches shorter than the two at his back, he is quite possibly the most handsome man I've ever seen.

Actually, no. Handsome isn't the correct word. He's downright beautiful, like an oil painting by one of the old masters you might find hanging above some rich person's fireplace.

Nia's fingers curl around my wrist. "This is just wonderful. I was hoping Nolan would bring the prince."

I swallow so hard, my ears pop. "Did you say *prince*?"

Her shapely brows lift, her eyes widening with shock. "Did I not mention that Nolan works for Prince Ronan Reve?"

"No, you didn't." That is definitely a detail I would've remembered.

"Nolan is Ronan's personal guard. The prince just turned twenty-seven last week. Rumor has it, he is finally on the hunt for a wife. The two of you would make the most stunning match!" She tucks the hair that has escaped my braid back behind my ears and then pinches both my cheeks. "There. Now, you're perfect."

Perfect.

Heavens, do I despise that word and the unwelcome weight it brings. Still, Nia means well, so I do my best not to let my smile falter.

"Oh! I almost forgot!" She takes both of my hands in hers and squeezes my fingers as she looks me dead in the eye. "Do not gawk when you look at the prince. He hates that."

Right. No gawking.

One final squeeze of my fingers and Nia slips off her stool, running straight into the arms of a man with dark chestnut hair almost as curly as hers.

It would appear Nolan *isn't* the one with golden curls after all.

How interesting...

Not that he's not handsome—he is. But when compared to the one in the front, I wouldn't look twice.

"If that's the greeting my guard receives, then I can only imagine how happy you are to see your favorite prince," the beautiful man drawls with a roll of eyes so blue, they'd make a cornflower jealous.

Prince Ronan Reve.

My jaw wants to drop, but I keep the hinge firmly locked.

Nia's giggle sounds a bit maniacal as she pulls away from Nolan and dips into a curtsy. "So good to see you again, Prince Ronan."

"You as well, Nia." The prince's gaze finds mine, and his eyes widen. "Who is this stunning creature at your table?"

Nia catches my arm and drags me off the stool. I land with a wobble, but the prince is there to steady me. The way his warm hands curve around my arms makes curtsying impossible.

Heavens. His eyes are even more arresting up close.

"This is my cousin Kerris Dawn, from Gravale." Nia's voice

drifts from somewhere else. Right now, it's only the prince and me and his beautiful, beautiful eyes. "She is twenty-five on the fourteenth of May and has come to Rosehill for a husband."

The prince's thumbs sweep back and forth against my skin, sending chills racing down my arms. "Isn't that fortuitous? I suddenly find myself in dire need of a wife. How would you like to be a princess, Kerris Dawn?"

Imagine *me*, a princess.

It's a good thing he's holding me upright; otherwise, my legs would give right out.

"I might consider it," I hedge, not wanting to seem too desperate.

The third man who came in with them steps out from the prince's shadow. Behind a pair of round spectacles blink kind green eyes. His chestnut hair curls slightly around his pointed ears in the most playful way. His gaze darts to me before settling on my cousin. "Nia, you're looking as beautiful as ever."

"You're too sweet, Trevor." My cousin gives the man's arm a friendly pat. "Kerris, this is Trevor Dillon. He works in the library as one of the city's most esteemed records keepers."

How interesting. And he works in a library? Sounds like heaven to me. When I smile at Trevor, his cheeks turn the most endearing shade of pink. "I love reading," I confess. When you're stuck on the side of a mountain in the dead of winter, there's little else to do. "Perhaps you would be willing to show me around the library some time?"

Trevor's glasses slip down his nose when he offers an eager nod. "It would be my pleasure, Miss Dawn."

"Kerris, please. Miss Dawn makes me sound like an old maid."

Ronan steps in front of Trevor, nearly stomping on his boot. "The library at the castle is twice as large as the one in the city," he says. "If you'd like to see it as well, I'd be more than happy to arrange a visit."

An invitation to Castle Rose on my very first night? I cannot wait to tell Father. "That sounds lovely."

A streak of pink flashes in my peripherals, and the woman we met outside Nia's cottage, Ivee Lynch, waltzes through a gap in the tables. The two women from earlier follow closely behind, as if tied to the bodice of Ivee's blush-pink gown.

"Prince Ronan! Oh, Prince Ronan!" Ivee waves a gloved hand toward the prince, sparing the rest of us not so much as a glance.

The prince's smile slips into a grimace, and I'm fairly certain I hear him groan.

Ivee doesn't stop until she has inserted herself right into the middle of our group. "What are you doing here, darling? You said that you were too exhausted to come out tonight."

Prince Ronan's teeth flash with his bright smile. "A prince is entitled to change his mind," he says. When he winks at me, my cheeks start to heat.

Ivee whirls, her eyes narrowing when they land on me. Her gaze slides down to my new gown, and she snatches a handful of my skirts, examining the fabric with a furrowed brow. "Is this a Madame Ella?"

"It is." I tug my skirt out of her grasp. Thanks to her strangling the silk, it's going to need steamed.

"But...she isn't taking new bookings until next year."

"Familial connections," Nia chimes in, hooking her arm through mine, creating a solid line of defense against Ivee's scowl. "If you'll excuse us for just a moment..." She sweeps me through a gap in the tables and straight into the privy.

The moment she turns the lock, she starts pacing from the sink to the toilet and back again, all while muttering under her breath. "That bloody witch has the worst possible timing. How did she even know the prince was here?"

"Does it matter?" Yes, she seems rude and awful, but we shouldn't let one person ruin our night.

"Of course it does! For the last two years, I've listened to that wretched cow boast over having her pick of the men. If she wins the prince, then she will be even more insufferable. Imagine Ivee Lynch as the next Queen of Willowhaven." Nia shudders. "If that happens, I might have to throw myself into The Divide. I was hoping you and Ronan would hit it off, but that cannot happen if she insists on showing up like a bad case of hemorrhoids."

While Ronan is handsome, I only just met the man. As far as I'm concerned, if Ivee wants him, she's welcome to him. "I don't want to be in competition with her." I don't want to be in competition with anyone.

Love is something you fight for, not fight over.

"Ivee will see you as competition whether you want to be or not. She is now our nemesis."

"Nemesis" seems a little dramatic. After all, there are twice as many men in this pub than women, so it's not like they're a rare commodity. Besides, just because someone proposes does not mean the other person must accept. Take my brother Theo, for instance. His first month in Applewood, he turned down four proposals.

If the prince wants to marry Ivee, wonderful. I wish them all the happiness in the world.

Nia's eyes widen. "I have an idea. Stay here. I'll be right back." She unlocks the door and slips back into the pub without another word.

I love my cousin, but I am not going to wait in a privy simply because she told me to. Instead, I return to our table where Ivee and her two friends have claimed our stools, blocking the prince and leaving me to stand awkwardly beside Trevor.

Nia and Nolan speak in quiet tones over by the wall while she casts furtive glances my way. Heaven only knows what she's telling him.

Trevor adjusts the spectacles on the end of his nose, his lips pursing. "The city library has a thousand more books than the one in the castle."

The way he says it, so matter-of-factly, makes me chuckle. I wonder what the prince would have to say to that—not that he's paying us any attention. "Does it? Well, your library sounds far more impressive to me."

When I catch him glancing at me, his blush returns full force. He reminds me of my father in a way, reserved and soft-spoken. He's not hard on the eyes, either.

"Would you like another cider, Kerris?"

"I would love one. Thank you."

The prince appears behind him, clamping a hand on Trevor's shoulder. "Save your coins for your new roof, Trev." From his pocket, he withdraws a heavy purse. "Let the royal treasury handle this round—and all the others—tonight."

4

"Even the richest fae use the privy."

— *A Seelie Guide to*
Happiness

I've been abandoned and I don't even care.

Nia and Nolan have absconded to some dark corner to get lost in each other, leaving me with Trevor, Ivee, her two shadows, Florence and Aurelia, and a monologuing prince.

Prince Ronan tells the most fascinating stories. He's been to every town in our kingdom—including Gravale when he was a little boy. Not only that, but he has also visited the other six fae kingdoms as well. He's seen so much in his twenty-seven years, and I've seen so little.

With every sip of cider he takes, his stories grow more fantastical. Part of me wonders if they're entirely true. Not that it matters, I suppose, when they're so entertaining.

Trevor drinks silently by my side. Every so often, I catch him peeking at me and offer him a warm smile. Mostly, I stare at the prince.

Probably not the smartest thing considering the way Ivee has attached herself like a leech on his arm, but I'm afraid it cannot be helped.

He's so beautiful. It really is too bad Ivee's head keeps blocking my view.

Nia stumbles back and swipes her drink, knocking it over in the process. Ivee's shriek cuts through the chatter as amber liquid splashes all over her skirts.

"Oops," Nia says with mock sincerity, her lips pressed to the side of her glass.

Ivee shoots her a glower oozing such hatred, I feel a chill in my bones. Her skirts swish as she whirls and stomps to the privy. Florence and Aurelia follow in her wake, assuring her they can "hardly notice" the stain.

Do they go everywhere with her? Imagine the three of them all curled in the same bed, snoring in perfect harmony.

Nia winks at me before skipping back to where Nolan waits and leaping on top of him with an exuberant kiss.

I giggle into my...*empty* glass?

Where did all my cider go?

When I glance back up, fae light flickers across Ronan's face, making him look positively angelic.

The prince leans in close, bringing with him the scent of cider and citrus. "Have you seen the Black Rose gardens yet, Kerris?" he whispers.

"Not yet." Truth be told, I didn't even know there were gardens.

The prince takes my glass straight out of my hand and gives it to Trevor. "Come with me and I'll show you." His hand falls over my fingers braced at his elbow as he brings me out a back door and into the moon-kissed night.

This isn't a garden; this is an entirely new world. One where roses rule and fuchsias abound. Redbrick paths cut through the maze of blooms, with the occasional bench tucked into shadowed alcoves.

"I've never seen anything as beautiful as this."

Ronan plucks a lilac from a branch, twirling the stem between his fingers before handing the flower to me. "And I've never seen anything as beautiful as you."

Warmth bubbles in my chest, threatening to spill out in a giggle.

"Tell me about you, Kerris. About life in Gravale."

Where do I even begin? "The village is small, and the population is aging. Most of those with children have relocated to the towns and cities off the mountains, where the land isn't as unforgiving." In Gravale, one wrong step or strong gust of wind, and you could find yourself plummeting to your death.

"That sounds atrocious. No wonder you left. Is your family still there?"

"My older brother Theo moved to Applewood six months ago. But my father loves the mountains, so he chose to remain. He raises goats." I think he might love the goats more than the mountains. "My mother..." That familiar ache pinches my heart. "She passed when I was five."

You'd think that after almost twenty years, the heavy weight of grief would have subsided. All it does is burrow deeper into your marrow, rearing its ugly head when you least expect it.

I don't want to be sad tonight, not when I'm lost in the moonlight with a handsome prince. "Tell me about your family, Prince Ronan."

"Just Ronan is fine. There's no need for such formalities between us." His fingers caress mine with soft, sensual strokes. "As for me, I have no brothers or sisters. Both my parents are still living —much to my mother's chagrin." Impossibly blue eyes lock with mine, wide pupils reflecting the waning moon. His head tilts, bringing us within a whisper of each other. "Can I tell you a secret —something I've never told anyone?"

Tell me all your secrets.

All your fears.

All your dreams.

I'll keep them safe in my heart.

"Of course."

His chest brushes against mine with his heavy exhale. "Part of me wishes I wasn't born a prince. My true passion—oh, never mind. You're sure to think I'm mad if I tell you."

"I won't. I swear."

"All right, then. My true passion lies in carpentry. In building things that will last forever."

The forgotten lilac still pinched between my fingers brushes against my skirts. How intriguing. A carpenter prince. "What sort of things do you build?"

The corners of his lips lift into the tiniest, most mischievous smile. "How about I call by your uncle's cottage on Thursday and show you?"

He wants to see me again. *Me.* The daughter of a goat farmer. When I tell Theo, he'll think I'm spinning yarns.

Could this night get any better?

"I would like that very much."

His perfect smile stretches across his handsome face as his gaze drops to my lips.

Is he going to kiss me? He is! Prince Ronan Reve is about to kiss me.

I've waited my entire life for this moment and now that it's finally here—

My lips are...they're too chapped. And my breath probably tastes like cider, and I haven't bathed since I left Gravale...

"I should get back to Nia," I blurt, my cheeks ablaze as my heart thunders against my breast.

The prince blinks at me from only a breath away. "W-what?"

What am I *doing*?

Why didn't I just let him kiss me?

I am such a dolt, but it's too late to take it back now. The moment is over; the spell broken. "Nia. She'll be worried about me." Has a more terrible liar ever existed? Nia probably doesn't even realize I'm gone.

The harsh sound of Ronan clearing his throat cuts through the quiet night. "Right. Of course. Let me bring you inside."

By the time we reach our table, his smile has returned, but mine is nowhere to be found. How did I muck that up so thoroughly?

Trevor darts a glance between us, a glass of cider clutched in his fist. "Here, Kerris. I bought this for you."

Ronan's brow furrows. "I said I would buy the drinks."

"You weren't here," Trevor clips as he takes a swig of his own.

"Thank you, Trevor. That was kind of you." Thank heavens for cider. My mouth is as dry as the Fairsing Desert.

Would you look at that? Ivee no longer wears a pink dress, but Aurelia's green one. Meanwhile, Aurelia looks utterly miserable as she clutches the front of her skirts to hide the cider stain. Ivee is too busy glaring at me to notice her friend's discomfort.

Trevor clears his throat, his cheeks growing rosier with each passing second. "Would it be all right if I called on you this Thursday, Kerris? I could bring you by the library. Or, if you'd prefer, we could go for tea. Or both. Or if you'd rather do something else—" His fingers drum an uneven beat against his thighs.

"Both sounds lovely, but the prince and I already have plans on Thursday. What about tomorrow instead?"

His mouth drops open, and his glasses slip down his nose. "No one goes to town on Wednesdays."

"Why not?"

Ronan throws an arm around Trevor, rattling the poor man so badly, his glasses fall to the ground. "That's the day my father has graciously allotted for the Unseelie to visit our well."

Trevor's blush ignites as he extricates himself and bends down to retrieve his glasses.

Unseelie fae.

The opposite of us Seelie in every way. We prefer spring and summer while they'd rather live in eternal autumn and winter. If we're light, they're darkness. We're the day and they're the night.

I always assumed that they kept to their side of The Divide, while we remained on ours.

There are countless legends about where The Divide came from. My favorite is the tale of an ancient Unseelie King who fell in love with the first Seelie Queen. He betrayed her with another, and in her rage, she cleaved the world in half, separating the two factions of fae for all of eternity.

"Why don't the Unseelie use their own well?" Every town has one—even Gravale. Here in the city, not only do they have a well, but also immortal water runs in their taps.

Ivee snorts. "Because the monsters prowling the other side of The Divide have drained their wells dry."

Trevor settles his glasses back onto his nose with a quiet huff. "That's a myth, Miss Lynch. No one knows what happened to their wells—or if there were even wells to begin with."

"Has no one ever thought to ask them?" Seems a simple enough solution.

"No one cares," Ronan says with a chuckle. "If it were up to me, they wouldn't have access to our well at all."

He must be joking. "They would die without immortal water." If we stopped drinking, our lives would wane after only a handful of seasons. With the water, we could live to see two hundred, even three hundred summers.

"And I'd say good riddance to the lot of them."

That seems unnecessarily cruel. The Unseelie might be different from us, but they're still fae. How would the prince feel if our roles were reversed? If they were the ones with the wells and we had to rely on their generosity to survive?

Ivee sidles closer to the prince, her head bobbing in agreement. "You're right, too. The Divide is an abomination, just like those Unseelie beasts."

Ivee is the only beast I see. "Well, I'd love to see it myself." They say The Divide is so large, it's impossible to see across to the other side. It's so deep, there is no bottom.

Nia appears to my right, swiping the glass straight out of my hand. "See what for yourself?" She takes a swig, then drags the back of her hand over her puffy lips. Behind her, Nolan's hair is sticking straight up, his own lips just as swollen.

I steal back my glass for one final drink. "The Divide."

Ronan's grin widens. "Why don't we go now?"

Nolan presses a hand to the prince's shoulder. "Sire, that isn't wise."

Trevor's face has gone green with horror. "Don't be reckless, Ronan. The Unseelie aren't the only monsters that lurk on that side of the canyon."

"You mean the wolves?" Ronan chuckles. "It's all a load of bollocks, if you ask me. There hasn't been a wolf sighting in over a decade. Father says they're all extinct."

Perhaps it's the alcohol talking, but the idea of seeing The Divide makes my heart beat a little harder. The rhythm of the unknown. Of adventure.

I take Nia's hand. "I'll go if you do."

My cousin chews on her lower lip, darting a glance at a narrow-eyed Nolan. "Why not?"

"It's settled, then." Ronan hooks an arm around each of our shoulders, drawing us against his warm body. "We're going to The Divide."

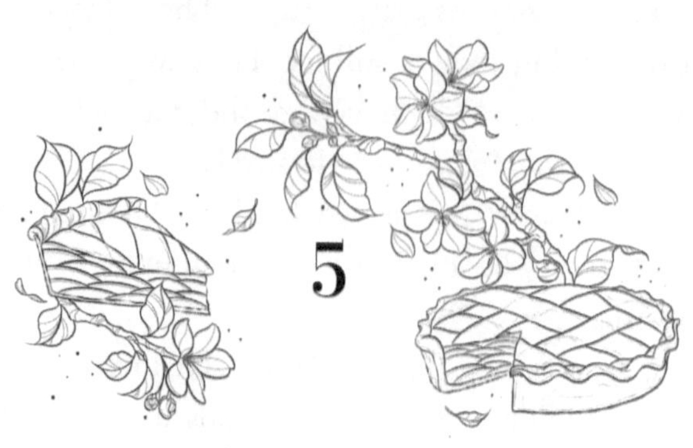

5

Despite Nolan's best attempts to deter the prince, Ronan escorts us out of the pub and onto the dark streets where gas lamps flicker atop curved iron posts. Trevor brings up the rear with Ivee and her cohorts tittering about how this is a terrible idea.

People dance and sing in the streets while passionate couples share clandestine kisses in alleyways.

Love is definitely in the air.

Grumbling a curse, Nolan leads us down the wide street to the square where the city's well waits atop three stone stairs.

Like everything else in this city, Rosehill's well is far more ornate compared to the one in Gravale, with carved arches that come to points beneath the slate roof.

Nia's skirts swish as she dances along next to me, her cheeks

30

ruddy with excitement. "Look at you, Kerris." She pokes my arm. "You're the belle of the night."

Please. "I am only a passing fancy."

"A passing fancy, my arse. You have caught the attention of not one but *two* of Rosehill's most eligible bachelors." She holds up two fingers and wiggles them in my face. "Ronan has been fending off offers of marriage for the last two years. Something tells me that is about to change."

As if he can hear Nia's whispered musings, Ronan turns and gives me a wink. My face ignites. "When we were in the gardens—"

She snags my hand, urging me to a stop next to a darkened apothecary. "You went to the gardens with Ronan? Do you know what this means? That is akin to a declaration of love. He is smitten, as I knew he would be. Queen Ivee Lynch will now only exist in my worst nightmares."

Please, the prince is far from smitten. Enamored, perhaps, but that is likely because I'm still a stranger to him. I'm not foolish enough to believe the daughter of a goat farmer could ever win the heart of a prince.

Nia keeps hold of me as we walk down the street toward looming darkness. Unease prickles inside my chest, a silent warning that I ignore. If the kingdom's sole heir is willing to come here with only one guard, I'm certain we'll be all right. "Have you ever been to The Divide?"

"Once when I was younger. There's a bridge the Unseelie cross when they access the well."

"Have you ever seen one?"

"Goodness no. I stay away from the square on Wednesdays. But one of Nolan's friends said the sight of them would turn your blood cold. They're big as giants and covered in warts, with hairy hands and fangs the size of your thumbs."

They sound terrifying, indeed.

Ronan falls back to drape an arm across my shoulder. "Fear not,

Kerris. If any one of those Unseelie bastards deign to show their faces, I'll protect you." He pats the bejeweled dagger hanging from his belt.

While I appreciate the sentiment, it's hard to imagine Ronan taking on a giant Unseelie warrior and emerging the victor. The prince seems more likely to use the dagger to butter his toast than to stab someone.

"What about me, darling?" Ivee whines from the back of the group.

"I'll protect you too," he says, but it sounds more like an afterthought.

The cobblestones end abruptly, meeting a dirt path cluttered with foot and hoofprints. Light from the final lamp post is no match for the darkness beyond. We come to a stop at the edge of that golden arc, peering into the night. Nolan withdraws his blade and then nods to Ronan. Together, they step into the shadows.

Nia clings to me as we tiptoe behind them, listening for any suspicious sounds in the silence.

The dirt gives way to a wide bridge of planks and rope that stretches across a black void. The weathered boards bow in the center, as if on the verge of snapping under any bit of weight.

My slipper grazes the stones clinging to the ledge, knocking one free. It tumbles into the abyss, vanishing completely. I listen for the sound of it hitting the bottom, but only silence answers.

"You've seen it. We should go back now," Trevor calls from the cobbles. Ivee and her followers wait next to him, their hands folded as if in prayer.

Ronan snorts. "Why? Are you afraid of the big, bad Unseelie fae?"

"Of course not."

"Prove it." Ronan tilts his head toward the bridge. "Cross The Divide."

"That is madness," Trevor shoots back. "No one crosses the bridge."

"*Really?* I seem to recall the Unseelie crossing every Wednesday."

"You know what he means," Nolan mutters.

Trevor's spine snaps straight. "Being afraid isn't the same as being weak."

"No? You sure about that?" Ronan nudges Nolan aside and steps onto the first plank. The wood groans and creaks, warning him to stop there.

Ivee whimpers from behind her hands. "Don't do this, Ronan. I beg you." Florence and Aurelia join in her pleading, their faces drained of color.

Perhaps it is my ignorance, but I don't believe the Unseelie could possibly be as awful as everyone seems to believe.

If they were that lawless, they wouldn't abide by a mere rule that keeps them from crossing the bridge any other day. If they were that murderous, there wouldn't be a bridge in the first place.

Ronan takes another backward step. "Come on, Trevor. I'll go with you. I'll even hold your hand if you want."

Trevor twists on his heel and stalks back toward the glow of town.

Nolan's fists bunch at his sides. "You've proven your point, Ronan. You can come back now."

Ronan keeps stepping back and back, throwing me a wink before turning around and continuing until he's nothing more than a silhouette, swallowed by darkness

Raking both hands through his hair, Nolan steps onto the bridge. "Ronan!"

There is no answer.

"Ronan! This isn't fucking funny," Nolan roars.

Is it just me or...is the bridge beginning to sway in the still air?

Nia's grip on me tightens. "Look at the bridge."

A distant howl pierces the silence, lifting the hairs at the nape of my neck.

"The wolves!" Ivee screeches. "They're back! They're going to kill my prince, and it's all your fault, Kerris Dawn!"

She's right...it *is* my fault. If I hadn't asked to see The Divide, none of this would've happened—

A shadow slices through the blackness.

Ronan sprints toward us, his face as pale as his shirt, his arms pumping up and down. "*Run!*"

Nia and I whip toward the city lights, but my feet get tangled up in my skirts and I go down hard, cracking my knees on the road and dragging my poor cousin down with me. By the time we stumble to our feet, Ronan has already raced past, a cloud of dust lifting in his wake.

So much for his promise of protection.

Like the fool I am, I look back over my shoulder to where three distinct shadows wait on the bridge. Not of wolves, but of men.

The shadows make no attempt to follow, but there is no doubt what they are.

Taller than any man I've ever seen, broad of shoulders, and dark as the night around us.

Unseelie fae.

"Kerris!" Nia shouts, her hand in Nolan's as he leads her back toward the cobblestones.

Hearing my name kickstarts my heart, and I hobble to catch up. We sound like a herd of cattle as we run toward the safety of the city to where the others wait beneath the streetlamps. Ivee grips Ronan's shirt with both hands. The poor man looks as if he's been chased by a ghost.

The prince tugs out of Ivee's iron grip and takes a halting step toward me. "Are you all right, Kerris?"

I press a hand to my pounding heart, forcing air into my

burning lungs. "I'm fine." Not that he seemed to care only a few moments ago.

"Did you see them?" Aurelia asks, her voice high and childlike.

Ronan shudders, bracing his hands on his knees as he gasps. "Yes, and they were disgusting. With horns and blood dripping from their fangs. And there were bones everywhere."

That does sound terrifying, except... I squint toward the darkness behind us. "Were there lights on the other side?"

Ronan shakes his head. "Only darkness."

If there were no lights, then how did he see them so clearly?

6

Everett

Maddox's legs swing off the side of the bridge, dangling into the canyon. "How far down do you think it goes?"

"Who the fuck cares?" Gryffin mutters, poking the end of his sword into the fire, sending sparks swirling into the fog.

"I the fuck care," Maddox shoots back, collecting one of the stones from the pile beside him and launching it into the void of nothingness that lives between our world and theirs. *The Seelie fae.* A bunch of colorful, smiley bastards who love nothing more than to show off their flat, useless teeth and their sprawling gardens.

The only thing that grows wild out here is death and despair. And wolves.

It has been years since one of the monsters that used to roam freely in these forests has been spotted. Still, we remain ever vigilant. It is either that or die.

I would rather be gutted by some wolf's snarling maw than expire due to decay.

The flames dance higher into the mist when Gryff stabs a blackened log. "I wish he would stop throwing those damn rocks."

Something soars over my head, hitting Gryff square between the eyes. He leaps to his feet, his muscles coiled, and his teeth bared in a growl.

Maddox does not even have the good sense to stand and meet his fighting stance. "Awe, is the big, scary fae going to hurt me?"

"Fuck off. Both of you." We are not here to piss around. We are here to do a job. A job we cannot do if they keep snarling at each other.

When a stone hits my back, I do not budge. I would sooner launch myself into the canyon than give in to Maddox's attempts to rile us. The man bores too easily for this position. He really should try tanning hides or join the barterers on their treks to the other Unseelie territories.

An idle Maddox is a menace, indeed.

"You need to lighten up, Ever. Would not want that pretty face of yours to end up in a permanent scowl like poor Gryff's."

Gryff drops back onto one of the flat stones encircling the fire with a huff, stabbing a little harder, no doubt picturing Maddox's grinning face in the flickering orange and red flames. Of all the males in our clan, Gryff is the one I would not cross. Maddox must not have a brain in his head because he does not have the same reservations.

Another one of Maddox's rocks is launched into nothingness, vanishing without a sound. "Have you given Leah Locke an answer yet?"

I nudge what remains of a femur with the toe of my boot,

scooting it back into place with the rest of the bones lining the path. "Not yet." If it were up to me, I would never respond. Maybe if I leave it long enough, she will forget she asked me in the first place.

Maddox tosses the next stone into the air, catching it once more without even looking at the thing. "Do me a favor, will you? Let her down gently so she does not hate the rest of us by association."

Gryff snorts. "Like Leah Locke would ever consider mating with the likes of you."

This time when the stone comes, Gryff is ready, snatching it from the air before it strikes his forehead. A rare smile crosses his face before his favorite expression of utter disdain for everything and everyone returns.

Maddox grins, his teeth a vicious flash of white in the darkness. "Who said anything about mating? I just want to bring her to my barrel-top, bend her over, and—"

I pick up the biggest rock I can find and throw it at his exasperating head.

Maddox rolls in the nick of time, and the stone cracks against the edge of a plank before vanishing into the abyss. "You bastard. That almost hit me."

"You should not talk about females like that."

He blinks at me, his brow furrowing. "Why not? Wren likes it."

Gryffin grabs another log from the pile we gathered, adding it to the top of the fire. "That is not what Ivan says."

"What does that mean?"

Stab. Stab. Stab. "Sounds like a question for Wren. I heard she proposed to him last night."

"Fuck off. She did not." Maddox looks to me for the truth.

"I am afraid he is right. When I saw her this morning, she bore his mark." There is sure to be an announcement soon.

My stomach grumbles with hunger; the venison we had for dinner was not nearly enough to keep me sated. I retrieve a piece of dried jerky from my pack and bite off a chunk, but the peppered seasoning burns the shit out of my tongue.

This is the last time I let Gryffin make the food.

Maddox catches a handful of stones and chucks them into the void. "Well, that is a knife to the bollocks..."

Flickering firelight dances in Gryff's eyes when they meet mine from over the fire. "Maddox is right, though. You should let Leah Locke down easily."

I love that the two of them think me completely heartless. Leah has been my friend since we were children. I am hardly going to make her feel like shit because she had the terrible idea to choose me as her mate. "Who says I will not accept?" Binding myself to Leah might finally silence the whispers that follow wherever I go.

Maddox's hoot of laughter makes my teeth grind. "No offense, but the orphaned son of the village pariah does not belong with the chieftain's daughter."

I would take offense if it were not true. I have done everything possible to shed the humiliating titles earned through no fault of my own. Trained harder. Volunteered for the most dangerous hunting expeditions. Stood guard day in, day out, doing my duty to my people.

Mating with Leah is my chance to finally make everyone see me for who I am and not as my parents' mistake.

The problem is that I feel nothing for the woman beyond friendship.

While that might be enough for most of the males of our clan, I am not sure it is enough for me. Especially when my mother's final words ring in my ears every night before I go to sleep and every morning when I wake.

"Find love, Ever. Promise me that you will settle for nothing less."

I made the promise, not knowing how difficult it would be to keep.

We are warriors created to survive the harshest conditions. Trained to kill.

Love is not meant for our world.

Maddox picks up another stone, tossing it into the air once before drawing his arm back and—

A distant sound pricks my ears.

"Wait!" I hiss.

Maddox freezes mid-throw.

Gryff straightens, his head turning this way and that before he falls still. "Voices."

I nod. The sounds are not coming from the forest or the well-worn path along the canyon. I point toward the bridge. "Across the canyon."

By the sounds of it, there are multiple Seelie. Male and female.

Gryffin grabs the bucket of silty sand, dumping it over the fire. Smoke dances from the ground, curling into the air before melting into the fog.

One moment, Maddox is on the bridge, the next, he is beside me, searching the ground for the one thing he should know better than to leave behind. "Where the fuck is it?" he hisses, combing the stones surrounding the fire.

Gryffin sidles up next to me, his dagger in one fist and his short sword in the other while Maddox scrambles and digs around in the darkness. "Which one of you bastards took my dagger?"

Gryffin shakes his head. "When he finds it, I am going to murder him with it."

Maddox leaps to his feet and shoves Gryff's shoulder. "That is my dagger. Give it back, shit bag."

"This is my fucking dagger. You left yours in the doe."

Maddox glances toward what is left of the deer we killed earlier this afternoon. Sure enough, the bone handle protrudes from between its ribs. He sprints over to free the blade, cleaning it on his trousers as he stalks back to where we wait.

Technically, our job is not to keep out the Seelie fae. Unlike us, they are welcome to cross the bridge any time they please. Fortunately, they usually have the good sense not to.

It would seem tonight, that is not the case.

Gryffin nods at the swaying planks. "They are crossing."

I withdraw my own dagger, the hilt smooth and familiar in my grip. We might not be able to keep them out, but we can sure as hell scare them shitless so they never want to come back.

Maddox bounces on his toes, tossing his dagger from one hand to the other.

A shadow appears in the mist. A lone male. Short. Broad shouldered.

Foolish.

Maddox cups his hands around his mouth and lets out a blood-curdling howl. The figure freezes. Gryffin catches a handful of discarded bones by our boots and launches them toward the intruder. The Seelie lets out a shrill yelp, turns tail, and runs back across the bridge, his footsteps stomping until he hits the dirt on the other side.

We follow him to the edge of the curling mist, ensuring those who linger think twice before crossing the canyon again.

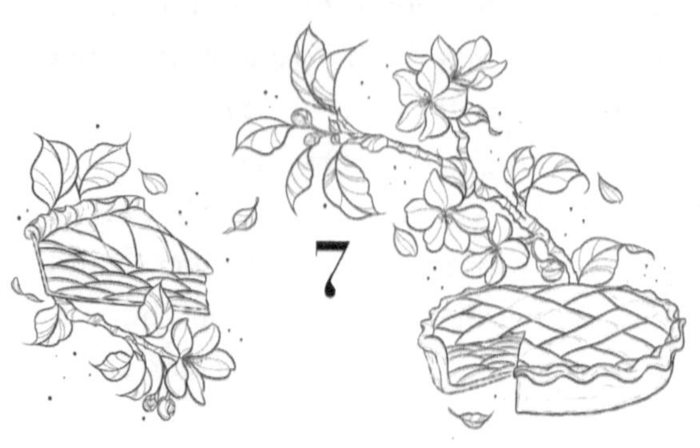

7

> *"When you find your heart's true mate, you will never desire another."*
>
> — *A Seelie Guide to Matrimony*

When we arrived home last night, Madame Ella had a white box bound in black ribbon waiting for me on the stoop. Inside, I found the most stunning gown— which was fortuitous considering the one I wore out already had a hole in the knee.

The buttery yellow skirts of the new gown slip like liquid over my stiff legs as I pace my uncle's living room. Nia sits curled up on the sofa, her feet draped over the rolled pillow, tapping along to music only she can hear. Quiet conversation drifts from the kitchen where my aunt and uncle enjoy cups of peppermint tea. By the sounds of it, they're discussing what to plant in the raised beds by the back fence.

With our bellies full of poached eggs and toast, Nia suggested we retire to the living room to relax. I've searched for a book that I haven't already read, but it would seem my uncle's small collection is the very same as my father's.

After being cooped up in a carriage for so long yesterday, my poor legs tingle and ache from disuse. All I want is to go for a walk. Back home, I'd have at least two miles done by now. Unfortunately, today is Wednesday, and apparently Wednesdays are for hiding.

How is no one else going mad? Look at the golden light streaming through the break in the closed shutters. It's ridiculous for everyone to remain inside simply because of a few fae using the well. We aren't anywhere near the damn thing, yet the doors are locked, and the downstairs shutters have been pulled tight.

"You're wearing a hole in the rug," Nia drawls from behind her book, flipping to the next page.

That's because I'm this close to losing my mind. "How can you stand being locked in here when the day is so fine?"

"Every day in Rosehill is fine."

That may be so, but it doesn't change the fact that no day should be wasted. Sitting in the dark with books we've both already read feels like a terrible waste. "I need to move."

"Isn't that what you're doing?"

"*Outside.*"

She finally lifts her head, her eyes as wide as they were last night when we heard that haunting howl.

"We can bring Madame Ella my other dresses." I'll only get away with wearing this gown so many times before Ivee comments on the lack of variety in my wardrobe.

Not that I care what she thinks. If I had my way, she wouldn't notice me at all. Since she has noticed me, I'd prefer not to give her more fodder for her viciousness.

"Madame Ella's and every other business is closed today."

I give Nia's bouncing feet a nudge, waiting until she moves them to fall beside her with a groan. "It's nonsense."

"It's safe."

Safe from *what?* If the Unseelie were truly monsters, they wouldn't have let a dilapidated bridge keep them from punishing the prince for trespassing on their territory.

Unless that isn't illegal. Are we allowed to enter the Unseelie city on Wednesdays as well? It seems only fair if they can venture into ours that we should be allowed to do the same.

I smooth my fingers down my overskirt, straightening the wrinkles as best I can. "How do you know they're dangerous?"

Nia closes the book with a snap. "Did you not hear Ronan? There are bones scattered across their side of The Divide."

When I was little and my mother would blow out the candle by my bed, I thought I saw monsters in the dark too. Turns out, they were only the piles of laundry I hadn't put away. "They eat meat, correct?" Unlike Seelie fae, the Unseelie diet consists mostly of animals. "Perhaps that is just where they discarded them."

If I wanted to keep people away, that would certainly do the trick.

Rolling her eyes, she shoves her chaotic hair back from her face. "I suppose the horns and fangs aren't anything to fret over either."

"It was dark out, Nia. Everyone knows shadows play tricks with your mind—especially when you're already afraid. Haven't you ever wondered if the legends are true? We could go and find out."

She tosses the book onto the coffee table, rattling our forgotten teacups. "Don't you understand? If my father discovers that I went to see the Unseelie, he'll have my head—and yours."

"We are almost twenty-five-years old. We do not need his permission."

"What do you propose we do?" She waves a hand toward the door. "Stroll into the square and throw a welcome party? Bring one of the neighbor's new calves as a sacrifice?"

"Now who's being ridiculous?" Although a welcome gift never hurt anyone. Perhaps that is something to consider. "Is it illegal to go to town on Wednesdays?"

Her hand falls to her lap with a quiet slap. "Well, no, but—"

"If the king was truly concerned for his citizens' safety, there would be laws in place keeping us from leaving our homes. Since there aren't, I can only assume that it isn't as dangerous as everyone believes."

It takes ten more minutes to convince her and another five for her to pick a pair of shoes to wear. Don't ask me why her choice of footwear matters when she's made me promise that we will stay hidden.

While I'm waiting, I straighten my wrinkled skirts and tighten the strings on my dress's corset top. I'm in love with the pale-yellow daisies printed on the silk, and the way the lacy sleeves of my shift puff over my shoulders like mushroom caps. It really is far too lovely a dress to waste on a day inside.

With her parents still in the kitchen arguing over what to bake with their cooking apples, Nia and I slip out the front door. Instead of leaving through the front gate where the neighbors might see, we creep around to the back gate and cross a field dotted with black and tan calves. Avoiding splatters of cow dung makes the crossing take far longer than it should, but eventually we reach the heart of the city.

Turning left at the library, we hurry down a skinny alley between the physician's office and an apothecary that spits us out into the square. The businesses are all shuttered, and the homes all have their blinds and curtains pulled. If I hadn't been here this time yesterday, I'd believe the city abandoned. Even the fountain no longer spills water into the wide pool below.

Doesn't look like the Unseelie are here yet. Either that, or we missed them.

There's a tug at the back of my skirt, followed my Nia's whisper. "This was a mistake. We should go back."

"Don't be silly. We'll be fine." I slip into one of the smaller alleys with the best view. Across the square waits the well, as silent as the rest of the city.

Excitement bubbles like the cider we drank last night, effervescent and light in my chest. When I glance over my shoulder at Nia, my excitement turns to guilt. Her hands tremble where they grip her skirts, and her teeth worry her lower lip.

Poor thing. She really is terrified.

I've had my walk. Perhaps it would be best if we went back. I can always sneak out on my own next week. "Look, if you want to go home—"

Her eyes widen, and her face drains of color as she takes a gulping breath. "It's too late. They're here."

I whirl back toward the square where horses, larger than any I've ever seen, with coats and manes black as pitch, slowly plod into the square. Deadly spikes protrude from the beasts' massive foreheads, gleaming like obsidian.

Not horses. *Unicorns.*

Here I thought the creatures of legend were all extinct.

Most of the unicorns pull small wooden carts laden with large clay jugs. It's hard to fathom crossing that rickety bridge on foot, let alone on horseback.

As fascinating as the unicorns may be, they're nothing compared to the fae sitting astride the beasts.

My heart pounds a little harder, climbing my throat, swelling with each rapid beat. *Heavens...*

Nia catches my arm, tugging me deeper into the alley, her labored breaths wheezing as she presses herself against the stone wall. "Shit. *Shit.* What are we going to do?"

"Take a deep breath. They're here for water, remember? Not us. We are perfectly safe." I pry myself from her strangle-hold and grip the gritty stones, peering around the wall to watch the Unseelie approach the well.

Nia leans over me, her fingers white as the mortar where they dig into the wall. "They're giants..."

Not giants, exactly, but certainly well over six feet tall. Taller than any of the men I met at the pub. "And would you look at that? Not a horn in sight."

Not a shirt in sight either, which I appreciate more than I'll ever admit. Unlike the softer Seelie men, the Unseelie look as if they've been carved from marble. The only hint of color is their greenish-gray skin that reminds me of a forest drenched in fog. While Seelie fae have hair of all shades and hues, the Unseelie's hair is black as a raven's wing. Some have the sides shorn so short, you can see the skin beneath.

Black rings climb their pointed ears, longer at the top than our own. They ride as if they're one with the creatures beneath them, all lithe grace and raw power.

All twelve come to a sudden halt. After a careful sweep of the area, they dismount as one.

The muscles in their arms flex and bulge when they lift the jugs from the carts, carrying them up the stairs to the well at the top.

"Can you see any fangs?" Nia asks.

"No. You?"

"Not from here."

Then again, their mouths are pressed flat, so it's difficult to tell.

Drawing water is a slow, tedious process and the trip back to the carts takes two, sometimes three men to carry each jug. If there weren't steps, they could wheel the carts right up to the well. Doesn't seem fair that they should have to carry them when all we do is turn on the tap.

The man at the front seems to be directing the others.

And he is magnificent.

Not handsome in the conventional sense like Ronan or Trevor. His jaw and cheekbones look sharp enough to slice through you.

But they're not nearly as cutting as his eyes. Even from this far away, I can see they're black as coal, and always alert.

Each man wears a dagger at his belt, the handle made from white wood. These weapons look nothing like Ronan's blade. The prince's was for show. I have a feeling theirs have tasted death.

Definitely not what I expected. "They're…"

"Monsters. I know. I did warn you."

Monsters? Hardly. "They're beautiful."

The man at the front turns his head toward us, and my stomach tenses, my lungs holding my exhale hostage. It's a coincidence, nothing more. There's no way he can hear or see us from all the way over there.

Even after I force out my breath and inhale anew, my head continues to spin.

"You are mad, Kerris Dawn," Nia whispers.

I might be mad, but I stand by what I said. Look at them. Even their flat stomachs are corded with ridges of muscle. They remind me of the bulls I've seen, alone in their pens. Not a pinch of fat on any of them.

"Why are there no women?" I whisper.

"Because they're born not of flesh and bone, but of darkness and shadows."

Nonsense. They look flesh and bone to me.

The longer I stare, the louder my heart sings inside my breast until Nia pushes away from the wall and tugs at my skirt. "Come on. You've had your gander. Let's get out of here before they eat us for dinner."

She's right, there is no logical reason for us to linger. Still, I find myself looking back one last time…

And finding a pair of black eyes trained on me.

Time stands still, the final grains of sand in an hourglass falling to their doom. My thundering pulse floods my ears as if I've been sprinting instead of standing frozen, staring back at the darkest eyes I've ever seen.

The Unseelie moves not a muscle, and neither do I, caught in a silent exchange where only the two of us exist.

Nia's tug of my skirt drags me back to this world. I duck out of sight, but the strange sensation of being watched follows me all the way to Nia's cottage. We burst through the gates, falling onto the soft grass next to a forsythia bush riddled with bulbous bees.

Saints above... I don't think I've ever run as fast.

"That was the most exhilarating moment of my entire life," Nia pants up at the downy clouds, the heel of her hand massaging her heaving chest.

Exhilarating, indeed. Although not nearly as exhilarating at locking eyes with that Unseelie fae. "I think he saw me."

Nia lifts to her elbows and peers down at me with her brow crushed up. "Who? One of the Unseelie?"

I nod.

"Heaven help us. If that's true, we're lucky to be alive."

Are we though? I felt no malice from the man, only the same curiosity that hums in my veins.

That night, when I finally manage to drift into sleep, I dream of shadows, black eyes, and blood-drenched blades.

8

Everett

"Leaving home without one's blade is a death wish."

— Surviving the Unseelie Lands, Author
Unknown

The day started out the same as any other, with the young, able-bodied males in our clan preparing to make the mile-long trek from the camp to the well, and yet an uneasy feeling in the pit of my gut followed me the entire way. I remained on high alert, scanning the fog for signs of danger that never materialized.

Then the soft scent of honeysuckle drifts through the air. The aroma isn't entirely outside the realm of normality considering everything in this damn place reeks like flowers, but there's something about the scent that calls to me.

A moment later, the sound of shuffling footsteps reaches my ears. The others must hear it too, because their movements aren't nearly as fluid as they should be. "We are not alone," I murmur.

"Alley to the right," Gryff says under his breath, hoisting

another jug onto the raised path surrounding the well while Ivan cranks the wooden lever until the bucket inside lifts. River fills the first jug to the brim and then he and Saint carry it back to the first cart.

Maddox stops beside me to bend down and tie the fraying laces on his boots. "What do we think they are doing?"

Can you see any fangs?

No. You?

Not from here.

My lips twitch. "They have come to gawk at us." If the women doing a piss-poor job of keeping to the shadows by that café want to see sharp teeth, I would be more than happy to smile at them. That would send them running back to the safety of their cottages of flowers and stone.

Maddox chuckles. "Then we should probably give them a show." He rights himself and stretches his arms toward the sky, twisting to give the Seelie a clear view of his stomach.

Gryffin calls him a gowl, but I notice Gryff flexing his arms as he stalks back to his cart to retrieve another jug. We have been hauling these things since we turned fifteen, so our movements are practiced, almost reflexive at this stage.

The potters of our clan made the jugs from the clays along the banks of the Ishka river—about five days north of our camp. Without them, we would be reduced to rationing like they used to back before the bridge was built.

The Seelie in the alley continue their conversation, unaware that we can hear every word.

They're…

Monsters. I know. I did warn you.

My teeth clamp so hard my jaw aches. I set my jug down with far too much force. Luckily, the thing does not crack.

"Monsters." A name I have been called since the first day I

crossed the bridge. When we were smaller, Gryff, Maddox, and I thought it would be a brilliant idea to sneak into Rosehill.

At twelve, we were already larger than the largest Seelie but too tall and gangly to look like much of a threat to the softer fae. The woman who saw us hid behind her male companion, whispering for him to tell the monsters to return to our side of The Divide.

I had looked around for wolves, but there were none.

That was when I realized the Seelie were not frightened of the true beasts.

They were terrified of us.

To them, we were the monsters.

"They're beautiful," the second woman whispers.

The hair on my arms lifts at the wonder in the stranger's soft, sweet voice. I should ignore the comment. Should finish filling these jugs and ride back across the bridge without looking back.

I should, but I do not.

Instead, I turn, finding a sweep of lilac hair and a pair of wide eyes the color of spring foliage.

You are mad, Kerris Dawn, the other Seelie says from where she leans around the wall, indignation rife in her tone.

Kerris Dawn.

The female's surname is that of light and the birth of a new day. The sun rising, stretching across their world, rarely touching ours.

I force myself to look away, to focus on the matter at hand. We need to load the carts with the filled jugs and make the laborious trip back through the cobbled streets, across the bridge, and to the camp where the jugs will remain until next week.

Why are there no women? The one with the sweet voice, Kerris, asks.

Her friend's response makes me chuckle. *Because they're born not of flesh and bone, but of darkness and shadows.*

"I will give them a bone," one of the younger men joining us for the first time sniggers to another.

Rage swells in my chest, a fiery inferno that paints everything in my vision the color of blood. "What did you say?"

He glances at his friend for help, but his friend steps back, leaving him alone.

"I-I was only talking about the Seelie fae."

"I know who you were talking about. If I ever hear you make another crude joke like that, you will be on bridge duty for the next month."

The pair have the good sense to bow their heads and walk away. They might be nearly as tall as me, but they only just earned their daggers and wear only ten bones around their necks between them.

Maddox stalks up behind me, nudging my shoulder with his as I continue to glower at the younger fae. Maybe I will stick them on bridge duty anyway.

"That was harsh." he whispers.

I cannot help but roll my eyes. "You are only saying that because you were thinking the same thing."

His grin sets me on edge. "True. But I had the good sense not to say it out loud within earshot of you."

There are many things I will tolerate, but when it comes to the treatment of females there can be no leniency.

Come on. You've had your gander. Let's get out of here before they eat us for dinner.

I glance over my shoulder to find the lilac-haired fae still watching, her plump lips fallen open as if in a gasp.

Maddox's breath hisses through his teeth. "Fuck me, that one is pretty."

Pretty does not begin to describe her. She has a face that would haunt a man. Made for poetry and sonnets. One that would break even the strongest fae warrior.

Although she slips away, her face has been burned into my memory.

If I were to close my eyes, I would see hers.

From this day forward, every time I come to this spot, I will be looking toward that alley, hoping for a glimpse of her.

Because a glimpse is all we can have. There is a reason our worlds are divided. Seelie fae have no natural defenses; they are soft in every sense of the word, and their chances of survival on our side of the bridge are non-existent.

As for one of us ending up here?

The Seelie have made it clear how they feel about the monsters across the canyon.

Still, I find my feet carrying me toward that alley, telling myself that I only want to ensure their safety. After all, if either of them meets a terrible fate between here and where they are living, we will be to blame.

"You are in charge," I tell Maddox.

Gryff casts a wary glance over his shoulder. "Ever?"

I will take shit for this later, but I am too far gone to respond, jogging into the alley where the most enticing scent lingers. I have never been one for sweets, but the perfume clinging to the air makes my tongue tingle and nostrils flare. I track the scent to a row of modest cottages southwest of the city, across from a stretch of farmland overflowing with grazing cattle.

For some reason, knowing the female does not live in one of the monstrosities up the hill makes me impossibly happy.

Keeping to the shadows, I catch a flash of lilac from a circular window on the second floor.

Kerris Dawn stands in the center, like a portrait in a frame, the sun playing on hair so long, it appears endless.

Unseelie females keep their hair short so that it cannot catch if they need to flee for their lives. Not that this female has such worries, living in a place where sheep and cattle laze in swaying grass, not so much as a thought spared for wolves or other predators.

She turns her head and says something I cannot hear before walking out of view.

Somehow, I manage to leave that gate, but whatever spell she has cast over me lingers all the way back to the well where Maddox and Griffin are loading the last of the jugs. Although they do not speak, the curious looks in their eyes say it all.

They are searching for an explanation.

If only I had one.

9

My reflection blinks back at me as I stare at myself in the mirror. The bedroom I've been given is like its own greenhouse, with ferns and ivy flowing like waterfalls from their pots affixed to the white-washed stones. Behind me, Nia hums off-key and without any recognizable tune as she finishes my hair.

She plaited the heavy strands into an intricate braid, weaving in a few of the ribbons she's so fond of. With her help, it didn't take hours to comb.

Nia sticks in another pin to keep the braid in place, scraping my scalp and earning yet another hiss from me. She might be a sorceress with my hair, but she's also a bit of a sadist with the bloomin' pins.

"Are you sure you want to cut it?" she asks. "I would kill for this length."

"It's impossible to manage on my own," I grit through a wince, my poor skull pulsing.

The corners of her lips lift. "If you marry Ronan, you won't be on your own."

True. A princess would have a whole bevy of servants at her beck and call, which sounds wonderful in theory. But I enjoy baking and mending—and even cleaning, on occasion. If there are maids and servants to complete all those tasks, what would *I* do all day?

If our forbidden excursion into the city yesterday tells me anything, it's that I am no good at sitting around.

I offer a non-committal "We'll see," to avoid hearing yet another monologue on the merits of being a princess.

There's no point dreaming of crowns and thrones when Ronan is bound to come to his senses and set his sights on someone more suitable, like a wealthy heiress or a foreign princess who already knows how to be royalty.

"What are your plans for the day?" I ask.

"I'm meeting Nolan for tea."

"Is that a euphemism?"

She whaps my arm with a giggle. "Oh, you! Stop that now. Nolan and I are very respectable."

"The way he wore your lip stain two nights ago would suggest otherwise."

Her skirts billow as she plops onto the edge of my unmade bed. "A few stolen kisses, that's all. Everyone does it."

If only that were true. "Not everyone," I grumble.

Nia's hand snaps out, her cool fingers encircling my wrist. "Wait. Are you saying you haven't kissed *anyone?*"

"Who was I to kiss? My brother or the neighbor's goats?"

"Oh, Kerris! You poor thing. You simply must kiss Ronan. I hear he has a wealth of experience and is well-versed in the art of lovemaking."

"I am not interested in Ronan's... *lovemaking*." Heavens, above. Imagine *me*, bedding a bloody prince. Utterly ridiculous.

A knock reverberates up the stairwell, and my pulse speeds at the noise. Downstairs, I hear my aunt offer a friendly greeting, followed by a familiar voice.

"He's here!" Nia launches to her feet and drags me to mine. "Your sleeves would look better down." She tugs them off my arms, exposing my shoulders.

"What are you talking about? They're supposed to be up." I put them back where they belong. There. Nice and respectable.

"No, they're supposed to be *down*." She yanks them down once more, and when I go to fix them again, she raps my knuckles. "Don't you dare touch them. You already insisted on lacing your corset all the way; give me this one thing. Please?"

I only insisted on lacing my corset because my breasts would fall out otherwise. I suppose my sleeves don't look *too* scandalous down. "Fine."

"Ah! Thank you! You are perfect, Kerris. Just perfect." Her warm hands come over my shoulders, squeezing tightly. "Remember: Ronan is the one who must work for your proposal, not the other way around." Her eyes sparkle. "And for the love of all that is holy, let that man kiss you."

I catch my skirts to keep from tumbling down the steep stairs and descend to where Ronan waits at the door with my aunt in a shirt as blue as his eyes. When the prince sees me, his mouth curves into an appreciative smile.

Let that man kiss you.

The thought of his lips on mine makes me nervous and excited and maybe a tiny bit sick to my stomach. Perhaps there is some merit to the idea. I don't have to marry the man to let him kiss me, do I? Don't I owe it to my future mate to have at least a little experience?

My aunt opens the door for us. "Have fun, you two."

Ronan inclines his head. "Thank you, Mrs. Quill. Are you ready, Kerris?"

As ready as I'll ever be.

The sleeves of his shirt have been rolled to his elbows, exposing a pair of tanned forearms. Taking his proffered arm, I let him lead me out into the sunny day. Wisps of white dot the blue sky overhead as we traverse the path to the bustling sidewalk.

"You look stunning," he whispers.

Heat blooms up my throat, burning a path to my jaw. "Thank you."

"How did you fare yesterday?"

My mind leaps straight to the tall, toned Unseelie we saw at the well. I press a hand to my fluttering stomach, willing my voice to remain calm instead of giddy. "I found it difficult to stay inside."

"But you did stay in, didn't you? There's no telling what those beasts are capable of. I couldn't bear the thought of something happening to you."

"I appreciate your concern." Although it is entirely unnecessary. The leader saw me, and nothing came of it.

Instead of continuing toward the city center, Ronan takes a sharp left, bringing me to an area of the city I've yet to explore. Each cottage is larger and grander than the one before it—so grand, I'm not sure they can be called cottages at all. The roofs morph from thatch to slate, the windows growing and growing until they become walls of glass overlooking gardens so magnificent, they belong in a storybook.

"Where are we going?"

He pats my knuckles with his warm, smooth hand. "Do you recall me confessing my secret passion in the garden?"

The garden where he almost kissed me.

Is he going to try to kiss me again?

"Of course I do."

His blue eyes glitter with his blinding smile. "I want to show you what I've been building."

We cut through a side street, emerging across from the treehouse I saw the day I first arrived. Lilacs tremble from bushes on either side of a wide staircase that climbs to a porch encircling the trunk. The door has been built into the bark, with the scrolled iron hinges painted black. Each of the thick upper limbs holds another level, the pitched roofs made not of slate or thatch, but of woven branches.

"That is the loveliest house I've ever seen." When I was a little girl, there was an apple tree in one of our fields that I claimed as my own. In the years after my mother passed, I spent more time in that tree than on solid ground.

"The inside is even more remarkable."

"Do you know the owner?" I'd love a chance to see it someday.

Ronan unlatches the gate. "Kerris, I *am* the owner."

This place is *his?* When he said he liked building things, I assumed he made toys or little wooden figures, not houses. "You built *this?*"

"No, but I designed it as a summer house."

A summer house twice as big as the cottage I grew up in by the looks of it. The sanded oak banister slips beneath my fingers, glossy and smooth with fresh lacquer. Up the stairs we climb, my excitement doubling with each step toward the intricate facade.

The main door leads to a modest foyer that opens into a larger living room with a black stove and a kitchen boasting deep green cabinets. Every detail has been carefully thought out, even down to the brass knobs shaped like twigs.

"Ronan, this is... It's remarkable." One room flows into the next, with small staircases leading to bedrooms and a bathing room perched at the end of a branch all by itself, overlooking Rosehill.

Ronan watches me with a shoulder propped against the doorframe. "Do you really like it?"

Who wouldn't? I trace my fingers along the carved headboard in the largest bedroom, marveling over each divot. "It's unlike any home I've ever seen."

He glances down, his cheeks flushing. "Do you really think so? My mother says it's too whimsical."

The queen couldn't be more wrong. Even if this home isn't her style or preference, there is no denying the talent it took to create something so beautiful. "It's perfect."

He pushes off the frame, stepping closer. "It could be yours, you know. If you were to marry me."

A tempting offer, but a house—even one as fine as this—doesn't make a marriage. It's the people who live in it. As talented as Ronan may be, we only just met. Yes, he is handsome and rich, but he is also a stranger.

Who is he deep down? Is he caring? Giving? Does he understand that true beauty doesn't live on the surface, but in a person's heart? In their soul?

I sink onto the end of the bed and tuck my hands beneath my thighs to keep from fidgeting. "I hear that you've been fending off marriage proposals for years. Why are you so interested in matrimony now?"

He pauses, as if genuinely considering his answer. "I feel as if I've been waiting."

I've been waiting.

I've been waiting.

I've been waiting.

When I speak, my voice is no more than a whisper. "Waiting for what?"

The legs of his trousers brush against the silk of my skirts. "For this house to be finished so that I have a place of my own."

Disappointment sinks like a stone in my stomach. Not that I expected him to say, "For you," considering we only just met. That would be madness.

Still, a small part of me had hoped for such a confession.

That someone would see me and *know*.

Ronan spends the rest of the walk into town pointing out who lives where, naming fae I've never even heard of. He is a wealth of information, responding to any questions I have about the city or the buildings with clear, concise answers.

When we finally reach the tea house, we're given a table along the cobblestone walk where the rich perfume of roses sweetens every inhale. I add honey to my tea, preferring it extra sweet. The peach and blueberry pie served with vanilla custard is transcendent, although the servings are so large, we cannot finish it all.

We talk about everything and nothing, life in the mountains and in the castle, the people we grew up with, and the people we want to be.

Ronan has just refilled our teacups when I catch a glimpse of his friend Trevor making his way up the lane. When Trevor glances at the tea house, our eyes meet, and his lips curve into a smile.

Then he sees Ronan sitting across from me, and his smile fades to a frown.

At first, Ronan doesn't seem to notice Trevor, but when he does, the prince waves him over to our table.

Trevor slips off his glasses, tucking them into the leather satchel slung across his chest before running a hand through his chestnut hair. "Good to see you again, Kerris. Ronan."

Leaning back in his chair, Ronan drapes an arm over mine. "Fancy meeting you here, Trev."

"You mean at the restaurant where I come for lunch every day? Yes. What a coincidence."

Hold on. Did Ronan choose this place *because* he knew Trevor would be here? If so, that was dreadfully underhanded. I might be out with the prince today, but that doesn't give him the right to scare away any other potential suitors.

"I'm looking forward to our tea tomorrow, Trevor," I say, making it clear that my decision has not been made. Yes, I had fun today, but I could have even more fun with Trevor tomorrow.

Trevor's whole countenance brightens, his spine and shoulders straightening. "I was thinking we could go to dinner instead, if that's all right with you?"

"Dinner sounds wonderful." When I get back to the house, I'll have to bring my mother's dresses to Madame Ella to see if she can alter any in time for the date. It seems such a silly, senseless thing, but I'd hate to wear the same gown two dates in a row.

Trevor deserves his own dress.

Trevor tells us goodbye and makes his way further into the tea house to sit at a table all by himself.

Setting my teacup down, I try to read Ronan's expression but come up short. "May I ask you something?"

He flashes me a blinding smile. "You can ask me anything."

I could tell him there's a bit of blueberry stuck between his front teeth, but that will depend on how he answers my next question. "Did you choose this tea house because you knew Trevor would be here?"

He glances away, his cheeks turning the slightest shade of pink that has nothing to do with the sun washing over us. "I didn't *not* choose it for that reason."

That's what I thought. "I am not a prize to be won, Ronan." I am a woman who deserves to make up her own mind.

He sits up, his hands finding mine. "But you are, Kerris. And if I must fight dirty for your proposal, I will."

I'm not sure whether to be flattered or appalled.

Perhaps a bit of both.

But since I do not approve of his underhandedness, I don't tell him about the blueberry.

After tea, Ronan makes a quick trip to the privy. When he returns, the berry has been removed from between his teeth.

He doesn't mention it, and neither do I.

The walk back to the cottage is pleasant enough, and as we stroll down the path, I decide that if the prince wants to kiss me, I'm going to let him.

When we reach the stoop, I linger instead of running straight inside.

His hands find my hips, drawing us closer. "Thank you for today. I truly enjoyed your company."

You can do this. You are a strong, capable woman. I force air into my lungs, dying with anticipation as his gaze drops to my lips. "I enjoyed your company as well," I manage to say with only the slightest tremor in my voice.

Slowly, ever so slowly, he lowers his mouth to mine. The warm press of his lips spins my mind like a top. He grips me tighter, using his mouth to part mine, and then something happens that is so unexpected, I let out a mortifying squeak of surprise.

Ronan sticks his tongue *inside* my mouth.

What am I supposed to do? Do I move my tongue? Do I try to hide it?

The moment his tongue retreats, I blurt, "I need to go," like a total loon, and then escape into the house.

The moment the door closes, Nia leaps off the sofa and starts bouncing on her toes, asking if I let him kiss me.

My cheeks burn even hotter. "I did."

Her piercing squeal rattles my eardrums, and she holds both of her fists in front of her grin. "*And?*"

"And he used his tongue. Is that normal?"

She doubles over in a fit of laughter. "Oh, Kerris. You are my favorite person in the world."

She is mine as well, but that still doesn't answer my question.

10

*"Of course you're supposed to use your bloomin'
tongue."*

— *Nia Quill, An Exclamation*

After an enjoyable dinner with Trevor, he asked if I'd like to see his home. So here we are, in an overgrown front garden studying the coziest cottage I've ever seen. The graying bench would look amazing painted buttery yellow to match the door and window frames. The brownish stone looks a bit dated and drab, but if I were to whitewash the exterior, that would really revive the place.

Trevor frowns up at the dark patch on the thatch, gone green with mold. "I know it doesn't look like much now, but after they lay the new roof and I clean up the garden a bit, it'll be the nicest home on the street."

"It's beautiful." Listen to that burbling brook in the background. It's like a slice of mountain solace carved into the heart of this bustling city. If I were to close my eyes, I could almost convince myself I'm back in Gravale.

Trevor's smile lights up his whole face, making him even more handsome. "Would you like to see inside?"

"I would love to."

He fumbles to pull his keys from his pocket and unlock the latch. The interior is a bit gloomy and smells damp, but the dark walnut floors and counters are immaculate. Having grown up with floors this exact shade, I appreciate how difficult it is to keep them clean. There doesn't appear to be even a speck of dust on the bookshelves framing the fireplace or on the coffee table. The living and dining room are one with the kitchen, the knobs on the ivory drawers and cabinets shaped like acorns.

I press my thumb against the tiny bumps on the acorn's cap. "I love these."

Trevor comes up behind me, bringing along the soft scent of ink and leather, as if he himself has been wrapped inside a book. "They're my favorite part of the kitchen. My grandmother picked them out when my grandfather built this place."

Trevor trails a finger along a pull, his nail tapping the little stem at the top. "If the whole house burned to the ground, and I could only save one thing, it would be one of these."

A tingle starts at my feet, traveling up my legs, the sensation familiar and unwelcome. Even knowing what's going to happen next, I'm still not prepared for the way my chest constricts, tightening, hardening, as if a boulder has been dropped on my sternum.

It's only a figure of speech. Stop being dramatic.

I rub idly at my chest, escaping from the kitchen into the lone bedroom on this level, focusing on what is in front of me, not the flashes of painful memories flaring in my traitorous mind.

A four-poster bed. A matching nightstand. A short chest of drawers.

Normal. *Safe.* Three pieces of furniture stuffed into a small room the way the air feels stuffed into my lungs. I slip into the adjoining bathing room to grip the edge of the claw-foot tub and try to get my breathing under control.

The air smells not of smoke, but of lavender and chamomile from the small bowl of potpourri sitting on the edge of the sink.

I'm fine.

Everything is fine.

I'm safe. Whole. Alive.

Trevor waits in the living room, his soft smile giving no indication that he noticed my brief panic spiral. When he offers to show me the upstairs, I nod, not trusting my voice to remain steady.

At the top of the staircase wait two more bedrooms and another bathing room, twice as large as the one downstairs, with an arched window that opens out toward the stream. By the time we return to the living area, the tightness in my chest is no more than a terrible memory.

Trevor shifts his weight from one foot to the other as his fingers tap against his thighs. "Do you..." He clears his throat. "Do you like it?"

"It's perfect." This is the sort of home I've always imagined myself in.

He pats a hand against the wall, his expression warm and full of memories as he gazes at the stone. "I know it's not a castle, but the walls are strong, and the foundation is sturdy."

"Who said I was looking for a castle?" I came to Rosehill for a husband, not a house.

When he smiles down at me, my chest feels warm and full.

"Do you think... What I mean to say is, can you imagine yourself living here?"

I can picture myself sitting on the slightly worn sofa, darning socks in front of a crackling fire. Cooking dinner in the kitchen while children race up and down the stairs, squealing and laughing.

I can imagine sitting by the stream reading while Trevor works in the gardens. It's a future that makes me feel hopeful.

His parents have both passed and his brother lives in Wrenwich, so they don't see each other very often. It would be just the two of us, building a life with no expectations but our own.

That makes me happier than I can put into words.

Our hands graze once more when I turn to face him. "That depends."

His brows arch. "On what?"

"On whether or not you'll let me change the curtains."

He blinks at me, the wrinkles on his furrowed brow slowly smoothing with his answering smile. "This home would be yours, Kerris. You could do whatever you want with it—as long as you keep the acorns."

"I'll keep the acorns," I promise.

Trevor inches closer, until the toes of his boots knock against my slippers where they peek from beneath my skirts. His hand lifts, hesitating for the briefest moment before he touches my cheek. "You are unlike any woman I've ever met. Most are swayed by Ronan's title and wealth, but you... You make me feel as if I have a chance at winning your hand."

He has more than a chance. After today, I'd say Trevor Dillon has a slight lead over the prince. He has been the perfect gentleman —not to mention excellent company. Unlike Ronan with his choice of cafés, Trevor appears honest and forthright in his words and actions.

I'm genuinely looking forward to spending more time with him.

"Would you permit me to take you out again?" he asks.

"I'd be upset if you didn't."

"Tomorrow?"

"Tomorrow is perfect."

His gaze drops to my mouth, then travels back up to my eyes. I wait for him to ask for a kiss, to make some sort of move. After the longest ten seconds of my life, Trevor takes a giant step away from me and clasps my palm for a stiff shake.

He lets go, says he will see me tomorrow, and then practically sprints toward the front door with his head bowed and shoulders fallen.

This just won't do.

I cannot marry him without kissing him at least once, right?

"Trevor?"

He turns, his eyes widening when he sees me following. I stop right in front of him, cup his cheeks, and press my mouth to his. Our kiss is soft and sweet, and while he doesn't use his tongue, when I pull back, I feel as giddy as I did after the prince kissed me.

Nia was right. I have been missing out. "I will see you tomorrow."

He blinks, his eyes hazy and unfocused. "Right. Yes. Um. Right. Tomorrow. Good day, Kerris."

"Goodbye, Trevor." Two kisses in two days. Who am I? I press my fingers to my lips as I slip back into the overgrown garden, my smile so wide, my cheeks hurt.

Whom shall I kiss next?

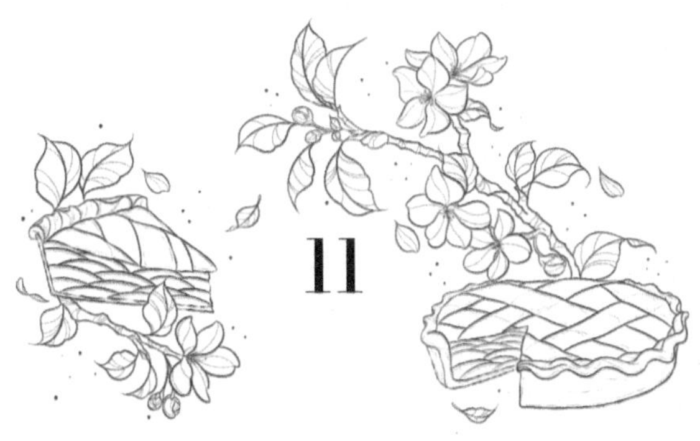

11

*"One should never arrive to someone's cottage
empty handed."*

— Celeste Hanson Dawn, An Observation

I shouldn't do it.

But that's my head talking, and when it comes to the war between my head and my heart, the latter tends to win.

My heart is telling me to open the gate and step into the field of swaying grass. To run far and fast until I reach the town square.

I've officially been in Rosehill for over a week, and after nights out with Nia and two more dates with both Ronan and Trevor, I'm no closer to choosing a husband.

Both of my suitors are wonderful, but neither have done much to sway me either way. My stomach flutters when I'm with them, especially when I let them kiss me.

But it feels as if something is...

I don't know. Missing?

There are flutters but no sparks.

Nia says I've lost my mind, that sparks belong in the hearth, not in the heart, and maybe she's right. Every day brings me one step closer to the biggest decision of my life, and I probably shouldn't let what's lacking matter more than what's there.

Ronan has proven charming and bold and shown that he is willing to do anything to receive my proposal.

While Trevor has proven attentive and cautious, his presence has been calming and solid.

In front of me are two very different lives, spread out like separate paths, yet here I am, stuck at a fork in the road without a bloomin' map.

Which brings me to today: Wednesday.

Nia is suffering from cramps, so she's spending the day in bed with a hot water bottle on her stomach, leaving me in front of a gate with a decision to make: Stay here where it's safe and secluded or venture to the well.

The thought of staying makes me feel as if I'm being locked away in a cage.

The thought of going makes me feel as if I'm being swept away in a rushing river.

When you look at it like that, there really is no other choice to make.

I reach for the latch, push open the gate, and spring across the field, my hair flying behind me and the pack on my back bobbing. Tonight, my hair will be full of impossible tangles, but I cannot bring myself to care.

Without Nia around to caution me, I choose an alley even closer to the well so that I can get a better look. A loud gong chimes through the empty streets, the clock in the clocktower ringing in the noon hour. As if summoned by the deep, reverberating sound, unicorns and riders emerge like smudges of black across the horizon, accompanied by the steady thump of heavy hooves, rising and falling with every strike of the bell. Part of me expected to see different men from last week, but as far as I can tell, they're all the same.

Certainly, the same leader, with the same slashing brows and serious, midnight eyes.

They fill their jugs in a show of muscles and strength, not so much as a conversation between them. It isn't until they carry the final jug to the final cart that I get up the nerve to do what I've been planning all week.

With a deep breath, I push away from the wall, straighten the pack on my back, and step into the square.

The moment my slipper meets the cobblestone, the man at the front stills. Twelve heads swing my way.

How on earth did they hear me? I didn't make a sound.

When they see me, their spines snap straight, making them even taller and more imposing. I take another step toward them, and another, encouraging my lungs to breathe as they watch me through curious eyes, silent as the cobbles.

Not wanting to frighten—or irritate—them by coming too close, I stop when I reach the well.

The man at the front clasps his hands at his back, and all the others follow suit. The movement pushes their toned chests forward.

Heavens above, I have never seen so many muscles in one place. The deep cuts of their chests, highlighted by the necklaces of white stones ringing their necks. The ridges of their abdomens. The indentations at their hips where those menacing daggers gleam.

Although my smile never falters, my nerves make my voice quake. "Hello."

The others exchange glances, but the man at the front doesn't look away.

None of the Unseelie smile or offer greetings of their own.

Perhaps they don't speak our language.

Why didn't I think of that possibility sooner?

I press a hand to my chest. "My name is Kerris Dawn. What's yours?"

One of the men to the leader's right steps forward to whisper in his leader's very pointed ear.

Whatever he says earns him a glower, but no one addresses me. All right.

I suppose that answers the language question. I slip my pack from my back, and the whole lot of them retreat a step, their hands falling to the hilts at their belts.

"Oh, I'm sorry. I didn't mean to startle you. I brought a gift." *They don't understand you, Kerris. They might not even know what a gift is.* I withdraw the box of almond biscuits we baked last night.

Back in Gravale, I had a cantankerous old neighbor who lost his son in an avalanche and his wife shortly after. For over forty years, he was all alone—and surlier than a cat with no teeth. Week after week, I brought him blueberry-lemon bread. After a few months, he eventually invited me inside for tea. I visited him every week until the day he died.

These men might not be old, but they do look almost as wary as I flip open the top of the box.

The men at the back of the group lift onto their toes to peer inside. The leader's chest expands, his nose wrinkling.

Perhaps he doesn't know what a biscuit is.

How tragic.

I lift one out and take a bite, showing them there's nothing to be afraid of and that they're safe to eat.

The one who whispered stretches out a hand only to have it smacked away by their leader.

I step forward and raise my head to meet the leader's narrowed eyes.

How is he so bloomin' tall? The top of my head barely reaches his collarbone.

No matter. Being the size of a giant doesn't necessarily mean he has the temperament of one. When I smile, his scowl deepens.

Hmmm... Perhaps I'm wrong.

Still, I withdraw another biscuit and hold it toward him.

To my shock, he stretches out a large hand and takes it from me. His hands aren't hairy at all, nor are they covered in warts. Besides being that strange green-gray hue, they're just like mine.

Just like mine if mine were gigantic.

He brings the biscuit to his nose and sniffs. His nose wrinkles once more even as he breaks the biscuit in two and pops one half into his mouth. The others watch attentively as he chews. There's something oddly sensual about the flex of his jaw and bob of his throat when he swallows.

I truly must be losing it. Whoever heard of someone having an attractive throat? My smile tightens as I meet his steady gaze, the onyx pools of his irises threatening to pull me under, an ocean of ink and darkness.

The one who whispered tries once more to reach into the box, but the leader swipes the box from my hand, twisting around with a deadly glower aimed at his fellow Unseelie. The most heinous noise rumbles from his throat, somewhere between a growl and a snarl.

The hairs at the back of my neck lift, and goosebumps prickle my arms.

The others back away, hands tucked behind their backs once more, casting wary glances my way until it's only the leader and me standing at the well, him clutching the box of biscuits to his chest as if he's a dragon guarding treasure.

The feral noise stops, and the others take to their mounts.

After a beat, the leader turns back to where I wait. His endlessly dark eyes lower to mine, and my heart starts to race the same way it did the week before when I thought he saw me from across the square.

Something stirs deep within me. Not in my heart, but in my soul. A flash. A spark.

Heat spreads through my veins.

My tongue darts over suddenly dry lips. His eyes sharpen like blades as he tracks the movement.

What would it be like to kiss *this* man?

The errant thought is enough to make me stumble back.

His gaze drops to the biscuits and then he twists to look at his unicorn. I wait for him to thank me, to say anything at all just so that I can hear his voice.

I bet it would be deep.

I bet it would rumble like that throaty growl.

I'm left wanting as he turns on his heel and stalks back to his mount, the muscles of his back shifting and rippling with each step. I watch with my heart in my throat as he shoves his boot into the stirrup and throws his long leg over the beastly unicorn, my biscuits still clutched in one hand as he grips the reins with the other.

With a click of his tongue, the animal beneath him springs to life, whipping its horned head toward the road leading out of town where the other Unseelie have all but disappeared. He and the others ride away, the wheels of their carts creaking as they vanish on the horizon.

I wait for the spark to die, but it burns the whole way home.

12
Everett

"Distractions are deadly."

— Surviving the Unseelie Lands, Author
Unknown

*S*he came back.

Those words pulse like a second heartbeat through my body.

Why did she come back?

And why did she give me a gift?

"Come on, Ever. Give me one," Maddox whines the moment he climbs out of the saddle and ties his mount to the post.

If he tries to stick his grubby hand in my box one more fucking time, I will cut it clean off.

"The ignorant Seelie clearly does not understand the implications of what she has done," Gryff points out, tying his reins next to Maddox's, his own beast snorting and shaking its massive head, just as surly as its owner.

Hearing him call Kerris "ignorant Seelie" makes me want to

deck him, yet my fists remain at my sides. "I know that." If she understood what it meant, she absolutely would not have handed the box to me—to any of us.

But the fact of the matter is, she *did*.

Now this gift is mine and if anyone else so much as sniffs it, their life is forfeit.

Maddox crosses his arms and props himself up against the hitching post as our steeds lap at the fresh water we added to the trough. Some might think giving animals our immortal water is a waste, and to those people, I say: try to haul the jugs from Rosehill without them.

"What if she *does* understand?" Maddox taps a finger against his chin as if deep in thought. I almost laugh. The words "deep" and "thought" do not suit him.

For some senseless reason, I find myself hoping that Kerris might have known what this gift means. The female may be Seelie, but surely, she would have been taught at some point what it means to give an unmarried Unseelie a gift of sustenance.

Not that I would consider the box of whatever these are sustenance, but they are almost edible, so I suppose they loosely fit the definition.

Maddox clasps my face between his hands, squishing my cheeks like the elders do to the younglings in camp. "What if she saw this face and fell instantly in love?"

I shove him away, and the bastard uses my distraction to steal the box from my saddle bag.

I sweep my leg, catching him off guard and knocking him flat on his ass. The box skids toward one of the many puddles, but I manage to snag it before the thing gets ruined. Clutching the gift to my chest with one hand, I whip my dagger from my belt with the other, pressing the blade to Maddox's bobbing gullet. "Touch them again, and I will slit your throat."

The maddening fool twists his head to shoot Gryffin a grin. "I think you are right, Gryff. There is no way she knew what that gift meant."

"Fuck you." He cannot know that. When Gryff chuckles, I turn on him. "Fuck you, too." They are supposed to be my best friends; they should be trying to help me figure this out instead of making fun of me.

I carry my box to my barrel-top and sink onto the stairs. The flat, round things inside smell strange. When I turn one over, crumbs skitter across my lap.

I take a bite and...

They are exactly as awful as they were at the well. The more I chew, the drier it gets, not to mention it is so sweet my teeth ache. By some miracle, I manage to swallow the chunk down without gagging.

Nyx nudges my shoulder with his muzzle, huffing and snuffling at the box. "You do not want one. Believe me."

However, the beast is insistent. Maddox's burst of laughter from whatever he just said to Gryff sets me on edge. Whether Kerris meant them as anything more or not, they were still a gift, and throwing them out is such a waste.

Although I would rather give the things to my mount than any of the other males in the camp.

So I lift the lid once more and hold one out to Nyx.

He takes the thing between his big, flat teeth and grinds them to dust, spilling even more crumbs down my trousers. One after the other, I feed them to him until they are gone, and then he goes back to the patch of grass between my home and Maddox's.

Maddox meanders over, flopping himself onto my bottom step and giving my knee a nudge. "All jokes aside, can I at least try one?"

"They are gone."

"Liar."

I show him the empty box.

"You are some bastard, you know that?" His scowl is short-lived, replaced by a glint in his eyes. "What is Leah Locke going to say when she finds out another female cooked for you?"

I had not thought about that.

If I am being honest, I have not thought about Leah since the moment I heard Kerris's name. I fiddle with the hilt of my dagger, this close to ramming the blade into his thigh. Would serve him right for sticking his nose where it does not belong. "Who is going to tell her?"

"Everett Gathin!" A woman's shriek pierces the overcast sky.

Maddox chuckles darkly, leaning back with his hands clasped behind his head like the fool he is. "Sounds like someone already did."

Never one to run from a fight, I toss the empty box into my house and prepare for the inevitable argument. If I ever find out who told Leah, he is going to regret the day he was born.

Leah stalks down the lane, the bottom of her brown skirt sweeping across the muck. She looks fearsome, with her short, straight hair the color of a midnight sky swinging against her sharp cheekbones.

"What is this I hear about some Seelie bitch baking for you?" she snarls, coming to a stop at my bottom step, her dark eyes alight with fury.

"Leah..."

"Do not 'Leah' me, you lying, cheating prick."

I might be a prick, but I neither lied nor cheated. "You and I are not engaged."

Her nostrils flare, and her ears darken with anger. "You think I want to be reminded that you still have not accepted my proposal? I gave you that jerky three weeks ago!"

I push to my feet and offer her my hand. "Come with me." There is no need to have this conversation where everyone and their brother can hear.

The problem with living in such close quarters to one another is that there is never any privacy.

Refusing my hand, she stalks ahead of me to the forest's edge. When she turns her back to the trees, fury paints every plane of her sharp features.

Leah knows as well as I do that what lives within these woods could tear her to shreds, and turning her back is akin to a death sentence.

What the beasts of the forest do not realize is, Leah Locke is more lethal than all of them put together. And right now, she wants my head on a pike.

"This is not about the Seelie, is it?" I venture.

Her chin lifts. "Of course it is about the cursed Seelie. I demand you tell me her name so that I can cut her from ear to ear. Give her a pretty, new smile."

The thought of Leah getting her hands on soft, sweet Kerris floods my stomach with icy dread. She might claim this is about the gift, but I would wager my best cooking pot that she is lying. "I am sorry I have not given you an answer yet."

"Then soothe my ire by giving me one now."

Leah might be the only female in our clan who sees me as something more than the son of the village pariah, but I would rather remain single forever than be tied to a woman whose temper rivals Gryffin's.

For some reason, she set her sights on me when we were ten years old and has not swayed since.

When I do not respond, she huffs out a breath. "Is this because of Robyn? Dammit. I told you I was sorry."

"You stabbed her." It is not me she should be apologizing to. If we had not had the water on hand to heal her, Robyn very well could have bled out and died.

If Leah's father was not the chieftain, she would have been exiled instead of being forced into laundry duty for six months.

"Because she brought you those almonds."

"Almonds I gave to the elders. As I said before, I did not reciprocate." Even if I did, it would have been my prerogative. "You and I are friends, Leah. Nothing more."

Leah takes a menacing step forward. "I see. And do you bed all your friends? Is that why Maddox and Gryffin are so loyal to you?"

"You know what I mean. You deserve better than me." Everyone deserves better than me.

"Maybe I do. But I want you, Everett Gathin." Her hands meet my chest, rough from countless hours churning butter and curing hides. "Think of all the good we can do for the clan. Think of the strong home we can build."

With only ten females of marriageable age in our clan and more than thirty males, it is an honor to be chosen. Yet the thought of marrying Leah eats away at me, which is why, when she moves closer, I step back in retreat.

The coy smile on her lips matches her honeyed tone. "Give me the night to convince you?"

For a moment, I consider letting Leah back into my bed; consider getting lost in her for the night. But then morning would come, and I still would not have an answer for her.

We would be right back where we are now, except maybe it would be a little worse, because, for those few hours, I know she would be dreaming of our mating ceremony.

So instead of giving in, I tell her, "Not tonight," and leave her to her rage.

Every time I close my eyes, I am haunted by visions of a woman with hair the color of a lilac bloom and eyes the shade of clover.

There is no sense wasting away abed when sleep alludes me, so I dress and head back to the forest, hoping something emerges that I can kill.

Foolish on my own? Undoubtedly.

But it is a risk I am willing to take.

Our first hunt cannot come soon enough.

We will be gone most of the summer, returning in the fall with enough to feed our people through the harsh winters that only seem to affect this side of the canyon.

Instead of taking the path pitted with footprints leading north, I follow the southern trail that curves deeper into the heart of the woods. The trees creak and groan and moss swallows the base of every trunk, silencing my footfalls.

With my dagger in my grip, I venture farther than I normally would, down to where the river meets the silty bank. A few years ago, I would not have been brave enough to go this far without the others, but tonight I feel reckless.

Restless.

Haunted.

Across the lazy water, silver strips of moonlight fall upon a glen. I am about to turn away when something small and iridescent catches my eye. If I did not know any better, I would say it was a flower, but flowers do not bloom in our forest.

Flowers need sunlight to survive, and this land of shadows has too little. My father used to say the Seelie stole it from us, but he was as bitter as he was cross, so I imagine he was full of shite.

The icy water barely registers as I step into the river, crossing the slippery stones carefully until I reach the far shore.

Not only are they flowers, but also, they are as silver as the buckle on my belt.

The urge to kill fades as I kneel to pluck one by the stem, carrying it back with me to camp.

I should probably give the bloom to Leah as an apology for

making her wait so long for an answer. But that would be an answer in and of itself.

For once a meal is offered, the male accepts with a gift of his own.

Maybe Leah is right in demanding our union. She is a strong female, the fiercest in our clan. Maybe I should give her what she wants. It is not as if anyone else will be lining up to mate with me after she stabbed Robyn. I have a duty to our people, to the Unseelie, to bring offspring into this cruel world, lest our line be eradicated.

The longer I stare at the flower, the more my chest aches.

Leah would not appreciate the gesture, only the outcome.

Would Kerris think this flower is beautiful?

Probably not considering it is as devoid of color as everything else this side of the bridge.

What if she understood?

Maddox's teasing comment from earlier drifts through my mind.

What if Kerris *did* give me that box for a reason? It seems impossible, but still, I wonder...

Before my destination registers, I am already mounted on Nyx and riding along the trail of bones toward the bridge where River and Rynan have taken first watch.

I dismount without a word, tying Nyx to the post furthest from the fire pit.

The men leap to their feet, exchanging worried glances. I pay them no mind and head straight for the bridge.

"Where are you going, Everett?" one calls.

All it takes is a glower to shut him up.

I do not answer to them. I do not answer to anyone but our chieftain.

Seeing as he is not here right now, I am free to cross the bridge into Seelie territory. The journey takes me twenty minutes, but eventually the house where I last saw Kerris comes into view.

The flower still clutched in my fist looks so small and insignificant in light of the finery of her home, I almost turn around. But something in my foolish heart urges me to leave the gift on her stoop. I wish I could be here when she finds it just to see her face.

Will it make her smile? Will she know it is from me?

Such whimsical thoughts. How in the world would she know the gift came from me? She does not even know my name.

What was I thinking? This was a fool's errand.

I am about to retrieve my gift when there is a clang from inside. Somewhere close by, a cat lets out a low mewl.

With my heart in my throat, I sprint all the way back to the canyon, feeling like the biggest fool who has ever lived.

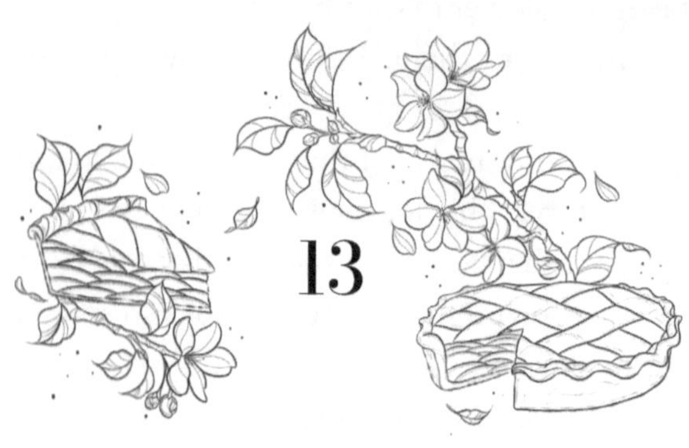

13

"Ronan. I wasn't expecting you this early." Thank goodness I bathed last night, otherwise it would be at least another hour for my hair to finish drying.

Today, my hair falls in soft waves over the blue and white pinstripe dress Madame Ella altered. Gone are the heavy sleeves my mother once wore, replaced by lace ties that refuse to stay up properly. The ruffles at the bottom of the skirt have been cut clean off, and she sewed on a length of baby pink fabric that grazes the tops of my matching pink slippers. I never would've paired the two together myself, but they create a stunning garment.

The prince grins from the stoop, one shoulder casually propped against the doorframe. "I couldn't wait until noon to see you."

Do they teach princes to be charming or is this an inherent trait?

From behind his back, Ronan reveals two boxes. The white one I recognize from Madame Ella. It's hard to believe she sent another dress already. She must be working round the clock.

The second is from the café where we went on our first date.

The pie inside appears to be the very same peach and blueberry masterpiece I enjoyed so much.

"You mentioned that you wanted to figure out how to make it yourself," Ronan says with a deep flush along his starched white collar.

The fact that he remembered not only what I ordered but also my desire to recreate the recipe means more than any words of flattery ever could. Now I can really test the flavors to figure out the ingredients—assuming I don't eat all of it first.

When I go to put the boxes on the hall table, I notice something shimmering in his pocket. Is that a flower? "Are you meeting another woman or is that for me as well?"

He glances down, then chuckles as he withdraws the bloom. "Oh, yes. Of course it's for you."

I spin the stem between my fingers, fascinated by the sunlight sparkling on the silver petals. "This is gorgeous." Quite possibly the most beautiful flower I've ever seen. The scent reminds me of a lily but isn't quite as strong.

"I'm glad you think so. I picked it especially for you, from the castle gardens."

"What kind of flower is it?" The petals look as if they've been dipped in moonlight.

"I'm not sure. I can ask the gardener if you'd like."

"Please, do. I would love to know." I thank him and bring my flower into the kitchen to retrieve a bud vase from the cabinet. The bouquet he sent me the other day sits in the windowsill, already wilting because the water has dried up.

It's silly, but this solitary flower feels even more special.

Not that I don't love bouquets as well, but a florist curated the bunch of roses and baby's breath, whereas he picked this one himself.

I add water to both vases but bring the silver flower upstairs to my bedside table. The petals are so delicate, so ethereal. Who knew Ronan could be so thoughtful?

By the time I return to the front door, I find not one suitor, but two.

Trevor stands shoulder to shoulder with Ronan, the two of them trading glares. In his hands, he clutches a brown paper package wrapped with twine.

"Trevor. Hi. I thought we were meeting tomorrow." Tell me I didn't get my days mixed up.

His head swings toward me so quickly, his spectacles slide to the end of his nose. "We are, but I bought you a gift and thought I would bring it by." He shoves his glasses back and then extends the package across the threshold.

So many gifts today, you'd swear it was my birthday. Less than five weeks left and it will be. Is one of these men my future husband? The thought makes my stomach burn with indecision. Good thing I still have time to choose.

Inside the package is a book. I run my fingers over the cracked leather binding and the faded gold foil title. *Unseelie Fae: A Scientific Study*.

Ronan snorts and folds his arms across his chest as he scowls at the tome. "Why the hell would you give her that?"

"Because she asked if the library had any books on the Unseelie. The only copy was already on loan, so I bought her this one."

"Thank you, Trevor. This is such a thoughtful present." And it couldn't come at a better time. After what happened yesterday, I'm more curious than ever.

"If it gives you nightmares, I'd be more than happy to keep you company after the sun falls," Ronan offers, pushing off the doorframe.

"I'm certain I will be fine." This is a book of science, not some terrifying horror tale. I set the book on the table next to the boxes and grab the parasol Aunt Cordelia loaned me. "Shall we go?"

Ronan offers his arm with a muttered, "We'll see you later, Trev," tossed over his shoulder. What he doesn't realize is that I can see him flashing my other suitor the middle finger.

There goes all the goodwill he earned with the flower and pie. "Actually, why don't you come along, Trevor? The more the merrier, right, Ronan?"

From the way he gawks, you'd swear I asked the prince to shave his head. It takes Ronan a whole ten seconds to stop blustering and respond with a choked, "Of course."

The walk is tense, one man asking me a question, followed by a completely unrelated question from the other. It's like holding two different conversations at the same time.

Ronan wants to know about my favorite food; Trevor asks if I have a favorite author.

Ronan invites me to have dinner with him the following evening at a restaurant overlooking the castle. The way he describes it sounds impossibly romantic.

Trevor asks if I'd be interested in a carriage ride to Glassmarsh to visit the greenhouse there. According to his brother, they have some of the most exotic plants in all the kingdom, including one that eats flies.

How fascinating. I definitely can't miss that.

By the time we reach the city center, my mind is spinning, and I've made enough plans with both men to last nearly to my birthday. I'm so relieved when we run into Nia and Nolan entering the same café that I give them both an exuberant hug.

Hopefully their presence will take some of the attention off of me.

The prince asks for a table at the back of the restaurant for privacy, and the server rushes to do Ronan's bidding.

Conversation flows like the expensive bottle of honey wine Ronan orders. The syrupy drink coats my throat in sweetness, sort of like the medicine I used to take when I would get sick as a child. The only differences are, it tastes a lot better *and* makes me feel like giggling even before I've finished my first glass.

Who would have thought that I would be sitting at a table with so many handsome men? Perhaps I should have come to Rosehill sooner.

"It really is too bad the monsters come to Rosehill on Wednesdays," Ronan grumbles. "Otherwise, we could've gone to the quarry for a swim yesterday."

"You mean the men." The Unseelie aren't monsters at all. Sure, they're taller, but I felt no malice from them yesterday, only mild curiosity. When I glance up, I find everyone staring at me as if I'd spilled the drink all over myself. "What?"

Ronan pats my knee, his smile tight. "You have only just arrived in Rosehill, Kerris. Your ignorance is understandable."

My ignorance. Is he joking? "Have you ever met them? Spoken to them?" From the way he carries on, I doubt it.

The prince's brows lift. "Have you?"

Walked straight into that one, didn't I? What is in this wine? "No. Of course not."

Nia shoots to her feet, her chair bobbling on the uneven stones. "I need to use the privy. Come with me, Kerris." She takes the glass out of my hand and sets it down on the table.

"I don't have to—" My cousin yanks me right out of my seat, hauling me toward the privy at the rear. "What is it with you and privies?" I mutter when she lets me go to lock the door behind us.

She ignores my question, her eyes flashing. "What the hell was that?"

All I can do is blink at her. Does she know how beautiful she is? And the dark kohl she added to her lashes makes them look impossibly long. I wonder if she'd let me borrow some the next time we go out?

"Kerris!"

"What?"

"Don't play coy with me. You defended the monsters across The Divide, and in front of the prince no less."

Again with the "monsters." She saw them, same as me. They aren't monsters at all. "All I did was say the Unseelie were men."

"*Dangerous* men."

Men all the same. I find myself shrugging, a little thrill zinging through my blood when I think of their leader's intense gaze.

Nia presses a hand to her forehead. "What did you do?"

The wine has made my lips feel a little too loose. "I may or may not have gone back to the well yesterday."

Her mouth drops open on a gasp, her face going white as her hair. "On your own?"

"No, with Ronan." HA! Imagine. "Of course, on my own."

"What happened?"

"Nothing, really. I mean, I spoke to them—"

"You did not."

A giddy little laugh climbs my throat. "I did."

"What did they say?"

"Nothing."

Her brows inch higher on her forehead. "At all?"

"Not a word. So I started wondering if perhaps the Unseelie speak a different language than we do." If that's the case, perhaps I could learn a phrase or two. "I had planned on going to the library to see if I could find out, but then Trevor gave me a book with more information about them." As soon as I get home, I'm going to read it from cover to cover.

With another huff, Nia props her hands on her hips, looking so much like her mother it makes me stand that much straighter. "You're here to find a husband, Kerris."

"I know." I'm here with two suitors, aren't I? "But since we aren't supposed to leave our homes on Wednesdays, technically, my interest in the Unseelie isn't interfering—"

"It doesn't matter! You cannot hope to make a good match if you flout the rules meant to keep us safe. If Ronan finds out, he will want nothing to do with you. Forget about them, Kerris. I'm begging here." Her eyes are so imploring, I find myself offering a tight-lipped nod in return.

I thought Nia would understand. That she would be up for this adventure.

Clearly, I was wrong.

"Focus on choosing a husband first," she says. "Once you are wed, *then* you can do all the research you want."

Scientific study, my arse.

I'm two chapters into Trevor's book and so far, it's filled with more conjecture than facts. There's no mention of the language the Unseelie speak or anything about what happened to their wells.

In the third chapter there are some illustrations that look nothing like the men I met. Beasts with elongated fangs that hang over rolled lips, coal-black eyes without a speck of white, and warts everywhere. The only part the illustrator got right were the longer ears, the greenish skin, and the muscles. Although in the drawing, their bodies are covered in coarse hair, kind of like boars.

And they... um...

The aren't wearing any trousers.

The only member of the opposite sex that I have ever seen undressed is my brother when we were children, so I understand how a man's anatomy differs from a woman's, but this illustration cannot possibly be correct.

My door swings wide, and I snap the book closed when Nia steps inside.

"It's almost three o'clock in the morning," she groans on a yawn, rubbing at her squinting eyes. "What are you still doing awake?"

"Nothing." I tuck the book under the covers.

She whips the quilt away and grabs the thing before I can stop her. Her eyes narrow. "Kerris, I thought I told you to put the Unseelie out of your—" She flips open the book, and the words die on her lips.

Even from my bed, I can see that she has stumbled upon the exact page that I've been staring at for the last twenty minutes.

Is it possible to die from mortification?

"Well," she breathes, her own face as flushed as mine surely is. "I can certainly see what's keeping you up in the middle of the night."

I hide my flaming cheeks behind my hands, stifling my laughter. "Go away, you menace. I am only doing research."

"Mmmhmmm. I see that. If I'd known this was the sort of 'research' you were doing, I wouldn't have protested so much."

I let my hands drop even though my face still feels as if it's been burned by the sun. "There's no way it's that big." Is there?

She tilts her head from one side to the other, then tilts the book, bringing the pages so close to her face that her eyes go crossed. "If it is, it's larger than Nolan's."

"Nia!"

Her cheeks dimple with her grin. "What?" She holds the book

out to me, tapping the page right next to...*it.* "Tell me that doesn't look like a third arm."

Swiping my book out of her hand, I clutch the yellowed pages to my chest. "Go back to bed and leave me alone."

"Oh, I see how it is. Do you and your book need some privacy?"

"You are incorrigible."

She saunters into the hall, but before she closes the door, she sticks her head back inside and wiggles her brows. "I'm not the one 'researching.'"

14

*"Research suggests the first Unseelie fae were born
of shadows and darkness."*

— Unseelie Fae: A Scientific Study

I'm about to break my promise to Nia.

I feel terrible about breaching her trust, but not terrible enough to turn back. Nia left for drinks with Nolan over an hour ago. She offered to let me tag along, but I declined. They deserved time alone together, and I needed her out of the house so she didn't realize that I had no intention of staying in my room.

Getting around the city without being noticed wasn't difficult. All I had to do was keep the hood on the cloak I borrowed from Nia's closet pulled over my hair and not trip over my skirts again. The dress Madame Ella sent yesterday was far too long. I would've thought she sent it to the wrong address if my name hadn't been written on the box.

Nia suggested bringing it back, but I don't want to be a bother.

Madame Ella is already doing me a favor by altering my mother's dresses, so I did my own hemming this morning.

The handful of people I came across were too drunk to even notice me skirting the shadows in my borrowed cloak. The downside is that, by the time I reach The Divide, I'm a ball of sweat underneath the thick wool.

The bridge waits like a silent sentinel, guarding the unknown.

There's nothing to be afraid of. I've already met the people who live on the other side, and the bridge can handle the weight of not only horses and riders, but also carts of water . These old planks won't have an issue with my weight.

It's going to be fine.

Everything is fine.

With cool air filling my lungs, I take the first step.

Beyond the quiet groan of the board beneath my slipper, nothing happens. I don't burst into flames or keel over dead. It's just a bridge. I cross bridges all the time. Couldn't reach the well in Gravale without crossing one.

Everything is fine.

I take another step. And another. Each one feels like a victory, a testament to my perseverance.

When I return to Rosehill, I'll be able to tell everyone with certainty that there is nothing to fear. That our neighbors aren't monsters out to dine on our flesh for supper. They have no intention of using our bones to pick their teeth clean.

Those are the sorts of nonsensical lies printed in the first few chapters of that ridiculous book Trevor gave me. I got so irritated by the falsehoods, I couldn't even finish.

No wonder everyone in Rosehill is terrified.

When I can no longer see any lamplight at my back, the bridge starts to sway of its own volition. I wait for shadows to emerge from the gloom, but nothing appears. Mist falls around me like a shroud, so thick I can hardly see the steps in front of me.

Despite the roughness cutting into my palms, my hands remain steady on the ropes holding the swaying planks. This isn't so bad. A little eerie, sure, but the more I walk, the easier it is to take the next step.

I swipe my hands down my skirts, thankful for the cool silk against the soreness. Surely, I must be almost to the other side by now. This must be the longest bridge in the—

My foot meets nothing but air.

I'm too far gone to pull back, and my body tips forward. My arms cartwheel, missing the rope on my way down. No! No! "No!" I flail for something to keep me from plummeting to my death, somehow managing to catch the brace where the board should have been attached. The rusted metal bites into my hands as I dangle, nothing but air and terror beneath me.

A scream rips from my throat as I beg for help. If I cannot pull myself up, I'm going to plummet to my death, my bones broken and entrails splattered over whatever waits at the bottom of the abyss.

Stupid, bloomin' weak arms.

My life flashes before my eyes.

My mother's laugh.

My father's smile.

My brother's teasing.

My fingers cramp, and I screw my eyes closed, praying to whatever deity is listening.

Nia will be devastated. My poor father and brother will never know the truth of my demise. My sudden disappearance will break their hearts.

Why didn't I stay home? Why didn't I listen to Nia when she told me to put the Unseelie out of my head? Why did I venture into this terrible place of darkness and shadows and death and—

Something clamps around my hand. My eyes flash open, meeting a pair of dark eyes set in a face I recognize.

The Unseelie leader, the one who took my biscuits.

I wait for him to peel away my fingers and let me fall to nothing, to be the monster everyone says he is.

Instead, he offers me a second hand. I cling to him like a lifeline while he lifts me as if I weigh nothing, right over the missing planks to where he stands. I collapse against his damp chest, gasping for breath, willing my thundering pulse to slow.

My palms and fingers ache and burn, but I don't even care because *I'm alive.*

I screw my eyes closed to stem my tears, but still they find their way through my lashes.

If he hadn't been nearby—

Brilliant. Now I'm sobbing.

Peering through watery lashes, I find myself face-to-face with a very bare gray-green chest.

I jump away to give him space and would've fallen back into that damn canyon if he didn't catch me again. This time, he spins me around and places me so that he's the one with his back to the hole.

What a bloomin' disaster. "Th-thank you for saving me."

The man's expression is as stony as ever, his eyes so solemn beneath the thick curtain of his lashes. "You should not be here." His deep voice rumbles with the slightest hint of a lilting accent.

Wait. He just spoke to me. He speaks our language!

I knew his voice would be deep and rough. I bloody well knew it—

Hold on. If he can speak our language, does that mean he understood everything I said Wednesday and chose not to respond?

How rude—not that I say that aloud considering he saved me from certain death.

Twice.

He blows out what sounds like a frustrated breath and props his hands on his hips. Suddenly, I'm very aware of every single hard line of his bare torso. His flat nipples, darker than the rest of him. His belly button amidst the ridges of his abdomen.

Stop staring at him, you loon!

You should not be here...

I force my gaze to meet his. "Is it illegal?"

His brow furrows as he shakes his head. "There is no law, but there are rules. And it is not safe for someone like you on this side of the canyon."

Irritation flares in my chest, heating me all the way through. "Someone like me? And what, pray, do you mean by that?"

"Someone so...soft."

"I am not *soft*." I mean, compared to him maybe, but I'm stronger than I look.

He arches a dark brow.

I liked him better when he didn't speak. "If it's so unsafe, then what are you doing out here?"

"Hunting."

"Without a shirt?" That doesn't seem very safe or smart. "Don't you get cold?"

He glances down at himself, as if he's forgotten that his chest is bare. When he looks back at me, his eyes have narrowed. "No."

"Not even in the winter?" I'd die without the heavy coat of furs that used to belong to my mother.

He shakes his head slowly.

Fascinating. Perhaps his skin is thicker than mine. If it wasn't wildly inappropriate, I'd ask if I could touch him again. Purely for research purposes, not because I want to, because that would be foolish.

Nearly falling to my death aside, I am not a fool.

A fool would want to run her hands down the planes of his chest or drag her fingertips over the ripples of his stomach or trace the deep cut of his hips—

But not me. Not at all.

The man stares at me as if I said all of that that aloud.

What I need right now is a distraction. Let's see... Wait! I know. "I brought you more biscuits." I slip my pack from my shoulders and withdraw the box. "My mother always said that you shouldn't arrive to anyone's house empty-handed." This might not be his house, but it is his territory, so I figured the rule applies.

He takes the box quicker than he did on Wednesday, reminding me of the cat I adopted back home. The thing hated me at first, clawing and scratching any time I got near. But after bringing it a bowl of milk every day for a month, the little ginger menace eventually allowed me to pet its matted fur.

Speaking of fur, this man has none. If the book Trevor gave me was wrong about that, were they wrong about everything else? My gaze drops to the man's dark green trousers for a split second before I realize what I'm doing and focus once more on his face.

A face that is still fixed in a scowl.

"This is a Seelie custom, then?" he says slowly. "To give a gift of sustenance to everyone you meet?"

I'd hardly call a few biscuits sustenance, but that is neither here nor there. "I suppose it is, especially when you're trying to make new friends."

For some reason, that makes his eyes widen. "You wish to be my friend?"

"Of course. But in order for that to happen, you should probably tell me your name." It feels strange to have met him twice now and still not know.

The Unseelie's chest expands as a heavy breath passes through his lips. He glances over his shoulder toward Rosehill like he can't wait for me to be gone. "My name is Everett."

Everett.

Everett.

Everett.

"That's a nice name." A nice name? Really? Did I honestly

come all the way over here to tell this man that he has a nice name and give him biscuits?

Nia is right. I have gone mad.

I look away, my cheeks blazing. That's when I notice two planks stacked behind me.

The planks weren't missing at all. They were removed.

Did he take them out because of Ronan trying to cross the bridge, or have they always been gone? If it's the latter, Ronan could've met the same fate I almost did. He's lucky to be alive.

I bunch my skirts in my hands and wince when I remember the soreness there.

Everett sets the box on the bridge and holds out his hand. "May I see your palm?"

For the first time since I arrived, I realize exactly how alone we are. He could push me through that hole in the bridge, and no one would ever know.

"I will not harm you," he says gently.

I know that, don't I? Otherwise, I wouldn't have snuck out to meet him.

With a deep breath, I set my hand in his.

The only change in his expression is a slight flutter of the muscles in his jaw. From his pocket, he withdraws a flask. He thumbs-open the lid and pours cool water over my sore skin. Not just any water—water that instantly heals the wound, erasing all redness and pain.

"Thank you." Cupping my fingers, I splash my other hand.

He returns the top to his flask and stuffs it back into his pocket.

Are those *cuts* on his shoulder? It looks like he might have been grazed by some pesky thorns. I hate it when that happens. Back home, they used to snag my skirts something awful.

Hesitantly, I raise my damp fingers to the small scratches.

Everett stiffens beneath my touch, and his nostrils flare. In hindsight, I probably should've asked his permission the way he asked mine. Oh, well. It's too late now.

Muttering an apology, I dry my hands on my skirts.

Everett drives a hand through his hair, sweeping the dark strands from one side of his forehead to the other. "Why have you come, Kerris Dawn?"

For some reason, knowing he remembers my name makes me feel as if I could fly all the way back to the cottage.

"It's just Kerris. We're friends so you don't have to use my surname. And to answer your question—"

A sudden wind whips across my cheeks, and Everett hisses out a breath, cutting off my explanation. He stalks past me to collect the missing panels, replacing them one by one, muttering, "You must return home."

"But—" I haven't even gotten to ask my questions.

Everett's dark brows slam down over narrowed eyes. "*Go. Now.*"

The urgency in his tone leaves me whirling for my side of The Divide. Even though I know all the planks are there, I still hold tight to the ropes, just in case.

When I'm safely standing on Seelie dirt, I turn to find Everett only a step behind. The man moves like a shadow, not even the boards creaking under his feet. He comes to a halt on the final plank, his dark eyes trained on the ground.

His fingers flex and stretch at his sides, the muscles along his chiseled jaw jumping.

"Do it," I say.

His head lifts and our gazes lock. Something deep and knowing stirs in my chest the same way it did the first day at the well.

"Go on. I dare you. Don't let me be the only one breaking the rules tonight."

With his gaze still on me, he takes the final step.

I don't know why, but this seems like a small victory after the monumental failure of my visit to the Unseelie fae.

To my delight, Everett doesn't stop there. He escorts me along the outskirts of the city, all the way to my aunt and uncle's back gate.

Once I close and lock the latch, he turns and disappears into the night, leaving me to sneak back to my bed, my heart filled with so much excitement it's bound to burst.

It isn't until I'm drifting off to sleep that I realize: Everett led me back home...

But I never told him where I live.

15

Everett

"The kiss of spring is all it takes to make the winter flee."

— An Unseelie Fable, Author Unknown

I run all the way back to the canyon. The moment I reach the bridge, I slow my pace so the fate that nearly befell Kerris does not claim me as well. If I had not heard her cry for help, she would have fallen to the bottom, never to be seen or heard from again. Dropped like one of those stones Maddox insists on throwing night in, night out.

On my way, I collect the box she brought for me.

Not for me. For whomever she happened to meet.

By the time I step back into Unseelie territory, my anger has been stoked into a flaming inferno. The three males laughing by the fire are about to know the true meaning of rage.

The box Kerris gave me crushes in my trembling hands. "Which one of you lazy shits removed the planks from the bridge?"

They stumble to their feet, but no one has the bollocks to fess up. Figures. These fools think they know everything, yet two of them have never even made their first proper kill.

"No one wants to come forward?" I seethe, vibrating with the force of my temper. It is not only anger boiling beneath my skin but also fear. If I had not been close by—

One male, with his hair skinned all the way to his scalp, plants his fists on his hips. Even with his spine stiff, he is still a good hand shorter than me. "Why does it matter?" he asks, sneering at the box in my hands.

It matters because I fucking say it matters. "One of the Seelie fae nearly fell into the canyon."

"So? If you ask me, there are too many damn Seelie anyway."

No one asked him because he is a sniveling little pissant who is about to have his nose broken.

Kerris did not deserve to die because these fools were too careless and lazy to do their damn job. We watch the bridge, not only to keep the wolves out, but also to track their movements and ensure none of them reach our camp.

That is what I have been doing since this afternoon. One of the lookouts at our northern post thought he saw a wolf prowling through the forest there. The most seasoned hunters set out immediately to search for tracks but found none.

Removing only one or two planks from the bridge would not be enough to keep the beasts from leaping across the gap and plundering the Seelie city. I have seen a wolf jump from one side of a river to the other without getting its fur wet.

"What is your name?" I demand.

"Joseph."

I cannot wait to see Joseph's face when he is called before the chieftain for such a catastrophic failure. None of them heard Kerris scream, which makes me wonder where the fuck they were when she fell.

"Those 'damn Seelie' allow us access to their well. How do you think you would fare if they found out we failed to protect them and revoked our privileges? Hmmm?" That shuts him up as I knew it would. "What about the rest of you? Does anyone else have an issue with this position? Would anyone else like to take shortcuts and leave their posts?"

All of them shake their heads.

That is what I thought. "If I ever come back here again and find you have abandoned your posts, you will be stripped of your mounts and exiled from camp. Do you understand?"

I wait until every one of them mutters his acquiesce before stalking back to where I left Nyx in a panic. There is no worldly explanation for how I knew the scream had come from Kerris, but in my bones, *I knew*.

I stuff the box into my saddlebag and stick my foot into the stirrup, my rage still choking me as I kick Nyx into a gallop down the bone-lined path. When I was young, I felt the same as Joseph, not overly concerned for the fae across the canyon.

None of them have ever mattered before.

But this is *her*.

Gryffin was right all along. The gift was not an offer of courtship, but a request for friendship. I touch the spot where she laid her fingers on my shoulder. I am not certain what I feel for the Seelie fae, but this attraction feels stronger than friendship.

The thought of any harm befalling her makes me want to become Kerris Dawn's own personal shadow.

I tug the reins before I hit camp, urging Nyx to slow down in hopes that my own hammering pulse will return to normal. When we reach my barrel-top, a dark shape waits on my steps.

The stairs creak as Leah descends and takes the reins from me, tying Nyx to the post. "Why are you back so late? The rest of the hunting party returned well over an hour ago."

"I stopped by the bridge to check the guard."

Nyx snorts with satisfaction as Leah pats his wiry black mane, scratching right below his horn just the way he likes. "You cannot keep burning the candle at both ends. At some point, even you need to take a break."

I dismount on the opposite side from where she stands, clipping my saddlebag so she does not see the white box hidden within. I do not have it in me tonight for another argument. "And I am taking one." As soon as she leaves, I am going to fall into bed and sleep until noon.

Leah's hand grazes my thigh as she drifts along next to me. "Perhaps I will take a break with you."

Can she not see that having her around makes me less inclined to agree to her proposal? "I am tired."

She sidles closer, "walking" her fingers down my chest to the buckle on my belt. "Then we can sleep until you are not tired anymore."

I catch her hand before she can unfasten the leather strap. "Go home. I am not in the mood."

Her hand falls, but her eyes flash. "You are never in the mood."

Exactly.

And that is part of the problem.

16

My lashes flutter open, and all I can do is stare up at the beams on the ceiling. What time is it? It feels as if I just closed my eyes, but according to the clock on the mantle, it's almost noon. The last time I slept this late was...

I can't remember ever sleeping through breakfast.

I throw the covers aside and sit up. The book on the Unseelie clatters to the carpet from where I must've dropped it in my sleep. My head feels heavy, as if filled with cotton wool. I slip out of the bed to retrieve the book, setting it on my bedside table next to the flower Ronan brought me two days before.

Thanks to the water in the vase, the shimmering petals look even healthier than they did yesterday.

As beautiful as the flower may be, when I think of the prince, there is a distinct lack of fluttering in my stomach. In contrast, when I think of a certain Unseelie, I have to clutch the sheets to keep the butterflies from lifting me clean off the floor.

This is a problem.

A big one.

One that could easily be solved by putting said Unseelie out of my mind.

But how am I supposed to do that when I can still hear the deep rumble of his voice and feel the dark sweep of his gaze upon my skin?

Thankfully, quelling the whine in my stomach provides the perfect distraction from these troubles of my own making.

By the time I dress and go downstairs, everyone is already sitting at the kitchen table for lunch.

Nia's lips twist as she dips her spoon in and out of her bowl. "Good morning. Or should I say afternoon?"

It's like she can see straight through me to those damn butterflies. "Sorry. I don't know what came over me. I never sleep this long." A sheepish smile insists on taking over my lips as I collect a bowl from the counter, filling it with hearty vegetable soup. When I find brown bread still warm from the oven sitting next to a dish of smoked salmon, my heart leaps. I snag two slices on my way past, carrying everything over to the table.

My aunt stretches a hand across the table, pressing a cool palm to my forehead the same way my mother used to when I'd complain of any ailment.

It's amazing how something so small and seemingly insignificant can make one's eyes burn.

"You do feel a little warm," she muses. "Hopefully you aren't coming down with something. I hear Mrs. Willis's youngest has had an awful fever for the last week."

Since I have no clue who Mrs. Willis or her youngest are, I assume I haven't caught whatever ails them.

If my family knew with whom I spent my night, they'd probably blame Everett for my lie-in and insist I bathe to keep the warts away.

The memory of how small my hand looked in his when he used his water to heal me sends my stomach fluttering anew.

This is a big, big problem.

Nia taps her spoon against her smirking lips. "Another dress arrived from Madame Ella this morning."

Hopefully this one fits. The skirt on the last one was far too long.

"And one of your admirers left something for you as well," she singsongs over her soup.

The prospect of a charming prince or a handsome scholar dropping off gifts doesn't excite me as much as it should.

Unless one of them brought desserts. Now, *that* sounds enticing.

Nia nods toward the solitary silver flower in the vase by the ice box.

"That's from Ronan." A heaviness that feels a lot like disappointment spreads through my chest. Perhaps I *am* coming down with something.

Nia's smile widens. "Nolan says that he has never heard of Ronan Reve giving anyone flowers before."

"You should consider yourself very lucky, Kerris," my aunt says with the barest hint of a smile. "Many women would kill to be in your position."

I should consider myself lucky, except...

A pair of dark eyes flashes through my mind, and my heart pinches at the memory of Everett so gallantly crossing the border simply to escort me home. I'm dying to tell Nia, but that would mean admitting to breaking my promise. They say all's well that ends well, but I'm not entirely sure that would be the case here.

The three of us chat about the upcoming Beltane festival over our stew. Apparently, the king considered changing the date of the celebration from the first of May to the second since the first fell on a Wednesday. Ultimately, his advisory committee voted to keep it on the same day. However, the Seelie are to stay inside until after five to be sure the Unseelie are all gone.

Did it ever cross their minds to invite the Unseelie? That this would be the perfect opportunity to come together in celebration of a new season?

Having slept through breakfast, I help myself to a second serving of soup to help me survive until dinner. Afterward, Nia and I clean the dishes while her mother rolls crust for a strawberry rhubarb pie. We offer to help, but she tells us there's no need on her way out to the chicken coop.

My mouth waters as I stare longingly at the flecks of sugar glittering atop the dough lattice. I'm not sure I can wait for it to be baked. "Would you like to go to town? I'm craving chocolate cake." Or raspberry macaroons. Or some gooey banoffee pie.

Perhaps I'll purchase all three.

"You know me. I never miss a chance to go to town."

Unless it's Wednesday, I muse silently, snagging the towel to dry my own hands.

Part of me wishes it was Wednesday so that I could sneak out to meet Everett.

I really need to stop thinking about him. If I'm not careful, this obsession is going to consume me.

The new silver flower catches my eye. Perhaps that will help.

I pluck the bloom from the vase.

When I tuck the flower behind my ear, Nia's eyes widen from where she waits in the doorway, parasol in hand. "Just so you know, Ronan will take that as a declaration."

Shrugging, I throw open the door. "He might."

"He absolutely will," she counters, skipping down the path beside me. "Does this mean you've made a decision? Are you going to be the next Queen of Willowhaven?"

"I doubt it. Besides, it's too soon to tell."

"That's not true. I knew Nolan was my soulmate the moment he smiled at me."

"How?"

"Where do I even begin? My stomach went all jittery, and my heart felt like it was going to leap from my chest. For the longest time, he was all I could think about."

See, neither the prince nor Trevor have that effect on me.

When I think of Everett, however, my insides feel all twisted up, which is inconvenient to say the least. What would Nia say if she found out the truth?

That it's *him* who makes my stomach flutter and heart leap.

That it's *him* I dream of at night.

Based on her assessment of soulmates, I should be proposing to Everett.

On our way into town, we end up running into Ronan and Nolan near the city fountain.

The prince beams, and although I find myself returning his smile, my heart does not leap and my stomach does not flutter, not even when he nudges my shoulder with his and invites me to visit the castle the following morning.

The prospect doesn't sound as enticing as it might've in the past. What is wrong with me?

Ronan raises his brows, his gaze imploring.

Right. His invitation. "I would like that very much," I say, telling myself that it's true.

The prince's chest puffs out, and his gaze traces my face,

landing on the flower behind my ear. "This is beautiful. I've never seen one quite that shade."

"Very funny."

His brow furrows. "Why is that funny?"

Is he serious? "It's from your gardens, Ronan. You left it for me this morning."

His eyes widen and he presses a hand to his forehead. "Oh. Yes. Yes, of course it is. How silly of me to have forgotten."

I step back, studying his face, noting the way he refuses to meet my gaze.

He's lying.

Why though? It's only a flower. Why would he take the credit when it wasn't from him? Have the flowers been from Trevor this whole time?

When Ronan asks if we'd like company at the cafe, Nia says yes before I can tell him no, so it looks like I'm stuck with the prince.

Not exactly the sentiment of a woman on the verge of proposing.

Nia and Nolan's joined hands swing between them, the pair grinning like lovesick teenagers at one another. I pretend not to notice when Ronan reaches for mine and tuck my hand into the pockets sewn into my skirts instead. His shoulders slump, but he quickly recovers, regaling us with a story about seeing lions.

He's probably lying.

Am I overreacting about this? It's only a flower, after all.

If he's willing to lie about something so small, will he tell the truth about the bigger things? The ones that truly matter?

The balmy breeze flutters the petals of the flower behind my ear, tickling my cheek. My yearning for dessert has evaporated altogether. Perhaps I should skip the café and visit Trevor instead.

You know what? That's exactly what I'm going to do.

When we pass the library, I tell Nia I'll meet her in a few minutes.

"Where are you going?" Ronan calls at my back.

"To see if Trevor would like to join us," I throw over my shoulder. It might make me a bad person, but I delight in the way the prince scoffs. Serves him right after playing me false.

I skirt around two women pushing prams and slip between the library's open doors. The familiar scent of ink, musty parchment, and worn leather fills my lungs, dampening my ire.

Never in my life have I seen shelves this high. With the way the shadows cling to the vaulted ceiling, you can barely see the tops. There are more books in this place than a fae could hope to read in ten lifetimes.

Quietly, I make my way to where a woman in a pinstripe suit sits behind a wide mahogany desk. When I ask for Trevor Dillon, she gives me directions to an office at the very back of the library.

I find Trevor bent over a large book with ornate script in golds and greens, glasses perched at the end of his nose and his hair falling over his brow. He looks so handsome, so quiet and studious, yet there isn't so much as a flutter in my stomach.

There used to be though. Where have all the flutters gone?

Trevor glances up, his eyes widening when they meet mine. The chair scrapes the ground as he pushes back from the desk and launches to his feet. "Kerris. What are you doing here?" He swipes the glasses from his nose, tucking them into the pocket of his tweed waistcoat.

He smiles and I feel...*nothing*. I press a hand to my stomach, willing the butterflies to wake up, but they remain dormant. "I was in town and thought I'd call in to see if you'd like to come out for a bite to eat."

His smile falters and his shoulders fall with his sigh. "That sounds lovely, but I am quite busy today."

What did I expect? That he would drop everything simply because I strolled in?

I should let him get back to work, but first, there is a mystery to solve. I let my fingers trail along the flower's silky petals as I tuck a few loose strands of hair behind my ear.

Trevor's lips press flat, his brow furrowing. "That flower you're wearing. What kind is it?"

If he doesn't know, then he probably isn't the one who left it for me either. God's tooth, this is so frustrating. I've met a handful of other men in Rosehill but cannot imagine any of them leaving flowers without so much as a card. "I was actually hoping you could tell me."

Fishing out his glasses once more, he gestures toward the bloom. "May I?"

I slip the flower from behind my ear and hand it over.

"It looks like some sort of lily, but I've never seen one with petals like this. Truly remarkable." After a few more moments of study, he tucks it behind my ear once more, his fingers lingering in my hair.

His wistful sigh warms my cheeks as he takes a step back. "I'm afraid I really must be getting back to work."

"Of course. I'm sorry for interrupting."

His lips tip up, and he sinks back onto his chair. "You never have to apologize for that. Would you like to meet for tea on Monday? I could come by your cottage around noon."

"I would love that."

I make my way back out of the library, more confused than before. If the flower didn't come from Ronan or Trevor, then who—

Maybe it was...

No, that's ridiculous.

Or is it?

None of the Seelie seem to recognize the flower.

Is that because it didn't come from our side of The Divide?

17

"Unseelie fae can scent their prey from a kilometer away."

— *Unseelie Fae: A Scientific Study*

Moonlight peeks through the clouds, kissing the silver petals of the two flowers thriving in my windowsill. *Everett knew where I lived.*

He brought me right to my doorstep without a word of direction. Is that because he's been here before, perhaps with a flower in tow?

I should leave well enough alone. I've already appeased my curiosity over the Unseelie, after all. But the thought of seeing Everett again makes me giddier than all my suitors combined, and I simply have to know.

One more visit to confirm my suspicion. That's all.

Then the husband hunt will truly begin.

I ease the bedroom door open and slip into the hallway, keeping to the side of the staircase to avoid any unnecessary squeaks. After visiting Trevor, I went to the café with the intention of forgetting the whole silly thing. Then I saw Ronan and just couldn't bring myself to hold an idle conversation with the man.

As I stood on the sidewalk watching the three of them laugh and joke, Ivee swept through the café doors and stole my seat.

Although I felt guilty for Nia having to endure her presence, not a hint of jealousy sparked in my veins. As a matter of fact, if Ivee had proposed to Prince Ronan then and there, I would've wished them well.

Not wanting to make things awkward, I returned to the cottage and stole away to my room intending on reading my Unseelie book. Unfortunately, the late night led to a nap, which means I'm wide awake at two in the bloomin' morning.

I tiptoe through the kitchen to the back door, unfasten the latch, and step into the moonlit garden.

Instead of crossing the field and ruining my slippers in the dew, I take the path through town. There are still a few people in the pub, but most appear to have gone home for the night. Now that I have my bearings, it's easy to keep to the shadows, and there's no fear of anyone following once The Divide comes into view.

When I reach the bridge, I do not hesitate to take that first step. Keeping a hand on the rope railing in case any boards have been removed, I slowly make my way forward, searching the mist for signs of the man I hope to find.

The heaviness in the air grows thicker, until I can barely make out my next step. I stretch my foot ahead, feeling for the plank instead of assuming it's there, continuing until my slipper meets solid wood.

The mist thins enough for me to see white bones scattered across the ground the way our gardens stretch in our front lawns, as if the bones have grown from the dirt. There is a path between them, and on that path stands Everett.

Was he this tall last night? He must've been, but saints above, he seems twice as large.

And twice as handsome.

I raise a hand in greeting, but he remains still.

Perhaps they don't wave on this side of The Divide. Then again, I'll not assume that is the case the same way I did about the non-existent language barrier.

I keep my head up, ignoring the harsh reminders of death that surround us. Despite his lack of a proper greeting, the way his dark gaze sweeps down my periwinkle dress leaves my heart ramming against my breastbone. When his eyes return to my face, they track a little higher, to the flower in my hair, and they widen ever so slightly.

His chest goes still, as if he's holding his breath, and somehow, I already know the answer before the question falls from my lips. "You recognize it, don't you?" I withdraw the stem from behind my ear, holding the silver bloom in the palm of my hand so there can be no mistake.

"It is a flower."

That *voice*. The deep, delicious rumble bathes me in goosebumps. "Yes, but what kind of flower is it?"

"How should I know?"

"Because you're the one who gave it to me."

His weight shifts from one foot to the other, but he does not deny my accusation. I was right! *Bloody Ronan.*

Now that I know Everett brought me the first flower after I met him at the well, that still doesn't explain how he knew where to leave it in the first place. "How did you know where I lived?"

They're monsters...

Dangerous...

Perhaps his intentions aren't so gallant after all. Just because I feel as if I know him doesn't mean I do. "Are you stalking me?"

"No. That is not what..." His hands flex. "*No.* You and your friend were in the city on your own that first day. I only wanted to ensure that you made it back home safely."

He could be lying, but from the sincere expression on his face, I don't believe that is the case. Didn't he do the very same for me last night?

"But why did you leave the flower?" All I did was give him a box of biscuits and an awkward greeting. He doesn't seem the type to carry around flowers, meaning he must've crossed The Divide a second time.

His toned shoulders lift and lower in a stiff shrug. "You gave me gifts, so I gave you gifts in return. Now we are even."

"I didn't bring you biscuits expecting anything back." That's considered bartering, not gifting.

His black brows come together over narrowed eyes. "Seelie do nothing without asking for something in return. They are not kind. They are not gracious. What do you want, Kerris Dawn? Do not lie and say *friendship*."

I have spent my day being lied to and disappointed by the men I've met in Rosehill; why would this one be any different? Who cares about the bloody flower? It meant nothing. He was only reciprocating because he thinks I'm like all the other Seelie fae who hate them.

I was willing to go out on a limb, to give Everett and the rest of the Unseelie the benefit of the doubt, and now he's throwing my kindness in my face.

Straightening my shoulders, I infuse my spine and tone with steel so he doesn't hear the tears clogging my throat when I say, "I want nothing from you." I crush the flower in my palm, toss it on the ground next to the bones, and turn and run away.

18

Nia sweeps into my room, a white box with black ribbon in one hand and a silver flower in the other. The box, she tosses on the bed and the flower she tucks into the vase with the first one Everett gave me. I wonder what he *expects in return* for the "gift."

My cousin's lips quirk as she stares down at me still lounging abed. "I should be mad at you, you know. You ditched me, which meant I had to spend the afternoon with Ivee bloody Lynch."

"I'm sorry."

She drops onto the mattress and starts to bounce with glee, her hair springing every which way. "You can make it up to me by telling me all about your date with Trevor. Spare no details. Did he bring you back to his cottage? Did you let him *keep your records*—if you know what I mean?"

"Stop waggling your eyebrows like that. You look ridiculous."

"I'll stop when you start talking."

"There isn't much to tell. I went to see Trevor, but he was busy working. Then my stomach started hurting so I came home and took a nap."

Nia's bouncing and waggling come to an abrupt stop. "I had to sit across from Ivee—*Ivee*, Kerris. The least you could do is have some sort of scandalous love affair with Ronan's rival."

If she wants scandal, perhaps I should tell her about meeting Everett, after all. Instead, I shrug. She has made her feelings on the Unseelie quite plain. "Sorry to disappoint."

"Kerris, dear!" my aunt calls from downstairs. "The prince is here to collect you!"

Collect me for what?

Oh, no...

I completely forgot that I agreed to accompany him to the castle today.

Nia launches off the bed, tripping over my discarded slippers on her way to the wardrobe. She flings open the doors and starts combing through my gowns. "What about this one?" She holds out the yellow one with the daisy corset.

How about none of them? "I don't really want to go."

"Tell me you're joking. Kerris, you have been given an audience with the King and Queen of Willowhaven. That is not something you cancel at the last minute unless you're dying."

It's not the king and queen I have an issue with. It's their deceitful son. Not that I can tell Nia that because then she will ask who gave me the flowers and that would lead to a conversation about Everett and then an argument.

I'm too bloody tired to argue.

So I roll out of bed, prepared to bite my tongue until the day is through.

She withdraws a deep violet gown from the back. "What about this one? It looks very regal."

It does look regal, but there's only one problem. "Madame Ella made the skirt too long."

Nia's lips purse as she holds the dress up to her willowy frame. Sure enough, the dress is too long for my cousin as well. "That's not like her. All the dresses Madame Ella has made for me have been perfect."

"The last few gowns she sent have been the same." There were a few in the mix that fit, but the others must've been meant for someone else.

"We can bring them back to her next week. Until then, you go brush your teeth and hair, and I'll get my needle and thread."

Ronan waits outside the cottage in a gilded carriage more opulent than any I've ever seen—even the wheels are golden. Once I'm settled, the driver cracks the whip and we're off, rolling down the cobbled streets while passersby stop to gawk and point.

I hate every second of it.

Who needs a golden carriage? It's utterly ridiculous, if you ask me. Surely there are better uses for one's wealth than this.

Ronan's hand falls to my knee with a reassuring squeeze, his smile making his eyes crinkle at the corners. "I missed you yesterday."

When I cross my legs, his hand slips off. "My stomach started hurting, so I went back home."

"How are you feeling now?"

Like I don't want to be here. "A little nervous, I suppose." Although I'm not sure why. It's not as if I plan on proposing to Ronan and need his parents' approval.

"Don't worry. My parents are going to love you."

We'll see about that.

His smile tightens as he turns to face me fully. "But you might do me one small favor," he says. "If they ask about your family, can you tell them your father is something respectable? Like an accountant?"

Something respectable? Is he joking? I can't lie to the king and queen. All they have to do is ask anyone from Gravale to find out the truth. There must be awful consequences for sowing such falsehoods.

Besides, I'm proud of my father's job. Raising goats might not be the most glamourous work, but my father is a good, honest man.

Ronan pats my knee once more as we roll to a stop at the base of the castle's marble stairs, seeming unfazed by having asked this of me. Meanwhile, I feel as if I'm a piece of muck unfit to cling to the prince's shiny boots.

All this time, I believed Ronan liked me for me, that he didn't care about my father's occupation.

I should've known better.

He has proven time and again that he is willing to lie about everything; why wouldn't he lie about this?

"Ronan, this is a mistake—"

The door opens and a servant in blue and gold livery appears, his hand extended toward me.

I can't exactly tell him to take me back now, can I?

My stomach twists as I step out of the carriage.

Everything is fine.

It's going to be fine.

I'm going to walk in, look around, and then put this place and this prince behind me.

Castle Rose is as lovely as its name, with rounded turrets and peaked, sky-blue roofs. According to Ronan, there are twenty-five bedrooms. Visitors range from foreign leaders and dignitaries to Ronan's extended family—his mother has six siblings, all with multiple children. I can't imagine having that many guests staying in my home with me and my family.

Not that it matters since I have no intention of marrying the prince.

Ronan leads me past the waiting servants into a spacious receiving room with black and white checkered tiles.

From the triple-height ceilings to the maze-like hallways, the palace is beautiful but also overwhelming. Servants bustle from one room to the next, while men in robes stroll past, so deep in conversation with one another that they barely notice us.

In the throne room, the King and Queen of Willowhaven sit atop a dais that overlooks a space so golden, I have to squint my eyes against the blinding brightness.

Ronan's fingers squeeze mine as he brings me closer, and it takes everything in me to keep from yanking my hand from his. When we reach the bottom step, he bows, and I drop into a curtsy.

"Welcome, son," a smooth, sweet voice greets. The queen smiles demurely from her throne. The prince clearly favors his mother, from the color of his hair and eyes, right down to the shape of their mouths.

His father's features are harsher, his deep-set eyes the light brown of a wren's wings and his hair matching his aubergine-colored waistcoat. The king says nothing but gives a tight nod of greeting.

Ronan sweeps a hand toward me, beaming. "Mother. Father. This is the woman I was telling you about. Kerris Dawn of Gravale. She is staying with her aunt and uncle in the city."

My mother and father might have taught me manners, but they never prepared me for how to properly greet a king and queen. It feels silly to curtsy again, so I settle for dipping my chin. "It's a pleasure to meet you both, Your Majesties."

"You were right, Ronan," says the queen. "She is quite the rare beauty. Who is your mother, Kerris?"

My molars clamp together. Is my mother's name respectable enough to share? "Celeste Hanson Dawn."

The queen leans forward, bracing a velvet-clad elbow on her throne's scrolled arm. "I believe I met your mother once. She and Madame Ella were good friends, no?"

"That's what Madame Ella said, but I lost my mother when I was young, so I never had the chance to ask about life in Rosehill."

"Pity."

Pity that I lost her or that I didn't get to ask her?

"What of your father?" the king asks, his tone intrigued as he stares down his nose at me, the golden crown on his head glittering with the morning sun streaming through the arched windows.

"He is thankfully still with us but chose to remain in Gravale."

"But what does the man do?"

Ronan squeezes my fingers.

Tell them your father is something respectable...

My family might not have had much, but I was lucky enough to grow up in a home filled with laughter and love—for the first five years of my life, anyway. Although we all felt my mother's loss acutely, we honored her memory by continuing to laugh whenever possible.

Standing in this room with its gilded ceiling and colorful tapestries, I feel so small, so insignificant, that I don't want to answer at all.

Tell them your father is something respectable...
An accountant.
A foreign dignitary.
A king of a distant land.

Would Ronan think *that* is respectable enough? If he's so ashamed of where I came from, why did he bother bringing me here at all?

Ronan might be ashamed, but I'm not.

"My father raises goats, Your Highness."

The queen's tittering laugh echoes, and she presses her fingers to her smirking lips.

Farming might not be the most glamorous position in society, but it is a vital one. Without people like my father, the castle kitchens would have no food to feed their royal mouths.

Ronan's grip tightens as he pulls me tightly to his side. "What she means to say is that her father owns the largest farm in Gravale."

That isn't true, but what else did I expect?

"Impressive," muses the king. "You couldn't pay me enough money to work on a farm here in the valley, let alone on the side of a mountain."

"Thank you, Sire. That is kind of you to say."

The queen's eyes narrow on her husband before her head swings back toward me. "What do you think of my son, Kerris Dawn?"

I think he is a liar. "Ronan has made me feel quite welcome in the city, and for that, I am truly in his debt."

"I see. And do you plan on marrying him for his money or his throne?"

Ronan's fingers dig into my palm, his jaw pulsing as he returns the queen's glower. "Mother..."

"What?" The queen shrugs her slender shoulders. "It's a simple question, is it not? The daughter of a goat farmer. Honestly, Ronan.

It's obvious the woman is only interested in what you can provide for her."

The king sits up straighter, a flush creeping up his jaw. "That is quite enough, Majella."

I don't care that this woman is the queen of our kingdom. I have done nothing wrong, and she does not get to treat me like dirt simply because she believes I am some money-chasing fae with a thirst for power.

"To be honest, I see his crown as a barrier to a future together." And I want nothing to do with it. "But to answer your question, if your son and I were to marry, it would be for neither his money nor his throne. It would be because I care for him and feel the two of us would make each other happy. That we make each other laugh."

"A princess who laughs," the queen scoffs. "Just what this castle needs."

The king offers me the first genuine smile I've seen since I stepped into this room. "I believe you're right. That is exactly what this castle needs."

Ronan's cheeks are as red as cherry pie filling, and I imagine mine probably match. If I had to live my eternity with this wretched woman looking over my shoulders, commenting on everything I said or did, I'd lose my mind.

No wonder Ronan built his own house. I wouldn't want to live under her thumb either.

Finally, Ronan finds his words, asking his father for permission to show me the private gardens.

The king inclines his head. "Of course. Kerris, it was truly a pleasure to meet you. I do hope we will be seeing more of you here at the castle."

While I appreciate the sentiment, I won't be seeing either of them ever again. "Thank you, Your Majesty." I bob a final curtsy, turn on my heel, and leave without another word.

Good riddance to this throne room.

Good riddance to this castle and everyone in it.

"Kerris? Kerris, wait up!"

I halt in the middle of the hallway.

Ronan skids to a halt, clutching the jeweled dagger swinging at his hip. "That was a disaster. Did you forget what I said about your father?"

Gone are the stars that have filled my eyes since I first arrived in Rosehill. This man may be a prince, but he is also a liar who would rather belittle me than build me up. I only hate that I wasted the last few weeks on him.

That ends today.

"Unlike you, I refuse to lie about who I really am." He can find someone whose lineage won't disgrace the crown and leave me to search for a husband whose family doesn't despise me on principle alone.

"I never lied—"

"I *know* the silver flowers didn't come from you."

He swipes his palms down his thighs, peering at me from beneath his lashes as a trickle of sweat races down his temple. "You're right. They didn't. When I saw them, I got so jealous that I lied. I'm sorry, Kerris, but you must understand that I'm not used to sharing a woman's affections."

This has nothing to do with sharing my affections.

Not only has Ronan Reve proven himself deceitful and untrustworthy, he also wants me to be someone I'm not.

"Allow me to make this easy for you then: I do not wish to marry you, Prince Ronan. Now, if you would kindly point me toward the exit, I would like to go home."

I came to Rosehill in search of a mate, and it would seem all I've found is disappointment.

19

Monday morning, I find a single flower on top of the latest box from Madame Ella waiting on the stoop. I pick up the box and stomp on the flower, leaving it there as a reminder that no good deed goes unpunished.

The dress doesn't fit, and when a note arrives from Trevor cancelling our date, I give up and go straight back to bed.

20
Everett

Keeping my head down, I make the trek across camp to where Gryffin's wagon sits closest to the forest's edge. Maddox and I have offered to make room for his between ours, but he has always refused, saying he does not like other people knowing his business. Which is something I can appreciate now that everyone in the whole camp knows that I have yet to give Leah an answer.

Whispers follow me everywhere, and it is annoying as hell. I can only imagine how Gryffin must feel.

I find my oldest friend on his steps, a stick in one hand and a chisel in the other, carefully chipping away at the graying bark.

"Who is that for?" I ask, gesturing toward the stick.

"Why does it matter?" he grumbles.

I suppose it does not matter at all. "Just wondering if you have a secret lover none of us know about."

He digs his chisel deeper, bits of gray coming off in flakes. "Funny. Is that why you came by? To tell jokes?"

If only. "I came because I need a favor." From the way Gryffin glowers, I have a sinking feeling this is going to be more difficult than anticipated. "I need you to convince Finn to give you his shift tonight."

He aims the chisel toward me, as if he is about to carve my skin from my bones. "You can fuck right off with that. I was on shift for three nights last week. The only way I am leaving camp tonight is if you hold a knife to my chest." Back to work he goes. Scrape, scrape, scraping the stick, revealing ivory flesh marked with deep grooves.

"I do not mean for you to work it. I will do it."

His chisel stills. "Let me get this straight: You want to work Finn's shift but will not ask him yourself. Why not?"

Because I do not want Finn knowing I am interested and asking the same fucking question. It is one thing for Maddox and Gryff to know my secrets, and another thing entirely for Finn to find out. As grumpy as Gryffin may be, he is a loyal friend and knows when to keep quiet. If Finn learned the truth, the entire village would catch wind by daybreak. And I do not want Leah—or her father—to find out.

Our chieftain might be fond enough of me to approve of his daughter's proposal, but our relationship will not matter at all if he learns I am secretly meeting with a Seelie fae. Not that I think Kerris will show tonight. But there is no shame in hoping, is there?

"This has to do with *her* does it not?" Gryffin asks.

There is no point denying it. He will only harp on until he gets the truth. "It might."

His eyes narrow. "What are your intentions?"

If only I knew.

"Do you plan on seducing her?"

My stomach tightens at the thought. Leave it to Gryff to come right out and say it. "It is not like that between us."

His lips press flat. "But you want it to be."

I bite my tongue until the coppery tang of blood fills my mouth. The last two days have been unbearable, all because I have wanted to see the Seelie fae so badly and she has not shown. I could have knocked on her window, but leaving her those gifts crossed enough lines. She already made the accusation of stalking once; I do not want her to be right.

"It does not matter what I want. I fucked it all up." Even if Kerris *did* come back, I am not sure what I would say to her.

How do I explain this heaviness in my chest when she is near? The way she consumes my every thought, waking or dreaming? This is not the way I should be feeling when Kerris Dawn has made it clear that she only wishes to be my friend.

At least she did want that. Now, who knows?

Gryff goes back to his carving, but instead of taking all the bark in that section, he turns the stick, creating a spiral pattern. "Figures."

"Not helpful, Gryff." I already have enough disdain for myself; I do not need his as well.

"At least this explains why you came to me and not Maddox."

I should have known he would figure it out. Maddox, for all his bravado and charm, thinks he knows what he is doing with females, but he has yet to receive even one proposal of marriage.

"What did you do?"

As I explain what happened, his face grows grimmer by the second, until he is full on cursing. "For an intelligent male, you have no damn sense. If you want this female, you need to let her know."

This would be so much simpler if she were Unseelie. Kerris would not appreciate me slaying a wild boar or a stag and leaving that on her doorstep like the females of our camp.

He points at me with his chisel, the blade coming so close to my chest that he nearly takes off a chunk of my skin. "Once she realizes your true intentions, you need to open up to her. Tell her exactly how you are feeling."

"Says the most closed-off man I know." I would rather kill something. I am good at that.

"Just because I do not share my feelings with you does not mean I never shared them with my wife." His voice thickens, his eyes glistening as he blinks rapidly. "I used to tell her everything."

He rarely speaks about his wife—rarely shows emotion at all, so I am not quite sure what to do with myself. If this were Maddox, I would make fun of him. But with Gryff, it feels as if I should turn and walk away, give him some privacy to work through this and find someone else to help me.

Except there is no one else.

Gryff swipes a fist under his eyes and clears the gruffness from his throat. "I will do it. On one condition: You give me your skillet."

"That belonged to my mother." If he takes it, I will have to make the three-day trek to Villers to get another one.

"I do not care if it belonged to the gods themselves. Mine is in shit, and I want yours."

His is only in shit because he does not know how to properly care for cast iron. My mother might not have been much of a cook, but she knew how to season a damn pan. "If you were a true friend, you would not ask for anything in return."

"It is because I am a true friend that I am not asking for all of your cookware."

What other choice do I have? To remain at home, and let one of the other males meet her at the bridge? To let her give them a box of inedible "biscuits" and have them think she is offering them more? "Fine."

"Then we have ourselves a deal." His nose wrinkles as he

glances down at my trousers. "Do us both a favor and bathe before you meet your Seelie."

"She is not mine." But maybe, if I do this right, she could be.

Not forever. That would never work.

But perhaps for a little while...

"She certainly will not be if you go to her reeking of blood and guts. What did you kill anyway?"

"Took down a mountain elk in the northern forest this morning." After what happened the other night, I had to kill *something*.

I leave my friend one pan poorer but with a spark of hope in my heart.

Kerris is not coming. I know that in my weary bones, but still I wait in the mist, clinging to the last vestiges of my dwindling hope.

I hate myself for the way I acted when we last met, like a youngling throwing a strop. The gifts were a pathetic apology. Tonight, I had planned on taking Gryffin's sage advice and explaining my frustration, telling her what that food could have meant, and gauging if she did understand but was perhaps too shy to speak the truth.

But as I stand on stiff legs and stare into the unending gray, it is clear the opportunity will never come.

I have broken something that was never mine to play with.

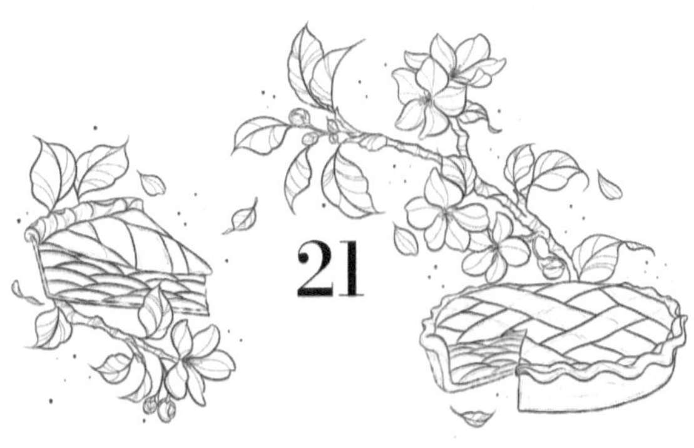

21

Reaching for my stockinged feet, I feel the muscles at the backs of my thighs pull tight. I may have overdone it on my walk today. Traversing the quiet fields gave me some semblance of peace, and by the time I returned home, I no longer wanted to scream at anyone, which is quite an improvement compared to yesterday.

Nia invited me to the theater with herself and Nolan, but I chose to stay in. She chided me, saying I wouldn't find a husband in the cottage, but at the moment, I'm not sure I even want one.

From the corner of my eye, I catch a flicker of movement outside my window.

Probably a bird or a bat, although it's too dark on this moonless night to know for certain. When the thing moves again, I sit up, realizing too late that it's far too large to be a bird. My heart begins to pound unsteadily as I inch forward.

What if it's a bandit? Or a murderer?

Oh, no...

What if it's Ronan?

My stomach twists as I slowly slip from beneath my covers and back toward the door. I'll just go across the hall and wake my uncle. He'll take care of whoever is—

My footsteps still. The shape is far too large to be Ronan, and when the person raps against the window, I'm pretty sure the skin of his hand is *green*.

Everett?

What in heaven's name is he doing here?

And why do the traitorous butterflies in my stomach choose this exact moment to wake up?

I whip my rose-printed silk robe from the back of the chair, throwing it on over my shift and bloomers before sneaking back over to the window to where Everett crouches on the roof, gripping the sill with both hands. I have to move the vase of flowers aside so I can unlatch the window and push it open a fraction.

"What are you doing here?" I hiss through the gap.

His dark eyes flit down to my robe before settling back on my face. "I have come to tell you that I am sorry." From his pocket, he withdraws a new silver flower, the stem longer than any of the others he's left at my door.

Why? I want to scream.

Why is he here?

Why didn't he just leave the flower and go away like every other night?

Why is he bringing me flowers at all?

"What do you want in return?"

Everett draws back as if I'd struck him, his gaze downcast and face solemn.

"Go on. I've been told the Unseelie are not kind, so why would you bring this to my window unless you're looking for something?"

"It is true. I am looking for something."

His quiet confession douses the fire in my chest. "You...you are?"

A nod. "I would like your forgiveness."

Right. Of course. That makes the most sense. What else could he possibly want from me?

"There is no excuse for the disrespect I showed you," he goes on. "I am ashamed to have spoken such horrible things aloud. I do not expect you to forgive me, but I need you to know that I did not mean a word of it. You are...different from the others."

As far as sincere apologies go, that was a pretty good one. I suppose I can give him one more chance, depending on how he answers my next question. "How am I different?"

His gaze locks with mine, unwavering in their intensity. "You intrigue me."

Definitely not the response I was expecting. Apparently, the butterflies in my stomach approve.

Is it possible that Everett feels the same pull toward me that I feel toward him? There's only one way to find out. "Would you like to come in?"

His eyes widen, and if I didn't know better, I would say he looks terrified. "You can't very well stay out there; you're liable to fall straight through the thatch." How would I explain a giant hole in the roof to my aunt and uncle?

This really is the most practical solution.

Everett's long fingers wrap around the window frame, and he pulls the glass wide enough for him to duck through. The space that had felt so large only a moment ago suddenly feels too tight. He hunches so that he doesn't knock himself out on the wooden beams overhead.

He turns in a slow circle, seeming to take everything in, from the plants on the wall to the wardrobe stuffed with all the dresses from Madame Ella.

Facing me once more, he slides his hands down his thighs before folding his arms behind him like he did at the well. "I waited for you at the bridge, but you did not come back."

"Because you were rude to me."

"I was. I let my frustration speak words my heart did not mean."

Such a simple, beautiful confession.

It's a good thing he's not Seelie; otherwise, I would be quite taken with him.

The floorboards creak as he shifts his weight. "In truth, I find your presence distressing."

That wipes the smile from my face, but he's too busy focusing on the floorboards between us to notice. If my presence causes him stress, then why is he here?

Quietly, he adds, "When I look at your face, my mind gets lost."

That might be the sweetest thing anyone has ever said to me.

"You smell like honeysuckle. I find the scent overwhelming."

Well, that's embarrassing. I guess I'm so used to the smell of my shampoo that I don't even notice it anymore. "I can open the window to let in some fresh air—"

His brow furrows. "Why would you do that?"

"Because you called my 'scent' overwhelming."

"You misunderstand. I like filling my lungs with you."

That probably wasn't meant to be erotic, but heavens, it makes my knees go weak. I sink onto the edge of my bed to keep from collapsing in a heap of hormones.

His head tilts as he watches me. "Your face is pink."

How can he see when it's so bloomin' dark in here? "I'm too warm."

He rushes for the window, throwing it open, and fanning the cool night air toward me. It's all so ridiculous, I can't help but laugh.

His hands fall and he watches me with an unreadable expression.

"What?"

"Your laughter pleases my ears and makes my cock stir."

Oh. My. Heavens. "Everett! You cannot say such things to me!"

His head tilts. "Why not?"

"Because it's inappropriate!" Do they not learn proper manners on the other side of The Divide? You cannot just come right out and tell someone they make you...*stir.*

"I am going to kill Gryffin," he mutters under his breath, carding a hand through his midnight hair. "He told me that I should share how I feel with you instead of keeping it all in. Now I have said too much."

I doubt this Gryffin fellow meant for Everett to take his advice quite so literally. I also doubt I will ever recover from hearing him say the word...*cock.*

The poor man looks mortified, which makes me feel guilty for laughing. He clearly didn't know any better.

Would he be as forward with an Unseelie woman?

Would she like it?

"It's all right. I...um...appreciate your honesty." Compared to Ronan, this man is a breath of fresh air. "But moving forward, perhaps you should keep any stirrings to yourself."

He turns back toward the window. "I think I should return to the bridge."

He probably should, but I don't want him to. Perhaps it's time I take a page out of Everett's book and let him know how *I* feel. "I would rather you stay."

He twists slowly.

"You...intrigue me too."

He smiles the first real smile I've seen since we met.

Which gives me an unobstructed view of his teeth.

Teeth that aren't flat like mine, but sharp points that gleam white as bone in the darkness. A vicious predator. *A beautiful nightmare.*

Although his lips cover his teeth once more, the memory will stay with me forever. I'm not sure if I'm more intrigued or horrified. Perhaps it's split down the middle.

"Do you spend every night guarding the bridge from us?" I ask, hoping he doesn't hear the tremble in my voice.

He folds his hands behind his back once more. "We do not guard from the Seelie. We are tasked with keeping what lurks in the forests from crossing our bridge."

Their bridge? For some reason, I had assumed the bridge was ours. "What lurks in the forests?"

"Wolves, mostly."

I raise a brow. "Mostly?"

His mammoth shoulders lift and lower in a shrug. "Mostly."

I remember tales of wolves once roaming our land, but assumed they were only stories to keep children in line. After all, it's hard to imagine a beast large enough to eat one's grandmother whole. "Have you seen one before?"

His eyes darken. "I have."

"And?"

"And you should be thankful they do not live on your side of the canyon."

First thing tomorrow, I am going straight to the library to find any information I can about the wolves and any other animals living in Everett's territory. To think, he and his people are out there, night after night, protecting us from danger.

Do the citizens of Rosehill realize the role these people they're so afraid of play in their safety? "That's awfully kind of you, watching out for us."

His lips flatten. "It is part of the agreement. We protect you in exchange for access to your well."

So *that's* why they're allowed to use the well. No wonder he assumed I wanted something in return for the biscuits. "What happened to your wells?"

"We have none."

Meaning they're wholly reliant on our goodwill.

A well should be for everyone, regardless of where they're from, but they can only use it in exchange for putting their own lives at risk. "Who protects you?"

His hand goes straight to the handle of his dagger. "I can protect myself."

That may be so, but it doesn't seem fair that they should have to live in constant fear just to survive. Meanwhile, right across the bridge, the rest of us walk around blissfully unaware of danger.

"May I see your dagger?"

He withdraws the weapon from its sheath and flips it over, catching the blade at the tip and offering me the handle. My fingers wrap around the worn wood, but when my thumb smooths along the bubbled section at the end, I realize it's not wood at all.

It's bone.

The dagger is lighter than I thought it'd be—not that I have much experience handling weapons. The only knives I'm familiar with are the ones that spread butter or slice pie. This one looks wickedly sharp.

Still, it's a wonder he needs another weapon with those teeth...

"Have you killed with this?"

His head tilts, sending a lock of hair falling across his brow. The piercings in his ears glimmer despite the darkness. "How else am I supposed to eat?"

He says it so simply, as if he can think of no other alternative. Perhaps he doesn't know any better. "I don't kill for my food."

The way his nose wrinkles makes me chuckle. "Vegetables taste like dirt."

"Only if you don't wash them." I picture Everett hauling a carrot from the ground and taking a big old bite. Another laugh bubbles forth, and he raises a skeptical brow. There's only one way to settle this. "You wait here, and I'll be right back."

I tiptoe out of my room, careful to close the door behind me in case Nia wakes up to use the bathing room. Downstairs in the kitchen, I find a bowl of leftover tomato soup in the ice box. The dish won't be as nice cold, but I cannot be caught heating it at this hour, nor do I want to take the time.

When I get back to my room, Everett is sitting cross-legged on my floor. "Here." I extend the bowl and spoon toward him.

He takes both, staring down at the reddish liquid with a grimace. "Why are you giving me this gift?"

"It's not a gift, Everett. I want you to try my food. The soup is meant to be served warm, but I don't think my aunt or uncle would appreciate me cooking at three o'clock in the morning."

He dips the spoon in and out, letting the liquid splash back into the bowl, watching like it's the most fascinating thing in the world. "So this house is not yours?"

"No. My brother and I grew up in the mountains." I nod toward the bowl. "Are you going to try it or keep playing with it?"

He scoops some up and takes a slurping sip.

"Well?"

His lips smack as he makes a face. "Not the worst food I have tasted."

I can't help but laugh when he hands back the bowl. I take a bite and decide the next time I want him to try something, it simply must be at the correct temperature. Setting the bowl on my dressing table, I sit, not on the bed, but on the floor with Everett, my back braced against the brass footboard. "Do you have a family?"

"No, I was born of shadows and darkness," he deadpans.

Nia told me the exact same thing that first Wednesday we snuck out, except when she said it, she was serious. "Funny." I'm not sure why, but I didn't expect him to have a sense of humor. "How old are you?"

"Thirty. How old are you?"

"I'll be twenty-five on the fourteenth of May."

For some reason, that makes him frown. "You have come to Rosehill for a mate, then?"

"I have." Although right now, the thought of choosing one makes my stomach churn. Or maybe that was the cold soup. "Is it the same in your kingdom?"

He offers no more than a nod, his dark gaze boring into mine.

My mouth suddenly feels too dry. When my tongue swipes across my lips, I swear his eyes follow the movement. "Do you belong to someone, then?"

His head shakes slowly. "Not yet."

Why has no one chosen him? He is handsome, strong, and funny. Perhaps he, like my brother, has been fending off proposals for years and hasn't wanted to settle down. What is he waiting for? Or does he simply have no interest in marriage?

"Do you...belong to someone?" he asks.

"I've been seeing a few men, but I'm not sure they're going to work out."

"Why not?"

Where do I even begin? "One is a liar and the other doesn't seem very interested."

"They are fools."

Nothing like coming right out and saying it. "I think you might be right." At least someone else agrees.

"I am. Any male would be lucky to have your attention."

Heat climbs my throat, and I know I'm staring but how can I not? Does he really think that or is he just trying to make me feel less miserable?

Everett stands suddenly. "I must go."

I scramble to my feet, still searching for my voice. He's not even gone yet and already I feel lonely. "Will you come back tomorrow night?"

"Tomorrow is my shift to guard the bridge."

Disappointment falls over me like a cool spring rain.

Until I realize that there is nothing to keep me from going to him. "Perhaps I will come to you then."

"You should not be wandering alone at night."

"I won't be alone, Everett. I'll be with you."

22

"The grandest gestures often go unnoticed."

— Celeste Hanson Dawn, An
Observation

All day I've been wound tighter than a spring, counting down the hours to nightfall. If Nia hadn't been following me like a shadow since the moment we woke, I might've tried to sneak out and go to the well.

Instead, I've been forced to wait until the house is asleep to see Everett.

Any male would be lucky to have your attention.

Those words play on repeat in my mind.

We're only friends but hearing him say things like that makes me wonder if perhaps we could be...*more.*

Not that it matters since I cannot possibly marry an Unseelie fae.

That doesn't stop my mind from imagining the two of us together. Especially since I know I make Everett...stir.

My body ignites and no amount of fanning can cool me down.

Tomorrow, I need to get back out into the city and find a mate who doesn't disappoint me at every turn. But tonight...

Tonight, I find Everett waiting on my side of the bridge, wearing the same solemn expression that seems to live on his handsome face.

It's a good thing I like him even when he scowls. "Are all the planks there tonight?" I ask, only half teasing.

"They will always be there."

For some reason, the slight edge to his tone makes my stomach flutter. "Afraid I'll fall, Everett?"

He shifts his weight, and his hands flex, as if bracing for a fight. "I will not let any harm come to you."

"I know you won't." Don't ask me how I know. I just do.

While I grip the rope railing, Everett strolls straight down the middle of the bridge, as if unbothered by the way the planks sway. He doesn't seem the least bit concerned by the silence that has descended between us either.

There are so many questions on the tip of my tongue, but I'm not quite sure how to start. I want to know everything about Everett and the Unseelie. What makes them different from us and what makes us the same.

Don't ask me why.

Perhaps one day I will write a book of true facts that will put that grossly misleading one Trevor gave me out of print.

Although, I'm not sure my drawings could do Everett justice.

Since I will never see him *disrobed*, they wouldn't be wholly accurate either. Imagine me, asking this man to remove his trousers. The very thought makes it almost impossible to swallow.

Everett comes to an abrupt halt. "Are you all right? You sound as if you are choking."

Someone push me off this bridge right now before I die of

mortification. "I'm just...um..." Just *what?* Picturing him naked, that's what.

Sod it. I might leap off this bloomin' bridge myself.

He waits patiently for me to compose myself, and when I finally do, all I can think to say is, "I'm having trouble breathing."

He steps closer, his brow crushed with concern. The heat of his skin and the smells of leather and warm spring rain that seem to cling to him isn't helping the breathing situation.

"Am I walking too fast? Do you need me to go slower?"

"No. No. You're perfect." Tell me I did not just blurt out that I think this man is perfect. *Get it together, Kerris.* "What I mean is, everything is fine. Please, proceed."

He studies me from head to toe. He mustn't find anything amiss, because he starts walking again, only this time his pace is considerably slower.

When we reach the other side, I hear the distinct sound of laughter drifting from the mist.

My heart shouldn't sink. After all, if I want to know all about the Unseelie, I need to meet more than just one of them. But part of me is gutted that Everett and I won't be spending the evening by ourselves.

A few more steps and we come upon a campfire where two Unseelie fae wait, not facing the flames, but turned toward us.

I recognize them from the well, but when I offer a tentative smile, neither of them returns it.

"Told you she would be here. Pay up," the one with long hair says to the surly-looking one, his palm extended toward him. The blazing fire at their backs makes their gigantic silhouettes appear even more imposing.

Everett's lips press flat when the man hands over a small knife.

How much did Everett tell them? Do they know we've been meeting in secret?

The one who won the bet rolls to his feet and saunters over.

"My name is Maddox Finch. You must be the Kerris Dawn we have heard so much about." He holds out a hand, but before I can give him mine, Everett growls at him.

Actually growls.

Chills race up my bare arms. Heavens, he can be intimidating when he wants to be. "You've heard about me, have you?"

Despite Everett's menacing glare, Maddox claps him on the shoulder. "Heard? This lad does not stop talking about you. It is all: Kerris Dawn this and Kerris Dawn that."

Everett's hands flex into fists. "If you do not stop speaking, I will throw you into the canyon."

Maddox huffs a laugh. "I have heard that before and yet here I stand. Welcome to our humble outpost, Kerris Dawn." He sweeps his hand to where the other Unseelie still sits, gnawing on something by the fire.

So this is where Everett spends his nights, guarding our land from the dangers in his. "It's lovely to make your acquaintance, Maddox." The third man still hasn't looked up from whatever he's eating. "What's your name?"

Maddox glances over his shoulder. "Oh, that is Gryffin Hew. He does not talk much—which is for the best since we are in the presence of a female, and he speaks mostly in curses and snarls."

"You speak enough for the lot of us," Gryffin mutters in a gravelly voice, not bothering to acknowledge my presence.

Is this the same Gryffin who told Everett to share his "feelings?"

Nope. *Nope.*

I am not thinking about that right now.

It's nice knowing Everett isn't out here all by himself. What a lonely life that would be, always looking out for people who don't appreciate your sacrifice. The next time someone brings up the Unseelie, I'll have to set them straight.

With a heavy sigh, Everett gestures toward the wide, flat stones encircling the fire. I follow him closer, the crackle and snap of the glowing logs unlocking horrific memories. Suddenly, the breeze shifts, blowing a plume of smoke toward me. My eyes start to sting, and my chest locks up.

Fires in a hearth are one thing, but a bonfire like this—

It takes everything in me to keep from dropping to the ground where the smoke cannot reach me, cannot remind me... "Can we sit somewhere else?"

Gryffin snorts. "Too good for us, Seelie?"

I don't owe the man an explanation—I don't owe him anything. But for him to believe this has to do with my dislike of them isn't how I want to start this night. I swallow past the lump in my throat, hating the tremble in my voice when I whisper, "My mother died in a fire, and the smoke brings back awful memories."

Everett kicks the back of the log Gryffin sits on, sending the man sprawling into the dirt.

Gryffin scrambles to his feet and whirls on Everett, his stark features twisted in fury. "What the fuck was that for?"

"I told you to be nice."

"How was I supposed to fucking know about her mother?"

Clucking his tongue, Maddox shakes his head. "Language, Gryff."

"Fuck you, too."

I expect him to stomp off, but instead he sits right back down and drags something from a leather satchel on the ground.

Everett holds out his hand. His long fingers envelop mine as he leads me to a spot far enough from the fire that the smoke doesn't reach. He scowls down at the sparse patch of grass forcing its way through the dirt. "I should have brought a blanket for you to sit on."

"There's no need." I unclasp my cloak and stretch it across the ground. Even after I settle myself with my skirts around me, Everett remains standing there looking like he doesn't know what to do next. "Aren't you going to sit with me?"

He glances to where his friends are watching, then back to me. After a few moments of indecision, he sinks down onto my cloak.

Maddox withdraws his dagger, balancing the tip of the blade on his index finger while Gryffin stabs the fire with a sword, sending sparks dancing into the endless gray.

"So this is what you do all night?" I ask.

Everett nods.

"Doesn't it get boring?"

Maddox flicks his dagger into the air, catching it by the hilt. "Sometimes we kill trespassers."

They do?

Everett shifts closer, bumping his shoulder against mine. "He is joking."

"Am I?" Maddox waggles his brows, a wicked gleam in his eyes and a smile twisting his lips.

Maddox is the comedian, and Gryffin is the grumpy one. What does that make Everett? As if he can feel me staring at him, he turns slightly. His dark, slashing brows lift, a silent question in his black eyes.

Who are you?

This is neither the time nor the place for that question, so I ask another. "What's with all the bones?" I nod toward the piles of white lining either side of the path.

"Most animals can smell death and avoid the area," he explains.

"So they're not to scare us off?"

The corners of Everett's lips tilt into an almost-smile. "An added bonus."

A chill dances up my spine, and it has nothing to do with the damp breeze.

His smile slips away. "You are cold. You should go home."

Something about the darkness and the shadows makes me feel bolder than ever before. Makes me want things I shouldn't.

Any man would be lucky to have your attention.

Right now, Everett has *all* of it.

"Or you could come closer and keep me warm."

After a brief hesitation, he shifts until his bare arm presses against mine. No wonder he doesn't need a shirt. He's as warm as that fire.

I reach out a finger to trace his necklace, right where it falls at his collarbone. "Where did these come from?" It's made of bones and teeth. *Fascinating.*

"That one is from the first elk I killed."

"And this one?" My finger slips from the tooth, grazing along the hollow of his throat.

His breathing hitches, nostrils flaring. "From a silver fox."

I didn't even know foxes could be silver. "Why do you keep them?"

"We try to use everything we can."

Such a different outlook compared to the Seelie fae, who drink in excess and leave behind far too much food. We're wasteful by nature. If the sparse vegetation I can see from here is any indication of what lies on this side of The Divide, there doesn't seem to be as much *to* waste.

"No box of food tonight, Kerris Dawn?" Maddox calls from his seat by the fire.

In my excitement to leave the house, the thought of bringing biscuits hadn't even crossed my mind. "I'll bring you some next time."

Maddox's bark of laughter only seems to make Everett's scowl deepen. Even Gryffin is almost smiling.

"Please, do not do that," Everett says through a grimace, his quiet plea almost lost to another round of laughter from Maddox. There is clearly something happening between them, but when I ask what it is, Everett rolls his lips together and his friends fall silent.

Did they not like the biscuits? Are they making fun of me? The heat of embarrassment washes over me.

But then Everett's thigh grazes my skirt, and I'm warm for an entirely different reason.

"How old were you when you lost your mother?" he asks in a quiet voice.

"Five."

His expression softens, soothing my raw heart. "My mother passed when I was five as well."

"So, you're not born of shadows and darkness, after all?"

The corners of his lips lift. "I am afraid not."

Who would have thought that Everett and I would have such a tragedy in common? Perhaps that's why I feel so drawn to him, because we have both suffered and have come out on the other side of loss different than before.

That's something the so-called experts on these matters never tell you. When you lose someone you love, the years don't fully heal you; they only give you longer respites between bouts of insurmountable grief.

"What about your father?" I ask.

The warmth in Everett's eyes vanishes. "The elders exiled him from camp, and he did not survive long after being cut off from their resources."

What could he possibly have done that was awful enough to warrant such a harsh punishment? As intrigued as I am, the shadows in Everett's eyes leave me swallowing my question.

He shakes his head, as if dispelling the bad memories. "What about your father?"

Ronan's voice cuts through my mind, unbidden. *Tell them he's something respectable. Like an accountant.*

I didn't lie to the king and queen; why would I lie now? "My father is a goat farmer."

Everett doesn't tell me I'm beneath him. He doesn't make me

feel less. He gives me one of his almost-smiles and says, "He must be proud of raising such a good female."

Such simple words, yet they mean more than he could ever know.

"I hope so."

Maddox hurls a stone toward The Divide. "I ate a goat once."

Gryffin snorts. "You did not."

"Did too."

"When?"

"A few years ago. You were not there."

Everett's quiet chuckle makes my stomach flip. "Neither was the goat."

23

Everett's footsteps make no sound as we traverse the fields behind the cottage.

Tonight was such an unexpected delight. Maddox is funny and Gryffin...well, he isn't the worst man I've met the last few weeks.

But Everett...

Where do I even begin?

We come to a stop outside the gate. "Thank you for a wonderful night, Everett."

He shifts his weight from one foot to the other as he frowns down at me. "My friends call me Ever."

Ever. I like that even more. Him referring to us as friends, however, I could do without. Yes, I was the first one to suggest friendship, but that was before I got to know him. I have a sinking feeling that the more I learn, the less interested in friendship I'll be.

"Would it be all right if I come to see you tomorrow night, *Ever*?"

"I will not be guarding the bridge tomorrow."

Oh, right...

"Perhaps...Perhaps I could come to you?"

A night alone, just the two of us? Even better. "I would like that very much."

From the pocket of his trousers, he withdraws a single silver flower. The petals are squished and flattened, but I love it all the same. He holds the flower out to me, and I take it with my heart in my throat. "Until tomorrow night, Kerris Dawn."

"Just Kerris, remember?" If he wants me to call him Ever, surely, he's capable of calling me by my given name.

"Kerris," he whispers like a prayer. Gently, he raises his hand, his fingertips grazing the curve of my jaw. His touch ignites a longing so deep, it takes everything in me to keep from stumbling back.

This is bad. Very, *very* bad.

The fire I'd hoped to find burns in an Unseelie's forbidden touch.

Clasping her hands beneath her chin, Nia bounces on her toes as the sunlight falls through my bedroom window, casting her snowy curls in a golden glow. "You simply must come along. It's the hottest day of the year so far, and if you stay inside, you're going to melt into a puddle. No one wants to marry a puddle, Kerris."

I want to be excited about the prospect of visiting the quarry, but I'm not for two reasons.

The first: I got only a handful of hours of sleep last night.

The second: Prince Ronan Reve.

Going to the quarry means being stuck in a carriage with him. No, thank you. "I'd love to but perhaps it would be best if you go on your own."

She arches a brow. "Because of Ronan?"

I nod. When I told her what happened, she was rightfully appalled.

"He will be the perfect gentlemen. I'll make sure of it."

I'm fairly certain she will be too busy with Nolan to do such a thing, but I appreciate the sentiment all the same. A day out could be exactly what I need to get my mind on something besides Ever. Heaven knows I could use a distraction.

Besides, I cannot stop living my life or hanging out with Nia because of the prince. He has already wasted the last few weeks of my life; I don't plan on giving him any more.

"I will agree as long as I don't have to swim." I don't care how hot it is outside; my clothes are staying *on*.

Nia squeezes my hand, her smile soft and understanding. "Do whatever makes you happy. I just want you with me."

Nia dons her swimming costume beneath an airy blue and white striped dress, while I select my lightest dress: a loose gown of peach linen and a silken shift with lace cap sleeves that give my skin plenty of room to breathe.

Before we leave, Aunt Cordelia insists we both wear sun hats with thick ribbons that tie beneath our chins. The moment we climb into Ronan's waiting carriage, we take them right back off.

As nervous as I am about seeing the prince again, he doesn't seem the least bit bothered by my presence as he regales us with the queen's plans for the most glorious Beltane festival of the century. There will be jugglers and acrobats swinging from makeshift maypoles, custom cocktails made from rare liquors, and a cake as tall as the town fountain.

He doesn't try to speak to me other than to exchange a few pleasantries. Every so often, I catch him staring, but that's to be expected in such a tight space.

With each turn of the carriage's gilded wheels, my mood perks up a little bit more, and as the carriage rolls to a stop between two others, I am downright excited about the prospects of today.

Ronan is the first out and offers his hand to me as I exit. Not wanting to be rude, I let him help me down the stairs, then promptly let go.

Shouts of delight and revelry echo through the glen, where a wide cerulean lake waits at the bottom of a large crevice.

Fae in various states of undress sit on a dock of wide planks, their bare legs and feet dangling into the crystal-clear water. Others drink from wine bottles on the shore or share picnics in the grass.

Nolan shoulders our basket and a floral blanket, stretching the latter onto a free patch of ground, half in the shade of an oak tree and half out. As much as I would love to feel the sun on my skin, it's too warm to enjoy the rays unless I plan on venturing into the water. Which I don't.

"This is the most glorious day," Nia muses, falling next to the basket, her chin lifted toward the sky and hair tossed by the spring breeze.

Nolan kneels next to the basket to pour us glasses of golden honey wine. I sink down as well, keeping to the shade as best I can.

All it takes is half a glass before the men decide to shed their shirts. Although they're both in fair shape, Nolan's physique is more toned than the prince's due to the hours spent training as a royal guard. Ronan's stomach is a bit softer, nothing at all like Ever's.

I tip my glass into my mouth and take a deep drink of wine to clear the memory of bare, gray-green skin from my traitorous mind. Each swallow pushes him a little further away.

Nia swipes the damp curls from her brow with the back of her hand. "Heavens, it's warm, isn't it?" Off come her slippers and stockings, followed shortly after by her dress, leaving her in nothing but her swimming costume.

The thought of stripping down in front of all these strangers makes me clutch my glass a little tighter. If I were alone, or if it were only Nia and me, then I might venture into the water.

Perhaps I can convince her to return on a day when it's not so crowded.

The men remove their boots and socks before suggesting a swim. When it's clear that I'm not going to give in to their relentless begging, the trio races toward the shore, their laughter getting lost in the sounds of merriment around me.

Butterflies flutter their painted wings as they land on the few wildflowers not stamped down by eager feet or blankets. This would be a peaceful setting if it weren't for all the screaming. Despite the warmth in the air, I imagine the water is still quite chilly.

From the looks of the stream feeding into the far side, it must run straight off the mountain. I know first-hand how frigid a mountain stream can be.

Thinking of the mountains brings an ache to my chest. I wonder how Father is faring without my brother and me. Perhaps I will write to him when we get back to the cottage.

Nia's screech pierces the serenity, followed by her laughter as Ronan and Nolan chase and splash her in the shallows. A woman with canary-yellow hair in a peony-pink swimming costume races down the shore to join them. *Ivee Lynch.*

I never thought I'd be happy to see the woman, but here I am, smiling because her presence means the prince will be entertained, leaving me to enjoy the day on my own.

This could be my life if I find a husband in Rosehill, spending long, sun-drenched hours lounging by a beautiful lake with my cousin and her man.

Has Trevor ever been here? I should stop by the library when we get back to see if he'd like to accompany me on his next day off. Assuming he's still interested in continuing our courtship. Although to be honest, I don't really care either way.

When did I become so apathetic?

Perhaps Nia and I should go for drinks somewhere besides The Black Rose so that I might meet some different suitors. With my birthday drawing ever closer, there is no time to waste.

Sweat tumbles down my brow and spine. It feels like I sprung a leak. When no amount of fanning myself seems to work, I push to my feet and meander through the blankets toward the water. I have to peel my shift from my thighs and puff my skirts to get some air flowing.

Hoping to avoid getting soaked by the relentless splashing on the shore, I climb the steps to the dock instead.

As much as I want to remove my slippers and stockings like everyone else, I keep both on. Instead, I dip my hands into the water and press them to my damp brow and the back of my neck beneath my braid.

When Ronan sees me, he leaves Ivee treading water to swim over to the dock. He draws himself up and out of the lake, landing in a wet heap beside me. His soaked trousers stick to his thighs, and droplets cling to the patch of golden hair on his chest.

Everett had no hair on his chest, only a thin, dark trail from his belly button to the top of his—

"Like what you see?" Ronan teases with a waggle of his brows and a pat of his stomach.

Not particularly. "The lake is quite lovely."

He scoots a little closer, the water from his trousers spreading on the planks, soaking into my skirts. "I meant me."

"Please, don't start." Let him fish for compliments from Ivee.

His face falls into a frown, and he kicks his feet in the water, sending ripples toward the other swimmers. Nia has her arms wrapped around Nolan's neck, both laughing hysterically, their heads thrown back with abandon.

What I wouldn't give to find a love like theirs.

Ronan nudges his shoulder against mine, leaving my lace sleeve wet and drooping. "You really should get in. After the initial shock, the water is quite refreshing."

"I'm not one for bathing in public."

"Ah, go on. I promise not to peek." The prince's smile grows, and he grabs my hand from my lap, giving it a tug.

"I don't like swimming." When I was little, I used to love going to the lake with my parents and Theo, but now...

He leaps to his feet, his tight grip giving me no choice but to stand as well. "Come on, Kerris. Let down your hair and do something fun for once."

"I'm having plenty of fun." At least I was before he came over.

"Nonsense. You must be roasting in all those layers. Please?"

"No." When I try to pull free of his grip, his fingers tighten. "Ronan, I want to return to the picnic. Let me go."

He catches my other hand, tugging me closer to the dock's edge.

"I said I don't want to swim." How difficult is that to understand? I told him no and I meant it, but when I try to twist out of his grip, he only clutches tighter.

"Come on. Live a little." He dips me over the water. I let out a piercing squeal, begging him to take me back to shore. I might be short, but I am by no means light, and if he lets go, I'll be soaked with no clothes to change into and—

His grip slips.

"*Shit!* Kerris!"

I'm holding nothing but air. Ronan swipes for my dress, and a terrible ripping sound rings in my ears as I tumble into the lake.

The icy water steals my breath, and my heavy skirts tangle around my legs, making it nearly impossible to kick my way to the surface. A pair of arms wraps around my waist, hauling me upwards until my head bursts through the water. The rest of the people on the dock clamber to see what all the commotion is about.

Ronan swims me to shore, but the moment my feet are beneath me, I shove him off, not caring who is watching. One of my slippers has been lost to the depths, and my body vibrates with so much rage, I cannot even feel the cold as I shove my soaked hair off my brow with a shaking hand.

"I'm sorry. I didn't mean to—"

"Didn't mean to what? Ignore my repeated requests to be left out of the water?"

He gawks at me, his hands splayed at his sides. "All you had to do was tell me that you don't know how to swim."

I *do* know how to swim, but I don't bother explaining that because the excuse serves my purposes, and this infuriating man doesn't deserve the truth. "I shouldn't have had to tell you anything. I said I didn't want to get in the water, and *you. Didn't. Listen.* I hope you listen to me now, Ronan Reve, because I am only saying this once: I do not wish to see you ever again." I turn on my heel and stomp for our blanket.

Ronan chases after me while Ivee chases after Ronan, calling his name. "Kerris, please. You cannot be serious. It was an accident."

Dropping me may have been an accident, but ignoring my wishes wasn't.

Nia catches up, and the glare she shoots Ronan could freeze the entire lake. When she turns back to me, her eyes soften. "Are you all right, Kerris?"

"I-I'm f-fine." Humiliated and angry and embarrassed but *fine*.

Ronan stomps off toward the mountain in a huff, the crowd parting in his wake as Ivee rushes to console him. Whispers fill the air, women saying how lucky I was that our prince would deign to consider a match with me. How I am a fool for turning him away.

They're all wrong.

I will never tie myself to someone who does not take my wishes or me into consideration, no matter how handsome or wealthy he might be. That is a recipe for a terrible life, and I refuse to spend eternity without a voice.

Nolan jogs over to our forgotten picnic to whip the blanket from beneath the basket and settle the coarse wool around my shoulders.

I appreciate their concern, but their attention is only making this worse. "I'm going back to the house."

Nia swipes her dress from the grass. "Give me a moment to change, and I'll go with you."

"There's no need. I can take one of the public carriages."

"Kerris—"

"Please. I want to be alone."

Thankfully, my cousin knows when to quit. She gives my hand a squeeze and tells me to be safe. The driver insists I'm too wet to sit inside the carriage for fear of ruining the cushions, so I'm forced to sit beside him on the stiff wooden bench at the front. By the time we reach Rosehill, my skin and dress have gone muddy brown from the thick layer of dust kicked up by the four horses pulling the carriage.

I'm mucky, freezing, and exhausted.

Heaven help the poor woman who ends up marrying Ronan Reve.

24

Everett

> *"Most people believe that dreams and shadows dance in silence. But if you listen closely enough, you'll hear their song."*

— Author Unknown

My skin feels tight from my bath in the river, but at least I no longer reek of death. It is a fruitless notion for me to wish Kerris finds my scent as pleasant as I find hers, but I wish it all the same. Which is why I stooped to borrowing the soap Maddox infused with pine needles and sap. It smells much better than I thought it would. Not that I would ever give him the satisfaction of admitting it.

Moonlight falls over Kerris's fine cottage like a beacon, calling me to her side. Maddox would not stop asking questions about her during today's hunt. What she likes. What she hates. What makes her different from an Unseelie female.

As if I would share anything with him.

Kerris might not be mine, but she certainly will never be his. I would run him through before I let him near her.

I scale her roof with ease, the stiff thatch cracking under my weight like a quiet threat.

Before I knock on the glass, I catch a glimpse of my reflection and stifle my groan. The back of my hair is not cooperating with the front. No matter how many times I press it down, the strands keep lifting right back up. As frustrated as I am, I refuse to let this deter me from seeing Kerris.

Her room is dark, so perhaps she will not notice my unruly hair.

My knuckles meet the glass pane in a discreet knock.

I listen for sounds of life but only silence responds. Where is Kerris?

Did she forget that I promised to call? Does she not wish to see me anymore?

Who would blame her?

She does not need you.

You are the one who needs her.

I allow myself one more knock. A desperate plea for more time in her warm presence.

Sounds of stirring drift from within. The rustle of a quilt. A quiet curse that pulls a smile from my lips. The stumbling of feet as her form appears.

The most beautiful face that has ever graced my eyes materializes like a vision in the glass. Her hair is a lavender riot, a thousand times more unruly than mine.

My fingers itch to push the silken strands back from her face as she struggles with the latch on the window. When she finally manages to open it, a waft of honeysuckle washes over me, and my cock swells in my trousers. Not that I say so out loud. I will not make that humiliating mistake again.

Kerris offers me her beautiful smile, and I tuck it away in my memory for when I am alone. "I'm so sorry," she says in her sweet voice. "I fell asleep waiting for you."

She must not have the same eagerness in her chest that lives in mine. I could not sleep tonight even if I tried.

Although I would like very much to spend the night with her again, I do not want her to be tired when morning arrives. She has her own life to live, and I will not have her think me a selfish thief for stealing all her hours for myself. "I am sorry for disturbing your dreams. I will go back to the canyon."

Before I can turn away, her soft fingers wrap around my wrist. "Don't leave."

Then I will not leave.

"Come inside. Please."

Kerris lets me go, making room so that I can climb through her window.

The sheets of her bed are as delightfully rumpled as she is, and the robe she wears gaps ever so slightly, revealing a hint of lace and silk and sun-kissed skin.

Bite your tongue.

Do not mention the stirring.

Kerris closes the window with another yawn. "Do you mind if we lie down? I'm exhausted." She climbs onto the mattress and slips beneath the covers without another word while I am rooted to the creaky floor.

Surely, I am misunderstanding her meaning. "You wish to share your bed with me?" The thought does nothing to quell this infernal stirring.

"There's no need to sound so scandalized, Ever. I promise not to take advantage of you."

She says my name so sweetly, like a sigh. The smile she offers is small, but I like it as much as the others. It feels like a secret just for the two of us.

"What do you mean by advantage?" In battle, having an advantage is when you possess the upper hand. We are both on the same level now, so neither of us has an upper hand. Unless you consider our size difference. Then I am the one with a great advantage.

"It means not to expect anything but cuddles," she says on a yawn.

"What is cuddles?"

"Get in bed, and I'll show you."

I like this demanding Kerris, the one telling me to come to her bed. This night is already better than I anticipated. At least she is not trying to make me eat more cold slop.

I remove my boots, careful not to disturb her as I climb into the spacious bed. Instead of scooting away, she slots in right next to me and wraps one arm around my waist. Her head, she tucks into the crook of my neck and her leg...

She drapes it over one of mine, but her soft thigh is dangerously close to something that she does not wish to discuss.

If I do not stop thinking about the way her supple body feels against mine, I am afraid there will be no choice but to discuss it.

"You smell good," she whispers against my neck, and I can feel her lips curve into another smile. "I enjoy filling my lungs with you."

Not nearly as much as I enjoy filling my lungs with her sweetness. "I have new soap." There is no point telling her that it belongs to Maddox since he is never getting it back.

"Well, I like it." It could be my wishful imagination, but it feels as if she presses herself even closer. "I missed you."

"You did?" How is that possible when she lives in such a grand place? It is a wonder she even remembers my name.

When she nods, her wild hair tickles my cheeks. "Today was an awful day."

"Because I was not in it?"

Her laugh is a puff against my neck and an arrow to my heart. "Someone is full of humor tonight."

I am full of many things. Humor, certainly, but mostly need for this female who wishes only for friendship. "What made your day so awful?"

Her fingers begin to trace the bones of my necklace the way they did at the outpost. Occasionally, the soft tips graze my skin, and I am set ablaze.

"I'm not sure I should tell you," she whispers.

Nonsense. "My ears are very good at listening."

"If only all men were like you," she murmurs under her breath, but I hear every word.

See. Good at listening.

"I was seeing someone briefly," she says a little louder, "and at one point, I thought the two of us might marry."

My hands tighten into fists at my sides. Perhaps I do not wish to hear after all. Curse these ears of mine. Why must they listen so well?

Kerris's hand falls to my chest, her palm landing on my heart. Does she feel how it beats for her?

"But it turns out," she goes on, "he is a liar and a wretch."

Thank the gods. If she were getting married, it would take all my self-control not to steal her away for myself.

She draws back to look me in the eye. Every time I see her face my breath flees my chest. "He pushed me into a lake."

For thirty years my ears have never failed me, but that might have changed because I swear Kerris said some male *pushed her into a fucking lake.* "What is his name?"

Her brows lift. "Why do you want to know?"

So that I can murder him. "No reason."

"You're not a very good liar, Ever."

"Thank you." Who knew a tired Kerris would be so full of compliments? It is a good thing we are in her bed and not at the outpost. If Maddox heard even one compliment, he would be on his knees at her feet, begging for more.

Her head returns to the crook of my neck, and her hand that was on my chest drifts lower, to my ribs.

Silence envelops the room as I settle deeper against her pillows. There are so many, it feels as if I am leaning against clouds. On her bedside table, there is a book. What sorts of stories does Kerris like to read?

Carefully, I pick it up.

Unseelie Fae: A Scientific Study.

Kerris is reading about us? Why?

As if she can hear the question in my head, she stiffens. "You weren't supposed to find that."

How could I miss it? It was right on her table. "Why do you have this book?" A terribly inaccurate book if this page about contracting warts is any indication of the information within. I do not have warts and neither do any of my kinsmen. Who wrote this nonsense?

She buries her head deeper into my throat. "I was curious."

I flip to where a dried flower has been pressed between the pages and scan the words there. "About mating ceremonies?" This knowledge should not make my heart skip, but it skips all the same, right around my chest.

"Not specifically. I wanted to know more about you."

"I am here now, full of knowledge about Unseelie fae. I have been one my entire life, you know. Ask and I will answer."

Once again, there is silence between us. I would think she fell asleep if not for the way she trails her nail along my chest, back and forth, conjuring gooseflesh. "Will you tell me about mating scars?"

Why would she want to know about that? Surely, she isn't considering—

I shake my head at the thought that almost crossed my mind. Her questions have nothing to do with a desire for mating. She is simply trying to learn about our customs like a friend would.

"When two Unseelie mate, they use their teeth to mark each other."

"Doesn't that hurt?"

"I have heard that the pain only fuels the passion, but I do not know from experience." I have never marked Leah, and she has respected my wishes to leave my skin unblemished by her own teeth.

"Where do you leave them?"

"Depends on how amorous the mating. Some only have one or two..." I dare to trace a finger where her shoulder meets her neck. Her sharp intake of breath is a strike to my heart. "Others have them all over." Like our chieftain and his mate.

"Oh..."

I already know that if we were to mate, Kerris's skin would be scarred from neck to toe. "Do you have more questions?" I rush before I can let that thought take root.

"Hundreds," she says on a yawn, burrowing deeper into me like a little rabbit. "But they might have to wait until tomorrow."

Then I look forward to tomorrow, because this means I will see her again.

My life has never been full of luck, but knowing this makes me feel like the most fortunate male who has ever lived.

"I hate that I'm so tired," she murmurs. "You can leave if you're bored."

How can anyone be bored with such a magnificent female wrapped around them? "I would like to stay a little longer, if you do not mind." After all, she might think of a very important question that requires an answer right away.

"I don't mind...as long as you don't mind me closing my eyes for a moment."

"Close them for as long as you want. I will keep watch over you."

No harm will come to her as long as I am around.

Cautiously, I slip my fingers into her silky hair. The strands are so long, she could wear them as a gown.

Shit. Now I am imagining her in nothing *but* this hair and it is a slow, painful death. Like being shot in the gut and left to bleed out.

So many brown specks dot her nose and cheekbones, like tiny grains of sand. Even breaths fall through the perfect bow of her parted lips as dreams steal my sweet Seelie fae.

As I listen to the silence, my gaze drifts over to where a rainbow of silk spills from her wardrobe. Kerris has so many dresses to choose from, much like she has Seelie men. Her options are endless.

Unwelcome emotions twist in my gut.

Kerris Dawn might not be meant for me, but in the quiet of this night, I let myself pretend.

"Kerris? Hello? Why is the door locked?" The knob
jangles in time with Nia's irritated voice.

My eyes flash open, meeting a pair of stunned
black ones.

Ever is here. In my bed. And there is *sunlight* streaming
through the bloody window!

Oh no.

Oh no.

Oh no.

"Just a minute!" I rasp, throwing the covers aside and scrambling over Ever to get out of the bed.

Thank goodness I had the foresight to lock the damn door
before falling asleep last night.

After what happened at the quarry, my energy had been

sapped. I'd bathed to wash away the dirt and lake water and then fallen straight into bed. It's a wonder I woke up at all.

But I did wake up and I...

My hands fly to my fiery cheeks.

I asked Ever to *cuddle* with me.

I can't even blame my boldness on drink. I simply wanted him to stay, and he did.

Now he's here and—

The way Ever's hair sticks straight up at the back is the most endearing thing I've ever seen. He might be a dangerous Unseelie warrior, but he is also an excellent snuggler.

For some reason, he isn't getting out of the bed.

"What's wrong?" Why doesn't he seem the least bit fazed by our current predicament? The sun is out and if he climbs down the roof now, the neighbors are liable to see him.

He frowns.

"Ever!" I hiss under my breath.

The muscles in his bicep flex as he drags a hand through his hair. "I am struggling with something that you do not wish to discuss."

His gaze makes an unmistakable sweep down the front of my robe—

Hold on. Where the hell is my robe? I could've sworn I put it on last night, but now I am standing in front of this man in nothing but my shift and bloomers. The cool morning air leaves my nipples straining against the silk. I fold my arms over my chest to try to hide them even though there's no point because he has obviously already had a good gander.

I am struggling with something that you do not wish to discuss.

Ever adjusts the covers over his lap, his pained wince transforming into a grimace. The meaning behind his cryptic words clicks, and I choke on the air evacuating my lungs.

His body is *stirring*.

Thump. Thump. Thump. "Kerris! Come on. Mother needs help with the pies."

Who can think of pies at a time like this?

Forcing my embarrassment aside, I look Ever dead in the eye. "You need to hide."

He glances from the bed to the wardrobe and back again. "Where?"

Where, indeed?

"Kerris!"

"I'm coming, Nia! Just let me get dressed."

Now it's Ever's turn to choke.

"Close your eyes and don't peek."

He rolls over in the bed and buries his face into the mattress. Trusting that he won't try to steal a glance, I quickly change into one of the gowns I've altered from Madame Ella. Instead of wearing the corset with the ribbons to the back, I keep them at the front so I can tie them myself.

"You can open your eyes now." Where are my damn slippers? I really need to clean this room. When I finally straighten, Everett is still staring at me.

"What is it?" Tell me there isn't drool crusted on my chin. After going to bed with my hair wet, heaven only knows what it must look like.

He shakes his head, as if dispelling cobwebs from his brain. "My heart aches at the sight of you."

It is too early in the morning to swoon.

The smallest wrinkle appears between his brows. "Are you too warm again? Your cheeks are as pink as the dawn."

"I'm not too warm. I'm—"

"Kerris!"

Why can't Nia leave me alone for one damn minute? I am trying to sort this out and it's difficult to think with the way Ever's eyes seem to drink me in. I grab one of the leather queues from my bedside table and pull my hair back from my face.

Ever watches like I'm the most fascinating thing he's ever seen.

"Do you think you can get out of here without anyone seeing you?"

"Of course I can. I am our clan's stealthiest hunter."

I glance out the window, skeptical. Still, he doesn't seem concerned, so perhaps my own worries are misplaced. "Will I see you tonight?"

He nods. "I will be waiting for you at the bridge."

I reach for the doorknob, but do not leave. When I turn and find Ever still sitting on my bed, an overwhelming urge washes over me. Before I can think too much about what it means, I hurry to his side and press a kiss to his cheek.

I leave in a flurry, my stomach leaping all over the place as I bound down the stairs to where my cousin waits in a floral apron, a second stretched toward me. "It's about time," she clips. "You've been asleep forever."

Aunt Cordelia stops rolling pie dough long enough to sprinkle extra flour over her rolling pin. "Good morning, Kerris. There are fresh blueberry pancakes over on the table if you'd like some breakfast. Nia, dear. Will you run outside and gather the eggs? We're going to need as many as we can get if we want to beat Mrs. Wilson this year."

Nia retrieves the basket from the edge of the counter.

I don't know who Mrs. Wilson is or why we want to beat her, but I do know that if Nia goes outside right now, she's liable to find Ever scaling down the roof.

"I'll get the eggs!" I swipe the basket right out of my cousin's hand.

Nia tries to take it back, but my fingers are locked on. "You need to have breakfast."

"I'm not hungry." My stomach chooses this very moment to moan, making me look like a liar.

Nia's gaze drops to my middle, and her brows quirk. "You eat, and I'll get the eggs."

"Why don't you both do it?" Aunt Cordelia clips.

Curse my aunt and her problem-solving. Nia takes advantage of my distraction and steals the basket, then she slips out into the garden.

I burst out of the back door behind her. "Isn't it a glorious day?" I say far too loudly, a warning for any Unseelie who might be trying to escape. From the corner of my eye, I see Ever freeze on the thatch.

So much for being stealthy. If Nia looks up, she's going to see him in all his bare-chested glory.

The next time I feel like cuddling, I will have to ignore the urge.

Nia stops dead and narrows her eyes at me. "What is wrong with you?"

"Nothing at all. Just loving the fresh air and sunshine."

With a roll of her eyes, she ducks inside the coop without noticing my Unseelie visitor. I wave for him to hurry up, which earns me a grin.

I cannot help but grin back.

"You're smiling like a loon," Nia remarks as I enter the coop behind her.

She's right, but I cannot seem to stop.

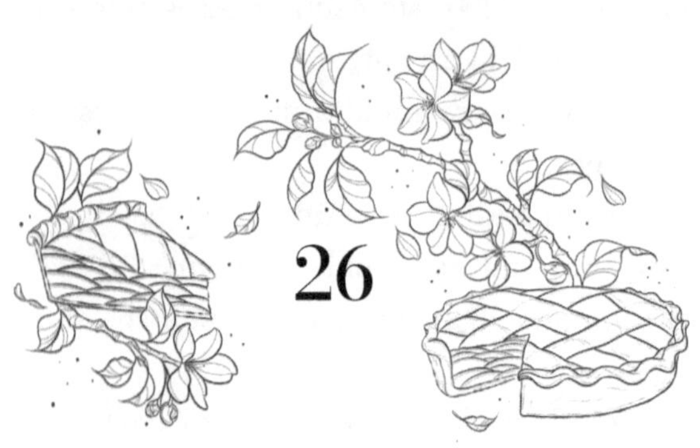

26

My heart leaps with joy when I find Ever waiting for me on my side of the bridge. He asks about my day, and I tell him all about the pies and fresh loaves of bread we baked. Aunt Cordelia's kitchen has turned into a proper bakery. If one more dessert gets added to the ice box, the thing is liable to explode. I swear the oven sighed with relief when we finished.

He listens intently, escorting me to where Maddox and Gryffin sit around the fire. A short distance away, a blanket has been stretched on the ground with two more stacked beside it.

Ever must catch me looking at them because he nudges my arm with his elbow and says, "You will not be cold tonight."

It's incredibly sweet that he remembered to bring them, but part of me mourns the fact that we won't need to sit as closely.

On the other side of the fire, Ever's unicorn stamps his hoof. Two more beasts have been tied to the same post, but their saddles aren't quite as intricate.

Hesitantly, I step toward the animal. They're almost like Seelie horses only bigger. Kind of like the Unseelie themselves. Then there's the spike on its head. Imagine finding yourself at the wrong end of that thing.

The unicorn watches me through careful eyes, much like his master. "He's beautiful. What's his name?"

Ever positions himself between the unicorn and where I stand. "Onyx, but I call him Nyx." At hearing his name, Nyx nudges Ever's shoulder with a snuffle.

Onyx. Suits him. "Hello, Nyx." The beast's ears twitch, his wide eyes landing on me as I inch closer.

Ever's lips flatten even as Nyx nudges him again. "He does not like many people."

Neither did my father's horse back in Gravale, but I still managed to make old Domino my friend. I stretch out my hand toward Nyx's nose. From over Ever's shoulder, the unicorn bumps my fingers with his muzzle. Ever's eyes widen as I dare to close the distance even more. Nyx sniffs my hair then nods as if he approves.

Probably because I smell like apple pie.

I can't help my smile as I pat his stiff mane more confidently. "I knew you were a good boy. So beautiful, aren't you?"

Nyx snorts happily, letting me pet him like I used to pet old Domino.

"I can be a good boy too," Maddox murmurs under his breath.

I bite my lip to keep from giggling.

"How would you like to explore the bottom of the canyon?" Ever snaps.

Maddox raises his hands in surrender, but his cheeky grin remains.

Gryffin doesn't look up from the fire.

Nyx swings his head back toward the sparse patch of grass where the other two unicorns tear at the vegetation with their teeth. Is there any good grass here for them? Imagine the grazing they could do in the field behind the cottage.

Ever gestures back toward the blankets. "Come. I made you a seat."

"I can see that. Thank you."

Ever folds himself next to me, sitting a little closer than necessary. The other two seem content to speak quietly in front of the fire. Every once in a while, the wind changes direction, blowing smoke toward the blankets. It takes all my effort to keep my breathing steady even as my eyes burn.

When Ever shifts, the dagger at his hip bumps against mine. Maddox and Gryffin seem to have similar weapons on their belts.

"Do you all have the same daggers?"

Ever leans back on his hands and stretches his endless legs in front of him with a shake of his head. "Younglings are given daggers of elk antlers. You only receive a wolf's bone dagger when you have killed one."

"All of you have killed wolves?" To think, I've lived my whole life protected from the harsh reality of their world.

They nod.

"How young were you when you first killed?"

Maddox puffs up his chest. "I slayed a squirrel on my third birthday."

The soft scent of pine and leather tickles my nose when Ever leans closer. "Maddox lies."

"I do not."

Gryffin shakes his head. "You were five, same as the rest of us."

"I was three," Maddox insists.

The two of them squabble like an old married couple while Ever watches silently. Always watching. Always alert. "As Gryffin said, we were five when we were allowed to hunt in the small forest near camp, but we are taught to defend ourselves as soon as we can walk."

They're taught as children, and here I sit without even the most basic knowledge of how to defend myself. *Soft*, just like Ever accused when we met. "Will you teach me?"

His dark brows come together over narrowed eyes. "Gryff, do you have an extra blade?"

From his pack, Gryffin withdraws a small silver dagger and tosses the thing right at us.

Ever rips it out of the air easily enough, like the hilt and his hand are made magnets. He flips it over, handing me the bumpy hilt. *Antler.*

The poor deer...

Ever's fingers come around mine, and all thoughts of cute, fuzzy animals flee my mind. "That's too loose. Hold it like this." He tightens his grip, forcing me to do the same. "Otherwise, if you miss your mark and hit bone instead, the blade might slip right out of your grasp. Keep your grip firm. There you go." He withdraws his hand, but I can still feel his touch as acutely as if his fingers were still tangled with mine. "Just like that. Now you can swipe across the throat or stab the eye and strike the brain." Taking my free hand, he presses my fingers to his bare chest. "Do you feel where this bone ends?"

Suddenly, my tongue is made of ash. "Yes."

"Being this close to your prey is not ideal, but if you are, angle the blade upwards to avoid the ribcage and strike the heart. Never hesitate. Always go for the kill. If you miss, it could cost your life. Even if what you are hunting does not seem dangerous, you must remain on your guard. A deer's antlers can be as deadly as a wolf's teeth."

Remain on your guard.

Never hesitate.

Always go for the kill.

Maybe Ever was right. Maybe I am too soft.

I return the blade and slide my hands down my silk skirts.

Ever's head snaps up and his chest rises with his deep inhale. Before I can ask what he smells, chaos descends.

With a vicious curse, Gryffin starts digging through his pack. He drags out a piece of brown cloth and tosses it onto the fire. Maddox scrambles to standing and unbuckles his trousers.

Ever launches to his feet, yanks a blanket from the stack, and wraps the scratchy wool around my shoulders. Then he picks me up like a child bundled up for bed and starts running toward Nyx.

"What's wrong? Is it a wolf?" Perhaps I shouldn't have given back the dagger.

"Quiet," Ever hisses as he puts me down and untethers Nyx.

Hold on. Is Maddox urinating over there?

Ever stuffs his foot into the stirrup and mounts in one fluid motion. When he extends his hand toward me, I let him haul me up in front of him. The way his body presses against my back as he reaches for the reins feels incredibly intimate, never mind the way his thighs squeeze mine as he kicks Nyx into a gallop.

Wind tears at my hair as we race away from the canyon, the thudding of Nyx's hooves matching the drum of my thundering heart.

A few minutes later, Ever comes to a halt beside a tree and dismounts. When he reaches for me, I let him lift me down to the ground. The wool blanket falls into a puddle on the dirt.

"Can you climb?" he whispers.

Nodding, I grip the lowest branch and haul myself up to the next one and the one after that, my arms and legs protesting the entire climb. This is far more difficult than I remember. Eventually, I reach a small platform hidden among the barren branches with sticks and twigs nailed to the walls. The space would be cramped for just one person, let alone both of us. By some miracle, Ever manages to fold himself into the tiny gap behind me. He grimaces as he tries to settle himself, but there's hardly enough room for him to stretch his legs without bumping into me, even though I'm trying to make myself as small as possible.

"Kerris?"

"Yes?"

"Come here." He holds out his hands, and I hold my breath as he settles me right onto his lap.

I try not to think about how close we are, how intimate the space feels, but it's all I can seem to focus on and if I don't distract myself, I'm going to do something incredibly foolish. "What just happened?"

"Riders were approaching the outpost."

Really? I didn't hear a thing beyond the crackling fire. Looks like Trevor's book was correct about Unseelie hearing.

"And Maddox was relieving himself because...?"

"We needed to cover your scent."

So the book was right about their sense of smell as well. "I thought it wasn't illegal for me to be here."

"It is not illegal, but our chieftain would not approve, and I would rather not have the entire clan knowing my business."

His words rumble from his chest, straight into my heart. His chieftain wouldn't approve and yet here he is, hiding me, protecting me, seeking me out anyway.

And I'm doing the same. If Nia found out, she would be so angry. If any of the other Seelie learned the truth of where I sneak off to every night, they wouldn't understand. But here I am, crossing The Divide night after night just to steal a few hours with this cautious, caring man.

The realization gives me the courage to turn around and ask him one very important question: "Am I your business, Ever?"

After the briefest hesitation, he nods. The look in his eyes says I'm more.

I think...

Heaven help me, I think I *want* to be more.

To know this man inside and out. To learn what makes him smile and how to cook his favorite meal. To feel the press of his bare skin against mine. I want...

I want everything I shouldn't.

Ever watches me with the same intensity that seems to live in his gaze. My heart beats double time as I continue to twist until I'm straddling his thighs. Ever's toned chest rises and falls with each deep inhale, brushing against mine.

Slowly, I bring my hands to the necklace he wears, tracing the bones and teeth. Evidence of the violence that lives in this beautiful man only to realize I don't want to touch his necklace.

I want to touch him.

"Kerris," he whispers.

"Yes?"

"I lied."

My hand stills. "About what?"

"I do not want to be your friend."

"Why not?"

"Because friends should not want to do the things I long to do to you."

No one has to know.

It's just the two of us.

The darkness is made for such truths.

"What sort of things?" I dare to ask.

Strong hands anchor around my waist. "I long to touch you when no one is watching," he whispers. "To mark you as mine."

I've wanted the exact same thing since I first read about mating scars.

His voice drops even lower as his hands slide to my hips.

Kneading. Insistent. "I yearn to taste your most secret places and feel your body shuddering around mine. To hear my name on your tongue when you shatter."

Desire sparks like a flame in my blood, burning through me until I'm a pile of wanton ash. All those things... I want them just as much. No, I don't want. I *need*.

"Ever..."

His hum is a delicious vibration in his throat.

Even knowing I would be a fool to give in, my fingers trail along his collarbone. I tell myself to say nothing. To put a stop to this before it's too late.

If only I'd known it was too late the moment our eyes met across that square. "I don't want to be your friend either."

He raises one hand, his eyes wild as they search for any hint of discomfort as he trails a solitary fingertip along my own collarbone.

An even exchange.

A stolen touch for a stolen touch.

No. Not stolen.

Given freely.

I move my hands lower, to the cut in his chest, and press my palm to his heart. Slow. Steady. Strong. So unlike my own beating like a hummingbird's wings.

Heat gathers low in my stomach, pooling as he flattens his hand and inches down *down down* until his own palm stretches over my left breast.

I don't know who disturbed us at the outpost, but I say a silent word of thanks for the interruption. Without them, I might never know the utter ecstasy of Ever's touch.

His nose grazes my ear, sending a delicious thrill zinging down my spine as he breathes against me, drawing my essence into his lungs. Warm lips dance down my neck as I move my hands lower, squeezing his chest, telling him without words exactly what I need.

That whatever he wants from me can be his.

His free arm bands around me, holding tightly even as his hand cups my breast. His quiet groan turns my bones to water.

Our foreheads press together and breaths eddy, caught between us in a haze of wanting. Gazes drop to lips, the space separating us slowly disappearing until—

"Psst! Ever!"

Maddox's quiet call is like a cold bucket of water poured over our heads.

My Unseelie stills.

"They are gone," he goes on. "You can come down now!"

Ever's hands fall back to his sides, but the fire in his touch gathers in his heated gaze. An onyx inferno burning just for me.

"Ever!"

"I heard you the first time," Ever growls.

"Prick," Maddox mutters, followed by the thump of hooves on hard earth.

This got out of hand far too quickly. He must think me shameless the way I threw myself at him. I slide off his lap and crawl toward the exit even as my body screams for more of his touch.

"Wait." Ever's quiet plea freezes me in place.

When I glance over my shoulder, I find him grimacing.

Say you want to finish what we started. Tell me not to leave this place until we know the taste of each other's lips.

Ever's head shakes as if he heard my silent pleas. "This is not over."

"Good." I'd never forgive him if it were.

With muscles protesting, I climb back to the ground where Nyx waits. The ride back to the fire might not be as quick as our exit, but it's filled with the tension of unfulfilled promises.

Maddox waves from where he ties his mount to the post while Gryff waits with his hands on his hips and his scowl in full force.

When I go to dismount, Ever stills me with a hand on my knee.

The casual touch reignites the burning beneath my skin. "Who was it?" he asks.

Gryffin folds his arms over his chest. "River. A pack of wolves was spotted near Villers. The chieftain wants his best warriors on the hunt. We leave tomorrow at noon."

A whole pack of wolves? And they're going *toward* the danger?

Ever nods even as his hand slips from my knee. "You must go back."

Somehow, I knew that would be my fate when we returned.

This is not over.

I cling to those words as Ever dismounts from behind me and helps me to the ground. I tell the other Unseelie goodnight, which earns a smile from Maddox and a grunt from Gryffin.

The walk back to the cottage feels desperately lonely, only the sounds of my footsteps and swishing skirts to keep my mind occupied.

Ever might be accompanying me, but he seems as lost in his own thoughts.

"How long do hunts usually last?" I ask, missing him already.

"A few days. A few weeks." Ever shrugs as he glances up at the stars winking above us. "There is no way to tell."

I might not see him for weeks?

Maybe this is a good thing. Maybe this forced separation will allow me to gain some clarity.

"You will be safe, won't you?"

"I am a skilled hunter. It is the wolves who should be afraid."

"I know. I just don't want anything to happen to you."

He offers a slow nod. "Would you weep if I did not return?"

"I'd be beside myself."

"Good."

Cheeky fae. I nudge his arm with mine, and the corners of his lips tug into the barest hint of a smile.

Suddenly, all I can focus on is the fullness of Everett's mouth as he stares down at me, his large hands hanging loosely at his sides. All I can think about is what it would feel like if he dipped his head and pressed those lips to mine.

Don't go.

Stay with me tonight.

Let's finish what we started.

Requests that never leave my lips as I watch him turn and head back the way we came.

"Ever?"

The muscles in his back flex in the most enticing way as he twists toward me, his brows raised in silent question.

"If you're back in time, will you come to the Beltane festival? I bought a new dress just for the occasion."

His expression gives nothing away as he sighs and offers a non-committal, "We will see," before melting into the shadows.

When I make my way to the back door, I can still feel the warmth of his gaze like a caress. This has been the most magical, most memorable night of my entire life. I don't think I'll ever get to sleep—

Something scrapes in the corner of the room, followed by the flicker of a flame. Nia sits at the kitchen table, a match pinched between her fingers, glowering straight at me. "Where the hell have you been?"

27

"Your voice will only be heard if you are willing to speak up."

— Author Unknown

Nia's question hangs as heavily as the fog across The Divide.

Where the hell have you been?

Falling for an Unseelie fae probably isn't the answer she's looking for, but it's the first one that springs to mind.

Because I have been falling, unbeknownst to myself, and what I feel for Ever is more than anything I've felt for another.

Not that I can tell her any of that.

So I slip out of my shoes and set them beside the door, pretending nothing is amiss. "My legs were feeling restless, so I went for a walk."

Her harsh breath extinguishes the flame; gray smoke twists toward her face in the filtered moonlight. "With an Unseelie fae?"

Drats and damnation. "Nia, I can explain—"

"I don't want to hear more lies. I want the truth."

"The truth is, I did go for a walk...to The Divide."

"Heavens, Kerris, it's one thing to venture there with your friends by your side, and another thing entirely to go to that cursed place without an escort. The Unseelie are killers, every last one of them. You're lucky to be alive."

"You're wrong about them." Everyone is wrong.

"Keep your voice down," she hisses. "There's no telling what will happen if you wake my parents."

She's right. I'm lucky my cousin was the one who discovered my secret and not my aunt or uncle. *This is a good thing*, I tell myself. A chance to quell her ignorance. "The Unseelie only kill to feed themselves—and to protect us. That bridge? They guard it every night so that the wolves and whatever other monsters prowl their land don't cross into Rosehill. They keep us safe." Without Ever and his people, there's no telling what sort of beasts would have infiltrated the city, and all anyone on this side does is spread hate about them.

"That doesn't change the fact that if anyone finds out you were with one, your reputation will be ruined beyond repair. You've already spurned the prince. Do not alienate yourself further by aligning yourself with one of them."

I think of Ever's hands on my body. The way his breath tangled with mine. The press of his lips to my skin. He is the only man who has ever made me feel this way, and all Nia cares about is my bloomin' reputation.

Swallowing my truth, I tell the biggest lie of all: "We're only friends. Nothing more."

Although her eyes narrow, she must not feel like arguing because she bobs her head and says, "See that it stays that way."

This morning, Nia's eyes feel as if they're burning a hole through my skull. I offer to do the dishes after breakfast to avoid having a conversation. That only gives me a brief reprieve, because when I finish, Nia sweeps into the room holding a box from Madame Ella's, her eyes narrowed into slits and a stern set to her jaw.

She shoves the dress at my chest, forcing me to take it. "This arrived for you this morning. Try it on."

"I will later." When she isn't in a strop.

"Do it now so that we can take it back if it doesn't fit. We need to collect our dresses for the festival."

Fine. I'll try it on to appease her. Hopefully a walk into town will brighten her sour mood.

I bring the gown upstairs to where the others I've yet to alter sit in a stack beside my wardrobe. Sure enough, the skirt on this one is too long as well. What's going on?

Nia enters my room without knocking, wearing a buttery yellow dress and a frown. "Madame Ella must be sending you someone else's dresses."

"I know." The first dress she sent was tailored to perfection, but all the others have been too big. I return the dress to the box and grab two of the others I've yet to alter. If she wants the rest of them back, I'll bring them another time.

With the parcels split between us, Nia and I make our way to Market Square. The sun warms my face and the air swirls with the delicious smells of spring and sugar.

Nia walks at a clip, seeming content to ignore me.

I despise the tension between us but don't know how to make it better. She will forgive me for sneaking around behind her back eventually, right? She must.

If only she could see what I see.

If Ever didn't have that hunt, I'd bring her with me across the bridge tonight. Perhaps when he returns, I'll introduce them... whenever that may be.

When we reach Madame Ella's shop, the place is as empty as it was the day I first arrived in Rosehill. The only sounds are our slippers on the marble floor and the hum of a sewing machine.

Nia and I set the boxes on the countertop next to the till, and Nia presses the bell.

The hum stops, followed by the click of heels. Madame Ella appears from behind a curtain, her cherry hair loose around her shoulders. "Welcome, welcome. So good to see you both again."

At least someone is happy to see me today.

"Your Beltane gowns are finally finished and, Kerris, I have three of your mother's dresses altered. Give me a moment to pack them up—" Her gaze falls to the boxes we brought, and her brow furrows. "Was there something wrong with the dress I sent?"

"I'm afraid the skirts are all too long."

"We thought perhaps they were meant for someone else," Nia chimes in, leaning a hip against the counter.

Madame Ella's bracelets jangle as she slides the ribbon off the top box. "How is that possible? When I removed the ruffled panels, I didn't change the length."

"Oh, no. The ones you altered are perfect. I'm talking about the new dresses."

Ella shakes her head as she lifts the lid. "I haven't sent any new —" Her soft gasp leaves us leaning over the box. "I didn't make these dresses for you."

Lovely. Now I feel awful for not coming to see her sooner. Some poor woman is out there waiting for her dresses and two of them won't fit her anymore. "I'm so sorry. I should've brought them right back the moment I realized they didn't fit. I thought maybe you had the wrong measurements, so I shortened the skirts on a couple others, but I didn't touch these."

She sets the top box aside and opens the one below it. "You misunderstand. I didn't send you these dresses at all."

Nia picks up the mauve gown to inspect the stitching. "They're not yours?"

"They are, but I made them...saints, it must've been over thirty years ago. They were commissioned by the king."

Just when I thought this mystery couldn't get any stranger. "Are you telling me I've been wearing the queen's dresses this whole time?" Has Ronan been secretly raiding his mother's closet? The thought makes me shudder. No wonder the woman despised me. I showed up to her castle wearing her bloomin' gown.

"I know the queen's measurements by heart, and this gown would never fit her. See. Look." She stoops behind the counter and stands back up with yet another box. She flings open the lid and withdraws a stunning navy gown edged in gold lace with sequins sewn on the overskirts. Nia holds up the mauve gown next to it and, sure enough, the navy one is at least a foot shorter and a good few inches smaller in the waist.

There is absolutely no way these two dresses were made for the same person.

If the king commissioned these gowns and they weren't for the queen and he has no daughter, then... "Do you think the king has a mistress?"

Madame Ella grimaces as she folds the queen's gown back into the box. "That's what I assumed at the time. He'd hardly be the first."

That still doesn't explain how the gowns ended up at my house.

Madame Ella leaves us to collect our Beltane gowns. While she's gone, I return the mauve dress to its box, tracing the contrasting black ribbon accentuating the fitted bodice.

"What should I do with them?" It feels wrong to keep the dresses, especially since I have no clue where they came from.

"What do you mean?" Nia scoffs. "They're vintage Madame Ella, Kerris. You keep them."

I suppose that's the best choice considering I wouldn't know where else to send them. "Who do you think they're from?"

Nia shrugs. "Does it matter? You received seven free dresses made by the most exclusive designer in the kingdom. Let's just hope they keep on coming."

28

Everett

*"The quickest trail to death is the one you walk
alone."*

— Surviving The Unseelie Lands, Author
Unknown

The softest swaying rouses me from sleep.

We were relieved of our posts a few hours before dawn and returned directly to a silent camp. When I think back to the night, my body comes alive. As irritated as I was at River's unexpected interruption, the opportunity to share such an intimate space with Kerris made the night a magical one, indeed.

If I breathe deeply enough, I can still smell her honeysuckle hair. If I close my eyes, I can still feel the way she felt pressed against me, the soft swell of her breast beneath my palm—

This damn hunt could not come at a worse time.

We need food to feed our people, and the threat of wolves is one we need to quash as quickly and quietly as possible, but there is somewhere else I would rather be.

With Kerris Dawn.

Female of my dreams who confessed to sharing the same yearnings that stir within me. Such a thing hardly seems possible, and yet I can still taste the sweetness of her honeysuckle skin on my lips.

Even my bones know that she is not meant for me. Not forever.

She will find herself a Seelie fae, one who laughs and smiles with her, who can provide all the luxuries she deserves. When that happens, I will sink back into the dark shadows where I belong.

Until then, I will take every smile and laugh that she gives to me. Every intimate touch. Every burning look. I will lock all of them away in my heart to keep me warm on the nights when the loneliness creeps in.

"Ever?" a husky voice calls.

My stomach sinks. *Leah.*

At least she waited until daylight to call instead of forcing me to turn her down once again. The upside to this hunting trip is that she will be staying here to protect the rest of our clan.

I roll out of the bed to drag on my trousers and fasten my belt. When I open the door, Leah is waiting on my staircase, a steaming pot in one hand and a smile on her lips.

"Good day, Ever." She raises on her toes to press her lips to my cheek.

The overly familiar greeting stuns me silent. She and I have shared kisses, but never in the light of day where anyone walking past might see. What is she thinking?

She holds up the pot. "I brought you porridge oats."

Not this again. "Leah..."

"Do not look so worried. This is not a proposal. I have cooked them for all the hunters leaving today. You will need a full belly for the long journey."

I glance over to where Maddox sits on his own stairs, tucking into a pot like the one in Leah's hand. When he catches me looking, he throws his hand up in salute.

After the long night, I am very hungry and the thought of eating more jerky when that is all we will have for the foreseeable future does not sound enticing.

"Thank you." I accept the pot.

She kisses my cheek once more and then strolls away, her dark hair swaying in time with her steps.

What a strange morning.

The strangeness continues. While I pack my saddle bags with supplies, I can feel eyes on me. When I turn to look, I catch the females washing garments in the center of camp staring. Maddox teases me as we ride out of camp, claiming that the soap he made is the reason for all the unwanted attention.

I am not so sure but decide to stop using the soap for the duration of our hunt, just in case.

"Did your Seelie fae mention your scent?" he asks as his steed trots next to Nyx.

What is it with his infernal questions? He needs to find his own Seelie and ask her instead of bothering me. "She did not."

The fool grins. "The ticking in your jaw tells me otherwise. Perhaps she will like my scent better."

Perhaps I will make a new necklace with his bones. "You will not get close enough for her to smell you."

"We will see."

No, we most certainly will not. If he even thinks about walking within sniffing distance of my Seelie, I will make good on my threats to toss him into the canyon. Let him fall like those rocks he loves to throw.

Thinking of Kerris brings back the same emotions I felt when we parted last night. Longing. Desire. Sadness. Confusion.

So much confusion.

"She asked me to the Seelie festival," I confess in a low whisper.

Maddox sits a little taller as he steers his mount even closer, his eyes wide as a rabbit's when it sees a fox. "Just you or everyone?"

"Me. But I will not go on my own." There is much danger in Rosehill for one lone Unseelie fae. Not that I would have difficulty handling myself against even their finest guards, but the ramifications for our people if a fight were to break out could be disastrous.

"Then I will accompany you," he says with a brusque nod. "And so will Gryff."

There is no telling how long this hunt will take, but I find myself hoping that we will return to camp in time to witness the festivities.

"Everett Gathin!" our chieftain calls from a short distance ahead.

He will not join our hunt but has chosen to accompany us to the border of our territory.

I nudge Nyx into a canter, and the other hunters shift their own mounts to the side, allowing me past to where our chieftain rides in the center of the pack. Wisdom and age run like silver rivers through his black hair, much like all of our elders'. Silver mating bonds cover his arms and chest; he wears them proudly, as he should. No one in our clan has as many scars as our chieftain.

"Have you found any tracks near the outpost?" he asks.

"Nothing bigger than a rabbit or whitetail."

This makes him frown. "The wolves do not usually come this close to camps, but this was a hard winter."

Meaning the beasts are hungrier than normal. This is the best explanation for why they would venture from the deeper forests into the clearings near Unseelie camps.

Everyone knows, the only thing worse than a wolf is a starving one.

I am about to fall back into line when his solemn eyes meet mine.

"Is it true that you have befriended a Seelie fae?"

How the hell did he hear about Kerris? Not Maddox or Gryffin, surely—

"River said one came to the well and spoke with you," he goes on.

Fucking River. Do the males of our clan truly have nothing better to discuss? "A Seelie did come to the well. She spoke to me there, but I did not speak to her that day."

"Good. You know what happens to fae who become ensnared by their webs."

He speaks as if Kerris is a spider when she is the sun bringing warmth and joy and life and happiness. Not that our chieftain would understand since he has been mated for over a century.

"I am well aware," I hedge.

"If the Seelie ask about the wolves, you are to tell them there have been no sightings. If they are spooked, they are liable to close the bridge. Our people would not survive without access to the well."

I know better than anyone what happens to fae who no longer have access to infinity water.

Kerris already knows there was a wolf sighting, but she will not tell anyone.

Of this, I am certain.

"I understand."

He dismisses me then, but instead of falling back to where Maddox rides, I urge Nyx forward. The last thing I need is for my friend to bring up Kerris again and have the chieftain discover that I am not being wholly truthful with him.

29

"Never underestimate the power of wounded pride."

— Author Unknown

The last four days were as slow as sap dribbling down a pine tree.

On Saturday afternoon, I forced myself to stop by the library to ask Trevor if he'd like to go for dinner. Unfortunately, he had to take an unexpected trip to visit his brother in Glassmarsh.

Which left me free for Nia to play matchmaker.

So far this week, I've been on three dates.

Sunday, I met Nolan's third cousin, Tobias McAfee, at a tea house. Tobias was pleasant enough when he managed to pry his gaze from my breasts long enough to look me in the eye.

Monday, I went for a stroll with Nia's former classmate, Samuel Tipton, which was moderately enjoyable until he kissed me goodbye and tried to choke me with his tongue.

Tuesday was the final straw. My aunt's friend's son Finneas

Clarke took me to the Rosehill greenhouse and had the audacity to grab my backside. Too bad I didn't keep Gryffin's blade. Finneas deserved a good poke in the ribs.

By this morning, I've given up on men entirely.

Seelie men, anyway.

If Nia didn't spend every waking moment on my heel, I would've gone straight to the well to see if Ever had returned from his hunt and ask how he fared.

Instead, I spend the afternoon helping Aunt Cordelia pack all her pies into boxes for transport. When evening finally arrives, I change into my new dress. Tiny flowers dot the ivory corseted bodice and lavender chiffon overskirt. The ribbons at the back are a celery green. I feel like a princess when I put it on—although finding a prince is the last thing on my mind.

With my hair curling down my back, I tuck one of the flowers Ever gave me behind my ear, just in case he's back and decides to accept my invitation. When Nia sees me, she asks if I've changed my mind about Ronan.

I tell her that the flowers aren't from the prince, and when she asks who gave them to me, I shrug and escape down the stairs with her flying down behind me like a banshee. Both of us come to a screeching halt when we see my aunt speaking to Trevor on the stoop.

My missing suitor offers a tentative smile. "Ladies, I apologize for barging in unannounced, but as I was telling Mrs. Quill, I just returned from Glassmarsh and had hoped to escort Kerris to tonight's festival."

Nia shoves me between the shoulder blades, and I careen forward, narrowly avoiding a collision with my aunt. "You go with Trevor, and I'll help my mother with the pies."

"I don't mind helping—"

My aunt waves me off as well. "No, no. You go ahead. We insist."

Those two are as subtle as a bloomin' plank to the forehead.

Reluctantly, I allow Trevor to lead me down the path to where everyone is emerging from their fear-induced hibernation.

Imagine being so afraid that you lose an entire day every week just to avoid your neighbors. Madness.

Trevor pats my hand where it rests in the crook of his arm, his smile warm and friendly. "I'm sorry I have been so inattentive of late. You deserve better."

Unlike Tobias, Trevor has the decency to look at my face when he speaks.

I tell him it's all right even though I'm not sure it is. Never making time for someone with whom you wish to start a relationship doesn't bode well for the future.

I'd appreciate a husband who wants to spend at least a little time with me.

Then again, perhaps this is what marriage is like in the city. Take my aunt and uncle, for instance. Uncle Arlo rarely arrives home from the counting house until well after dinner and yet my aunt seems happy, baking away to her heart's content.

Perhaps I was spoiled by my parents' relationship and should lower my expectations.

Have low expectations ever begotten true happiness?

Do I really want to settle when there's someone out there for whom my blood sings?

The closer we get to the square, the more packed the streets become. People must've travelled from miles around to attend tonight's festival.

Maypoles have been erected around the fountain, with ribbons fluttering and flowers spilling from pots affixed to the tops. Children race toward the poles, fighting for their favorite colors. I remember doing the same when I was smaller, before the families with children moved off the mountain. Theo would never participate, even when I begged.

A few people we pass comment on the stunning silver bloom behind my ear, their gazes bouncing between Trevor and me, rife with curiosity. More than once, I hear them whisper about the prince, but I ignore them all.

With whom I choose to spend my time is none of their business.

Trevor and I meander through the vendors selling pies, buns, cakes, and biscuits of all flavors. We find Nia at one of the stalls, helping her mother arrange pies. When she sees us, she skips to my side, our argument from last week finally forgotten.

"Will we go for drinks?" she asks, bonfire light sparkling in her eyes.

It's one of the first times since our fight that she has looked at me without animosity. How I've missed her smile. The three of us head over to where the line meanders in front of the temple. To my eternal delight, Ivee arrives a moment later in a flurry of lacy pink skirts.

For once, she doesn't glare or glower at us, which immediately makes me suspicious. "Did you hear the news?" she gasps, her cheeks as pink as her gown.

Nia manages to control her scowl as the three of us shake our heads.

Ivee leans closer. "William told Shiela that the Unseelie didn't come to the well today."

Why is Nia looking at me like that? This is hardly my fault.

They're probably still hunting. Or maybe something went wrong. I hope Ever is all right. If there weren't so many people, I'd venture to the bridge to find out myself.

"Of course they didn't," a mocking voice says from behind me. My shoulders stiffen as Ronan and Nolan join our group. "We all know the Unseelie are allergic to happiness," Ronan continues, his eyes narrowed on where I cling to Trevor's arm.

After some speculation, mostly between Ivee and Ronan, we

finally reach the front of the line. *This wine cannot come soon enough.*

Despite Ronan's protests, Trevor insists on buying the first round. When he tries to hand the prince his drink, Ronan looks down at the glass as if it's filled with lava.

Petulant prince.

If anyone wants to know what a sore loser looks like, they need look no further.

I swipe the glass for myself and then drain them both before discarding them in one of the rubbish barrels.

Ivee might be the one hanging on Ronan's every word and clinging to his arm like a barnacle, but I can feel his eyes on me.

The simplest way to escape is to join the dancers.

For once, I'm the one dragging Nia into the fray. By the time we finish the reel, we're both breathless and our stomachs ache from laughter.

My smile falters when I catch Ronan leaning toward Trevor, their expressions grim as they converse. From the way Trevor glances my way, I have a sinking feeling they're talking about me.

Heaven only knows what Ronan is saying. The prince really has become a thorn in my side. The sooner he marries, the better.

When we get back to our friends, Trevor hands me a fresh glass of wine but keeps me at arm's length. Each time I try to step closer, he takes a step in retreat, until he nearly collides with one of the tables surrounded by merrymakers.

Enough is enough. "Have I done something to offend you?"

He suddenly finds the cobblestones very interesting. "I don't know what you mean."

What is it with these Seelie men and their penchant for lying? "I saw you speaking to Ronan, and now you're acting as if I'm covered in smallpox. I demand to know what he said to you."

"Do you mind if we continue this conversation tomorrow? I'm suddenly quite tired—"

"*Trevor.*"

My date grimaces even as his gaze darts around the crowded square. "I'm dreadfully sorry, Kerris. If I'd known you and Ronan were still involved, I never would have offered to escort you tonight."

"We're not involved. We haven't been in ages."

His brow lifts as if he doesn't believe a word I'm saying. "Look, I am quite fond of you, but you don't know the prince the way I do, and I cannot afford to be his enemy."

The prince's enemy? What in the world is he talking about?

"Did he tell you not to pursue me?"

Trevor grimaces.

That *swine.*

"You are unbelievable." He must not hold any true affection for me at all if he is so easily put off. "Ronan Reve is a bully, and I want nothing to do with him." And if no one else speaks up, he will only get worse. Petty princes make petty kings. "Until this moment, I thought you and I might have a chance at a relationship, that perhaps your hesitation was due to shyness." Turns out, I was a fool all along. "Now I see that you are a coward, Trevor Dillon, and I do not wish to tie myself to someone who isn't willing to fight for me."

Yes, I am a strong, independent, capable woman and can fight my own battles, but it does not make me weak to want a partner to stand up and fight by my side.

Trevor's cheeks flush a deep scarlet. "He threatened to have me removed from the library. I care for you, Kerris, but my job is my life."

He did *what?*

That manipulative *snake.*

I turn on my heel, scouring the crowd for the prince. Ronan Reve is about to get a piece of my mind, and he isn't going to like what I have to say. So much for enjoying the rest of my night. The moment I finish saying my piece, I'm going straight back to the cottage to stew in my rage.

Nia watches me through wide eyes, and I'm not sure whether she overheard everything, but from the way she scowls at Trevor, I assume she heard enough.

"Where's Ronan?" I grit out.

"With Nolan over by the fountain. Why?"

"Because I'm going to tell him that he is a no-good, conniving weasel."

Her hand snaps out, her cool fingers encircling my wrist. "Calm down."

Ha! As if that's possible right now with my blood boiling. "He threatened to get Trevor fired from his job if he continued seeing me." For that, he's getting a piece of my mind. No, not a piece. The whole bloomin' pie. I don't care who his father is, Ronan doesn't get to treat people like this.

The music comes to an unexpected halt, as if the musicians overheard my plan. Gasps and curses rise from the crowd as I search for Ronan's golden hair. I feel like ripping it all out, strand by strand until he's bald as a bloomin' mole.

Nia's hands fly to her mouth. "Oh, no."

"Oh, yes." I'm going to kick him in the shin. *Both* shins. I might even slap him. Let him walk around the festival with my handprint on his no-good face.

Nia points to something behind me. "No, Kerris. Look."

I whirl, finding Ever sitting atop his black steed. The rest of the Unseelie appear from the shadows, carts of jugs rattling behind them, staring back at us.

30

He's here.

I can't believe Ever is actually here!

My relief at knowing he's safe is like a living thing growing in my veins.

When Ever's gaze finds mine, my breath releases with a soft *woosh*, my heart picking up speed until the relentless pounding is all I can hear.

Every bit of disappointment and ire melts from my bones. The drama with Trevor and Ronan no longer matters. *None of it matters.*

I asked Ever to come to the festival, and he *did.*

"Come with me." I grab Nia's hand, pulling her toward the riders. It's time to allay her fears once and for all.

She tries to tug free, but my grip does not falter. "I couldn't possibly—"

"Please. I want you to meet him. To see what I see."

Ever dismounts, one hand on the reins and the other patting his unicorn's thick neck, hushing Nyx and watching us approach with an unreadable expression.

Nia stays behind me, her harsh breaths tickling the back of my neck as I come to a halt in front of him. "You came."

His gaze never strays from mine, but there is the slightest lift to his lips that I'm calling a smile. A smile just for me. "The female who invited me was quite persuasive."

Maddox appears from nowhere, stepping around Ever and clapping him on the shoulder. "Far be it for Ever here to turn down an invitation. I am Maddox, by the way." He stretches his long-fingered greenish hand toward my cousin.

Nia's hands remain pinned to her sides, her face devoid of color as she stares at him.

"This is my cousin, Nia Quill," I say, urging her forward.

Gryffin joins us, not a hint of humor on his stony face. "Did we come to chat or are we going to do our fucking job and bring water across the canyon?"

Right. The water. Of course, Ever didn't *just* come to see me.

"Would you like something to eat while you collect water?" There's more than enough to go around.

Nia lets out a strangled, choking sound before snatching my hand and dragging me away from the well. "You can't give him food," she hisses.

"Why not?" I brough plenty of coin.

"Did you read the book Trevor gave you or just stare at the pictures?"

"I read some of it." The first ten chapters, anyway. In my defense, the pictures were far more intriguing.

She presses a hand to her brow, her curls vibrating as she shakes her head. "Clearly you skipped the part that says giving an unmarried Unseelie food is akin to courting him."

Courting him?

Is *that* why Ever kept asking about the biscuits?

No.

Is it?

And I brought them twice.

"I didn't know that," I whisper.

"Just be glad that he didn't give you a gift as well."

He *did* give me a gift. A gift I'm wearing in my hair as we speak. My stomach flutters as my gaze drifts over Ever's strong back while he hefts a jug from the cart all by himself. "What would happen if he gave me a gift?" I force through dry lips.

"Then it means he accepts your offer of courtship."

I gave him food. He gave me flowers.

Am I unknowingly courting an Unseelie fae?

I do not wish to be your friend.

This is not over.

Bloomin' hell. I think I am.

What's more, the idea of being properly courted by Ever makes me giddier than it probably should.

A hand slips around my wrist. Ronan tugs me back to where the rest of the Seelie are watching, a crimson flush painting his jaw and neck.

When I try to pull from his grip, his blunt nails bite into my skin. "Let me go, Ronan." I might as well be talking to the bloody cobblestones for all the attention he pays me. "I said—"

He whirls on me, his blown-out pupils reflecting the fae lights strung above us. "What the fuck do you think you're doing?"

I flinch at the venom in his tone. How dare he speak to me in such a vile way.

"I'll not have my woman cavorting with some Unseelie bastard," he grits through clenched teeth.

"I'm not *your* woman, and I think I've made that perfectly clear." I wrench my hand, but still, he holds firm. "Let go of me."

"After I brought you to meet the king and queen, you insist on making a mockery of me?"

"You're making a mockery of yourself."

His mouth opens to spew some other hateful remark, but then

his head lifts and his eyes widen. I've never seen a ghost, but I imagine its complexion would match Ronan's right now.

A deep voice washes over us, vibrating with barely contained rage. "If you want to keep your hand, I suggest you let the female go."

Ronan drops me like I'm on fire, stumbling away from where not only Ever stands at my back, but also Maddox and Gryffin as well, hands on the hilts of their bone daggers and vicious smiles on their faces.

Those gathered in the square titter and gasp, retreating farther down the street.

Ever's lips fall over his sharp teeth, and he looks down at me through solemn eyes. "Are you all right, Kerris?"

Besides the red mark on my wrist and my indignation: "I'm fine."

"He never should have touched you without your permission."

The others nod and then fold their hands behind their backs.

They've done the same thing every time, and I've never been able to figure out why. "Why do you always stand like that?"

"To show that we are not a threat to you," Ever says, as if the explanation should be obvious.

While the meaning behind the gesture makes me feel all warm and gooey inside, those daggers and their hands aren't the only weapons at their disposal. "What's to stop you from biting me?"

His lips twitch, and he eases forward, his breath fanning against my cheek when he whispers against the shell of my ear, "If you would like me to bite you, I would prefer we did not have an audience."

Holy heavens.

I think I might faint.

One of the men by the well whistles, and Maddox and Gryffin leave us to help unload the rest of the jugs.

Ever straightens, his sigh rife with regret. "I should get back to work."

He's not here for me. This is a coincidence.

No matter how many times I repeat the sentiment in my mind, it never feels true. I suppose there is one way to find out. "Why did you come to the festival?"

Ever looks past me to the emptying square. When his gaze returns, he cards a hand through his midnight hair. "I am not here for the festival," he says slowly, and I do my best to hide my disappointment.

Of course, he didn't come for me.

He's here because his people need water to survive.

"I came to see your new dress," he says, making a slow, deliberate perusal from my corset to my slippers and back again. And then he winks and walks away.

"Bloomin' hell..." Nia murmurs.

Bloomin' hell is right.

"He is..." Her words drift away.

He is everything I've ever wanted in a mate. "I told you, didn't I?"

I didn't think it possible to care for Ever more than I already did, but I was wrong.

So bloody wrong.

Most of the guests have abandoned the square, including the musicians. Those who remain no longer dance or laugh but sit hunched over their drinks or desserts, watching the Unseelie fill their jugs through narrowed eyes.

Ronan seethes from a bench near the fountain. Ivee joins him, but he never seems to look away from the Unseelie. When the jugs have all been loaded back into the carts, they don't leave straightaway. Instead, they sink onto the edge of the well and the carts and stare right back.

I mill around somewhere in the middle, next to my aunt's

booth, still laden with pies. You could cut the tension in the air with a bread knife. Is this how Beltane is to end? With a bloomin' staring contest? "This is ridiculous."

I'm not going to stand here and let these ignorant people make our guests feel unwelcome. Enough is enough.

Giving an unmarried, Unseelie food is akin to courting him...

I grab a pie and fork, bringing them over to where Ever sits, one foot braced on the edge of the well's low wall and his elbow resting atop his knee.

"Here." I hold out the pie and watch his slashing brows lift toward the dark hair sweeping across his furrowed brow.

Behind me, a vicious curse echoes through the square. Ronan launches to his feet, his face contorted in fury and his hands bunched into fists.

It's a good thing I don't care. Let him see what it's like to have someone ignore his requests.

Ever blinks down at the pie, then back up at me. "Did you not hear your cousin?"

"I did." This time, I understand exactly what it means to offer him this gift.

He accepts the pie and the fork, holding my gaze as he takes a bite. The muscles in his sharp jaw flex in the most enticing way as he chews, and when he swallows, the bob of his throat makes my knees weak.

Behind him, Maddox sniggers. "Tell Nia Quill that I prefer blueberry," he says with a flash of those sharpened teeth.

"My least favorite fruit," Nia shoots back from a few paces behind me.

Gryffin glances up at the clock tower above the library, his scowl deepening. "It is nearly midnight."

Meaning Wednesday is almost over.

The Unseelie seem to rise in unison—everyone except Ever. He clutches his pie plate against his chest, as if anyone who tries to pry it off him would lose their arm. Only when the plate is empty does he set it aside. When he stands, he moves with purpose, and I wait with bated breath as he reaches into his saddle bag and withdraws four silver flowers.

"Why are there so many?"

His lips twitch. "One for every day I was gone."

My heart skips around in my chest, beating with the knowledge of exactly what this means.

I have made him an offer of courtship; one he has just accepted.

When I take the flowers from him, his gaze drops to my lips, and I know in my pounding heart that he isn't going to kiss me in front of all these people, but oh, how I want him to.

"Come to the bridge tomorrow night?" he whispers.

All I can do is nod and watch as he mounts his horse and leads the group of Unseelie into the darkness.

31

Everett

"Murder has its merits."

— Everett Gathin, An
Observation

"I should have killed him." Should've cut that Seelie bastard down right there in the city square. Painted the cobbles red with his blood. Impaled him on one of those strange poles with all the ribbons.

Gryffin pats his mount's head, scanning the fog for signs of trouble as the rest of our group disappears into the thick layer of gray, making the slow, painstaking trek back to camp. "You never should have gotten involved in the first place."

"And that pig never should have laid a hand on Kerris without her consent." If that had happened on our side of The Divide, any witness would have been honor-bound to take the male's hand. Instead, I was forced to stand by and do nothing but make threats.

Gryff's head swings toward me. "And if he laid a hand on her *with* her consent?"

212

Then I still would have killed him, but in secret. Nice and slow. Bled him within an inch of his life, then healed him with water from the well and gutted him like the animal he is, feeding his entrails to the beasts that roam these woods.

Maddox nudges his mount closer to mine. "Do you even know who he is?"

No, and I do not care either. "All their males look the same to me." Soft middles, round faces, and tiny, flat teeth.

"That, my friend, was Prince Ronan Reve."

Gryffin curses and folds a hand over his forehead with an exasperated huff.

It would be my luck that the Prince of Willowhaven set his eyes on the only female I have ever truly wanted. My only solace comes from the fact that, if Kerris were interested in him, she would not have given me that disgusting pie after her cousin explained what it meant.

"I do not care if it was the king himself." No one should be allowed to get away with treating a female like that.

Gryff snorts. "You do realize that all they have to do is destroy the bridge and be done with us, right?"

That is exactly what I said to those fae who left their posts all those nights ago. How quickly I forgot myself...

Maddox shakes his head. "They would not dare. We have a treaty."

A treaty that is nothing more than ink on paper, easily destroyed, much like the bridge connecting our world to theirs.

"If it is all the same to you, I would rather not find out," Gryff shoots back.

Even if I had known he was the prince, I still would have intervened. Having a crown does not give him the right to put his hands on a female whenever he wants, especially when she expressly forbids it.

Kerris looked so small against him, so helpless.

If anything, tonight should have proven that I have no business even entertaining the notion of her.

Tell that to my stubborn heart.

I can feel Gryff's gaze boring into the side of my head, no doubt judging me for all that has happened. "Did you know the two of them were involved?"

"No." Although it should not surprise me. Kerris is a rare beauty, and her heart has no malice. Any male would be a fool to look past her and not at least consider her as a mate.

"This complicates matters," he goes on. "Kerris Dawn is not just some random Seelie female. She is being courted by the heir to the throne. One day she might be queen. What can you offer her?"

I try to ignore his question, but the truth in his words pulses through my ears like a drumbeat.

"He makes a good point," Maddox chimes in, still smiling but not quite as widely. "Your cock will only get you so far."

What do I have to offer Kerris besides a life in exile from her friends and family? She would never survive on our side of the canyon, and I would never be welcome on hers.

The reality of our situation has never seemed so bleak.

I am too keyed up to return home, offering instead to take over guarding the bridge from River and Rynan. They gawk at me as if I ordered them to eat rocks. Although I would rather be left alone with my thoughts, Maddox and Gryff insist on keeping me company. Maybe their bickering will help take my mind off the hopeless situation with Kerris.

I toss another log onto the fire, and sparks shoot into the sky while the gray smoke curls toward the layer of mist hanging above us. Maddox holds out his hands, offering me a giant flat rock. "I have baked a pie for you, Ever. Here. Take a bite. You know you want to."

I shove Maddox back, and his "pie" goes flying. "You are one to talk. 'Oh, Nia, blueberries are my favorite.'"

He shrugs, not the least bit irritated by my retort. "What is so wrong with that? She is beautiful."

"She hates you."

"She only hates me because she does not know me."

Gryff shakes his head, unstrapping his dagger to stoke the coals beneath the fresh log. "And if she ever has the misfortune of getting to know you, she will hate you even more."

"Fuck off. You do not know that. Kerris Dawn is smitten. Maybe her cousin wants to cross the bridge for a taste as well." The way Maddox rubs his hands together makes it look as if he is plotting something terrible. May the fates help whatever female has the misfortune of choosing him as a mate. "Just wait till Leah Locke finds out."

Shit. Shit. Shit.

In my elation, I completely forgot about Leah.

I will have to be on alert in case she tries to cross The Divide. There is no telling what Leah would do to Kerris if she found her. This situation is becoming more complicated by the minute.

The thump of hooves echoes in the distance, growing louder with each passing breath. Whoever approaches is in a hurry.

The three of us stand to greet them.

Our chieftain arrives in a cloud of dust, leaping from his mount with the energy of a youngling. "There's no need to stand on my behalf. I only came to speak to my new son."

He has a daughter, not a son.

Perhaps his mind is not as keen as it once was.

He stalks over to where I stand, grips both sides of my face, and presses a dry kiss to my cheek. "Leah told me the good news, and I was waiting for you to return from the hunt to congratulate you."

Now I know he is confused. "Congratulate me for what?" I have done nothing of note that I can recall.

"Accepting my daughter's proposal of course! She showed me the skillet you gave her. Why did you not tell me when we last spoke?"

Accept her proposal? Skillet?

"I..." I do not have a fucking clue what he is talking about.

He claps me on the back once more, sending me stumbling a step forward. "Tell me, how was the hunt?"

How does he expect me to speak about the hunt when I am still trying to figure out why he thinks Leah and I are to be mated.

"We took down two bears, five elk, and a handful of foxes," Gryffin clips. I can feel his glower but cannot bring myself to face him.

Our chieftain beams with pride. "Well done. That should feed our people for weeks. Any sign of the wolves?"

"No." Not so much as a track.

"Excellent. After you have rested, I expect you to come to my home for a celebratory drink."

All I can do is stare as he slaps my shoulder once more and then stomps back to his mount and rides away.

Maddox and Gryffin turn toward me, their jaws hanging open.

Gryffin's eyes blaze when he shakes his head. "Tell me you did not accept Leah's proposal."

Maddox's hands flex at his sides. "What the fuck, Ever? You cannot have a mate at home and court another across the canyon."

I do *not* have a mate. "I never accepted Leah's proposal. I swear it." The chieftain said she showed everyone *my* skillet, but all my cookware is locked in my barrel-top. Unless she broke in there is no way—

Wait. There is one skillet that was not in my house. "Gryffin? What did you do with the skillet I gave you?"

His faces twists into a grimace. "*Shit.*"

"Did you give it to Leah?"

A nod. "She asked if she could use it while I was gone. We were not going to be here, so I thought nothing of it."

I drag my hands through my hair. We were supposed to be friends. How could she do this to me? "I must set the record straight."

Gryffin scrubs a hand down his face, his scowl deeper than I have ever seen before. "If you break it off, her father will lose his mind. He is not known for his forgiveness. You are liable to end up exiled."

"Maybe it is for the best," Maddox chimes in. "It is not as if it would have worked out with the Seelie anyway. What were you going to do? Move to Rosehill and start farming goats?"

I do not know how or even if Kerris and I would have made a relationship work, but at least it would have been our decision to end things instead of having someone else force our hands.

There is only one way to make this right.

Bones crunch beneath my boots as I stalk toward Nyx.

"Where are you going?" Maddox calls.

I am going to make this right.

I am going to clear things up once and for all.

"I am going to speak to Leah."

My fist threatens to break through Leah's unpainted door. I do not care who hears the deafening rattle. This is a conversation that cannot wait until morning.

She answers with a coy smile that sets my teeth on edge. Does she not realize what her lies have done?

"Hello, Ever."

"You will call me Everett Gathin." Only my closest friends call me Ever, and she has proven that she is no longer among them. I duck beneath the doorframe into her barrel-top. Her home is as stark as my feelings this night, without adornment or personalization. Unlike some females, Leah Locke has never been one to fuss over decorations. To my knowledge, she has never fussed over anything.

She closes the door behind me and leans a slender hip against the lone chair next to her table. "You have heard the happy news, then."

More like tragic news. "Your father came to the outpost to congratulate me. What were you thinking?"

Her chin lifts with defiance. "I was thinking the male I chose has strung me along for long enough. Everyone in the camp was laughing at me."

"They were not."

"How would you know? You are barely here. Only to sleep and then leave again on your hunts and to guard the bridge. You do not have to face their scorn."

She is hurting, and I should feel more sympathetic. Maybe I would if she had not put me into such a hopeless position. "I am sorry for making you wait so long. I can see now that my hesitance to give you an answer put you in a terrible position. In truth, I did not know my own mind, but now I do."

My mother's words ring true in my ears as clearly as the day she spoke them to me.

I will not settle for anything less than love.

Love that I feel for a Seelie fae with the sweetest face and kindest heart.

"I reject your proposal."

Leah's smile fades like the light at the end of every day. "How *dare* you turn me down. Your father was a disgrace, and your mother was a whore, yet I chose to look past your inferior parentage to see the man you have become, and you *reject* my proposal? I am the chieftain's daughter. I could have anyone—"

"Then choose someone else. Someone more deserving than me. Someone whose *parentage* is not so beneath you." I knew others in our clan felt that way about me but never Leah.

How could she think I would want to tie myself to her now that the truth has been revealed?

"And become the laughingstock of camp once more? Absolutely not. You and I will be mated."

I was hoping to appeal to her rational nature, but it would appear as though Leah Locke has forgotten all reason. "Then I will go to the chieftain and tell him the truth."

She jerks back, ramming into the cupboard. The skillet she claimed was from me clatters to the floor, barely missing her toes. "You wish to tell my father that you revoke your acceptance of his only daughter's proposal?"

"I never accepted!"

She rips the skillet from the floor, waving it in my face. "The skillet on my stove says otherwise. Who do you think my father will believe, Ever? You or me?"

Our chieftain might like me well enough, but no amount of affection could compare to the way he feels about his only daughter.

If Leah refuses the truth...

Then I am deep in the shit.

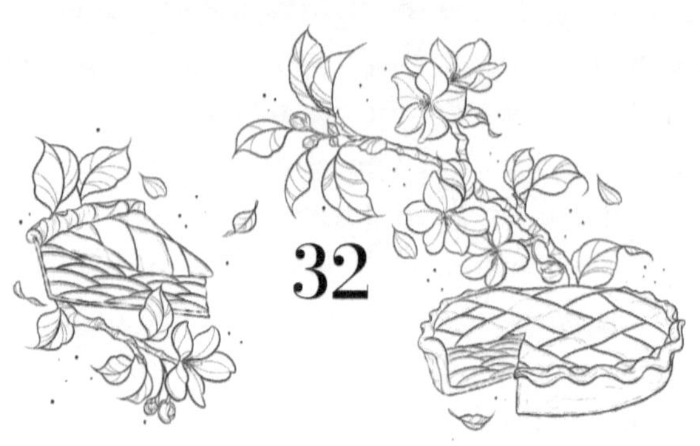

32

"Beware of enemies appearing where friends once stood."

— An Unseelie Fable, Author Unknown

Nia and I race back to the cottage, giggling through the maze of streets that already feel like home. Inside my aunt and uncle's hushed conversation drifts from the kitchen, but neither of us stop until we are safely ensconced in her bedroom.

"Oh, Kerris. I cannot believe you did that," she manages between gasps, her color higher than I've ever seen it before as she fans her face with both hands.

"Whatever do you mean?" I tease, twisting to give her access to the laces at my back.

Nia tugs at the knot, a smile in her voice. "You, Kerris Dawn, gave an Unseelie warrior a whole damn pie in front of the entire city!"

The corset loosens, falling to the ground so I can step out of it.

"I sure did." And if I had to do it all over again, I wouldn't change a thing.

I motion for Nia to twist around. The ribbon on her corset is tied in a double knot that takes a little work to undo.

"I thought Ronan was going to lose his life."

She sounds utterly delighted by the prospect, which strikes me as odd considering only a few days ago she was trying to convince me to forgive the man.

"I still cannot believe the wretched way he spoke to you." Her hair tickles my fingers when she shakes her head. "You should've seen Everett's face when the prince grabbed you. He had murder in his eyes. I was half afraid he was going to run Ronan through. Serves the ass right. He never should've touched you like that."

I trace a finger along my sore wrist, still marked from his iron grip. There will definitely be a bruise come morning. "I'm afraid it's official: I won't be the next Princess of Willowhaven."

Nia whips around, catching both of my hands as her corset falls to the floor. "No. You're going to be the next Mrs.— What's Everett's surname?"

"I don't know. I never asked." But when I see him tomorrow night, I will.

"It's so romantic, isn't it?" Nia spins me around the room like we're back at the festival, dancing to a fiddler's tune. "The way he gave you those flowers. Flowers that happen to match all the others in your room."

Everything about Ever is romantic. Being around him makes me feel as if I'm floating on a champagne cloud. "He is the most amazing man I have ever met."

"I never thought I'd see you so smitten. And the fact that he forced himself to eat that pie means he must be smitten as well."

"What do you mean?" I had a piece myself earlier in the night and it tasted like blackberry bliss.

She flops back on her bed, her arms splayed across her quilt.

"For a woman on the verge of bedding an Unseelie, you certainly don't know very much about them."

"I'm not on the verge of bedding him," I choke. Visions of those illustrations in Trevor's book dance through my mind. I wouldn't even know what to do if he were to *disrobe* in my presence.

I bet Ever would know…

Her only answer is a shrill, slightly maniacal cackle.

I swat her leg. "The pie?"

She toes off her slippers and then works her stockings down her thighs, adding them to the pile of discarded clothes on the floor. "The Unseelie don't enjoy sweet things."

"How do you know?"

"Do us both a favor and read your damn book. I'm sure you'll find plenty of things that'll keep you up at night. I think you'll find chapter seventeen particularly interesting."

I leave Nia to her giggling and cross to my own room to retrieve the book from beneath my bed. First, I flip through the table of contents to the chapter about the Unseelie diet. Sure enough, they prefer savory food to sweet. If this author is to be believed, the sugar irritates their throats.

Out of curiosity, I flip to chapter seventeen next.

The Unseelie Tongue.

Nia was right.

This is *riveting*.

The next morning, my aunt remains quiet over breakfast, eating her porridge without attempting to engage in conversation with either of us. Twice, Nia asks if she's all right and twice her mother claims that she is only tired after the festival. When a heavy knock rattles the front door, Aunt Cordelia slips from her chair while Nia and I follow her out into the foyer to where a young man waits with an armful of fliers clutched to his chest.

He hands my aunt a page from the top of the stack, and then retreats down the steps, through the gate, and over to the neighbor's house.

Nia leans over her mother's shoulder for a peek. "What does it say?"

"The king has called a meeting today at noon. All households are required to attend."

"Does this happen often?" I ask.

Both Nia and her mother shake their heads.

A niggling feeling grows in my stomach. Something must be wrong. Why else would the king want to speak to us?

By the time we arrive to the meeting, the city square is already filled with whispering fae, all of them speculating over the reason for us being called together. Some think the king is going to announce a new holiday. Others believe this has to do with last night's unexpected guests.

"Do you think this has to do with the Unseelie?" I whisper to Nia.

She nods. "Definitely."

What could the king say? The Unseelie arrived on a Wednesday, as was their right. It wasn't their fault that we happened to be holding a festival at the same time.

Speaking of the festival, the decorations have yet to be removed. Colorful ribbons still dance in the air, clinging to the forgotten Maypoles.

A wooden platform has been erected in front of the library, where the king and queen sit on their thrones. Ronan has a chair to his mother's right. The golden crown on his head gleams in the sunlight. When our gazes meet, his eyes narrow and his hands ball into fists in his lap.

I curse the moment I met the man. If not for him, my time here in Rosehill would've gone very differently.

Ivee, Florence, and Aurelia appear on our right, too busy tittering with one another to notice Nia and me. Trevor stands in front of the library doors along with a few other staff members I recognize.

When the king stands and clears his throat, a hush falls over the crowd. "Thank you all for joining us on such short notice," he says. "I'm afraid the news today is quite grave. It would seem as though our neighbors have been shirking their duty."

A man in plain brown cotton trousers and a grubby tunic climbs the stairs to the platform. In his arms, he cradles a small goat with ivory fur.

The man, a farmer by the look of his mud-caked boots, gently lays the animal on the wood. Its limbs flop akimbo, its small, horned head lolling to the side, revealing crimson-stained fur across its throat and another gash across its belly.

The crowd draws in a collective gasp.

That poor, sweet creature. Who would do this sort of thing?

The queen rises to her feet, her voice ringing with finality when she speaks. "The wolves have returned to Rosehill."

That's impossible...isn't it?

"Your children might not remember what it was like the last time a wolf found its way across The Divide," she goes on, "but many of you do."

The murmuring around us grows louder. A portly fae with crinkly lips and wild gray hair sprouting from beneath a straw sun hat mutters that she doesn't think it was wolves at all, but the Unseelie themselves who killed the goats.

No wonder the fae are so closed-minded, with vicious slander like that swirling around.

Everett said no wolves have been spotted anywhere near the bridge. Could he be mistaken and one slipped past? Or was the goat killed by something else?

"What if it's not the wolves?" a man to my right shouts. "What if that's what the Unseelie want us to believe?"

The queen raises a bejeweled hand, silencing the crowd once more. "Now, now, let's not jump to conclusions." Although her words are meant to placate, her twisted smile incites more bellows of agreement. "I think we can all agree that we must remain vigilant until the culprit is caught. That is why the king and I are proposing a curfew. All fae must return to their homes by dusk."

The younger fae curse and groan, no doubt more annoyed about missing out on socializing than any genuine concern for their own safety.

The king's lips purse as he glances over at his wife. When she doesn't meet his gaze, he turns back to the crowd. "We thank you for your cooperation and look forward to the day this beast is caught so that we might live in safety once more."

"First, we're not allowed out on Wednesdays, and now this?" a young man in front of Nia grumbles to the one next to him. "Fucking Unseelie. Ruining everything."

My nails carve crescent moons into palms as I glower at them. They need to stay inside when it gets dark. So what? Ever and the rest of his men are responsible for staying *outside*, on their own, watching the bridge in exchange for bloomin' water.

I'm sure they'd be more than happy to stay in the warm comfort of their homes instead of spending every damn night in the wretched darkness.

The king and queen step down from the platform and are quickly whisked away in their golden carriage. Ronan launches from his chair and makes a beeline to where Nia and I wait with no hopes of escape, blocked in by bodies and stone walls.

The prince's cornflower eyes bore a hole into my forehead. "Might I have a word with you in private, Kerris?"

Nia's fingers slip into mine, and she whispers, "You don't have to speak with him if you don't want to."

As if he's going to let me leave without talking to him. I wouldn't put it past the man to follow me all the way home.

The sooner I deal with him, the better. "It's all right, Nia. I'll meet you at the cottage."

She moves aside, and I follow Ronan to the back of the dais where only a few people linger. "Do you have anything to say to me?" he grits out.

I have plenty to say to him, but none of the words on the tip of my tongue are ones he'd be happy to hear.

"Last night you made a fool out of yourself, Kerris. What's worse? You made a fool out of me."

It's good to know where I stand in his list of priorities.

Blowing out a breath, he straightens his waistcoat, threaded with gold. "You're not from Rosehill, so your ignorance is understandable. You clearly don't realize how dangerous that Unseelie monster is."

In this case, not being from Rosehill feels like a blessing. Otherwise, I would probably be as prejudiced as the rest of this city. But I am not the ignorant one. "Everett isn't a monster; he's a man. Same as you." Only taller, leaner, kinder, more respectful, more handsome, and more intriguing.

"Don't be daft. He is nothing like me."

First, I'm ignorant and now I'm daft. Why am I still standing here, letting this small-minded man call me names? "Perhaps that is why I am so taken by him."

His jaw hinges open as he gawks at me. "You cannot be serious."

"I am quite serious. Now, if you'll excuse me, I'm going to go find some company that doesn't insult me at every turn."

"Kerris..." His tone holds a warning.

A warning I ignore as I twist on my heel and stalk away.

If his goal was to keep me from seeing Ever, he is about to be severely disappointed. All it's done is make me want to race across that bridge in the light of day.

33

"The Unseelie tongue is most fascinating, from its impressive dexterity to its surprising texture."

— Unseelie Fae: A Scientific Study

Night descends, the light in the sky giving way to a deep-blue blanket of twinkling starlight. With the rest of the house asleep, I slip out through the back door only to find a man wearing all black waiting at the gate. He tells me to return to the cottage or I'll be taken into custody for defying the curfew.

Since I don't fancy spending the night in a jail cell, I do as he says.

I can't sleep until the late hours of the night. When I peel my eyes open the next morning, my windowsill is empty.

34

Everett

I waited all night on the bridge like a lovesick fool, but Kerris never showed. Her choice should come as no surprise. No doubt, her cousin and the rest of her family explained the realities of our situation, and she decided I am not worth the hassle.

She is right, of course. I have unwillingly been pledged to another, and the consequences of breaking that promise would be dire, indeed. I should be happy that she saved me the trouble of explaining, but I am not happy.

I am fucking miserable.

Some would say it is because I barely slept after my shift, but the truth is that part of me believed we might find a way to make this work.

Maddox sits outside his barrel-top, stirring whatever rubbish he is cooking in the cast iron pot hanging above an open fire. When he sees me emerge from my carriage, his hand stills and nose wrinkles. "If you are getting sick, do not come near me. I am taking Aurora to the river later and she will never forgive me if I cancel."

"I am not sick." I am heartbroken.

"I do not believe you. Sit over there." He nods to a log well away from him, which is a blessing, really, because whatever he is making smells like boiled death.

Dampness seeps through my trousers the moment my arse meets bark. Maddox looks on, a clear question in his narrowed gaze. I glance around, making sure no one else can hear our conversation before explaining the reason for my melancholy. "Kerris did not show up last night."

"And?"

And it should be pretty fucking clear that I am upset about it.

Maddox slips the spoon from the pot, clanging it so loudly on the edge that my head starts to ache. He tosses it aside in exchange for a shaker of heaven-knows-what, sprinkling it over the boiled muck. "Poor Ever has too many females vying for his hand. I really should leave you to your gloom," he mutters, putting the shaker down to resume his stirring. "But since you are one of my best friends, I suppose I will put you out of it. The king has called for a curfew in Rosehill."

That cannot be true. There has not been a curfew in decades. "Why would he do that?"

"A couple of cute little fuzzy animals killed and whatnot. Probably a weasel or fox by the sounds of it."

"How did you find out?"

"River told me this morning."

"And you did not think this was something I would like to know?"

He lifts a shoulder. "I did not think you would care because you already have a mate."

A mate I never wanted in the first place. I should march straight over to the chieftain's home and explain everything. But then that would mean pitting myself against his daughter.

Even if she told him the truth, he might not forgive me for the role I played in stringing her along.

I had hoped that Leah would get tired of waiting and choose someone else, not force my hand.

All he will see is betrayal after betrayal.

"The Seelie did not institute a curfew for a fucking weasel or a fox." There is only one beast that would result in such a panic. "They think a wolf crossed the bridge." If a wolf *did* somehow manage to cross the bridge, then no one in Rosehill is safe.

Kerris is not safe.

I need to go to her. I need to—

He shoves the spoon toward me, reddish-brown liquid dripping like blood down the wood, splattering into the pot. "Sit your ass back down. No wolves crossed the canyon. Everyone in this camp knows how imperative it is to protect the bridge. I asked those who were on duty while we were gone if they have seen signs of a wolf, and do you know what all of them said?"

I bet he is going to tell me.

"They said there have been no tracks in the forests or on the paths. Whatever did this... it was not a wolf." He tosses the spoon into the pot. "I have a theory though. But you are not going to like it."

I do not like many things I have heard over the last couple of days but that has not stopped me from listening. "Tell me anyway."

His eyes narrow. "I do not think the curfew has anything to do with wild animals at all. I think they are trying to keep an Unseelie fae from stealing their prince's bride."

35

The stiff wood of my window ledge digs into my backside as I stare into the night, wishing I could see Ever.

Eventually, they will catch the wolf that prowls our streets, then the curfew will be lifted, and life can go back to normal. Until then, all I can do is try to find a semblance of patience and fill my days with plenty of walks so my legs and mind are tired by nightfall.

My plan hasn't worked thus far, but there's always tomorrow.

According to the books I checked out of the library earlier today, the wolves can grow as large as a horse. After reading the Unseelie book, I don't have much faith in the tome's accuracy.

Still, for this beast to shut down an entire city, it must be fearsome, indeed.

As if conjured from my deepest, darkest imagination, a shadow stirs down in the garden. I press my hand against the cold window-pane, holding my breath as the shadow takes the form of a gigantic wolf—

No, not a wolf. *A man.*

My heart hums inside my chest, beating faster when I realize who is in my aunt's garden.

What in the world is Ever doing here? Doesn't he realize it's not safe? How did he get around the guards? I fumble for my robe and throw it on over my shift.

The way he prowls through the hedges reminds me of a mountain lion I once saw on an adjacent cliff back in Gravale.

He scales the trellis with grace, keeping to the shadows as he slips along the thatch to my window. I open the latch and ease the barrier aside; the cool kiss of spring air wafts over me.

"If someone catches you, there's no telling what they'll do." I search the street for signs of the guard. He's out there somewhere.

"No one is going to catch me," Ever says with a smirk and more confidence than anyone has a right to possess.

While I appreciate his bravado, he clearly doesn't understand what's happening on this side of The Divide. "There's a guard at the gate and more patrolling the streets. We're not allowed out of our homes after dusk because of a wolf."

"Nonsense. No wolf has crossed The Divide."

"Are you certain?"

A nod. "The forest has been silent, and there are no tracks anywhere near the bridge or the village. Either the wolves sprouted wings, or they have not returned."

If the wolves aren't what killed that poor goat, then what did?

My fingers tighten on the sill as I shift closer to where he perches. "Do you want to come in?"

His gaze darts to my darkened room before settling back on me. "I thought perhaps we would do something special tonight."

"And what is that?"

"Come with me, and I will show you."

Far be it from me to turn down such a generous offer. I grab my slippers from beneath my bed and then climb out the window behind him. My robe threatens to come untied as I scoot down the roof like an awkward toddler. Meanwhile, Ever saunters to the end of the thatch and leaps silently onto the ground.

If I tried that, I'd probably break my neck.

On my way down the trellis, my hose catches on the thorns, and they must cut me because I can feel wetness dripping down my leg. Isn't that lovely? Hopefully the blood doesn't ruin my shift.

Ever offers to help me, but I insist on doing it myself because I am a fool, and by the time my slippers meet solid ground, I have at least two splinters and my knee has been raked clean. Heaven only knows how in the world I'm going to get back up.

Instead of taking the main path into town, Everett leads me through the back field where the tall grasses sway like dancing phantoms. We don't go left, to The Divide, but right, out of Rosehill. Ever holds my hand the entire time, and although it's a small thing, my heart soars at his touch.

This is not over.

Is this the night he finally makes good on that promise?

Ever stops suddenly, his nose lifting into the air.

When I do the same, all I smell is grass and cow dung. "Is it a wolf?" Tell me it isn't a bloomin' wolf. Although, if I had to face a wolf with anyone by my side, I'm glad it's Ever.

"I smell blood." His head falls, eyes narrowed on me. "Are you bleeding?"

He can smell my blood? That's disconcerting.

"It's only a scratch."

Letting my hand fall, he braces his fists on his hips, his expression far too grim for the current situation. "Let me see."

"No."

With a beleaguered sigh, his eyes trace my outline as if he can see through the fabric of my robe.

"Even the smallest wound can turn septic, Kerris. Show me so that I may heal you."

A few weeks ago, his scowl would've cowed me, but now all I do is scowl back. "I don't want to."

His dark hair tumbles over his furrowed brow when his head tilts. "Why not?"

A lie is on the tip of my tongue, but I stop myself.

If tonight ends up where I think it might, he's going to find out the truth anyway. Better for him to know now than to have him discover my secret in the heat of the moment.

If he turned me away then, I'm not sure I would ever recover.

"I'm afraid," I confess. And it makes me a coward, but there's nothing I can do about that, now, is there?

He leans down, his knuckle grazing beneath my chin as he applies the slightest pressure, lifting my face to his. "I would never hurt you."

"I know that."

The tiniest wrinkle appears between his knitted brows. "Then why are you afraid?"

For the same reason I didn't want to swim in the quarry.

When you spend your entire life listening to everyone tell you how "beautiful" and "perfect" you are, the last thing you want is to disappoint them with the truth.

Ever has been nothing but honest with me, and he deserves the same courtesy.

So I lift the hems of my robe and shift, exposing the cut on the back of my calf. It's a bit deeper than I thought, and my hose are shredded to bits.

Everett kneels in the dirt, his eyes lifting to where I wait, teeth pinning my lower lip and my breath stalled in my lungs. "May I remove your stocking?" he asks with a slight tremble in his voice.

All I can do is nod.

His hands graze up my calves, but before he reaches the top, his movements falter. I watch his brow furrow and then realization dawn as his eyes widen. "What happened to your legs?"

Only those closest to me know this shameful secret. And now Ever is one of them. "When I was five, there was a fire in our home. My father and brother were camping in our back garden, so they weren't inside at the time." They used to love sleeping under the stars. "My mother fell asleep putting me to bed in the loft. By the time we woke, there was no way out. She threw herself on top of me, saving me and sacrificing herself."

By some miracle, I made it out alive.

My mother did not.

"The burns were so deep, not even the water in the well could heal them properly." Leaving behind mottled, dimpled skin from my feet up to my thighs.

Ever stares up at me, a myriad of emotions playing on his handsome face. I wait for the disgust to settle in, but it never does.

Instead, he peels down my stocking and presses a tender kiss to my hideous knee. "In my world, scars are worn with pride. They are a testament to a fae's strength and resilience."

If only that were true on this side of The Divide. "In my world, they're just ugly."

"Nothing about you could ever be ugly."

He doesn't realize how much those words mean to me. How much I needed to hear them.

Tears slip silently down my cheeks as Ever withdraws the small flask from his pocket and twists open the lid. He pours water over the small wounds until all that remains is the stain of blood on my stocking.

Ever's fingers curve around my calf, his thumbs making idle sweeps, as if memorizing each hideous dimple. "Do they still pain you?"

"Only when I'm idle for too long." That's why Wednesdays are so difficult. When my legs start to burn, walking is the only relief.

With a heavy sigh, Ever draws my stocking back up my thigh. When he stands, my skirts fall back into place, hiding my scars once more. He takes my hand without a word, leading me farther from the city. Further from the rules that govern us. From the thoughts and fears of others.

Until we are in a world that is entirely our own. One where a symphony of crickets fills the night with their song. Where moonlight paints the landscape silver. Where a lake stretches across the dark horizon, the starlight making the water look like a sheet of glass.

"It's beautiful." That word doesn't begin to describe the serenity of this place. "How did you know this was here?"

"My mother used to sneak me over the bridge when my father was away on a hunt." Ever's fingers tighten around mine as he helps me navigate the rocky shoreline to where the water laps at the stones. The man is like a mountain goat, not slipping once on the algae-covered rocks.

I try to imagine a tiny Ever sneaking across The Divide, but it's difficult to picture him as anything but imposing. "Tell me about her."

His lips tug into the smallest smile, his eyes taking on a faraway glaze as he stares into the distance. "She was beautiful. Kind." His smile falters. "Too soft for life in the forest."

Soft, like me.

He slips his hand from mine to collect a stone from the ground. "She longed to live in Rosehill. Always claimed she had a Seelie heart beating in her Unseelie chest." He launches the stone into the air. A few seconds later, there's a quiet *plop*.

How sad that she wanted to live on our side but never had the chance. People should be allowed to live wherever they choose.

"I do not know why she married my father," he goes on. "He

used his fists when he was angry. By the time the chieftain found out, she could not be healed. My father was exiled the very next day."

I cannot imagine how devastating that must have been for him, to lose his mother so tragically and at his father's hands, no less. No wonder he was so irate over Ronan grabbing me.

"I'm so sorry, Ever."

Wounds, even ones made long ago, may heal but the memories can still turn septic. Look at the scars on my legs. Because of what happened, I can barely stand to smell smoke from a fire. The nightmares that once plagued my dreams may not come as often as they once did, but they never completely go away. Haunting my mind with visions of my mother's lifeless body covering mine. The stench of burned flesh. The unending pain.

Perhaps that pain is what connects me to this beautiful man. My brokenness calling to his.

Water licks at the shore, leaving the stones on the bank shining like gemstones. "Is the water safe?"

For some reason, my question makes him smirk. "Asks the woman who befriended an Unseelie monster."

"Befriended" seems like such an innocuous word for this bond growing between us. Has he already forgotten about the pie I gave him? "We aren't friends, though...remember?"

His eyes seem to ignite at the reminder. "I remember."

What would it be like to truly belong to Ever?

To kiss his mouth. To share his bed. To let him mark me as his.

How I long to find out.

I look back out at that water, my over-heated skin beginning to tingle with anticipation.

Why not now? Why not tonight?

The silk ribbon keeping my robe fastened slips through my fingers, slow, tantalizing, and luxurious. "Would you like to go for a swim with me?"

He nods solemnly, fixated on my every move as my robe falls into a silken puddle on the stones. His eyes ignite as they sweep down my lace and silk shift.

"Am I to be the only one undressed?"

Ever toes off his boots and removes his socks, then slowly slips the leather strap of his belt free from the buckle and slides off his trousers, revealing a pair of dark short pants beneath.

Short pants that conceal a very obvious bulge.

My cheeks flame as I step back into the cool water, the damp silk at my thighs sticking to my bare skin beneath.

The drawings in my Unseelie book flash through my mind as he enters the water, sending ripples of lust through me. Tonight, I am going to know what it's like to kiss this beautiful, quiet man.

Something tells me that afterward, I will never be the same.

I swim a little deeper, forcing Ever to come to me.

He swims with the same grace that he does everything else. Moving with purpose, strong muscles pushing him through the water.

When he reaches me, I splash him in the face. He looks so indignant, I can't help but giggle as he swipes a hand down his cheek, clearing the drops there.

I expect him to splash me back, but instead he catches my ankle and drags me toward him. I let out a yelp and make a half-hearted attempt to get away, only to have him pull me closer, until I'm within the safety of his arms. "You caught me."

He rolls his eyes. "Did you doubt I would?"

"Never." I think I could swim all the way across the lake, and he would still come after me. When I lick my lips, I taste the briny water clinging there.

I wrap myself around him. Legs around his hips and arms around his shoulders. "Now that you have me, what are you going to do with me?"

"I suppose that is up to you."

Our chests brush, and the bulge beneath his pants thickens. I pretend not to notice, but the sensation of him settling against where I ache is impossible to ignore. His confession from all those nights ago drifts through my mind. Secret desires that mirror my own.

"I want you to touch me like no one is watching," I whisper, my heart pounding in my breast. "To mark me as yours. To taste my most secret places and fill my body with yours. To hear my name on your tongue when you shatter."

Ever groans, his forehead falling against mine as his calloused hands bracket my thighs and slowly glide up to my hips until he's clutching my backside with only my thin undergarments between my skin and his.

My legs tighten, grinding my aching center against his hardness—

Heavens...

That feels...

I move again, harder, stoking these flames erupting between us. *Yes. More. Yes.*

Ever's lips skate along my neck as he uses his grip on my backside to rock me against him. His hips roll, creating the most mind-bending friction even as his tongue swirls over the hollow of my throat.

A tongue that isn't smooth but scratchy, like a cat's.

There probably are a thousand reasons why I shouldn't be with him but in this moment all I can think about is the reason I should.

Because I need to know what it feels like to give in, to take for myself.

So I fill my hands with his hair, tug his head back, and slam my lips to his.

Ever's fingers dig into the flesh of my backside, pressing me closer as he opens his mouth to devour me.

He kisses with the same controlled violence I've sensed in him from the very first day I caught sight of him at the well. He could destroy me, crush me, kill me in one practiced move, yet he holds me with such reverence as his tongue slips past my parted lips, finding and scraping against mine.

I can't get close enough; even the silk separating our chests is too much.

This is what I've been searching for.

What I've been missing.

To choose anyone else would be settling.

I don't care if the whole of Rosehill turns against me, I want this man and no other—

A broken sound climbs his throat, and he jerks back. Ever reaches behind his head, unclasping my hands, his hold vanishing as he lets me drop back into the water. "This is wrong."

"No, it's not. I have never felt anything as right—"

"I belong to someone else."

36

I *belong to someone else.*

"What do you mean?" He cannot belong to someone else. He belongs with me.

"I am to be mated with a female in our village."

"That's not true." It can't be. Why would he bring me here, why would he lead me on if he was going to marry someone else the whole bloomin' time?

"I am sorry, Kerris."

He's sorry? He's *sorry*? Not as sorry as I am.

Who is she? Why would he choose her over me? Is she more beautiful?

I hate the nameless, faceless woman. I hate her more than I've ever hated anyone. More than Ronan Reve.

Damp air floods my throat as I gulp for my next breath, my eyes burning with tears I refuse to shed. "Why didn't you tell me?"

Ever—*no, Everett,* just stands there, his face devoid of emotion. "Because I did not know—"

"Didn't know what? That you were getting *married?*" Poppycock.

"No. I mean, yes." Like everything else that concerns this man, I feel his huff of frustration in my bones. "She asked me weeks ago, and I never gave her a response. So she took matters into her own hands and told everyone that I accepted."

"Why didn't you turn her down?"

He cards his hands through his hair, his handsome face stricken. "Because she is a good match for me. Strong and capable. Independent and fierce."

All things that I am not.

"But then I met you and..."

And I took too long to figure out what I wanted. For weeks I tried to be content with the men on this side of The Divide, but my heart and mind kept drifting across the canyon. Why didn't I say something sooner? Why didn't I chase after what I truly wanted instead of wasting all my time trying to adhere to ridiculous conventions?

"Call it off." Surely, we can figure out how to make this work between us.

"It is not that simple."

"Why not? Do you love her?"

He jerks back as if I slapped him. Part of me wants to. "Of course not."

"Then why in heaven's name are you marrying her?"

"Because I am thirty years of age, and it is my duty to my people to accept a mate."

To hell with duty! To hell with everyone else. In my heart, I know it's meant to be him and me. In my *soul*.

Everett drops his head back, as if sending a prayer to the heavens. "I have never wanted anything more than what I have been given. And then you..."

"Then I what, Everett? Go on. Tell me what I did that is so wrong."

"You made me want what I cannot have!"

Can't he see? If he wants me, I'm his. I'm standing right here with my heart in my hands and yet he insists on turning me away. On keeping a promise he didn't even bloody make.

Heavens above, I care about this man more than any other, but he isn't mine...and now he never will be.

Not mine to kiss.

Not mine to want.

Not mine to love.

And now I am more than a fool. I am a fool who has fallen for a man promised to someone else. Another man refusing to fight for me.

"You should have told me the moment you came to my window."

"That is what I planned on doing. But then I saw you and...I did not want to let you go."

Yes, well, it's a little late for that, now, isn't it? At least if he told me before I wouldn't look like such a fool for throwing myself at him.

I turn and wade toward the shore, the stones slippery beneath my feet and water sloshing behind me. I scoop up my robe and slippers, clutching them to my chest before Everett reaches his own discarded clothes.

Then I run. Away from him—away from everything—all because my heart has been stolen by a man who cannot keep it.

Everett calls my name, but I don't slow down.

He could catch me if he wanted. His legs are more than long

enough, and he doesn't eat extra helpings of pie after every dinner. He doesn't even *like* pie.

If I'd known that from the beginning, I would've realized the two of us would have never worked.

How can you trust a man who doesn't like pie?

With my lungs blazing in my chest, I reach the back gate. Although I cannot see the guard, I can hear him shuffling around on the street. Dirt and grass cling to my feet as I climb the trellis, ignoring the scrape of thorns against my legs. The stinging doesn't ebb as I scramble onto the roof and slip back into my room.

Nia sits up from where she's curled on my bed, rubbing her eyes as she blinks at me.

"Kerris?" she whispers, her voice thick with sleep. "What's wrong?" Her brow furrows as her gaze sweeps down my form. "Are you *wet?*"

I pick up the flowers, vase and all, and throw them from my window. The sound of shattering glass explodes in the night. I hope the guard goes to investigate and cuts his feet to ribbons. I hope Everett is watching from the shadows and sees exactly what I've done with those infernal blooms that felt like they meant everything only to mean nothing now.

A gift as empty as all the others.

Once the window has been slammed shut and latched, I let myself crumble to pieces. Sobs wrack my body and tears flood my eyes, splashing into the puddle my soaked clothing leaves on the wooden planks. "H-he's engaged."

"Oh, Kerris." Nia sinks onto the floor next to me, pulling me into her chest.

"You don't want to do that. I'm s-soaked through." She feels so warm and steady, I can't bring myself to draw away.

"I don't care about a little water." Her arms tighten around me. "How did you find out?"

"We went to a lake. It was so romantic. I kissed him." Replaying the joyous moment is like death by a thousand thorns. "It was the most beautiful kiss of my entire life." I will dream of it for the rest of my days.

"The tongue?"

"The t-tongue." I'd wanted Everett's mouth to cover every inch of my body, to consume not only my mouth, but to also consume me. *He's not yours. He's not yours.* "Then he pulled away and told me he's to be mated with someone else. W-what am I going to do?"

She runs a hand down my soaked hair, careful to avoid the many tangles. "You cry until you have no more tears, and then you dry yourself off and get some sleep."

If I sleep, I'll dream of *him*.

You made me want what I cannot have.

If only I'd told Everett from the beginning that if he wanted me, I was already his.

37

Everett

"A king's line is rarely straight."

— Author Unknown

A sharp, shattering sound pierces the night. Even from where I wait by the back gate, I can see the glass glittering around the discarded flowers. Kerris's window remains dark, and I know I need to get home before my absence is noticed, but I cannot bring myself to leave this spot because, once I do, I will never be back.

This affection that has grown between us is over.

It must be.

Just because the thought of walking away feels like I am choking on that broken glass does not mean it is not the right choice.

There is a reason our worlds are separated—and I have witnessed the consequences of flouting the rules firsthand.

With Kerris gone, there is nothing left to hold onto.

The pain in her eyes the moment I told her the truth of my situation was the same pain that I saw when she spoke about the tragedy that befell her mother. I never should have let it get this far. Never should have crossed the damn canyon to appease my own curiosity.

My fingers skim over my lips, still feeling the blissful pressure of hers. Her taste will forever live on my tongue, the sweetness of her innocence and kindness.

When I turn and drift away, it feels as if I am leaving a piece of myself behind.

To avoid the guards patrolling the streets of Rosehill, I am forced to keep to the dark side of the city, where the shadows stretch their invisible fingers toward the orange glow of the streetlamps. With everyone so frightened of a non-existent wolf, it is easy to cross without being spotted.

The two men guarding our side of the bridge stand when they see me coming, their hands falling to the daggers at their belts. Daggers that they earned for doing what they had to do. Just as I will earn my place in our village by putting my own selfish desires aside for the greater good.

I do not need a female who weeps at the sight of a flower.

I need one who stomps them dead beneath her boot as she races toward her prey, killing to provide for her family. To protect.

My mother was like Kerris, a delicate bloom. And she wilted right before my eyes.

My heart grows a little harder with each step I take down the bone-lined path, all the way to the camp. I climb the stairs to my barrel-top and duck beneath the low door. A fire blazes in the stove and a female waits in my bed, her hair as black as midnight and eyes as dark as the shadows surrounding us.

Leah sits up, the sheets falling to her bare waist. She takes one look at me and her eyes narrow. "Where have you been?"

A thousand lies spring to my mind. On a hunt. Checking the outpost. With Maddox and Gryff. Walking the trails. Collecting firewood.

So many lies but only one truth: *Cutting out my own heart.*

"Everett?"

The voice that calls my name is not the one I long to hear. Am I to exist for the rest of eternity wishing for a different life?

Do not settle for anything less than love.

Will I one day break beneath the weight of this love I carry for another? How am I supposed to do this? How can I move forward when I am so stuck on *her?*

The answer is so fucking simple.

I cannot.

I collect Leah's dress from where she draped it over my chair, tossing it onto the bed. "Put this on."

For once, she listens. Only once she is covered do I drop onto the edge of my mattress.

"What is it?" She gathers her hair into a queue, tying the short strands back from her face.

She is a good female. A strong, faithful female. I should just accept my fate. Learn to live this life spread in front of me. Except...

Forever is a long time for a male to live without a soul.

Even knowing the consequences of my actions, I steel my spine and speak my truth. "I cannot mate with you." From the moment she asked, I should have known I was not meant to accept. "I want more, Leah."

Once, I believed I could survive on friendship alone, but it is not enough. Curse me for my desires, but now that I know what it feels like to be utterly captivated, I cannot go back to the way things were.

She presses a hand to my chest, where my heart beats for another. "Then let me give you more."

"You cannot."

Realization crosses her face as I remove her hand from me. "You want more from someone else."

My nod feels like the greatest betrayal of all. Not only am I about to lose a mate; I am about to lose a friend.

On this side of the canyon, friends are hard to come by.

Leah shoots to her feet, pacing from the door to where I sit, every move stiff. Calculated. "What is her name?"

I will not be giving Kerris's name to Leah or anyone else, no matter the consequences.

"Her name, Everett Gathin."

I clamp my jaw shut, prepared to take this secret to my grave. There is no telling what Leah would do if she found out.

Her hands ball into white-knuckled fists. "It is the Seelie bitch, yes?" Although I am certain my expression gives nothing away, her eyes widen, as if she can see into my mind. Into my heart. "I wonder if they need help collecting water this week."

I push to my feet, ready to show her out before she says something that we will both regret.

Leah's father would never allow her to cross the bridge. The females in our village are too precious to risk, and as peaceful as Rosehill might seem, that city is as dangerous for us as our side of the canyon is for them.

"I am sorry, Leah."

"You are *sorry*, are you? What is that pathetic apology supposed to do? Make me feel better?"

"I am not the one who lied about our relationship. This is a bed of your own making."

"By not speaking up sooner, you were complicit in the lie. My father will never forgive you."

"If you tell him the truth—"

"And disgrace myself even more than you have disgraced me? No. I wish to see you abandoned just as you have abandoned me."

"Leah, please—"

She holds up a hand, her eyes as cold as death. "No. You do not get to say my name. You do not get to speak to me ever again. You are just like your wretched father, and when our chieftain hears about this, I have a feeling your fates will be the same."

She stalks into the night and slams the door in her wake.

There is nothing to do now but suffer the consequences.

38

Nia waltzes into my room with fire in her eyes as she rips the covers from my languid form. "We're going to town."

When she throws open the curtains, I hate that I search the windowsill for a flower.

A flower that isn't there.

Damn this light and the sun that gives it. "It's too bright." I catch the end of my covers and drag them over my head. Why does it never rain in this cursed city? I want it to rain so hard that the streets flood and wash everything away. So that it's perfectly acceptable to feel this melancholy and remain indoors for the foreseeable future.

"There's a bath waiting for you. When you're finished, come downstairs for breakfast."

"I don't want a bath." Or breakfast, for that matter. I don't want anything but sleep and darkness.

"Too bad. I'm not going anywhere with you smelling like scummy pond water."

That's fine with me because I don't want to go anywhere with her either.

She steals my covers like the irritating woman she is, rolling them into a ball and flinging them into the corner where I cannot reach them without getting out of bed. "Let's go. Up you come."

Why must she be so bloody insistent? I push to my feet, my stiff legs refusing to bend as I hobble toward the bathing room where steam curls from the copper tub. I strip bare but as I sink into the water, all I can think about is the way it felt to be in the water with *him*. Everett has even taken the enjoyment out of a bloomin' bath. How insufferable is that?

I hate him.

Tears trail down my cheeks, and I press the heels of my palms to my eyes to staunch the flow.

No, I don't. I only wish I hated him. Then I could find a way to move on. As it stands, I might never marry.

All I can hope for now is contentment.

Bland, boring contentment.

I slip lower and lower, until water closes over my face and silence fills my ears. When my lungs start to burn, I have no desire to search for air. Perhaps I'll stay here, where it's dark and quiet and—

A hand catches my shoulder, and Nia forces me back to the surface. I blink through the water and my tears, drained of life. Of energy. Of enthusiasm.

With a disappointed *tsk*, my cousin forces me from the tub, towel dries my hair, and plaits the heavy strands. Back in my room, I stare at the dresses in my closet, not even caring which one I put on. What's the point? There is only one man I wish to marry, and he is pledged to another. For all I know, he might have married her already.

My hands start to tremble at my sides.

He's gone.

Gone. Gone. Gone.

Nia must notice me faltering and selects a pale pink gown with tiny rosebuds sewn into the bodice that reminds me of the vines outside my window back home.

Maybe I should go back to Gravale and hide in the mountains until I'm able to exist without shattering.

I force a tasteless croissant between my lips as we step outside where the sun caresses my bare shoulders, reminding me of the heat of Everett's lips. Drifting along next to Nia, I barely pay attention to anyone or anything around me.

She stops at a tea house where Trevor and Nolan wait at a table set for four. When Trevor sees me, his face brightens, and he pushes to his feet to slide out my chair for me. He brought a bouquet of wildflowers, their long, jagged stems tied with twine.

He hands me the bouquet with a chagrined smile. "I want to apologize. You were right in calling me a coward. I never should've given in to the prince's demands."

No, he shouldn't have. Not that it matters now.

I thank Trevor for the flowers and set them on the table beside me.

Why must there be so many? They feel so impersonal.

Trevor either doesn't notice my misery or he doesn't care. He just sits there drinking his tea with a small, *contented* smile on his conventionally handsome face.

A face I might have loved if it weren't for *him.*

Nia and Nolan keep the conversation light, discussing the

upcoming summer festivals and the new café opening on the other side of town near Madame Ella's. Apparently, they specialize in fish. Not sure why anyone would want to go somewhere that offers only one type of food on the menu, but what do I know?

Trevor orders a pear and rhubarb tart, offering me half.

I don't even want food but when the waitress drops off the plate, I force myself to eat so that I don't have to join in the conversation. Bedtime cannot come soon enough.

Trevor dabs the crumbs from his lips with his serviette. "What news from The Divide, Nolan?"

Nia's brow furrows as she glances at me, and then to the man holding her hand. "What is he talking about, dearest?"

I hate how much my ears perk up at the mention of the canyon. I try to appear nonchalant, but my knuckles have gone white where I grip my fork.

Nolan clears his throat, a flush creeping along his jaw as his gaze darts between my cousin and me. "This information does not leave this table," he says quietly, his expression grim. Once we've all nodded, he continues. "One of the men on patrol last night was mauled to death by a wolf."

But Everett said there were no wolves on our side of The Divide.

Had that been a lie?

No. Everett wouldn't have lied. Not about this.

Maybe he wasn't lying, but wrong.

Either way, a man is dead. Why would this be a secret though? If the people of Rosehill aren't safe, shouldn't they be told?

The three of them continue speaking in low whispers, but all I can do is sit back and stare into my milky tea, wondering if there really is a wolf loose in Rosehill.

I leave the restaurant without making plans to see Trevor again, ignoring the way his head hangs as he returns to the library to finish his shift.

Nia takes my hand as we stroll back to her parent's house, plying me with question after question about why I was so dismissive of Trevor.

She's so determined to find me a husband in Rosehill that she's forgetting one very important thing: This is going to be *my* husband, not hers.

I cannot tie myself to someone so cowardly.

Nia's skirt brushes mine as we walk, our hands swinging. "I still cannot believe a wolf killed one of our own. I never thought I'd say it but thank heavens for the curfew. I'm not sure I'll go out at night ever again."

It could have been me.

If I'd gone to The Divide last night, I could've been the wolf's victim.

It could have been Everett.

I hope he made it home safely.

Her fingers grip mine a little tighter, her eyes pleading as she slows to a stop, forcing me to halt as well. "Kerris, please. I know you're sad, but you didn't honestly believe there could be a future for the two of you."

That's just it. Part of me did start to believe in us.

"I'm sorry, Nia. I will be back on track tomorrow. I promise." And if I don't, I'll send a letter to Theo asking if he'd like some company in Applewood. Perhaps the men there won't be such an overwhelming disappointment.

Inside the house, the tangy scent of lemons hangs in the air.

My aunt waits on the sofa, her apron spotted with flour and batter. When she sees us, she launches to her feet. "Oh, good. You're back. Come in and have a seat."

The sofa's springs squeak as Nia and I both sink onto the cushions.

Nia doesn't lean back against the ruffled pillows, her posture rigid as a plank. "What's wrong?"

"Nothing is wrong, honey," Aunt Cordelia assures her with a quick pat on the knee. "Your father and I were simply discussing what to do with all this wolf nonsense."

What can any of us do? Start a hunting party? The thought is laughable. What weapons would we use? Butter knives?

My aunt's gaze slices toward me. "Kerris, dear, we think it might be best if you returned home."

Wait. What?

Nia catches my hand as if I'm about to race off to the mountains this very second. "You cannot send her away, Mother. She hasn't found a husband yet."

"She would be more than welcome to come back after it's safe."

Although I hear what she's saying, what she's *not* saying is even louder.

I curl my toes in my slippers, careful to keep my expression passive despite the indignation burning through my chest. "That's not true, is it? You don't want me to ever come back."

I don't know why I feel so betrayed. Wasn't I just contemplating leaving?

"Out of concern for your safety. Nothing more."

Poppycock. She wants me gone and it has nothing to do with my bloomin' safety. "Then I assume you'll be sending Nia to Gravale with me? Or is your daughter's safety not as important as my own?"

Nia crosses her arms, her chin lifting as she narrows her eyes at her mother. "Yes, Mother. Which is it?"

"Nia is more than welcome to visit you after she finds a husband."

"Unbelievable," Nia scoffs.

"Is it, really? You know as well as I do what everyone is saying about her. Do you want your cousin's poor choices to hurt your prospects for a husband as well?"

I never even considered how my connection to Everett would impact Nia. *Am* I hurting her prospects? That's the last thing I want to do, especially when she is so keen to marry Nolan.

Nia launches to her feet, her tight fists banging against her thighs. "Any man who doesn't want to marry me simply because of who I'm related to isn't worth my time. Unlike *you*, I don't want a coward for a husband."

"Nia Quill. You will hold your tongue." Aunt Cordelia snaps her fingers, her cheeks a ruddy shade of red.

It's my turn to stand and take Nia's hand—after I pry her fist open. "It's all right." Her mother is only trying to protect her. I'm certain that my mother would have done the same for me. "Aunt Cordelia, I can assure you that my dealings with the Unseelie have ended. But if you still want me to leave, I will."

Nia strangles my hand, her voice trembling. "Kerris, no."

My aunt's wariness lives in the lines on her face. "If you can assure me that you are no longer entertaining the notion of aligning yourself with the Unseelie, then you are welcome to stay."

After all that has happened, I'm not sure I *want* to stay. But for my cousin, I make the promise, wishing it weren't true.

39

Nia groans from the sofa, her head thrown back on the cushion and hands folded over her stomach. "Do you want to go to town?"

I glance up from the book I'm pretending to read. No matter how long I stare at the words, none of them register. I might as well be staring at an ancient text written in a foreign language. "Town is closed on Wednesdays."

It's funny that she would forget a rule only a few weeks ago she'd been so adamant to keep.

She pushes herself upright, dropping her feet from where they were propped on the coffee table next to a tray of uneaten biscuits. Normally, I love shortbread, but ever since Everett told me the awful news, food doesn't taste the same. Which is a travesty considering how much I used to enjoy sweets.

"You know what I mean." She shoots a glance over her shoulder toward the empty hallway before scooting so close, our knees knock together. "The guards don't patrol the streets during the day, so I thought perhaps we could go to the well."

Why would she suggest such a thing when she knows I'm barely holding myself together as it is? "I don't want to go to the well."

It's a damn lie and we both know it. I want to see Everett so badly my soul aches, but there is no point torturing myself.

"Come on, Kerris. No one has to know."

I'll know.

Besides, I made a promise that my dealings with the Unseelie were through. If I go back on my word, they'll ship me right back to Gravale as husbandless as I arrived. When I leave, I want it to be my decision, not because I was kicked out by my own family.

"I don't want to go to town," I insist, flipping to the next page and staring down at the text.

I expect a lecture or some sort of bargain. Instead, Nia nods and rolls off the couch, leaving me alone with a book I have no desire to read and memories of a man I'll never see again.

Thursday arrives on a breeze and leaves on a gale.

Friday is still as death, as if someone has put an invisible lid on the world.

This morning, a letter from my brother arrived, saying that he would love a visit from his favorite sister. As I trace his handwriting scrawled across the parchment, my chest pinches at the thought of seeing him again.

I'll stay with Theo for a month, maybe two, and try my hand at finding a husband there. Perhaps he has a friend who might consider a match with me.

Now to find a way to tell Nia.

Speaking of Nia... Where is she? I haven't seen her since breakfast. Probably because I came back to my room to wallow.

As if I called her name, Nia bursts through my door, her cheeks flushed and curly hair wild. "Do you still want to find a husband?" she blurts.

The longer I put this off, the harder it's going to be. I need to tell her the truth, to give her time to adjust before I leave. "Yes, but not in Rosehill."

"What do you mean, 'not in Rosehill?'"

From beneath my leg, I withdraw my brother's letter. "I've decided to move to Applewood."

She opens the missive with trembling fingers, her lips moving as she silently scans my brother's letter. When she looks back at me, her expression is as dark and threatening as a thunderstorm. "So that's it? You're giving up."

Rosehill gave up on me first. "No one has called to our door all week." Not even Nolan has come by to visit her. When I asked about his absence, she blew me off with a wave of her hand, saying that he was busy hunting for the wolf.

A wolf they still haven't caught.

"Because you haven't left the house!" Nia tosses the letter onto the bottom of the bed. "Ivee is telling everyone that she plans on proposing to Ronan at the end of the month, and as soon as the prince accepts, the rest of the men will come out in droves. You'll be beating them off with sticks. Just be patient."

If only this were a matter of being "patient." "Don't you see? I have no desire to tie myself to someone who won't stand up for me. Someone too scared of the prince's wrath to go against his wishes. The men of Rosehill aren't worth my time."

A knock reverberates from downstairs. Nia and I trade looks

before we both hurry into the hallway to watch my aunt saunter out of the kitchen, her serviette still clutched in her hand as she fixes her hair. When she sees us at the top of the stairs, she asks if we're expecting any callers.

I shake my head.

Nia smirks. "Perhaps not all the men of Rosehill are cowards after all."

Please. Whoever is at the door isn't there for me. It's probably Nolan coming to apologize for neglecting her.

At least I hope it is. If she loses him because of me, I will never forgive myself.

Aunt Cordelia pins on a pretty smile and swings the door aside. At her loud gasp, Nia and I both stumble down the stairs to where my aunt sways like a tree in a gale, her face as pale as porcelain. Nia tries to get to her, but it's too late. Aunt Cordelia faints in the foyer.

The man at the door lunges, catching her right before she hits the ground.

When I notice the green-gray tint to his skin, for a second, I think it's Everett, but then I see his longer hair and realize Maddox is here.

In my aunt's house.

In Rosehill.

In the middle of a bloomin' Friday.

"*Shit.*" Maddox's arms strain as he awkwardly eases Aunt Cordelia onto the floor. "I think I killed your mother."

Nia rushes to Maddox's side, waving him off. "I'm sure she's fine." She kneels, looking more annoyed than concerned. "Mother? Mother!" She presses her hands to her mother's gaunt cheeks. "Can you take her to the sofa?"

Maddox slips his hands beneath my aunt, lifting her as if she weighs no more than a child.

"The living room is this way." Nia leads Maddox from the foyer and into the living area, catching the cushions and placing them so that her mother can lie flat on the sofa.

Maddox has to duck so he doesn't hit his head on the door frame. I can only imagine how large Everett would look in this room. *I miss him so much.*

It's mad how someone you've known for only a short amount of time can have such an irrevocable impact on your life.

When Maddox stands, his face crushes in concern. "Should she be waking up?"

Nia shakes her head. "Not as long as you're here. Perhaps it's best if we have this conversation elsewhere."

Maddox throws one final concerned glance at my aunt before ducking beneath the doorway and following my cousin through the kitchen and out the back door.

He's so like Everett in his coloring and movements but so different. Not as severe. *Not as achingly beautiful.*

Stuffing my own feelings deep down, I steel my shoulders and follow them into the garden where Nia and Maddox whisper to one another, which is odd.

"Care to tell me what's going on here?" I gesture between the two of them. As far as I know, the only time they met was at the Beltane festival. Now it looks as if they're...friends?

Nia glances between Maddox and me, her lips pressed into a slight grimace. "Don't get mad."

Irritation stirs in my chest. Something tells me I'm better off not making that promise.

She steps toward me, leaving Maddox to frown at her back. "It's just that...you haven't been the same since...well, you know."

I do know, but that doesn't explain why there is an Unseelie standing in her back garden.

Her curls shudder when she blows out a breath. "I went to the well on Wednesday, but Everett wasn't there, so I spoke with Maddox instead."

Maddox lifts his eyes toward the cloudless sky, a smirk playing on his lips. "Nice to know I was not your first choice."

She pinches his arm. *Actually* pinches him.

"Ouch, *dammit*." Maddox rubs his arm. "Careful, Seelie."

Nia rolls her eyes. "He was *supposed* to meet me at The Divide, not come to my home and try to murder my mother."

"I meant your mother no harm," he says with so much sincerity that my heart aches. The Unseelie I've met have been such genuinely good people; it really is such a shame that the Seelie are so determined to hate them on principle alone.

Nia's lips tilt into a smirk. "Just tell her what you told me, all right?"

Maddox braces his hands at the cut of his hips, and I catch Nia stealing a glance at his bare chest. *Interesting.*

"Ever has been exiled from camp for calling off his engagement with the chieftain's daughter," Maddox announces. "We tried to warn him, but he has not been in his right mind since the two of you parted ways."

Hold on. Did he say Ever has been exiled for breaking off his bloody engagement?

"As I am sure he told you, our lands are dangerous. Because of his decision, he is no longer welcome in our camp and has been cut off from our resources."

No longer welcome in camp...

Cut off from resources...

"This is my fault."

When Maddox nods, Nia pinches him again.

He bares his sharp teeth in a snarl. "That fucking hurt."

"Good. Next time, don't blame my cousin for your friend's mistakes."

They can squabble later. Right now, there are more pressing matters at hand. "How do we help him?"

Maddox's face falls into a frown. "Once you are exiled, there is no coming back."

What about forgiveness? What about mercy? Ever makes one mistake and is expected to pay for it with his life? "So he's supposed to live on his own for the rest of eternity?"

Maddox's shoulders sink even lower as his hand falls to the bone-handled dagger on his belt. "Ever is more than capable of surviving, but it will not be for eternity."

But we're all immortal as long as we drink from a well.

Cut off from our resources.

"The treaty with the Seelie only applies to those within the community," he says, confirming my worst fears.

"What contract?" Nia asks.

"The one that lets them access the well on Wednesdays," I whisper.

Maddox nods.

And now, because of me, Ever is going to die. He may be young and healthy for the moment, but his youth will fade and that's the best-case scenario. For all I know, he could have already fallen prey to a bloody wolf.

There must be some way to undo this. Some way to save him from himself. Maybe if I speak to him—hell, even speak to his chieftain, he will change his mind.

One thing is for certain, I cannot sit around and do *nothing*.

"I need to see him."

Maddox nods. "I can bring you."

Nia's hand grazes mine. "If you cross now, everyone will see you."

She's not telling me not to go, simply alluding to the consequences. If anyone sees me crossing The Divide alongside Maddox, no man in the city will come near me. I won't be welcome in my aunt's home.

"Let them see." I refuse to hide my feelings any longer.

I'm in love with an Unseelie fae and I don't care who knows it.

40

*"While most Lethan wolves live alone, some have
been known to hunt in packs."*

— Surviving The Unseelie Lands, Author
Unknown

With Aunt Cordelia still passed out on the sofa, I race upstairs to pack some essentials into a bag. There's no telling when I'll be back...*if* I'll be back.

Maddox and I take the most direct path to The Divide, which brings us along the edge of Rosehill. There are only a few cafés, but they're packed to the brim. The fae inside gawk, their whispers following us the entire way.

Maddox is no longer the teasing man who let my cousin pinch him. He's a predator, one hand on his dagger, his black eyes scanning the sea of faces for trouble.

Thankfully, we find none.

When we reach The Divide, I'm thankful for the persistent mist that swallows us whole, drenching the world in silence.

Toward the end of the bridge, Maddox stretches an arm across, stopping me in my tracks next to a stack of boards and a hammer. It takes ten minutes for him to tack them back into place, a moment for us to cross, and another five for him to remove them again.

When I ask why they're gone, he simply says that they're not taking any chances.

"Because of the wolves?"

He offers a grim nod. "We have not seen any, but the guards on the other side swear they have, and we all know who the king believes."

Ever's life isn't the only one on the line. One word from the king and the Unseelie's access to the well could be cut off too. What would they do then?

In the gray light of day, the graveyard of bones on the other side looks like the setting of a horror novel. Skulls of all shapes and sizes line the path along with empty ribcages and other bones. Some are nearly as tall as me. Thank goodness whatever terrifying creatures they belonged to are dead.

Here, Maddox moves with an easy confidence, striding far too fast for me to keep up. When he realizes, he apologizes and slows down a fraction, but I still have to walk at a clip. We take a right at the mammoth skull of a horned beast, then a left at a pile of tiny skulls.

All of a sudden, the silence is replaced by the low hum of conversation. Voices grow louder, deeper. The mist slowly subsides, revealing twenty or so painted carriages, all parked in a circle, with their backs facing one another.

Beyond is a forest of trees taller than I've ever seen before.

"Where's the village?" I whisper to Maddox.

His brow furrows. "This is the village."

This is where the Unseelie live? There are no paved streets, only dirt paths. No cafés or libraries or pubs. A group of women hunker around a fire, turning a spit holding some sort of dead animal. Two of them bear silver scars shaped like kissing crescent moons along their necks and shoulders.

Unseelie mating bonds.

The others' gray-green skin remains unmarked. Is one of them Everett's fiancée?

Former fiancée.

The woman who lied to trap him.

The reason he is all alone.

I wish I knew her name so that I could give her a piece of my mind.

When the women see us, they fall silent.

Their clothes are plain earthen tones of grays, browns, and greens.

If I'd known what to expect, I would've changed out of this canary yellow gown.

Loathing oozes from their stares.

Is this how the Unseelie feel every time they cross the border into Rosehill? It's awful.

A handful of children screech, running in the center of the circle of carriages, chasing each other in a game of tag.

At least something in our worlds is the same.

We continue out of the "village" to the edge of the forest where the trees creak, their branches so high, I have to squint to see them. Ancient and stoic but providing very little shelter to anyone living here.

A short distance up ahead sits a turquoise wagon, the weathered boards painted with colorful flowers.

Maddox halts next to a boulder blanketed by moss. "This is as far as I will go."

"Why is that?"

The crease in his brow deepens. "Unlike Ever, I would like a mate one day. If the others catch me speaking to him, they will shun me too."

"I thought you and Ever were friends."

Maddox's scowl deepens. "Siding with Ever means certain death."

It might not be right to judge Maddox when I'm not facing the same dire consequences, but I judge him all the same. If Nia were kicked out of her home, you'd better believe I'd be right next to her. Hell, I don't even know how to survive in this land and I'm here for Ever.

With nothing more to say to Maddox, I leave him by the boulder. My ire slowly melts into despair as I approach the lonely carriage. The door swings open on squeaking hinges, and Ever appears, filling the space. When he sees me, his eyes widen and his gaze flies to where Maddox stood only a moment ago.

His nose lifts, and he inhales deeply. "Maddox?"

I nod.

His knuckles whiten where they grip the doorframe. "He knows better than to bring you to this place. It is not safe."

"And yet I'm here all the same."

His brows jump beneath the dark strands of hair falling across his forehead. "Why?"

Because I'm halfway to loving you, you big, prideful fool. "Because you have no one else."

Ever blinks at me, saying nothing as his gaze makes a slow glide from my braid to the dirty slippers peeking from beneath my skirt. Slowly, he steps aside, a silent invitation into his home.

The stairs whine as I climb to the entrance and duck beneath his arm. The roof is just high enough that he can stand upright. Barely. A crackling fire blazes inside a tiny cast iron stove with the pipe affixed to the wall. To my right are a handful of cabinets, all painted with the same flowers as the outside. At the very back is a bed.

I swallow thickly, working through the emotion climbing my throat. How does he live in such cramped quarters? And everything is so... *frilly*. There are ruffles and flowers everywhere, from the walls to the quilt on his bed.

Ever's bed.

With my stomach fluttering like mad, I trace a daisy on the cabinet, the petals gone yellow with age. "This is beautiful."

The carriage rocks when Ever shifts his weight. "My mother's touch."

"Is this where you've always lived?"

A nod.

"No brothers or sisters, I presume?" Heaven knows there wouldn't be room for them.

His head swings toward the little square window framed with yellowed lace curtains. "We are only allowed one child."

"Why?" I can't imagine life without my brother.

He slips his hands into the pockets of his trousers, the muscles in his bare arms flexing with even the slightest movement. "It is easier to keep one safe than multiple."

Because these lands are so dangerous.

Yet Ever and the rest of his people spend night after night guarding us against horrors we cannot even fathom.

I slip the pack from my back and set it on the wooden slab that serves as a counter of sorts.

"More biscuits?" He sounds almost hopeful.

"Something better." I withdraw the flask filled from the tap and hand it to him.

He sets it right back on the counter with a murmur of thanks.

"You should drink it." If what Maddox said is true, then he hasn't had any water from the well for over a week.

He shifts once more, his eyes brimming with shadows. "Why have you come, Kerris?"

"I missed you." Although I try to smile, there is no sincerity behind it. How can I feign happiness when my heart is broken for all Ever has lost?

He must understand the words I cannot bring myself to speak aloud, because his head drops and he says quietly, "Maddox told you everything, then?"

"He did."

"So you know that I have nothing to offer you."

Doesn't he see? "All I want is you."

"I am not enough."

"You are—"

"Stop. Please. You do not understand. I have nothing but what is in this carriage."

"*You* are in this carriage, Ever. I don't need anything else."

He cards a hand through his hair, sending the thick strands every which way. "And when I leave for days on end to hunt for food? Who will protect you from what lurks in these forests then?"

"I can stay inside." Even as I say it, my legs begin to ache. Surely there must be plenty of exercises I could do to remain active in such a tight space.

"For weeks?"

The walls feel as if they're closing in on me, pressing from all sides. It would be fine. Worth it for a chance at happiness together. "I would manage."

His head falls even as it shakes. "I would rather you hate me now than resent me for the rest of your days."

I could never hate him.

Would I miss the chance to have a house and garden of my own? Of course. But perhaps, in time, we could acquire the materials to build one for ourselves. If not, then we will find a different way to make a happy life inside this carriage. The other Unseelie have done so, haven't they? We can figure it out together.

Still, it strikes me as odd that he would give up his chance to remain part of the village, to continue drawing from the well, if he planned on remaining here, alone. Did he even think of coming for me after he called off his engagement?

I swipe my clammy hands against my thighs, gripping the silk with trembling fingers. "Why didn't you marry her?"

His deep voice is like a breath of air for my drowning heart. "You know why."

"Maybe I need you to say it."

He turns fully to face me, dark eyes locking with mine. "Because I love you, Kerris Dawn. And I do not know how to stop."

The air rushes from my lungs and a smile lifts my lips even as tears prick the backs of my eyes. "Then don't. Because I love you too. And I don't plan on stopping any time soon."

41

"To bear the mark of another is a sign of unwavering devotion."

— Author Unknown

Everett takes my face between his hands, holding me as if I'll shatter, belying what the world says he is and every single lie I've been told about the Unseelie fae.

"You are certain about choosing me?" He searches my face for any hint of hesitation, but he will find none.

"Forever," I vow even as I cling to his broad shoulders, holding on so I don't faint away. Reminding myself that every moment of this perfect dream is real.

His fingers slipping into my hair. *Real.*

His head lowering until we're only a breath apart. *Real.*

I lift to my toes and anchor my lips against his. My fingers dig into the muscles of his shoulders, demanding he take whatever he wants. Ever angles my head, giving himself better access for the slow, thorough assault of his sandpaper tongue against mine, plundering like a pirate, conquering like a king.

I press my body into his, until every part of me feels the sensual heat radiating from his bare torso. His taut stomach. His sinewy thighs. His groan of pleasure vibrates against my mouth as he shifts his lips to the side, dragging them down the column of my neck. Licking and nipping at my pulse. The wing of my collarbone. The hollow at my throat.

This man and his persistent mouth steal every thought from my head, the strength from my body, and the breath from my lungs.

Ever urges me toward the bed, stopping when my legs collide with the mattress.

His thumb drags along my bottom lip as he stares down at my mouth. "Do you remember all the things you asked for that night at the lake?"

My throat tightens as I nod, desire pooling low in my belly.

He eases forward to whisper against the shell of my ear. "Do you still want them?"

Yes. Yes. "Yes."

With his hands bracketing my hips, he drops to his knees in front of me. "You wore this dress the first day I saw you." He tugs on the end of the ribbon holding my corset closed, loosening the knot. "You looked like a ray of sunlight."

And he looked like an ancient god of war, striking a handsome yet fearsome figure atop his onyx steed.

My corset falls to the floor. He holds out a hand, helping me step out of the silk before folding the garment atop the table. He handles the skirt with the same care, until it, too, is folded and forgotten.

Calloused hands skate up my thighs, bracing around my waist as Ever wordlessly turns me so that his back is to the bed. The mattress whines when he sinks onto the edge, pulling me between his spread knees. Everything about him makes me feel delicate and dainty—and those are two words I would have never used to describe myself before.

His fingers trail along the edge of my shift's lace sleeves, slowly peeling them down my shoulders, chasing every inch of my skin with his lips. "These have driven me mad since the night you first came across the bridge. Every time they fell, you insisted on fixing them. You cannot imagine how badly I wanted to tell you to leave them be."

"You should have." I never would've covered my shoulders again.

His soft hum vibrates against my neck; his tongue darts out, dragging along my collarbone.

Heat spreads like liquid fire between my thighs.

My shift falls to the floor in an ivory puddle, and I stand before him with nothing more than a scrap of lace between my thighs.

His pupils swallow his dark irises, his chest rising and falling as if he's been running too fast for too long. He traces my ribs and along the swell of my hips, all the way to the mottled skin of my thighs.

"When I look at you," he begins, taking my hand and pressing my palm to his chest, "I am overwhelmed."

To think that I could overwhelm someone like him is ridiculous, yet I hear the sincerity in his voice and feel the way his pulse skips. He drags the backs of his knuckles down my neck, between my breasts, all the way to the line of lace. "You are so soft. So delicate. Every part of you is beautiful." His head lifts, dark eyes meeting mine. "May I touch you? I promise to be gentle."

I nod. Waiting. Anticipating. Desire licking at my skin as he toys with the tips of my breasts, skimming and stroking with featherlight fingertips. Gripping and kneading. Groaning as he finds me with his tongue. Teasing. Tasting.

I melt deeper into his embrace, relaxing against him as his lazy fingers make their way to the juncture of my thighs. "Has anyone ever touched you here?" he rasps.

"No one but me," I confess as he delves deeper, massaging. Exploring. Tantalizing.

His teeth drag against where my neck meets my shoulder. I think of those women in the village. Of what he told me about Unseelie mating bonds.

I tip up my chin, giving him more of me. All of me. A willing sacrifice. "Mark me as yours."

He draws back, his nostrils flaring and eyes searching. "Kerris..."

"Please, Ever. I want to belong to you in every way."

Still, he hesitates. "You are certain?"

"Yes."

He kisses where my neck meets my shoulder. Softly. Softly.

When he finally clamps down, the mix of pleasure and pain is so heady, my heart feels as if it's about to burst through my chest. "Again." A demand. A plea.

Ever moves lower, to my breast, nipping and then soothing the sharp ache with a devious flick of his tongue. My head falls back as my hips surge toward his, searching for friction. As if he knows exactly what I need, Ever spins us around and urges me onto the mattress.

The soft quilt smells like it's been dried in the fresh air.

Kneeling between my thighs, he tugs on my knickers. I lift my hips, allowing him to remove my final layer, baring myself to whatever wickedness he has in store. His teeth graze my upper thigh. His tongue swirls over my hip, dangerously close to where I ache. And when his mouth finds that most perfect spot, my spine arches off the mattress.

His grip on my thighs tightens as he buries his tongue deep inside me. A low, rumbling groan of male satisfaction lances through my core. "You taste as sweet as the biscuits you bake."

The way he flicks his tongue might just be the death of me. It certainly isn't making coherent thoughts very easy. "I thought you... didn't like...sweet things."

"I found an exception."

The delicious purr of his voice. Each heady stroke of that sandpaper tongue.

It's too much.

It's not enough.

I lose my hands in his hair as he loses himself in me until I cannot keep it together any longer. A dam about to break.

And when it does, his name falls from my lips in a desperate plea.

Ever holds me tightly against the onslaught of pleasure ripping through my body, his growl of pleasure rumbling over pliant flesh.

The most violent of my shudders subsides, but the aching returns the moment I catch a glimpse of Ever's tousled hair as he grins from between my thighs.

I cannot let this stand. No, this will not do.

"Trousers off. Now." I don't want to be the only one to have lost control this day.

Sharp teeth flash with his widening grin. "You are an impatient Seelie."

"You've kept me waiting long enough." I'm done. Finished. Through. I want to belong to this man in every possible way.

Ever rises to his full height, his disheveled hair sweeping along the curved wood of the ceiling as he slips the leather strap of his belt through the buckle. When he unfastens the buttons on his trousers and the rough wool falls to the ground, my jaw hinges wide.

He is long and thick, and the way he grips himself, as if wielding another weapon, reignites the fire in my deepest recesses. Stroking his length, he stares down at me, his face drenched in shadows and lust.

He pauses for the briefest of moments. "You are certain? There is no going back."

There was no going back the moment I realized he was the one who gave me that flower. Our worlds may have been cleaved in two, but we will find a way to weave them together. Create a world of our own where no one else exists.

"Yes."

The veins in his forearm pop where he holds himself, a pearl of wetness glistening at the tip of his manhood. "It will hurt."

"I can take it."

The mattress dips beneath his weight. With one hand braced by my head, Ever drags his thick crown through my folds, coating himself in my desire before notching himself at my entrance. He eases inside, the muscles of his stomach tensing as he disappears, inch by glorious inch. My body tightens around his and my legs begin to quiver.

He was right. It does hurt. It hurts, burns, and aches so much that tears spring into my eyes.

"You are doing so well." He kisses my forehead. My cheeks. "Breathe. There is no rush. I love you, Kerris."

I smile against his bobbing throat, the backs of my eyes stinging. *Overwhelmed.* Just as he said. By my love for this man. By his love for me.

Calloused hands roam over my bare chest, sampling, seducing. Giving me time to adjust to his size.

"Move down," I whisper.

He drops his hips, positioning himself lower against me. "There?"

"Lower."

This time, when he moves, I feel my body start to relax. "Yes. Right there. Try now."

When he eases forward, he slips deeper and *deeper*, until our bodies are flush, the dusting of dark hair covering his muscular thighs tickling against the backs of mine. His ragged breaths feather against my temple, and his arms start to shake where they hold his weight.

"Ever?"

"Hmmm?"

"I think you're meant to move."

"I know."

"Are you all right? You sound as if you're in pain."

"Kerris?"

"Yes?"

"If I move right now, I'm going to end up fucking you straight through this wall."

A smile curves my lips. "You say that like it's a problem." I love that he's on the verge of losing control. It makes me feel powerful. Invincible.

His pained wince only makes my smile grow. "I promised to be gentle."

"And I told you I could take it."

He scowls down at me, and I smile even wider. His scowl deepens, and I laugh.

He pulls out a fraction, then drives deeper.

I gasp and then hold on for dear life as he bucks his hips harder, thrusting deeper and deeper. So deep, I feel as if I'm being split in two. My heels dig into his backside as the whole cart starts to rock, and if there were a headboard, I've no doubt it'd rattling the whole forest awake.

Together, we find a frantic rhythm, becoming one body. One pounding heart. One bleeding soul. I cling to him just as he clings to me, riding a tidal wave of pleasure as it hurtles for shore. Cresting. Crashing. Falling into nothing.

Into each other.

Ever grips my thighs as he bucks, a lustful frenzy overtaking us both. When my body finally gives out, he withdraws with a curse, grips himself in his fist, and spills onto my stomach.

That was...

Heavens, it was unexpected. I anticipated my first time being awkward and painful, but right now I'm smiling so wide my face hurts and I'm so happy I could burst.

Specks of blood paint his hand and my thighs. Beautiful evidence of our joining.

From the bed, Ever reaches into one of the kitchen drawers, withdrawing a cloth to clean me off before falling down beside me.

With an unsteady finger, he traces one of the marks he left on my skin. "Even in my wildest dreams, I never imagined that you would ever want to be mine."

I melt deeper into his embrace, relaxing against him, content to stay in this spot for the rest of my days.

"I should have sent you back home," he whispers even as he draws me closer, tucking my head between his collarbone and jaw.

A contented sigh falls from my lips. "You're my home now, Ever."

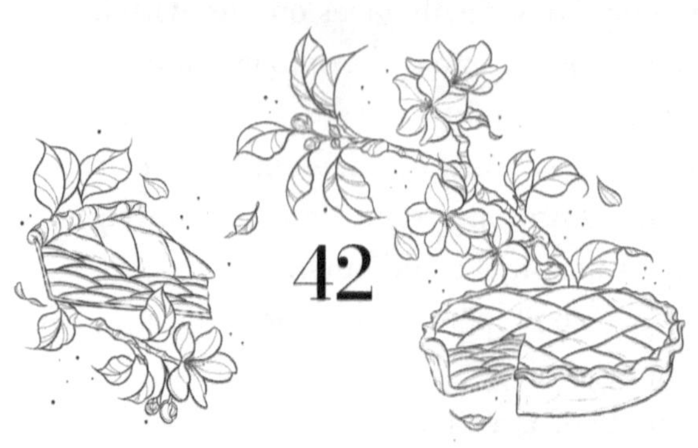

42

*"Summer's heat can burn the flesh of winter's
fiercest warrior."*

— An Unseelie Fable, Author Unknown

My body is thoroughly wrung out and yet sleep eludes me.

How can I rest when Ever's bare skin is molded to mine, his arm tucked beneath my neck as the most perfect pillow? He traces one of the more amorous marks left by his teeth at the swell of my hip as I run my fingers up and down the ridges of his abdomen.

"If you leave these much longer, they will scar," he says quietly, his words drifting into the curtain of night falling around us.

"At least when I look at them, they make me happy." Blissfully so. Unlike the mottled skin covering my legs. Thank heavens the sheets are keeping them out of sight.

"I wish you would let me heal you."

And waste all his water from the well on me? I don't think so. If we are to live together on this side of The Divide, then we must be frugal with what little resources we have. "I wish to wear your marks for everyone to see." For this world to know who I've chosen for myself.

"Do you plan on walking around without clothes, then?" he murmurs against my ear, cupping my breast and skimming his thumb over the mark alongside my nipple.

My back arches, pushing myself further into his grasp. "Would you like that?"

"Mmmm..." He replaces his hand with his mouth, his tongue dancing across the stiff peak. "Although if any wayward hunter were to stumble upon you, I would be forced to kill him, so perhaps you should wear clothes."

Wearing clothes is the last thing on my mind as a familiar ache gathers between my thighs. Surely it is too soon for a repeat of our lovemaking. We've only been laying here for half an hour.

Ever's erection nudges against my hip. Or... maybe I am wrong. I slide my hand under the sheet, finding the heat of his stiffness. When my fingers clasp around his rigid length, his breath hisses against my cheek.

"Is it too soon?" I whisper as he presses closer, the weight of his body falling over mine as he uses his knee to separate my thighs.

His rasped, "Never," breaks as I guide him home.

I expected some soreness, but not the utter euphoria of his body once again moving inside mine. Unlike the frenzy of our first coming together, this time his hips work in slow tandem with mine, the ebb and flow of a pleasure-fueled tide. Rolling and rocking until our panting breaths grow labored. Stilted. Overcome with the sheer bliss of release. I'm entirely boneless by the time Ever drops to the mattress beside me, his face painted in shadows and satisfaction, no doubt the mirror of my own.

If this is what eternity with Ever looks like, I just might be the luckiest woman alive.

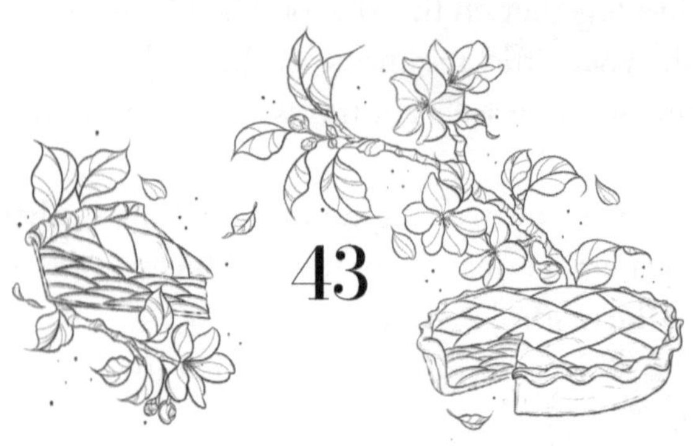

43

Hunger yawns in my stomach, as deep and as wide as The Divide. "If I don't get food soon, I'm going to turn into one of the beasts that roam these woods." I curl my fingers into claws and do my best impression of Ever's growl.

Ever swats my backside with a hearty laugh. The joyful sound warms me all the way to my toes. "Careful, Seelie. I eat beasts for breakfast."

"Not if I devour you first." I bite his shoulder the way he bit mine, earning myself a loud yelp.

Long fingers encircle my wrist, pinning my hands to the mattress above me. "There will be plenty of time for that later," he murmurs, his nose dragging down the column of my throat to press a kiss at the hollow. "Stay here. I will return with sustenance, beastie."

With that, Ever rolls off the bed, throws on his trousers, and ducks out the door, leaving me to my own devices. Although the fire has been stoked and a log was added at some point in the night, a chill persists in the air. This is going to take some getting used to.

Wrapping myself in sheets, I push off the bed to explore my new home.

Ever owns exactly three mugs, three plates, and three sets of cutlery. The bottom cupboard in his kitchen holds one pot and one small cast iron skillet. What I'm most interested in is the bow and quiver of arrows hanging beside the door.

Perhaps he'll teach me how to shoot.

Not that I have it in me to kill anything, but it wouldn't hurt to learn. Having distance between my prey and me might help as well. The last thing I want is for Ever to think I cannot take care of myself.

Two pairs of trousers soak in a bucket beside the fire.

Laundry.

Now, that's something I know how to do. All I need is some laundry powder...which I cannot find, so the bar of soap filled with pine needles will have to do.

Using the washboard and soap, I scrub his trousers along the metal ribs until my arms feel like they're going to fall off. Then I twist and squeeze the fabric with all my might and hang them outside on a line that runs from a tree to the front of the wagon.

Ever hunkers by a small fire, his broad back on full display as he cooks us breakfast. I wouldn't say it smells good, but my stomach grumbles all the same. At this stage, I'll eat anything.

Not wanting to wear a sheet for the day, I meander back inside.

The dress I wore yesterday doesn't exactly suit the current landscape. Perhaps I'll be able to purchase something more practical on Market Street. I could pick up some supplies as well, like bakeware and sugar and cinnamon. And bread. At least three loaves.

Maybe Ever has a shirt that I can wear in the meantime. I kneel down and peek beneath the bed. Sure enough, there is a flat trunk stuffed under there. It takes some maneuvering, but eventually I extricate the heavy box.

When I open the top, a waft of floral perfume tickles my nose.

Two pairs of worn trousers rest atop four pairs of thick wool socks and boots that have seen better days. I add a new pair to my mental list. That is, if they make them this large.

Unfortunately, there isn't a shirt in sight.

There is, however, a stack of white boxes tied with black ribbons bearing Madame Ella's insignia on the corner.

I remove the lid on the first one, revealing a stunning gown of emerald satin and lace. How did he get this dress? When?

"What are you doing?" Ever stands in the doorway, his brows drawn together.

Was his father part wraith? I didn't even realize he'd come in.

"I'm sorry." I rush to replace the lid. "I wasn't snooping." Not intentionally, anyway. "I only wanted to see what we needed from Rosehill."

His lips press flat as he pushes off the frame. "You are going back?"

"Only for supplies and the rest of my clothes."

He nods slowly but his frown remains.

"These are beautiful." The ruffles on the silk undulate like waves in the sea. "They're Madame Ella's."

"No, they belonged to my mother."

My hair tickles my bare back as I shake my head with a laugh. "I mean Madame Ella designed them."

"Well, they are yours now."

"Really?"

He lifts his shoulders in a shrug. "They are hardly going to fit me."

I hold up the gown to my chest. The skirt is a bit long, but other than that it should fit—

Wait.

The skirt is *too long,* just like all the dresses that have mysteriously shown up on my doorstep. This cannot be a coincidence. "Have you been leaving dresses at the cottage?"

"Of course."

"Why?"

"We already discussed this, Kerris."

"We most certainly did not." That is something I would absolutely remember.

"You gave me a gift, so I gave you one in return."

"I thought the gifts were the flowers."

His lips purse. "I do not think a flower pulled from the dirt is a fair trade for an entire box of biscuits."

"I only baked biscuits twice." And I cannot even remember how many dresses he gave me. Seven? Eight?

A shrug. "They were going to waste beneath my bed, and no Unseelie female would be caught dead in Seelie gowns." He nudges the toe of his boot against the trunk. "Knowing you might one day wear something that belonged to me made my heart happy."

This man. Here I didn't think it was possible to love him more. "Thank you, Ever."

He glances away even as a small smile plays on his lips.

I hold up the dress once more. This skirt needs a hem if I'm going to wear it outside. If I were back at the cottage, I'd bring it to Madama Ella for altering, but since I'm here—

Madame Ella.

She said these dresses were commissioned by the king himself.

For his *mistress.*

Does that mean Ever's mother was having an affair with the king?

If what Ever said was true, and no Unseelie would be caught dead in Seelie gowns, why did his mother have so many?

Ever's fingers drum against the doorframe. "Breakfast is getting cold."

At the mention of food, my belly lets out a hollow grumble and all thoughts of dresses and kings fall by the wayside. There will be plenty of time to figure out the mystery *after* we eat.

Ever has a picnic set up on his little porch. In the center of the wool blanket rests a plate of roasted meat on a spit.

"I do not know if you will like it," he says with a grimace. "All my spices are gone."

"That's all right." I'm hungry enough to eat...whatever this is whether it's seasoned or not.

Ever slides the dark meat from the spit and then extends the plate in my direction. The brown chunk feels squishy when I pick it up. Hopefully it tastes better than it looks. With a deep breath, I pop the bite into my mouth and chew. And chew. And chew.

Not too bad.

Not too good either.

The texture is strange. Definitely not as tender as a well-cooked carrot. At least it quells my hunger. Would be better with some salt and pepper and maybe a bit of clove.

Ever watches as if me chewing is the most interesting thing he's ever seen. "Does the face you are making mean you hate it?"

I wouldn't say I hate it—not out loud, anyway. "I'm just not used to it." Still, I eat as much as my stomach will allow and once I've had my fill, Ever devours what's left. It's hard to believe such a small portion is enough for him, but he insists it is, and an argument seems silly, so I let the issue drop.

"What happens now?" Back in Rosehill, Nia and I would

usually spend our afternoon exploring the city or lounging in the sun-drenched garden with books from the library. Here, there is no city, no books, or sunlight.

"Since you already washed my laundry—which I did not expect you to do," he mutters with a stern look, "we should probably wash ourselves."

A great idea. I could do with a nice, long soak. "Where is the bathing room?"

His face falls into a frown. "There is a river."

Surely, he doesn't mean the river beyond the fire. "Isn't it cold?" Just looking at it gives me shivers.

"I try not to linger."

Do I want to bathe in a river? Absolutely not. But I also don't want Ever feeling like what he has to offer isn't good enough. Because it is. Life on this side of The Divide is just different and will take some getting used to. Bathing in a river could be fun. Right?

Mischief sparkles in his dark eyes as his smile returns. "If we bathe together, I could warm you up."

Now, that does sounds like fun.

Ever disappears inside to grab the soap, then takes my hand and leads me to the shore. The river is large but moves lazily enough so there's no fear of being swept away with the current.

He strips off his trousers and walks straight in without so much as a hitch in his breath. Seeing him disrobed in the middle of the day feels very different from seeing him last night. Heavens, he is magnificent. How could I believe for even a moment that I would be happy with a Seelie husband after meeting him?

With the water kissing Ever's waist, he twists, sending ripples toward the shore where I wait.

I can do this. I used to swim in the early spring on the mountain when I was younger, didn't I? This is no different.

"I can boil water if you would prefer a sponge bath instead."

Yes, please. "There's no need. I want to do this." To prove to myself and Ever that I'm not too soft for life in the Unseelie lands. But first. I glance over my shoulder at the wagon, my stomach sinking even lower. "There's no privy, is there?"

He shakes his head.

No matter. I'll go over by that boulder. Be one with nature.

Once I've relieved myself, I return to the river and slip out of my shift. Ever's onyx gaze tracks my every movement, a predator studying his prey. Nerves flutter in my stomach as the icy water closes over my feet. My ankles. My calves. How is he just standing there without moving?

Are my lips blue? If they're not yet, they will be soon.

When I reach my waist, the shivers start. *Oh heavens. Oh heavens. Oh heavens.* How is it getting colder? This is it. This is how I die. Turned to a block of ice in the middle of a bloody river.

Ever closes the distance between us in a handful of strides. His arms come around me, instantly infusing my body with his heat.

"Hold your breath," he whispers against my temple.

My feet disappear from beneath me and water closes over my head. Hypothermia. That's what this shock is. I am dying from hypothermia.

"I h-hate y-you," I splutter when he brings us back up for air.

For some reason, the venom in my tone makes him laugh. "Then turn around so that I can make you hate me less."

Doesn't he see that there is nothing that will make me hate him any less—

He gathers my hair along with the soap and starts to massage my scalp. The tension in my muscles slowly eases despite the frigid temperatures. Warmth collects low in my belly and between my thighs.

"Is it working?" he murmurs against my cheek, his chest slipping against my wet back.

"Maybe." He brings the bar of soap down my neck to my breast. *Definitely.*

Steady hands scrub and massage until the cold is so far from my mind, it might as well be the dead of summer. When he finishes, it's my turn to steal the soap and do the same for him.

Ever leaves the water to collect three towels. One for him, one for my body, and a second for my hair. He insists on carrying me back to his house so that my feet do not get dirty, and I find myself set in front of the woodstove with a beautiful brush inlaid with mother of pearl in my hand.

"Your mother's as well?" I assume.

"Yes."

A mother lost as tragically as my own. A mother who might've been having an affair with the King of Willowhaven.

I'm about to ask him again about the dresses, but something stops me.

Does the truth even matter? Why dredge up a painful past when it has no bearing on our future? Ever's mother had beautiful dresses. Dresses that he gave to me. Beyond that, it's none of my business.

Resolute in my decision, I drag the brush through my hair, but between Ever's rigorous washing technique and the cold water, the heavy strands are more matted than they've ever been.

No wonder the women in his village keep their hair short. I yank the brush out and start again, this time from the bottom. "I should get my hair cut." At least then, it would be easier to manage.

Behind me, Ever dries himself with quick swipes of his towel before donning a fresh pair of pants, trousers, and wool socks. "Do what pleases you," he says, fastening the buckle on his belt.

Even watching him complete the most mundane tasks stirs desire within me. I twist a curl around my finger, so unlike an Unseelie woman's midnight strands. "Would it please you?"

He surprises me by sinking onto the edge of the mattress and gesturing for the brush. I nearly collapse in delight when he begins to comb through small sections a little at a time.

"Shorter hair is more practical," he says. "But I would mourn the loss. The first day I saw you, I thought your hair looked magical." He drapes the straight section over my shoulder and starts working on the next. "I must confess to fantasizing about you in nothing but your lavender tresses."

If he likes it, then perhaps I will keep it for a little while longer. At least until it becomes too much. Then again, if he continues pampering me like this, I might never cut it. "You're very good at that."

"My mother wore hers longer than most females in our clan. I would help her brush it sometimes."

I imagine a miniature Ever combing his mother's hair. How devastated he must've been when he lost her. "Who took care of you when she passed?"

"I took care of myself."

"But you were only five." I'm nearly twenty-five and some days I still feel incapable of taking care of myself.

A shrug. "Some of the elders would bring me their leftovers, but everyone had their own families to feed."

And there I was, balking at bathing in a river. Imagine having to survive on your own when you're barely out of nappies. It's a miracle this man is alive.

"What now?" he asks, setting the brush aside and admiring his handiwork.

"It's easier to manage when it's braided." My arms tend to get tired when I fix it myself, so it's easiest to lie on the bed and let my hair hang off the edge of the mattress while I do.

Ever begins to separate my hair into three sections.

"You know how to braid?"

He twists the part on the side around the center section, weaving with careful concentration. "Rope."

Not sure how I feel about my lover referring to my hair as rope, but that is neither here nor there.

When he finishes, he fastens the bottom of my hair with a leather queue from the trunk. I'm so relaxed, I could fall asleep right here on this chair, especially when Ever begins to trace along one of the scars on my shoulder. "Tell me of your Seelie mating traditions."

Where do I even begin? Most of what I know came from my mother's copy of *A Seelie Guide to Matrimony*. It all seems so silly now. So unnecessary. So shallow. Who cares about selecting the perfect bouquet? Why does it matter if you don't create a seating chart for the reception? I would marry Ever right here, right now, with the trees as our witnesses and be perfectly content.

"Instead of scars, we exchange rings." That's one tradition I wouldn't mind keeping.

He reaches into the trunk and starts rummaging around. When I ask what he's doing, he doesn't answer. After a few moments, there's a small golden band pinched between his fingers. "Rings like this?"

"Exactly like that."

"What happens next?"

"Your family and friends come from all around to attend." I'd love for Theo and my father to meet Ever. Maybe someday they will.

His jaw drops. "They *watch* you mate?"

"No! Heavens, no. They come to celebrate with you during the wedding ceremony. The...*mating* takes place in private afterward."

He turns the ring over in his hand, as if studying the way the firelight flickers on the gold. "Tell me more of this ceremony."

"Well, the bride usually wears white. And then you vow to love and cherish each other forever."

His lips flatten. "You are wearing white."

My stomach flutters as I glance down at my shift. "I am."

With a nod, Ever pushes to his feet and reaches for my hand, helping me to mine. Still holding onto me, he slips the ring onto my middle finger. I don't bother telling him that he has the wrong finger and the wrong hand because everything about this moment feels too perfect.

The quiet rumble of his deep voice washes over me, drawing tears to my eyes. "From this day forward, every beat of my heart belongs to you, Kerris Dawn."

I'm not yet twenty-five. We have no license and no witnesses, but none of that feels important as I stare into Ever's eyes. This is what a marriage should be: Two people who love each other coming together, vowing to honor and cherish each other until their dying day.

I straighten my spine and tell him all the promises in my heart. "I love you Everett—" *Wait.* "What *is* your last name?"

A smile. "Gathin."

Everett Gathin.

Kerris *Gathin.*

"I love you Everett Gathin, and I vow to never love another. From this day forward, you are my one and only."

Our kiss seals the vows spoken in the cool morning air, and when his hands find the small of my spine, urging my body closer to his, something occurs to me.

"We might have to visit the river again sooner than I hoped," I murmur against his hungry mouth.

Ever's smile curves against mine, followed by a nip of his teeth. "I am afraid that we shall become like the fishes who never leave."

44

— Unseelie Fae: A Scientific Study

Pressure on my bladder rouses me from a dreamless sleep. It isn't until I open my eyes that I remember where I am—and whose massive arm is draped across my stomach. Ever clings to me, his head resting over my heart, holding me so tightly, my lungs can barely expand. I never want to leave this spot but doubt he would appreciate me relieving myself in his bed. It takes all my strength, but I manage to lift his arm and slip from beneath him. His face crushes up, so fierce, even in sleep.

With my shift nowhere to be found, I throw on my dress to hide my nakedness.

The fog outside is thick enough to stir with a spoon, the tiny droplets of water soaking into the silk gown, gluing the skirt to my thighs as I descend the stairs. No birds chirp in the trees. No squirrels dart or tarry. The only sound is that of the quiet trickle of water in the river beyond Ever's wagon.

Not trusting myself to find my way back in this fog, I keep close to our camp, stepping behind a boulder to take care of my business. Perhaps we can fashion some sort of privy for ourselves nearby or purchase a chamber pot from the city.

Primitive, I know, but anything is better than the indignity of having to squat.

By the time I've finished, water droplets roll down my chest. The hair escaping my braid tightens into springy curls.

Something snaps behind me, and the hairs at the back of my neck lift at the unexpected sound. Slowly, I turn to see what made the noise only to find myself staring into the bloodred eyes of the biggest animal I've ever seen.

Not just an animal... *A wolf.*

The beast's lips curl back from its teeth; blood drips down its maw, splattering the curled, brown leaves at my feet. I don't know what it just killed but I know what it's going to kill next.

Me.

Carefully, and without taking so much as a breath, I back toward the wagon, making it three steps before the muscles in the wolf's shoulders tense.

"Ever," I whisper even though there is no way he will be able to hear me.

Why didn't I wake him when I left? Why did I think it would be safe to go outside? Didn't he warn me of the dangers of this forest? And off I went without a care in the bloody world.

"Ever," I call, louder than before, but fear steals the power from my voice. I take another step back. And another. And another, loath to take my eyes from the wolf to search the ground for something to use as a weapon, to give me some sort of chance against the beast.

The wolf's ears flatten, its eyes glazing over with feral rage. A growl starts low in its belly, lifting the hairs on my arms and sending my heart into overdrive.

I whirl to run but my escape is foiled by my feet tangling in my skirts. I screw my eyes shut and wait for the inevitable pain.

A pitiful yelp cuts through me and my eyes fly open, finding the wolf collapsed at my feet, blood pouring from where a dagger with a bone-hilt protrudes from its crimson eye.

Ever leaps in front of me, yanking the dagger free and dragging the blade across the wolf's throat. Blood sprays from the wound, splattering all over my bare feet and dress.

With the beast slain, he rushes to where I've fallen, cradling my face, but all I can see is the blood. Its coppery tang taints every breath. Ever's lips are moving, but the ringing in my ears muffles his words.

Something warm and wet dribbles down my cheek. More blood. His hands are painted with it.

The ringing suddenly stops, and everything around me comes into sharp focus.

"Did it hurt you?" Ever demands.

"N-no." But it could have. It could have ripped out my throat and torn me to shreds and Ever would've been none the wiser and he never would have forgiven himself.

He lets me go, carding both hands through his hair, his expression a tumultuous storm of rage and fear. "Why were you out here?"

Why was I out here? I can't even remember. "I-I had to use the privy."

"You should have woken me."

"I'm s-sorry."

"You could have been killed," he says, as if I wasn't already painfully aware of that fact. As if I can't still see the promise of death in the beast's eyes. Feel the heat of its blood-drenched breath against my cheeks. "If that wolf had gotten to you first, not even all the water in the well could have saved you."

I want to shout, but all my trembling voice is capable of seems to be another pathetic, "I'm sorry."

"You are sorry?" Ever murmurs, his head hanging and proud shoulders falling in defeat.

"I'll do better." I'll prove to him that I can survive on this side of The Divide. He can give me a dagger. Teach me to use the bow. I'll never be defenseless again.

He yanks the blade from the ground and twists the hilt in his hand, scarlet drops splattering on his bloodstained boots as his head shakes. "You will go back to your people."

"No." How can he even consider such a thing? I won't let him throw us away because of one foolish mistake. "Ever, I love you."

He looks me dead in the eye and says, "Take your love and return to Rosehill."

Finally, I find my voice. My courage. My backbone. "No. I'm not going back there." I refuse to leave him.

"I do not want you here."

"That isn't true." I know it's a lie, but his words are like a heel to my heart. Breaking. Crushing.

He shoots to his feet, his dagger clattering to the ground next to the carcass. "Don't you see? I cannot protect you! Maybe before, but now, it is only me. This is the way it must be."

I can feel the fight leaking from my bones, leaving me hollow. Cold. Shaken.

"Please, don't do this." I'm willing to plead with him until my dying breath, but something in the hard set of his jaw and the flint in his eyes tells me it's no use.

He stalks into the carriage, returning with my slippers, leaving bloodied handprints on the pristine silk. "Put these on."

"No. I won't leave you."

"Put them on. Please. I am begging." Just when I think there is no way for him to force me to put on those shoes, I see the tears glistening in his eyes.

He is truly afraid of losing me, and instead of fighting for me, he's giving up.

On me. On us. On the future we planned only a few hours ago.

When I look away, my gaze catches on the dead wolf.

Fear swells like a scream in my chest. I haven't even been in this territory for two whole days, and already I've met one of the beasts that prowl these forests. With Ever out hunting, foraging, searching for food to sustain not only himself, but also me , my life would be confined to that wagon. If we were ever blessed with a child, how could I possibly hope to keep a son or daughter safe in this place?

Compared to Ever and the rest of his people, I have been raised in the lap of luxury; I don't know how to fight. I know how to bake desserts the man I love doesn't even eat. I don't know how to cook meals for him, so he will have to either teach me or do that himself as well.

In this world, I am entirely out of my depth.

I am no good to him.

He needs someone stronger—deserves someone who can defend herself. A partner, not another burden.

I take my slippers with trembling hands and slip them onto my feet.

Ever swipes the dagger from the bloody grass, clenching the bone handle in his fist once more, his jaw set as he scans the forest. If it's not safe here for me, then he shouldn't be here either, especially not without access to the well.

"Come with me."

Dark eyes lock with mine.

"You have no one else." I swipe my fist beneath my watery eyes. "We will find a way to make it work. Just don't push me away. Please, Ever. Please."

My heart clatters against my ribs as he takes my hand in his and leads me out of the forest, past the Unseelie village, all the way to the bridge where Maddox and Gryffin sit by a fire, chatting quietly. When they see us, they lurch to their feet.

"What the hell happened?" Maddox asks me, not sparing Ever so much as a glance.

Ever clears his throat. "Wolf."

Maddox's dark gaze darts to Ever, but all my love does is stare straight ahead into the empty gray.

"You never should have brought her here," Ever grits out. "Take her home."

Maddox's gaze returns me, his jaw popping as his teeth grind together.

I cling more tightly to Ever's hand. "No. You're coming with me. Please. *Please.*"

He pries open my fingers, removing himself from my grasp, his sorrowful gaze falling over my face. "I am sorry I failed you. It will not happen again."

"Ever, please... Don't do this."

He presses his lips to my forehead, then turns and drifts away.

45

*"Your knees will buckle under the weight of a
broken heart."*

— Kerris Dawn, An Observation

Maddox comes to a sudden halt before we reach the end of the bridge. "*Shit.*"

I peer around him to see what caused the holdup. There, in the distance, stand two guards. Their backs are to us so they don't know we're here yet, but there's no telling what they'll say or do if they see Maddox.

He must be thinking the same thing because when he turns, he wears a wince.

"I can go on my own," I tell him. It's really not that far. Besides, it will be easier to traverse Rosehill unnoticed without a giant Unseelie escort.

Although he shakes his head, relief flickers across his face. "Ever asked me to take you home."

"I'll not let you get into trouble for my choices." Heaven only knows what his fate might be if those guards find out—or his chieftain.

I push past Maddox before he sees the tears burning my eyes and take the final few steps until my slippers meet dirt. "I'm home. Your job is done."

Maddox blows out a breath, casts one final wary look toward the guards, and then nods. He opens his mouth, as if to say something, but must think better of it because he turns and vanishes into the mist without a word of goodbye.

We were never friends, but we were at least acquaintances. Surely, I deserve more than silence. Then again, perhaps he blames me for the terrible fate that has befallen Ever. And for good reason. If Ever and I had never crossed paths, he'd be marrying an Unseelie woman, protected by the village.

Now he's all alone in a forest full of monsters waiting to devour him.

Monsters with red eyes and blood dripping from their razor-like teeth.

I press a hand to my racing heart, forcing myself to breathe through the panic rising in my chest. Knowing I'm safe now doesn't ease the unending ache. Not when Ever is still in danger.

Voices carry from where the guards continue to converse. Two more appear over the horizon, flaming roses emblazoned on their black armor. Instead of going left where they're congregating, I swing right and take the ring road around the city.

The state of me; if anyone sees there's sure to be talk. If only Ever had given me time to wash the blood from my clothes. *If only I'd convinced him to let me stay.*

"Good heavens, Kerris. Are you all right?"

My head snaps up and I see Trevor standing at his cottage gate, his jaw hanging open as he stares at the bloody smears across my silken skirts.

Are you all right?

No...I couldn't be further from all right.

A sob tears from my chest, and my legs give out, leaving me in a heap in the middle of the cobblestones.

He's gone. He's gone. He's gone.

I barely hear Trevor's curse over those two words poisoning my mind.

Warm hands gently clasp my elbows, helping me to my feet, escorting me on unsteady legs into the cool darkness of Trevor's quaint cottage. He doesn't stop until we reach the tiny dining area. When he drags out a chair for me, I fall onto the seat with a garbled thanks and drag my sleeve beneath my runny nose. I need to get myself together, but all I'm able to do is fall apart.

From the tap, Trevor fills a glass of water and presses the drink into my hand. "Take a deep breath, have a sip of this, and tell me what happened."

Rogue drops of water roll down the smooth glass to where my fingers tighten. Water that heals. Water that extends our lives. Water that Ever isn't allowed to access. "There was a... a w-wolf."

Trevor sucks in a breath, the color draining from his face. "Are you hurt? There's a physician down the road—"

"No."

He freezes, his hands outstretched toward me and brow furrowed. Slowly, he lowers his arms to his sides, and his lips flatten into grim line. "We must go to the king straightaway."

If we go to the king, he's liable to cut off all access to the well. I cannot be the cause of an entire village's downfall as well as my own. "No," I say again, stronger. More resolute.

"Kerris—"

"I said *no*. The wolf wasn't on our side of The Divide. It was on theirs. And it's dead." The Seelie are safe which means the king doesn't need to know a blessed thing. Besides, there are four guards watching the bridge. They would kill any beast before it made landfall in Rosehill.

Trevor blinks at me for a moment, but then his eyes widen, followed by a slow nod.

I take another sip, willing my hands to stop trembling. How am I supposed to walk through town looking like I've been shredded to ribbons? Word is bound to reach the king, and I cannot have anyone else finding out what happened. "I know I have no right to ask you this, but will you help me? I need you to get Nia and ask her to bring me a change of clothes."

He bobs his head. "Yes, of course. I'll go straightaway."

"Thank you." Although it'll do no good to put on a clean dress and still have blood on my hands. "Do you mind if I use your bathing room?"

"Not at all. Help yourself to what's there. There are fresh towels in the closet."

"Thank you, Trevor."

His boots fall heavily against the wooden floor as he hurries toward the exit, leaving me in bitter silence, drowning in memories. Forcing myself to my feet, I drift toward the bathing room to fill the claw-foot tub. Such a simple convenience that I've always taken for granted. With a shuddering exhale, I shed my clothes and sink into the water, its healing properties doing nothing to save me from the images in my mind.

Of the wolf.

Of *him*.

My eyes sink closed, and I let my tears melt down my cheeks and disappear into the bath. Eventually, the water goes cold, but I cannot find it in me to rise.

Hinges creak, and Nia steps into the room, a colorful carpet bag slung over her shoulder. "Are you all right?" she whispers. "You look as if you've seen a ghost." She steps closer. "Heavens above, Kerris. Is that *blood* on your forehead?"

I drag a hand across my brow. The dried blood turns pink in the water. "I'm..." I cannot bring myself to say I'm fine.

The bag clatters to the tiles, and Nia grabs a cloth from the sink, kneeling beside me to dip it into the water. Carefully, she smooths the soft terrycloth down my cheeks. Her brow furrows as she traces one of the scars on my neck. "Something bit you."

So much for not crying. "Ever." There's no sense trying to hide the truth when it's been painted in silver crescent moons upon my skin. My soul.

Nia's hand finds mine beneath the water. "What happened?"

I shake my head, cursing these damn tears that refuse to stop falling. "His people abandoned him. He's all alone in that forest and those wolves are...they're monsters, Nia. I would've died if he hadn't saved me."

She braces her hands on my shoulders, giving me a little shake. "But you didn't die. And neither will he. We'll figure this out."

What's there to figure out? I cannot survive across The Divide and Ever refuses to live here. This situation is as hopeless as it always was; I just didn't want to believe it.

Her mouth flattens as she shakes her head. "Stand up. You're shaking like a leaf." She grabs the towel from next to my dress and holds it open the way my mother used to.

Gripping the sides of the tub, I slide my feet beneath me before standing.

"Heavens, Kerris. They're *everywhere*."

It takes me a moment to realize she means the scars. They cover my arms, my breasts, my stomach, and even my thighs.

"Your man was quite thorough, wasn't he?" Clearing her throat, she envelopes me in the towel and tucks the end beneath my arm. "I'm not sure the dress I brought will cover them. I wonder if Trevor will mind you borrowing a shirt?"

"He told me to help myself to whatever I need."

She bustles around the room, drawing the plug from the bath and spreading out the cloth on the edge to dry. "He's a good man."

"He is. But I can't marry him." Perhaps before, I might have been content with a safe match, but now that I've tasted true passion, the kind of connection you find only once in a lifetime, I will settle for nothing less.

Her shoulders fall with her sigh. "Your life would be so much easier if you did."

Nia leaves me to finish drying, returning with a soft white linen shirt to wear as a sort of jacket over my dress. She scoops up all the soiled garments along with my abandoned towel and drops them into the wash basket.

By the time we return to the sitting room, Trevor is pacing from the sofa to the front door and back again. When he sees us, his brow crushes with concern.

Nia squeezes my fingers with a quiet, "I'll wait for you outside."

It feels like another lifetime when I imagined myself living in this quaint cottage. A lifetime that feels so far out of reach. "Thank you for your kindness, Trevor."

"Consider it an apology. I haven't done right by you, Kerris. For that, I am dreadfully sorry. If you could find it in your heart to forgive me, I would love nothing more than to prove myself to you."

Your life would be so much easier if you did.

One yes is all it would take to make all of this go away.

One yes that will never fall from my lips.

How can I possibly even consider moving on with the taste of Ever's skin still living on my tongue? With the vows we exchanged in the darkness still ringing in my ears?

"I'm sorry, Trevor. But I do not love you."

"I wouldn't expect you to. Love takes time to cultivate."

Some love can take time, like Aunt Cordelia and Uncle Arlo's.

But the love I've found is made of fire, all-consuming and devastating, leaving scars on my body and my heart. Scars that will never heal. There is no going back for me. "What I mean to say is that I am in love with someone else."

Trevor blows out a resigned breath. "Pity. I thought you and I could make an excellent match. But if your heart lies elsewhere, then there is no hope for us."

Truer words have never been spoken, and yet I feel my heart break a little more anyway. For the simple life I've thrown away in favor of a beautiful disaster. Of a love and life that can never be. "Thank you for being such a good friend. I hope you can find someone to be happy with someday."

When he smiles, it doesn't quite reach his eyes.

When I smile, neither does mine.

46

Everett

*"Mingled souls breed mangled hearts.
Sometimes it's best to remain apart."*

— An Unseelie Fable, Author
Unknown

Kerris is gone.

No matter how many times I tell myself those three words, they refuse to sink in. I do not walk back to my barrel-top, I drift. People in the camp stop and stare, but I cannot even lift my head to meet their curious gazes. For the briefest moment, I had everything.

And now everything is gone.

Maybe I acted too rashly. Maybe I should race across the canyon and beg her to come back. Tell her I did not mean what I said. That I would protect her with my own life until my dying day.

But seeing the wolf's carcass still lying where I felled the beast, its teeth bared in a silent snarl, destroys any thought of reconciliation.

I almost lost the most precious gift I have ever been given. I cannot bear the thought of Kerris leaving me of her own accord.

Of watching her grow to despise and resent me.

This is the way it must be. She lasted two fucking days before her life was in danger. If it had not been a wolf, it could have been a panther or a basilisk. Hell, even Leah is a threat to her safety.

I knew all these things, and yet I allowed myself to believe the lie. To pretend that I could keep her for myself.

Come with me.

For the briefest moment, I allowed myself to consider her earnest offer.

It is not as if I would be losing anything. I no longer have any friends, and all my belongings would fit inside my mother's trunk.

But then reality hit me like a kick in the teeth.

What happiness could I possibly offer Kerris in Rosehill? I highly doubt anyone would be in search of a hunter. Even if I brought my barrel-top with me, I own no land to leave it on.

My Seelie deserves the sun, moon, and stars, but I am as penniless as the trees in these woods.

So here I stand, alone once again, staring at a wolf as lifeless as I feel.

I want to burn the beast. Actually, no. I want to revive it and kill it all over again. To bathe in its blood and let the crimson flood wash away my rage.

But there is no sense wasting meat when I barely have enough to feed myself for the week.

When I finish gutting the wolf, I tie a rope around its neck and use my pulley to hang it from one of the trees so I can skin it. The pelt would fetch a good price up north, but it would take me three days to get there and three days back—and that is if the rain stays away. The roads are treacherous enough on dry days; in mud, they are downright deadly.

Distant leaves stir, crunching on the barren ground.

I smell my former friend before I see him.

Maddox is only stealthy when he wants to be, and apparently today is not one of those days. He comes to a stop at the edge of the forest and turns his back on me.

His shunning hurts more than it should. I chose this fate for myself, after all.

Maddox and Gryffin still have their lives ahead of them and they would be fools to side with me after what I have done.

"I took her across the bridge, but there were guards," Maddox murmurs to the high branches, his voice no more than a whisper.

At least Kerris made it safely across the bridge. "Thank you."

His head falls and he turns ever so slightly, casting a wary side-eye my way. "You love her."

"I do."

"And she loves you?"

All I can do is nod. She loved me last night, but I cannot be sure if our newfound affection is strong enough to withstand my sending her away. My heart might be hers until eternity, but she is like my friends. She has a future ahead of her. Any male would be lucky to be chosen by her.

The thought of someone else holding her, someone else loving her blurs my vision and ignites a fire in my blood. What can I do but stand here and burn?

Maddox kicks a clump of dirt with the toe of his boot. I wait for him to say something else, but all he does is sigh and leave me to turn to ash.

All that remains of the wolf is bone and sinew. Instead of leaving the thing hanging and attracting scavengers, I drag the carcass to the middle of the forest and leave it there. In a few months, I will return to add the bare bones to the perimeter of my camp. If I dry the meat, it should last me a week or two if I ration it. Considering I do not feel like eating anything, that should not be a problem.

Back at camp, I build a fire and cook the meat, so it does not go off. A squeak chirps from the path toward the village, too high-pitched to be an animal.

I catch a glimpse of a carriage moving through the trees. Maddox sits atop his steed, navigating his home through the broken logs and boulders. Behind him, Gryffin leads his unicorn and cart as well.

They come to a halt next to my carriage.

Maddox dismounts, giving the animal's thick neck a pat.

All I can do is stare as he ties the beast next to my own, offering not a word of explanation.

"What do you think you are doing?" I finally ask.

Maddox shrugs and swipes a skewer from the fire, blowing on the meat before taking a bite. "Moving. Staying in one place too long makes me itchy."

Gryffin steals one as well, not bothering to blow on it before stuffing the thing between his lips.

"You are moving too?"

He nods.

"Life at camp has been shit without you. Boring as hell too." Maddox steals another skewer, leaving me with only one left for dinner.

"By all means, help yourself to my food," I say dryly, blinking through the sudden stinging in my eyes. Must be the smoke from the fire. Yes. That is exactly what it is.

"It is not very good," Maddox mumbles around another bite. "Needs seasoning."

"I do not suppose you brought any?"

"As a matter of fact, I did." He climbs into his carriage,

returning a moment later with a shaker. He sprinkles his own skewer with a ridiculous amount before offering the shaker to Gryff.

In his haste, he left the door to his carriage ajar. When I catch sight of a familiar shape, hope stirs in my chest.

I take a halting step forward for a better look. "Is that a jug?"

Maddox tosses a glance over his shoulder before taking my seat as his own. "We cannot get water if we do not have something to put it in."

The burning in my eyes grows stronger. Curse Maddox and his damn spices.

I do not deserve their friendship or their loyalty, but I will cling to both until my dying day.

Gryffin claps me on the shoulder, and then drops to the ground next to the fire without a word and steals the rest of my dinner.

I am still miserable and despair hangs over my head like a fog, but at least I am not alone.

*"Secure your own happiness first.
Miserable fae are difficult to love."*

— A Seelie Guide To
Happiness

No conversation dampens our footfalls as Nia and I make our way back to the cottage. Instead of cutting through town, we traverse the path nearest The Divide. While it's going to kill me to see the bridge, the thought of running into anyone else we know and being forced to hold a conversation makes me want to curl into a ball and sob.

The guards I saw when Maddox brought me across are no longer by the lights, but standing at the entrance of the bridge, swords drawn and expressions blank. I only recognize one, but even he doesn't spare us a glance.

Nia comes to a halt. "Nolan?" Her skirts flutter as she rushes over to where her love waits with the other guards. When he sees her, he says something to the rest of them and meets Nia in the middle of the dirt path.

"What are you doing here?" she asks.

An excellent question considering he's meant to be Ronan's personal guard.

Nolan darts a glance at me before responding. "We've been ordered to guard the bridge. No one is to cross without the king's permission."

Meaning even if Ever changes his mind about us, he won't be able to come to me. "Crossing the bridge isn't illegal."

"Yet."

"What does that mean?"

He gives me his shoulder, sidling closer to Nia. "I shouldn't even be speaking to you."

Nia reaches for his hand, squeezing his fingers. "Nolan, please."

He stares for far too long at their connection before drawing away, putting distance between all of us, a small gap that feels as wide as The Divide.

Nia's face falls at the slight, her eyes glittering with unshed tears as she watches Nolan grip the sword at his hip. "If the queen gets her way," he says, "there will no longer be a bridge."

"She can't do that."

"I assure you, she can." He leaves us without another word, the sun glinting off his armor as he takes his place next to the other guards.

To remove the bridge would be damning all those innocent people to death. Maybe they could travel to one of the other villages along the canyon that have a similar arrangement with the Unseelie. Or maybe all the Seelie will follow suit and they'll be cut off entirely.

This isn't fair.

It isn't *right*.

The Unseelie have done nothing wrong, and the queen wants to go back on their treaty. No doubt, she'll convince everyone that this decision is solely to ensure the safety of those in Rosehill.

There is no hope of stopping this, unless...

"I need to speak to the king." Perhaps he will be willing to show some compassion to Ever's people.

Nia swipes at the tears running down her cheeks. "What makes you think he'll grant you an audience?"

After what I did to his son, he probably won't.

His son. That's it! "Ronan."

"He won't help you."

Probably not. He doesn't seem like the forgiving type. Perhaps I can appeal to his softer side—assuming he even has one.

Nia swipes at her eyes with her fist. "Maybe if we make him believe that you want to speak with the king for some other reason?"

What other reason would I have to speak to the king? I am no one. He owes me nothing. We only met the one time, so he might not even remember me.

Her eyes narrow. "I can think of one, but you're not going to like it."

At this stage, I'll do anything.

"If you were to apologize to Ronan for slighting him, convince him you're interested in marrying—"

"Absolutely not." The thought of even pretending to enjoy Ronan's company—his touch, his *kiss*—makes it feel like there are spiders crawling over my skin.

"Do you want to save Everett or not?"

Of course I want to save him, but to pretend to court Ronan to make that happen? I'm not even sure I could be convincing.

Unfortunately, I cannot think of any alternative. "Where do you think he'll be?"

"Either on his way to the Black Rose or already there."

The Black Rose is as busy as I've ever seen it, with people everywhere smiling and laughing, not a care in the world, oblivious to the dire situation unfolding for their neighbors. My hands want to tighten into fists, but I force them to remain relaxed at my sides as I push through the revelry in search of a prince who may very well hold the fate of an entire village in his careless hands.

I find Ronan near the back door with Ivee hanging on his every word as he regales her with some fanciful story. Two guards I don't recognize stand a short distance away, scanning the crowd for trouble through somber eyes.

As if she can hear my pounding heart, Ivee turns her head slowly, her gaze widening when she sees us. A sneer pulls at her painted lips, but Ronan doesn't so much as spare us a glance.

This is going to be much harder than I imagined.

Nia steps in front of me, her eyes narrowing as she trades glowers with Ivee. "Good evening, Ivee." She lets out a little gasp. "Oh, dear."

"What?" Ivee rushes.

"It's nothing, really."

"Tell me."

"You just have a little something right between your teeth."

An indignant screech bursts from Ivee before she reins it in with tight lips. She slides off her stool and twirls toward the privy.

One problem solved. Now to deal with the next.

Ronan collects his pint from the table, drinking deeply while staring into the crowd, a blatant slight that doesn't even sting. If I had my way, I'd never see the man again.

Still, I force my legs forward, erasing the gap between us. "Prince Ronan? I was wondering if I could have a word?"

He rolls his eyes like a child. That's what he is. A spoiled little boy trapped inside a man's body. "Go on then."

What I have to say—what I must do—requires a little more privacy. "Could we go outside?"

With another eye roll, he carries his pint to the back door leading to the gardens but doesn't bother holding it open for me after he steps through.

Unlike the first night he brought me out here, the sun is high, waiting to boil me alive. Ronan stops next to a bush laden with white hydrangea blooms and takes another drink, his foot tapping out his impatience.

The door opens once more, and the guards step through. Thankfully, they remain far enough away that they might not overhear.

Here goes nothing.

"I wanted to say that I am dreadfully sorry for what happened between us and for treating you so poorly." That sounded sincere, didn't it?

He sips from his glass, his gaze roving over me. Gone is the man who cared—or at least pretended to, leaving in his wake a cold, calculating prince. "Let me get this straight: Your Unseelie used you, then tossed you aside, and now you're crawling back to me?"

Annoyance prickles my spine. Ever didn't use me. He may have sent me away, but it was for my own safety. Because he loved me. If I hold onto that knowledge, I just might find a way to survive this. "That isn't true."

He yanks Trevor's shirt from my shoulder, exposing the scars from Ever's teeth. "Do you want to try again?"

With my face burning, I drag my sleeve back into place. What's the point in continuing this farce when he knows that I have no intention of rekindling our relationship? "I need to speak to your father regarding a very urgent matter," I say, remaining calm despite the panic gripping my chest. *Please let this work. Please.*

Ronan's nail taps against the glass, condensation sliding down the smooth surface, dripping onto the toes of his boots. The silence between us rings through my ears. Deafening in its emptiness.

His lips twist into a sneer. "You're trying to save the bridge, aren't you?"

Might as well come clean and pray this man has a heart somewhere in that arrogant chest. "Without access to the well, the Unseelie will die."

"So?"

"So, they are people too."

"They're not people. They're monsters. Now, if you'll excuse me, I have somewhere else to be." His shoulder bumps mine on his way past. I should follow him, beg him to reconsider.

All I can do is stand here, fighting for my next breath.

They're all going to die.

I failed them.

This is my fault.

The door opens once more, but I can't even bring myself to turn and see who it is.

A hand slides over my shoulder. "What did he say?" Nia asks.

"He won't help me." No one will. If I'm going to fix this, I'll need to find a way to do it myself.

"What now?"

There's only one thing left to do. "I'm going to the castle anyway."

The public carriage drops me right at the castle gates, where the guards refuse me entry. Their response comes as no surprise. Why would they let a random stranger through? Still, I don't know what else to do so I stand at the gilded gates, staring at the stone castle in the distance, pleading with the fates for an audience.

The sun sinks in the sky, the shadows growing larger, more formidable, yet another barrier to overcome. Then I see a gilded carriage tearing up the lane, drawn by four horses.

The king.

Finally, something today is going right.

Two guards rush to open the gates, while a third keeps track of me. I've had plenty of time to go over what I want to say, how best to appeal to the king. I only have one shot and cannot fail.

The carriage rolls to a stop where I stand, but my hope vanishes the moment the curtain swings aside and I find the queen sitting inside.

"Kerris Dawn. What a surprise. I was under the impression that my son was no longer courting you."

And from the smile in the queen's cool tone, the thought pleases her. Yet another reason to be relieved my dealings with that cad are through. "I'm not here to see Ronan. I would like to see the king."

The queen tugs on her lace gloves, adjusting the hem at her wrist. "My husband is a very busy man. Is there something that I might be able to help you with?"

How can I ask for help when she's the one who wants the bridge closed?

What other choice do I have?

"I heard a rumor about the bridge being closed and am concerned about the wellbeing of the Unseelie across The Divide."

"And what of the wellbeing of those in Rosehill? Or do our lives matter less than theirs?"

"Of course, not—"

"Then you must know that, as Queen of Willowhaven, it is my duty, first and foremost, to protect my people. That bridge has brought nothing but trouble since the day it was built."

"Please. I'm begging you. If access is cut off, you'll be damning them all."

Her smile returns. "Good day, Miss Dawn." She calls to the driver. The whip cracks, and the horses lurch forward, the carriage gliding away on gilded wheels.

I leave without even a spark of hope in my veins.

The bridge has been closed and there's nothing I can do to stop it.

48

"Sometimes there is nowhere to go but down."

— Author Unknown

I don't bother hailing a carriage to bring me back to Nia's, instead using the time it takes to reach her street to compose myself and rack my brain for solutions. I'm empty, completely drained, my steps trudging, my heart floundering.

My aunt and uncle are outside, along with Nia and a few of the neighbors.

Aunt Cordelia must be sick over my disappearance, and now I'm going to have to explain where I've been or come up with some other plausible excuse for going missing. If she learns the truth, she is sure to kick me out.

Nia breaks away from the group, running toward me. It isn't until she's nearly at my side that I see the tears tracking down her ashen face. "Kerris! Oh, thank heavens you're back safe. I've been at my wits' end."

"Why? What's the matter?"

A man steps out from the crowd, his dark curls damp against his brow and eyes red-rimmed. Why is Nolan crying as well?

Heavens, whatever happened must be terrible, indeed.

Nia's hand envelopes mine, her voice breaking. "It's Trevor. He's dead."

He's dead.

He's dead.

He's dead.

No... That cannot be true. "We just spoke to him a few hours ago."

"I know. I know we did—"

Nolan lays a gloved hand on Nia's shoulder, silencing her with a stern look. "Kerris? I need you to come with me."

"Why?"

"The inspector has questions." A muscle in his jaw feathers as he withdraws a pair of silver manacles from his belt. "I do not want to detain you but will if I need to."

Nia shrugs him off, stepping between us, her spine rigid and tone biting. "You must be joking."

"Step aside, Nia. This does not concern you."

"It sure as hell does. She's my cousin, and—"

"And she was the last person to see our friend alive," he grits out, his voice breaking.

"I was there too. Are you going to threaten to detain me as well?"

"You said you left the two of them alone in the cottage."

"Well, yes, but—"

Can't she see? Nolan doesn't want to be here; he's only doing his job. "It's all right, Nia. I didn't do anything wrong, remember? I'll be fine." Perhaps I'll be able to help them find whoever did this. Not that I know where to begin, but if I can assist in any way, I owe it to Trevor to try.

"You're damn right you will, because I'm coming with you to

make sure of it." She links our arms, but from the incredulous look on Nolan's face, it's clear that he isn't going to let that happen.

I pat her hand before prying free. "It's best if I go on my own." The fewer people that know of her involvement, the better.

I promise to be back soon, hoping it isn't a lie.

Although he doesn't chain me up, Nolan and two other guards escort me through the center of town like some sort of criminal. Although the town is mostly empty because of the impending curfew, there are still a few fae leaving the pubs and restaurants. When they see us, they fall silent. By morning I'll be even more of a pariah than before.

We don't stop until we reach Trevor's cottage, where another ten guards scour the dark garden.

Just inside the open door, I can see a body covered by a sheet. *Poor Trevor.* Who would ever want to hurt him? He was a good man. Kind and caring. And now he's gone.

Ronan appears from around the back of the cottage, speaking in low tones with an elderly man sporting a bushy mustache and a silver pin on the lapel of his black coat. When the prince sees me, he says something to the man before stomping toward the gate, his expression darkening like a storm cloud. "What the hell is she doing here?"

Nolan shifts his weight from one foot to the other, his face falling into a grimace. "Kerris was the last person to see the victim alive."

"The *victim?* Are you kidding me? That's our friend Trevor in there, not some nameless, faceless person."

"Ronan—"

The prince holds up a hand, stopping Nolan mid-sentence. "Save it. We both know she didn't kill him, so I'll ask again: Why is she here?"

Kill him? Nolan said they had questions, not that they thought I was responsible. "I would never—"

Ronan clicks his fingers. "Not another word. I will handle this." He stalks back toward the man with the mustache. The two of them exchange tense words with lots of serious glances cast in my direction.

I don't know what they're saying, but from all the frowning, it doesn't look good. Eventually, Ronan and the man shake hands, and he comes back to me. "Leave us."

Nolan and the other guards exchange confused looks.

"I said leave us!"

They scatter, but don't go far, the manacles on their belts jangling as they watch from behind the hedge with the rest of the guards.

Blowing out a breath, Ronan drags his hand through his golden curls. "I'm afraid it's serious, Kerris."

Of course it's bloody serious—our friend is dead. "Could it have been a wolf?" I know Ever said that no wolf crossed The Divide, but perhaps he was wrong and one made it through. Maybe it was in our kingdom all along.

The prince shakes his head. "Unless wolves know how to slit a man's throat, this wasn't a wolf."

The memory of Everett doing just that to the beast that attacked me this morning flashes through my mind. The hot spray of blood. The sightless look in the animal's dead eyes.

And someone did the same thing to poor Trevor. "Who would do such a thing?"

His jaw works as he stares hard at me. "The inspector thinks it was you."

"That is preposterous."

"You were the last person to see him alive."

"That doesn't mean I *killed* him!"

"Keep your voice down," he hisses with a menacing step toward me.

It takes everything in me to stand my ground. Not only has this been the worst day of my life, but also it's been the longest. Tears sting the backs of my eyes. There will be plenty of time for crying when I'm alone.

"I thought a lot about what you said earlier, and I think I've come up with a solution that would give us both what we need."

I'm not sure what Ronan needs right now, but I sure as hell need a solution because I'm all out of answers and fight.

He steps closer, the legs of his trousers brushing my skirts. "If I tell them that you spent the night with me, all of this goes away."

Give us both what we need.

That lie only helps me. "And in return?"

"Your birthday is in a few days, isn't it?"

What does that have to do with anything?

"If you were to propose to me—"

"No. Absolutely not."

"Perhaps you should consider your response before turning down my offer." He leans in to whisper against my ear, "I think it would look very bad if the inspector were to find the dress you left in Trevor's bathing room. You know, the one covered in blood."

Heavens... I did leave behind the dress, didn't I?

A cool sweat breaks across my brow. Leaks down my spine. "It's wolf's blood," I say through trembling lips, realizing this day could, in fact, get even worse.

"Maybe..." He inclines his head toward the man with the badge. "Maybe not."

Only a few hours ago, he wanted nothing to do with me. What changed between now and then? Even if I did propose to him, why would he willingly tie himself to me for all of eternity? It makes no bloomin' sense.

"Why would you help me?"

Malice sparks in his too-blue eyes as his mouth curves into a mocking smile. "Do you know how it feels to be rejected by a woman with *nothing*? The daughter of a fucking *goat* farmer? To have her cast you aside in front of the entire city in favor of a fucking monster?"

He cannot be serious. "This is about your wounded pride?" Does he even care that Trevor was murdered? Is he truly so selfish that he would use his friend's death for his own benefit?

"Do you know what I heard when you left the pub earlier? People were saying that you're the only woman in Rosehill I couldn't have. And despite the way you've treated me, I still want you."

"I'm not going to marry you, Ronan."

"Then by all means, plead your case with the inspector. Maybe he'll believe you about the wolf's blood. Maybe he won't. Or *maybe* he'll think your Unseelie lover killed Trevor in a fit of jealous rage. Who knows." He shrugs as if he doesn't care either way.

I'm willing to take a chance with my own life, but gambling with Ever's is out of the question. "Everett didn't do this." Of that I'm absolutely certain. "There are guards who can attest that he hasn't crossed the bridge."

Ronan bares his teeth in a snarl. "What makes you think they aren't willing to lie?"

He wouldn't do that... He *wouldn't*.

"Marry me or watch your Unseelie swing from the gallows. Those are your options."

He would.

My life in exchange for Ever's.

A simple choice, one I would willingly make time and again if it saved the man I love.

Agreeing to marry Ronan might give me an audience with the king. I could plead with him to keep the bridge open. I would have a voice.

I would have time to figure out how to get out of this.

Ronan sneers, knowing already that he has won.

I came to Rosehill looking for a husband...

And to my misfortune, I have found one.

49

*"Traditional white attire on one's wedding day
symbolizes purity, honor, and truth."*

— A Seelie Guide to Matrimony

By Tuesday evening the curfew has been lifted. An interesting development considering they never caught the wolf that everyone was so worried about. My aunt still won't speak to me, but she has yet to kick me out. Probably because the prince has been calling at the house every day to court me.

And by "court," I mean ensure that I still intend to hold up my end of our bargain.

According to Nia, the guards still patrol the bridge—not that I've seen as much with my own eyes. Every time I've set foot outside the cottage, at least two guards accompany me.

A prelude to my life as Princess of Willowhaven.

At noon on my twenty-fifth birthday, in the middle of the crowded Black Rose pub, I propose to Prince Ronan Reve.

Much to Ivee Lynch's dismay, he accepts.

Ivee isn't the only one shocked.

Nia gawks at me, and when those closest to us have finished offering their congratulations, she drags me into the garden to ask what the hell I'm thinking. I tell her Ronan's fabricated story, that he and I bonded over our shared grief and made amends.

We don't speak at all on Wednesday.

First thing Thursday morning, Ronan sent a carriage to whisk me away to his home in the tree where guards have been posted day and night. He claims it's for my safety, but we both know it's a lie. I'm being held hostage and there's nothing I can do to stop it.

Two days later, I'm sitting on Ronan's plush sofa, all alone, wishing there was some way to escape this nightmare that has become my life.

Knowing the bridge remains open on Wednesdays is the only solace I have. Perhaps one of the Unseelie will take pity on Ever and give him some of their water.

The front door eases open, and my stomach sinks the way it always does when Ronan comes over. He's still living in the castle, but after our wedding, that will change.

Instead of the prince stepping into the room, another familiar figure waits in the doorway. I rub my eyes. Can it really be?

"Father?" I launch off the sofa and race across the room to throw myself into his waiting arms. His embrace feels as safe as I remember, and he still smells like pipe smoke and chilly mountain air. It's a relief to know that some things don't change.

"Goodness, my girl." His chuckle rumbles in his chest. "Here I thought you forgot I existed." He eases me back, his brow furrowing as he studies me through the spectacles perched on the end of his nose.

Just like Trevor.

Perhaps that's why I felt so safe with my friend. Why I liked him so much.

And now he's gone.

"What is this? Why are you crying?" My father's thumbs trace reassuring circles against my shoulders the way they used to when I was small, and my burdens felt too large to carry.

Because the world is falling apart, and I don't know how to fix it. "I just missed you, that's all. What are you doing here?"

"You'll never believe it, but we received an invitation from the queen herself. She sent a carriage to collect us and everything."

"Us?"

"Do I not get a look in?" a deep voice grumbles from the foyer. Either my ears are deceiving me or—

My father steps aside.

"Theo!" My brother is here as well. I let go of Father to hug my brother. If this weren't the worst time of my life, it would be one of the happiest.

Theo lets me go and gestures toward the porch. "Kerris, there's someone I want you to meet."

A pretty young woman with hair the color of aubergines steps into the room, her eyes the most striking shade of aquamarine.

"Kerris, this is my wife, Cora."

Wait just a minute. Did he say this beautiful woman is his *wife?* "Since when did you get married?" He never mentioned a woman in any of his letters.

Theo stuffs his hands into his pockets, a splash of pink spreading across his freckled cheekbones. "Since last week."

"And you didn't think to tell me?" Or, I don't know, invite me to the bloomin' wedding?

Theo shrugs. "I've been a little busy."

Heavens... I never thought I'd see the day my big brother settled down. I take both of Cora's warm hands in mine and return her smile. "It's so lovely to meet the woman who has finally convinced my brother to marry."

"It hardly took any convincing at all." Cora's blush matches my brother's as she shoots him a smile full of secrets.

When they look at each other, their love shines in their eyes. What must it be like to marry the person you love and not be blackmailed into a union?

I twist Ever's ring around my middle finger.

If only I knew.

Theo grins down at me, looking so much like our mother that my chest aches. "I hear congratulations are in order for you as well."

More like commiserations...

My father's calloused hand squeezes my shoulder. "My baby girl is finally getting married."

"And to a prince no less," Theo adds with a wink.

Father's eyes start to glisten as he looks between us, his lips curving into a watery smile. "Your mother would be so proud of you both."

Not if she knew the truth.

Nia and her parents join us for an impromptu celebration of my impending nuptials. Fortunately, my husband-to-be is detained at the castle and cannot join us. Nia scrutinizes me from where she sits on the sofa, her lips pinched as she dips her teaspoon in and out of her teacup. It's as if she can see straight through the lies that I've been telling everyone since I proposed to the prince.

I try to encourage Theo to tell us the story of how he and Cora met. Unfortunately, my family keeps wanting to turn the questions back on me.

"When do we meet the lucky man?" Father asks.

Never, if I have my way. "At the wedding." If they see the two of us together beforehand, they're bound to recognize there's nothing but animosity between us and try to put a stop to this.

There is no stopping my fate.

Theo takes his wife's hand, lacing their fingers together and pressing a tender kiss to her knuckles. "When is that?"

"Wednesday." It's no coincidence that Ronan chose a day the Unseelie will be in Rosehill to conduct the charade. Even though Ever won't be at the well, the news will surely reach him by the time the other Unseelie return to their village.

I must take solace in the fact that the bridge is remaining open —for the time being at least. If I play my part well, perhaps the threat to the Unseelie will vanish altogether.

Father's brow furrows. "So soon?"

I shrug. "That's what happens when you're in love."

A lie has never tasted as bitter.

Nia chokes on her tea. She sets the cup down so hard, it rattles the others. When she shoots to her feet and stomps for the winding staircase, I excuse myself and drift along after her. If she cannot keep her emotions under control, our family is going to grow suspicious.

She comes to a halt in my bedroom. Birdsong drifts through the window, but the joyful song falls flat.

"Nia, please don't be like this." Life is difficult enough right now. I need my best friend by my side if I am to make it through.

She whirls on me, her eyes blazing and fist clenched, ready for a fight. "Don't you dare tell me you love Ronan. We both know that's a load of bollocks."

What can I say? She's right.

"I cannot help you if I do not know what's going on."

That's the problem. "No one can help me."

She takes me by the hand, her expression softening. "What has he done?"

It's all too much, keeping these secrets. Am I to take them to my grave? I can trust Nia—she's been with me from the beginning of this downward spiral. Perhaps I'm being foolish not enlisting her help. Even if we cannot find a way out, at least I'll have a shoulder to cry on. "Ronan found my dress at Trevor's. He threatened to blame me for Trevor's death."

Sinking onto the end of my bed, Nia presses a hand to her forehead, her face milky pale. "Oh, Kerris... What are you going to do?"

"I'm going to marry him."

"You can't."

I can and I will because: "I don't have a choice."

50

Everett

— Everett Gathin, An
Observation

Time passes in a blur—I am not even sure what day it is. All I know is that it is another day wasted without *her*. I have tried to keep myself busy. Having the lads here helps, but the nights stretch on forever, empty and lonely, and there is no hope of it ever getting better.

That is why I have made a very important decision.

Maddox crests the hill, his boots slipping on his way down to where a rare patch of sunlight breaks through the trees. He comes to a stuttering stop, his nose wrinkling as he takes in the state of my trousers. "What are you doing?"

"What does it look like I am doing?" Sometimes Maddox asks the most idiotic questions.

I am kneeling in muck, there is a dagger in my hand, and a dead stag by his boots. Not the kill I had hoped to make this day, but at least we will not starve while I try to collect as many furs as possible.

The Seelie love furs, especially in winter. If I spend every waking moment hunting, I will have enough pelts to pay for a small house across the canyon. Kerris deserves a castle, but if she was willing to stay in my barrel-top, she would not mind some place small until I can afford to give her something larger.

I will resign myself to living the rest of my days being hated in her sun-drenched world if it means I get to share a life with her.

He cards a hand through his hair, his bare chest heaving as if he ran all the way here. "You have not heard?"

Gryffin jogs into view, his feet sure as they eat up the distance between us. "What the hell are you doing?" he bellows.

"He does not know," Maddox throws over his shoulder.

Gryffin skids to a halt next to Maddox, perspiration dripping down his furrowed brow.

Looks like I am the one missing something here. "What do I not know?"

All they do is grimace, which tells me fuck all.

Maddox nudges Gryff with his elbow. "You tell him."

"You are such a fucking coward," Gryff mutters with a roll of his eyes.

"I prefer to give good news instead of bad."

"Will one of you tell me what the fuck you are talking about?" Or else I am going to stab them both with this blade and leave their bodies for the scavengers prowling this forest.

Gryffin blows out a breath. If he is hesitating, it must be very bad, indeed. "Kerris is getting married."

Kerris. Kerris. Kerris.

He says more words, but all I can seem to focus on is the fact that they are speaking about *her*. The two share another look, one that makes my heart stall.

The rest of Gryff's sentence hits me like a hurricane, knocking me back a step.

Kerris is getting married?

It feels like I am being held under water, my next breath nowhere to be found. What did I expect? That she would remain unattached?

I hope she finds happiness. I hope she—

Fuck. No, I do not wish any of those things. I want to drop everything, race across the canyon, and beg for her forgiveness. Explain that I am ready to make the move.

But now it is too late.

She found someone else.

The dagger's hilt bites against my calloused hands. "To whom?"

They trade a look, and my stomach sinks even lower.

This time, it is Maddox who stabs me with his words. "Prince Ronan Reve."

No. No fucking way is Kerris marrying him. Kerris would never tie herself to that arrogant prick. "When is the wedding?"

"Tomorrow."

No. No. *No.* "I need to go to her." I stumble to my feet, the ground like quicksand, threatening to swallow me whole.

They both take a collective step back, their noses wrinkling, but it is Maddox who speaks. "You are covered in blood."

"I do not care." After I speak with her, she will call off their mating just as I did to Leah. Then we can start our lives together.

Gryffin catches my arm in his unforgiving grip. "Take a minute to think this through."

How can I think when my mind is in tatters? I fill my lungs and force out a breath. Two. Three.

They are right. I cannot show up to her home looking like I sleep in the dirt. Her family will never accept me then. "How did you find out?"

Maddox lifts his chin. "I have my ways."

Gryff snorts. "River overheard some Seelie guards talking about it."

"Dammit, Gryffin."

I leave them to their squabbling, running back toward our small camp. When I reach the river, I leap straight in and scrub the blood and dirt from my body and clothes.

Water sloshes as I wade back to shore, goosebumps breaking across my skin. Not from the cold, but from fear. Fear of losing Kerris forever.

Gryffin hands me a towel from the line, and I mutter my thanks as I dry off and stomp into my barrel-top to throw on some clean trousers. When I return, both of my friends are waiting for me.

"What are you going to do?" Maddox asks.

"Stop the wedding." Is that not obvious to him? I am hardly going across the canyon to ask to be added to the list of guests.

"Then what? Are you going to stay there? Because you know she cannot live here."

"I know."

Gryff stands up straighter, his expression growing grimmer as he realizes my meaning. "Maybe..."

"Maybe what?"

"Maybe it is for the best? The prince can give her a good life. A safe life."

If that is what Kerris wants, then I will let her go. But I need to know for certain that what we shared no longer lives in her heart.

I take Nyx to the bridge, but cross on foot. When I reach the other side, four burly men stand guard, swords drawn as if expecting a wolf to emerge from the mist at any moment.

If they are startled to see me, they hide it well. The only movement between us is their hands flying to the hilts of their swords. Not the short daggers usually favored by the men who patrol this territory.

These are weapons of war.

"Turn back," the one in front growls, a head shorter than me but nearly as broad across his shoulders.

"We have orders to slay anyone who crosses," another bellows through whiskers as dark and thick as the west wood.

Slay me, will they? They will have to catch me first—

I hear the telltale creak of someone at my back a split second before a hand clamps on my elbow. Gryffin and Maddox glower at the guards, but after a tense moment, they turn those glowers back on me.

"Getting yourself skewered and tossed into the canyon helps no one," Gryffin says under his breath. Maddox nods his agreement.

They should have stayed away and minded their own business. I cannot fight men on both sides of this fucking bridge.

Although I yank my elbow from his grasp, I turn away from the Seelie guards and stalk back toward the mist.

One way or another, I will make it across this bridge, even if I have to run someone through to do it.

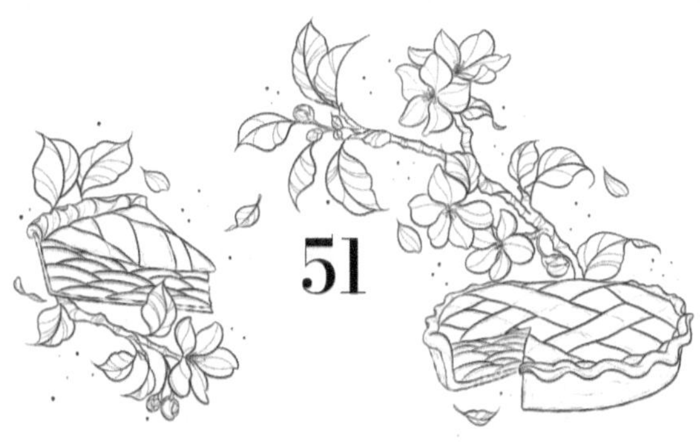

51

"Your wedding will be one of the best days of your life."

— A Seelie Guide to Matrimony

The gown squeezing my waist and hips may be white, but it feels as if it's covered in muck. I didn't buy it, nor did I pick it out. A garment bag had arrived from Madame Ella's yesterday, along with a note from Prince Ronan telling me where and when to meet him for our wedding.

My lace veil conceals the tears in my eyes as my father helps me down the stairs of Ronan's treehouse and into the gilded carriage.

Ronan chose to hold the wedding in the square, claiming that he wants all the people of Rosehill to be present for this farce.

I know the truth: he doesn't give a whit about any of our citizens. He only wants the Unseelie to bear witness to our union, to carry the news of our nuptials back to Ever.

Guards have been posted throughout the crowd and next to

alleys. They wait at each corner of the dais, and more stand guard along the edge of The Divide.

The king's golden throne sitting on the dais looks like the one from the castle. A crown rests on his head, gleaming in the sunlight. Does he know what his son has done?

If only I could have begged for his help before it was too late.

Turning away from the carriage window, I yawn into my fist. The last proper sleep I had was in Ever's bed. The only good thing about him being exiled is that he won't be at the well. Won't have to see me marry this wretched man.

My father adjusts the bow tie at his throat and sweeps a hand through his navy hair. "It's almost time."

The beginning of the end of my life.

"I'm ready." It's a lie but won't be the biggest one I'll make today. I'm about to promise to love and remain faithful to the worst man I've ever known. A man I despise with every fiber of my being.

Father catches the handle and throws the carriage door aside, climbing from within and extending his hand toward me.

My hand slips into his, and I step into the sunlight. My diamond-encrusted slippers meet the regal red carpet that stretches down the aisle between seated guests and enough flowers to fill the royal greenhouse.

Ronan waits upon the dais, a trellis of climbing roses arching high above him. Music from the stringed quartet near the well drifts through the air.

Not even the beauty of the day can hide the ugliness of this lie.

My father lifts my veil, silver tears lining his lashes as he leans forward to press his lips to my cheek. He passes my hand to Ronan, and the two share a smile.

Doesn't he see the hardness in the prince's eyes? The way my future husband's jaw works? Even if he did, what could he possibly do to save me from this fate?

Not a damn thing.

"Good of you to come," Ronan murmurs under his breath when my father leaves us to take his chair next to my brother and his new wife.

"I didn't have a choice."

His teeth flash with his wolfish smile. "No. You didn't."

The priest begins with a long, drawn-out monologue about duty and honor and faithfulness—three things Ronan Reve knows nothing about. The crowd stares on, smiles painted on their faces and their expressions enraptured. The kingdom's lone heir marrying a woman as common as muck. A fairytale in the making.

I can't do this.

I just can't.

Maybe if I make a run for it, I could reach The Divide before anyone catches me.

I'd rather live among the wolves than marry this manipulative wretch.

The music falls silent, and then I hear it.

A high-pitched squeaking. Faint at first, growing louder with each passing second.

The priest must hear it as well, because he glances over his shoulder to where unicorns and riders emerge from between armed guards.

The crowd begins to shift and murmur, glancing at one another before shooting looks of hatred toward the newcomers.

"What the hell are they doing here?" the queen hisses to her husband. The priest's wan smile twists into a grimace.

Ronan's own smile never falters. "Don't fret, Mother. I think it's bloody brilliant that our neighbors from across The Divide have decided to join us on this most wondrous occasion."

Poor Ever is sure to be heartbroken when he hears.

If only he hadn't sent me away...

Ronan's brow furrows as he searches among the Unseelie. "Where is he?"

My heart swells knowing this victory won't be nearly as sweet for him without Ever present. "Are you looking for someone in particular?"

"You know damn well who I'm looking for."

The queen grips the arms of her throne with pale fingers. "Ronan, why are you hesitating? Marry the girl and be done with it."

"Not yet," he snaps.

"Don't speak to your mother like that," the king snaps under his breath.

The murmuring crowd grows louder, and a few folks at the back vacate their seats. For the most part, though, they remain tethered to their chairs, witnessing the events unfolding like the scene of a play.

The queen's expression tightens as she turns to the priest and urges him to continue.

"I said *not yet*," Ronan grits out. "Not until he's here."

The first genuine smile I've had since all this chaos began finds its way to my lips. "He's not coming."

The king glances between us. "Who isn't coming?"

The only man I want to marry. "Why don't you ask your son?"

Ronan's nostrils flare, but he offers no explanation. The priest clears his throat while the crowd's murmuring turns to mutters of discontent.

I might not have found a way out, but at least in this, Ronan will not win—

The Unseelie part, and Ever steps through.

No. NO!

What is he doing here? He's in exile. He shouldn't even be allowed to cross the bridge.

I expect him to storm the dais, but he just stands there, dark eyes drinking me in, hands loose at his sides. Why isn't he drawing his dagger, threatening everyone standing between us? Why isn't he coming for me?

"Everett Gathin," Ronan says in a whisper, his lips twisting, his expression one of sheer delight.

The king's face drains of color as he slowly rises from his throne. "Gathin?" he whispers.

Ronan sneers at the king, a malicious gleam in his eye. "What's wrong, father? Is there something familiar about that name? Perhaps you've heard it somewhere before?"

The king grips the top of his throne, his other hand flying to his trembling lips.

Suddenly, everything clicks into place.

If Ever's mother *was* having an affair with the king, could that mean the king is...

No. Ever's father was an exiled Unseelie, not the king of Willowhaven.

Although now that I see them in the same space, there are some distinct characteristics they both share. The sharp lines of their eyebrows. The shape of their mouths. The proud lift of their shoulders.

If what I'm thinking is true, then this wedding was never about me, nor was it about Ronan's pride.

It was about drawing Ever across The Divide. Ronan never would've been able to do that if I hadn't agreed to this farce.

I was right in thinking that the prince had no desire to marry me.

I was never the prize.

I was the bloody bait.

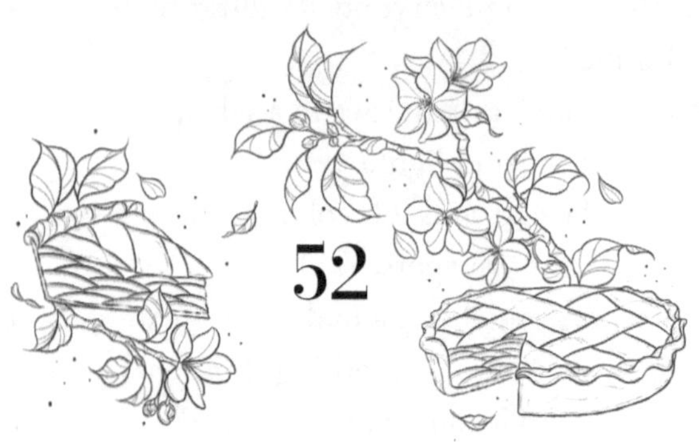

52

"Treachery comes in many forms."

— Author Unknown

With a wave of Ronan's hand, armed guards pour from the alleys, swarming like locusts toward the man I love. Ever does not fight when they take hold of him, nor when they drag him toward the dais.

The rest of the Unseelie remain frozen, their hands clasping their daggers and empty jugs at their backs.

The wedding guests leap to their feet; women and men dressed in finery twist and turn as if trying to find a way out. With the exits all closed off by guards, there is no escape for anyone.

The king looks as if he's seen a ghost, his blanched face devoid of all color.

The longer I stare, the more similarities I see.

Their cheekbones... The shape of their jaws...

Ever's father *is* the bloody King of Willowhaven.

That would make Ever Ronan's half-brother—his *older* half-brother. If I'm right, then Ronan isn't the heir to the kingdom.

Ever is.

Ever can't stay in Rosehill. He needs to get as far from this place as he can. "Run!" I scream.

Our eyes connect, and he must recognize the panic pulsing through me because his heels dig into the cobblestones. The guards holding him falter, trying and failing to drag him closer.

In a blink, Ever is free, but instead of doing as I commanded, he sprints toward the dais.

To save me.

I wave my hands even as I race toward him. "No! Go back to The Divide!"

Ronan lunges only to catch my veil. The comb holding it in place flies out of my hair as I leap to the ground. The rest of the Unseelie unsheathe their weapons, forming a circle to defend themselves against the Seelie guards. A circle that doesn't include the man I love.

I don't care how fearsome they are, they're wearing no armor, and their daggers are a lot shorter than the guards' swords. They're not prepared for this battle.

What am I even thinking? This isn't a battle.

It's a bloomin' ambush.

Screams fill the air as people hunker behind their chairs and run up the street, away from the melee. Footsteps pound an uneven beat behind me, growing closer and closer. Ronan grabs my hair, yanking me back against his chest. His golden blade meets my throat, and I freeze under its sting. I manage to catch a glimpse of the ornate hilt between his clenched fist. There, in between the gemstones, is the unmistakable crimson stain of blood.

Ronan does not hunt, nor does he eat meat.

Why would his dagger be bloody?

Did he cut himself?

Or did he cut someone else?

Ever's gaze locks with mine, and he goes utterly still. Rage burns in his narrowed eyes, his muscles coiling like a cobra prepared to strike. He roars for the rest of the Unseelie to drop their weapons, and although they don't look happy about it, they lower their daggers.

The guards pass all of them, circling Ever instead. They catch his hands and chain them behind his back.

I buck my hips against Ronan's hold, but he only presses the blade deeper into my windpipe. "You're a coward," I wheeze out. "Using me to get to him."

"I am merely a practical man. When I see a problem, I find a solution."

"What do you want?" Clearly, it's not me. What is Ronan's end goal?

"Just wait and see," he breathes against my cheek.

The guards drag Ever to the dais. The queen pushes to her feet, her face a mask of ethereal calm while the king gasps for breath, still clinging to the throne. He unfastens the clasp on his mantle, letting the heavy fur fall to the ground as he fumbles with the buttons on his collar.

Nolan emerges from the crowd, his eyes as cold as death as his voice booms through the square. "Everett Gathin, you are under arrest for the murder of Trevor Dillon."

Ronan finally loosens his hold on me and cleans my blood from his blade against his thigh.

Don't they see? "Ever didn't kill anyone." I whirl to where the king still hasn't said a bloody word. "Please, Your Highness, you must stop this. You know who he is."

The king's jaw drops, beads of sweat dripping down his brow. "I have never met that man before in my life."

"*That man* is your firstborn, heir to the throne of Willowhaven."

Those still within earshot gasp while the Unseelie trade confused glances.

"Lies," the queen seethes, a red flush climbing her jaw.

Even if I'm wrong, at least I've given them pause.

Ever's gaze falls to my neck, and he whips toward Ronan, leveling the prince with a menacing glower. "You are a dead man."

Chuckling, Ronan holds out his hands to where the Unseelie have been cowed and the rest of the crowd is still hiding. "Have you looked around? You're in no position to make idle threats."

Ever's sharp teeth flash. "You will see how idle they are soon enough."

The king swipes a handkerchief across his brow and takes a step forward, still studying Ever. His eyes grow wider with every step. Now that they're standing so close, their kinship is painfully obvious. Even Ronan shares some features with his older brother. I'm a fool for not seeing it sooner. For not asking more questions when Ever showed me his mother's dresses.

The king stands up straighter, his shoulders rigid as he twists back to Ronan. "Son, whatever you've planned, it stops now. Your duty is to honor this kingdom, not to disgrace it."

"You wish to speak of disgrace?" Ronan throws his head back with a barking laugh. "That's fucking rich."

"You will heed my warning. I am your father and your king."

"You are a disappointment, failing time and again to keep your people safe from the monsters that lurk across The Divide. The wolves are back, Father. But you've been too busy hiding in your castle to give a shit." Ronan taps his dagger against his thigh, adjusting his grip on the hilt. "I've never understood why you insisted on keeping the bridge open when such danger lurks just on the other side. But the moment I met *him*," he swings his blade toward Ever, "I *knew*. You kept it open because you were fucking one of them."

The queen looks too calm. Too poised.

The king's eyes bulge as he turns to stare at his wife. "You knew he was going to do this?"

Her chin lifts, and although she doesn't respond, the answer lives in the angry set of her jaw and the rage snapping in her eyes.

A whoop echoes through the square and Maddox charges through the crowd, a blade swinging over his head. The rest of the Unseelie join in the charge, fighting their way through to the dais. Nolan stumbles, and Ever leaps free. The chains on his wrist jangle when he tries to grab me, but Ronan gets to me first.

If only I had some sort of weapon to incapacitate him, some way to break out of his grasp, but I'm as helpless as I was before, only this time, my eyes are open to the truth.

Maddox yanks Ever back, but Ever fights him every step of the way until Gryffin takes him by the other arm and drags him toward the rest of the Unseelie still holding off the guards.

Tears spill down my cheeks as they haul Everett away to safety.

Among the mayhem, a lone guard walks onto the dais and dumps my bloodied dress onto the worn planks. Not just any guard; the one with the mustache that I saw outside of Trevor's cottage on the evening he died.

The cold slap of iron clamps around my wrists. "Kerris Dawn of Gravale, you are under arrest for the murder of Trevor Dillon."

It doesn't matter what happens to me as long as Ever is safe.

Even from this far away, I can see him struggling to get back to me as more guards flood the streets, heading not for Ever, but for me. He lets out an ear-shattering roar that turns my blood to ice.

Ever manages to get free, but it's too late.

The guards have set the bridge on fire.

The Unseelie abandon the fight, their mounts, and their wagons, scrambling to make it back to their side before the bridge falls into the canyon, vanishing into the mist.

I'll never know if he made it or if he fell into the abyss.

The king crumples to the ground, clawing at his throat, his face the shade of a ripe blueberry. Foam bubbles from his white lips as his eyes turn hazy.

The queen kneels beside her husband, taking his hands away from his throat. I expect tears or words of sadness, but she does not cry. She leans close and whispers, "You unfaithful wretch. Of course I knew. You built her a fucking bridge." She lets his hand drop to the dais. On his wrist he bears two crescent scars.

Unseelie mating bonds.

The queen removes his crown and stands. "King Bandon Reve is dead. Long live King Ronan."

Ronan inclines his head so the queen can replace his crown with the king's.

The handful of people still in the square sob and wail as they slowly bow for their new king, none the wiser to the treachery that has taken place.

Ronan smiles at me, his too-white teeth gleaming in the waning sun. "I always get what I want."

53
Everett

"Strength lies on the path to forgiveness."

— Author Unknown

N^{o...}

NO!

No matter how I fight, Maddox and Gryffin refuse to ease their grips on my arms, dragging me farther and farther from Kerris as the crackle of flames feasting on our bridge roars in my ears.

"Let me go, dammit!" When our boots meet solid ground, I finally wrench free. They block the path back to her, an impenetrable wall of muscle and flame as the rest of the Unseelie stumble for safety.

"What were you thinking? I could have saved her."

"Are you fucking serious?" Gryffin waves his arms over his head, his jaw set. "We were outnumbered ten to one. You are no good to Kerris Dawn if you are dead."

That may be true but, in this moment, I am no good to her alive, either. Not with flames engulfing the bridge, burning away the only way to reach the woman I love.

"They arrested her!" I can hardly bear to think about the consequences of her actions. How she defied the prince. There had been murder in his eyes, and without me there to suffer his wrath, he will turn that rage on her.

"Better her than you," says Maddox, withdrawing something from his pocket. A key. Where did he get it?

"Kerris Dawn is Seelie," he goes on. "Whatever crime they charge her with will be a slap on the wrist. She will be back at her house by nightfall." He motions for me to hold out my bound hands and unlocks the manacles at my wrists.

I hope he is right. *Please*, let him be right.

"If they would have taken you, you would not have even seen a fucking trial," Gryff adds, watching the flames with the rest of our people, each one wearing the same grim expression.

The bridge connecting our worlds still glows where it clings to the edge of the canyon, the planks falling one by one as the flames eat at the ropes holding them together. The wagons and mounts remain on the other side, along with all of our empty jugs.

Not only have I damned myself, but also I have damned everyone else as well.

Since we were children, we were taught that no good could possibly come from seeking the affections of a Seelie fae. Yet I chased one anyway.

I hunted her down and asked for things that I had no right to take. Her time. Her affection. Her heart.

There is no telling what the prince will do to her now, and she has no one to protect her.

I stay by the canyon until there is nothing but ash falling into the void, empty and without hope. A light rain begins to fall, extinguishing the few flickering flames that remain. For the first time in my life, I feel the cold. Its bitterness burrows deep into my bones, into my marrow, and not even the fire Gryffin has built back at our camp can stave its chill.

I have failed the woman I love.

I have failed the people who raised me.

I have failed myself.

Gryffin urges me to take the stone between himself and Maddox. Instead, I drift toward my barrel-top, unable to look at those flickers of orange and red without seeing the bridge being consumed.

"Everett Gathin," a gravelly voice calls from the clearing's edge, a voice I know all too well. One that has saved me and damned me.

Our chieftain waits by the trees, the mammoth trunks dwarfing one of the tallest males in our clan. With my shoulders high, I march toward my fate. Instead of anger twisting his features, he remains carefully neutral, almost impassive, as if he spent the last few hours lounging in his carriage instead of watching our hope of survival vanish into ash and smoke.

I come to a stop just out of reach, realizing belatedly that Gryffin and Maddox have joined me, halting a few steps back, blades in hands and scowls on faces. It is strange to see Maddox doing anything but smile.

The chieftain spares them no more than a glance, a flicker of something crossing his features before settling into indifference. "Is what they say true? Are you the son of the Seelie king?"

My father had accused my mother of being unfaithful during one of his many tirades. I had never believed her capable of such deception.

Until I stumbled upon the small trunk tucked beneath the bed.

I still remember the first time I dared to open it. What I found within made no sense.

Dresses, brightly colored and finer than anything I had ever seen. At the time, I knew little of wealth, but it was clear from the silken fabric to the golden thread that those gowns had cost a small fortune. There was no way my father would have had the means to purchase them, let alone the opportunity.

Never had I considered that the person who gave her those dresses could be the King of Willowhaven.

"I believe there could be some truth to the accusation, yes."

His dark brows jump up his forehead, and he drags a thick hand down the sharp line of his jaw. "Did you know?"

"I suspected that my mother might have had an affair with a Seelie nobleman but did not know that he was the king."

Although I do not turn around, I can feel the lads' eyes boring into the back of my skull. No doubt they are wondering why I never disclosed my suspicions. In truth, the story was not mine to tell, but my mother's.

One she had taken to her grave.

It was not my responsibility to resurrect such things.

The chieftain's low curse hangs in the mist between us. "That makes you the heir to the throne of Willowhaven."

"I am heir to nothing."

Slowly, he closes the gap between us, his eyes beseeching as he lays a heavy hand atop my shoulder. "Do you not see, Everett? You can help our people."

"Only a few days ago, you said I was a disgrace to our kind." I do not wish them ill, but none of those in the camp stood up for me when I was faced with exile. They have known me since I was a child, watched me grow up, helped mold me into the male I have become, and like the flick of a switchblade, they abandoned me without remorse.

The chieftain's hand falls to his side, his jaw flexing as he considers his words. "For that I am sorry. I judged you in anger and blamed you for my daughter's misery. You did not deserve exile for being truthful about your feelings."

No, I did not. If Leah had been anyone else, I would have received a month's shunning and nothing more. Instead, he handed me a death sentence.

I give him a brusque nod.

"If you claim your birthright," he says, "you can give us access to the well."

If the birthright is even mine.

Who is to say for certain? And even if I were the king's heir, there is one tiny fact that negates all of it. "There is no more bridge." The link between my world and hers has been irrevocably broken. All that remains is smoke and memories.

A slow smile spreads across the chieftain's face as his head swings toward the tree, his dark eyes alight with something akin to hope. "Then we shall build a new one."

54

"I am not afraid."

— Kerris Dawn,
A Lie

The only thing more fake than my wedding five days ago is today's trial. The judge doesn't consider any of my perfectly logical arguments nor the timeline I presented. My words have fallen on deaf ears ever since the blasted inspector handed over my blood-drenched gown. Worse still was the fact that they found a vial of deadly nightshade in the pocket.

The exact poison used to kill King Bandon.

Did I forget to mention that they pinned that crime on me too? There were witnesses who saw me at the castle gates, distressed and begging to see the king. None of them could say whether or not I made it inside, but what other reason would I have to request an audience if I wasn't there to assassinate him?

I face my jury with my head high, Ronan and the queen

watching from the balcony, their expressions giving none of their treachery away. Would this have happened if I had never crossed The Divide? Never pursued Ever? Had any of the romantic words Ronan once spoke to me been real? Had he ever truly aspired to share his life with me?

Had he cared for me at all?

It takes all of twenty minutes of deliberation for the judge to hand down a guilty verdict.

My sentence: Death by hanging.

My father sobs so loudly that his wails can probably be heard on the mountains of Gravale. What I wouldn't give to be back there now, among the goats and peaks, all thoughts of husbands and betrayal eclipsed by burbling streams and trees to be climbed.

"They're wrong. They must be wrong. My daughter would never kill anyone." Father's voice cracks as Theo leads him out of the courtroom. My brother casts me a sorrowful look from over his slumped shoulder. They both came to see me this morning, hoping for a proper resolution, believing that an innocent woman would never be put to death for such heinous crimes she did not commit.

I knew that this battle was lost before I stepped onto that platform. With Ronan on the throne and his wicked mother at the helm, there is nothing but darkness ahead.

I chose my side in this fight, and unfortunately, it wasn't the winning one.

I'm brought back to the prison cell where I spent the last few days awaiting trial. The cell isn't what I imagined it would be, with its fine mattress and single bedside table. There's even a private privy. The view of the city far below is peaceful, serene, and Nolan has ensured that the guards on duty keep me well fed. He even stopped by with some of the tarts I liked from one of the cafés in the city.

I'm not under any illusions that he's doing this for me.

Ever since my arrest, Nolan has been trying his best to get back into Nia's good graces, but she is still giving him the cold shoulder.

Nolan is only doing his job. There's no telling what his fate would have been if he'd defied Ronan. For all we know, he might've ended up standing next to me in that court today.

A kind-faced young man with peach-fuzz dusting his jaw trudges into view, torchlight flickering off his black leather armor. He looks at me in stolen glances, his cheeks coloring with splotches of pink every time I catch him. "You have a visitor," he says, fumbling for the keys at his belt.

Nia steps into view and slips through the door, her head bowed and eyes red from tears. The door closes quietly behind her, but the sound of the key in the lock cuts through the silence.

My cousin and I stare at each other, her gaze scanning as if searching for any signs of mistreatment. If not for the bars and guards, this place could be mistaken for an inn.

"I'd offer you tea, but I'm afraid all I have is water and a stale scone." They delivered my breakfast hours ago, when the sun was barely kissing the horizon. I was too nervous for my trial to eat. Now that my fate has been marked, I'm too despondent.

Nia's lips pinch, her curls swinging as she steps forward. "How can you make a joke at a time like this?"

Because come tomorrow, there will be no time for jokes.

There will be no time for anything.

When she pushes back her cloak, I notice she's strangling a book. "What have you brought?"

She captures my hand, leading me to the bed where she sinks onto the mattress. I fall down beside her, waiting as she sets the tome on top of the blanket and flips through the pages to one marked with a strip of ribbon.

"I went to the library," she says, pressing a finger to one of the lines midway down the page. "Read this."

The section in question speaks to the succession of the throne of Willowhaven. Apparently, if Ronan and his mother were to both fall, the crown would pass to the eldest male cousin. If there are no cousins, then the high chancellor—the king's head advisor—would be crowned king and his line would continue to hold the throne until such a time that there are no heirs, and the same thing would happen.

All very interesting, but hardly helpful at present. "I don't understand."

She closes the book with a huff, clutching the worn leather to her chest. "We have scoured every book in the library on the subject and there is nothing that states the King or Queen of Willowhaven must be Seelie. If Everett can prove that his father was King Bandon, then he would be the rightful heir to the throne."

And as king, he could rebuild the bridge. "Nia, this is excellent work."

"I can't take all the credit. Your brother and his wife have been neck-deep in research since Nolan took you away."

"He didn't have a choice," I remind her.

Her eyes harden even as her hands flex around the cover. "He *did* have a choice. He could've stopped working for Ronan the moment he found out the prince was a corrupt piece of shite, but he chose to bite his tongue. It's disgraceful and I shall never forgive him."

"Never is a long time to hold on to your anger." And my cousin is too full of life, too full of joy to lose that spark. "Don't forgive him for his sake; forgive him for yours."

Her curls spill over her wool-clad shoulder when her head tilts. "When did you become so philosophical?"

"Since I found out I'm to be executed tomorrow at dawn."

The book clatters to the bed, falling open to a page of the royal family tree.

How fitting.

"They cannot do that, not before Theo has filed your appeal. I won't let them."

Theo won't have time for his appeal, and Nia cannot do anything about it.

No one can.

I've made my peace with what's to come—at least I've tried to. "Will you do me one favor though? Will you promise me that you will find a way to get this book to Ever? Willowhaven deserves better than that heartless wretch Ronan as its king."

The glassiness in Nia's eyes spills down her cheeks when she nods. "This isn't the last time we'll see each other."

It's not. But tomorrow will be a day of mourning. Tomorrow I won't get to tell her these words.

I fold my arms around my cousin, her snowy curls tickling my nose as I press my face into her jasmine-scented hair. "I love you, Nia."

With the book pressed between us, she wraps one arm around my back, her body trembling with emotion. "I love you, Kerris."

The guard returns, his expression giving nothing away as he unlocks the door to let Nia out.

Her sobs haunt the stone hallway on the long, narrow walk toward the prison's exit.

Choking back tears of my own, I turn toward the rays of sunlight streaming through the bars and peer toward The Divide, wishing I could see my love one last time.

The gallows have been erected where only a handful of days ago I stood in a white dress, expecting to marry a prince. My wedding gown has been replaced by a fitted gray muslin so long it sweeps the cobblestones as I trudge toward the raised platform, escorted not by my father but by four armed guards.

This crowd is even larger than the one that came to watch the wedding, which says so much about the true state of this city. For all its sunshine and blooms, there is still too much darkness.

I climb the stairs. One. Two. Three. Standing face-to-face with a man as tall as he is wide wearing a black mask over his face, my heart beats firmly in my chest.

"Kerris Dawn, you have been sentenced to death for the murder of our great king, Bandon Reve, and Master Trevor Dillon. Do you have any last words?"

Only this morning, I had so many things to say. But now, all I can think about is how poorly these small-minded people have treated their neighbors. They deserve to know the truth about their leader, to be given a chance to decide for themselves.

I straighten my spine, throw back my shoulders, and say as loudly as I can, "Ronan Reve isn't the rightful heir to the throne. Everett Gathin is."

Ronan's face turns as red as a robin's breast, the vein in his forehead thumping as he glowers from his throne. Beside him, his mother smirks, ever the cold, calculating queen.

The masked man drags me by the chains still binding my wrists, forcing me to climb atop a rickety stool as he fits the length of coarse rope around my neck and tightens the noose at my nape.

I'm not scared.

I'm not scared.

I'm not scared.

I take my last breath.

I'm not scared.

I'm not scared.

My eyes fall closed.

A low rumble sounds in the distance. A swarm of tiny birds lift into the cloudless sky on colorful wings, a glorious farewell.

The guards posted at the edge of the crowd take off toward The Divide, to where dust swirls like a cyclone.

Everett Gathin emerges from the muddy cloud, dagger drawn and his long legs eating up the distance.

My heart soars as I gasp, and—

The stool is kicked from beneath me.

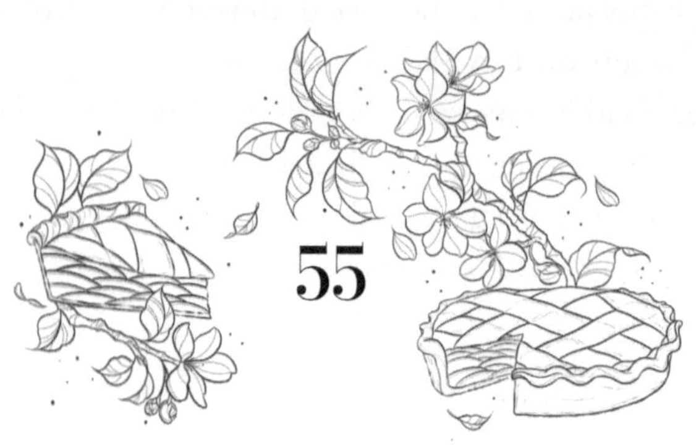

55

— Author Unknown

I hear him over everything else, the screams and cries, the slap of boots on cobblestones and clang of clashing metal. Ever shouting my name is the only sound in this world that can pry open my lids as consciousness fades. Amidst the black spots that speckle my vision, I see him sprinting toward me. Arms and legs pumping, fear wild in his midnight eyes.

As fast as he is, he won't be fast enough to save me.

My heart begins to slow, my throat straining against the rope cutting below my jaw.

My feet kick but there's nothing except air beneath me.

Blackness swells, swarming until all I see is a pinprick of light and the panicked face of the man I love.

Something brushes my legs. Squeezes and lifts. The pressure on my throat eases. Through the haze I find Nolan gripping my legs, holding me up as I gasp, filling my lungs with sweet air. The other guards watching the dais don't seem to know what to do. Their heads swing from their new king, to me, to the onslaught of Unseelie fae emerging from the settling dust.

Ronan launches to his feet, bellowing for the men to kill the Unseelie warriors.

There must be *hundreds*.

Everett's village had seemed so small. Where did they all come from?

One man towers over the rest, leading the charge, shouting orders of his own in a language I've never heard before.

Ever moves like lightning, and when I open my eyes again, he's here, his bone-handled dagger slicing through the rope still holding me aloft. Nolan stumbles under my weight, but Ever catches me, cradling my trembling form in arms as steady as the ground beneath us.

Carefully, he cuts away the length of rope, tossing it aside with a growl. "Kerris?" he breathes, his dark eyes desolate and his calloused hands cupping my cheeks. "Speak to me."

"You came for me." The words break from my lips, jagged and hoarse. This man found a way to traverse the treacherous Divide without a bridge.

He *made* one.

His lips twitch, followed by a flash of sharp white teeth. "Always."

"Guards!" Ronan roars, desperation in his demand. His plans are falling apart around him and there's no telling what he'll do to try and keep things together.

There's been too much death already.

Why can't he see that he's been beaten—

A haunting howl lances through the melee and the whole world stills. Men with swords raised, fae running for cover—it's as if time itself stops.

There, on the far side of the square stands a red-eyed wolf with a string of drool clinging to its gaping maw. Its head reaches nearly to the top of the fountain, as tall as the unicorns the Unseelie usually ride.

The terrifying beast isn't alone.

Four more wolves emerge from the alley, their sharp teeth painted red.

The closest one lunges for a Seelie guard, its teeth closing around the man's arm. The guard lets out a terrifying scream as he's dragged away and his cries for help fall silent.

The other guards tremble in their armor, their swords swaying like branches in a breeze.

All this time, I thought the threat wasn't real.

And all this time, the wolves must have been lying in wait...on *our side* of The Divide.

The Unseelie leader shouts, and the Unseelie fae shove past the guards, creating a perimeter around their Seelie neighbors.

Ever flips his dagger and extends the hilt toward me.

"Don't go," I beg, clinging to his arm.

Ever presses his dagger into my hand, forcing me to take it. "You remember how to use this, yes?"

Don't go. Don't go. Don't go. "Y-yes. But—"

"Listen to me, Kerris." He cups my face with steady hands. "I once said that you were soft, but I was wrong. You have the fiercest heart that I have ever known."

He's wrong. I'm not fierce. I'm terrified.

Nia's scream cuts through me like a scythe. She and her mother huddle under chairs as the wolves stalk around the crowd, selecting their next victims.

The dagger's hilt bites into my palm as my fingers tighten.

You have the fiercest heart that I have ever known.

Ever wouldn't lie to me. Not about something like this.

I might be afraid, but that doesn't mean I cannot be fierce as well.

Today, I looked death in the eye and emerged the victor. I did not survive execution to lose those I love to some bloody wolves.

Ever's hands fall away. "Keep your grip tight and always go for the kill."

The kill.

The kill.

The kill.

He presses a kiss to my forehead with a whispered, "I love you."

Before I have a chance to return the sentiment, he's slipping away, running toward where Maddox and Gryffin wait with steady swords and matching grins. Gryffin tosses Ever one of the two blades he carries.

Ever shouts and his friends launch forward, swords raised and a battle cry tearing from their throats. The wolves attack with ferocity, snapping out with teeth and claws, but they're no match for the Unseelie. The warriors move in tandem, almost graceful, like they're in a complicated dance. They slice with precision, cutting down the first wolf before attacking the next.

The second beast falls to the sounds of cheering fae.

The Seelie guards recover, surrounding the third wolf while Ever starts for the final beast still circling the crowd.

Crimson paints the cobbles, running in rivulets between the stones.

A woman's screams tear through the square as the queen is ripped from between two fallen guards. She goes down in a flurry of satin and blood while Ronan clutches his bejeweled dagger beneath the throne where he hides.

The queen's cries fall silent, followed by the sickening crunch of bones and the spray of scarlet across the wood and stones. Seelie guards try to save her, but they're no match for this wolf.

Then its head swings toward where Nia clings to her mother.

Go for the kill.

Stumbling to my feet, I race toward the wolf.

The last beast I met got the better of me, but I vow to the chaos that this one will not. I will do whatever is necessary to save my family.

Ever's words from when we sat by that peaceful fire all those nights ago drift on a coppery breeze.

Keep your grip firm.

You can swipe across the throat.

Stab the eye and strike the brain.

Angle the blade upwards to avoid the ribcage and strike the heart.

The wolf is so focused on Nia that it doesn't seem to notice me sprinting right for it. Not until it's too late. The wolf's head turns, but I'm already guiding my blade into its eye. The wolf snarls and whimpers, its hind legs knocking chairs aside as it stumbles back. An Unseelie fae leaps onto its back and drives his blade into the side of the wolf's neck.

Maddox.

Blood sprays like rain, painting Nia and my aunt in gore.

My aunt collapses to the ground in a heap while Nia trembles, staring slack-jawed at the fallen beast, her face as white as her hair beneath the blood.

It's too soon to celebrate victory. Not when we don't know if more wolves stalk these streets. "Get under the dais. Hurry!"

Together, Nia and Maddox drag her mother's limp body toward the wooden platform where my father, Theo, and Cora crouch. I motion for those closest to follow, keeping my grip firm on my dagger as I scan for more beasts.

Ever appears through the mayhem, blood splattered across his bare green chest and a smile on his face as he runs toward me. My dagger clatters to the cobbles, and I throw myself into his embrace.

With his strong arms banding around me, I let myself break. "I did it. I stabbed the wolf." My blow might not have killed the beast, but it certainly slowed the monster down.

"My brave Seelie fae. I am so proud of you." His sharp intake of breath hisses against my temple. When I draw away, I find him wincing. Before I can ask what's wrong, I see the gash in his side.

One of the wolves must've gotten him.

"Water..." Ever needs water. Carefully, I lift his arm over my shoulder and help him shuffle toward the well, only to find Ronan and a handful of guards blocking the path.

This must be some sort of sick joke. "Get out of the way, Ronan."

"It's not Wednesday," our new king snarls, dragging a hand beneath his red-rimmed eyes. "The treaty expressly forbids any Unseelie from accessing the well on any day but Wednesday."

He cannot be serious. "They saved us."

"They *failed*. The wolves killed my mother and countless others. They will never drink from the well again."

Can't he see this isn't time for an argument? There are too many wounded fae. Too many barely clinging to life. The Unseelie didn't have to help, but they did anyway.

Clearly, there is no reasoning with this man. "As a Seelie fae, it is my right to access the well."

"You are a traitor and a murderer. Guards! Arrest this woman!"

Nia stands next to me, her face smeared with dirt, blood, and tears. Behind her, Maddox clutches his bleeding arm. "I am a citizen of Rosehill, and I demand access to the well."

"I demand access to the well," my father's voice booms as he sidles up behind us.

Followed by another fae I've never seen before. And another. And another.

The guards exchange wide-eyed glances before the one at the front steps forward. "Sire, don't you think—"

"Hold your post, General, or you will be branded a traitor and relieved of duty."

A woman appears from what remains of the crowd, one I recognize from Trevor's favorite café. In her trembling hands, she holds a cup of water. "From my bakery," she says, extending the glass toward Ever.

Slowly, he reaches for the water, as if worried he'll scare her away. "Thank you for your kindness," he says, taking the cup and drinking his fill.

She offers him the smallest smile, then pushes her way through the people, back into the café.

A man and woman emerge from a building in the square clutching canning jars filled to the brim with water. They come to a halt in front of us, offering one to me and one to Maddox. I use one to wash and clean the wound at Ever's side. Worry doesn't lessen its grip on my chest until the gash starts to knit back together.

More Seelie race into buildings, emerging with glasses and mugs and pitchers of water from their taps. Water they offer to the wounded Unseelie fae.

Ronan calls us traitors, threatening all manner of punishment.

No one pays him any heed.

Gryffin stomps toward the well, scowling at the guard who tries to stop him. The man must realize the threat because he quickly steps aside. Once his flask is full, Gryffin goes to where Ivee whimpers, her right leg drenched in blood. She snatches the flask without so much as a word of thanks, dumping its contents onto her tights.

"*You*," Ronan snarls, hatred bleeding from his hardened blue eyes as he glowers at me.

Nolan limps over to his friend, his eyes narrowed. "Kerris didn't kill Trevor Dillon. Ronan did."

Nia's hands fly to her pale cheeks, but I'm too stunned to move. To breathe.

How could the prince do such a thing to his own friend?

Ronan turns his scowl on his former guard, the veins in his neck bulging with rage. "What the hell do you think you're doing?"

"What I should have done the moment I realized what a twisted bastard you were."

The general's head swivels between Ronan and Nolan. The guards who aren't nursing their wounds stalk forward, not to Ronan's defense, but to Nolan's.

"King Ronan ordered us to kill any Unseelie fae who crossed the bridge," a guard with a bushy beard announces.

"Lies!" Ronan spits, his backside ramming into the well as he tries to back away from their accusations.

"King Ronan went to the victim's house on the night of his death," another chimes in.

Where were all these cowards when I was being faced with charges of murder? How could they let me die for the prince's crimes?

"Who are you going to believe?" Ronan warbles. "These traitors or your king?"

The crowd presses in on all sides; the blinders they've been wearing have fallen away. The Unseelie aren't the monsters they feared. The true monster has been hiding in Castle Rose all along.

Ronan's cornflower eyes find mine once more, narrowing into slits. He tears the sword from the general's grip and lunges for me.

Trips.

And lands on the blade.

A pitiful gurgle falls from his lips, blood gushing out in a macabre pool.

The guards step back to keep the king's blood from staining their black boots.

King Ronan Reve dies at our feet, a sword protruding from his back and Ivee's screams tearing through the blood-drenched air.

He deserves this, I remind myself even as tears prick the backs of my eyes. He came to this square today to watch me die. So I swipe the tears from my eyes and turn my back on him the same way he turned his back on me.

Ever watches with a solemn expression on his handsome face. When he opens his arms, I fall into them, and the world in chaos falls quiet as I listen to the steady beat of his heart beneath my ear.

The bodies of those lost are covered and left for the mortician to collect while the rest of the fae watch in stunned silence as the Unseelie drag the wolves' carcasses back toward their makeshift bridge.

With his arms still tight around me, Ever orders the Unseelie to follow the wolves' tracks to make sure no more haunt our city and to find out how they reached Rosehill in the first place.

The temple doors swing wide on groaning hinges. A bearded man in red robes emerges, walking through the macabre scene as if it doesn't exist. How many other fae were hiding in their homes, watching their neighbors be slaughtered?

When he reaches us, he comes to a halt. "Are you Everett Gathin?"

Ever nods. "I am."

"Are the rumors true? Are you King Bandon's eldest son?"

"He is," Nolan announces, joining the robed man. "There are letters from Everett's mother to the king among the queen's private correspondence. They were intercepted before the king could read them."

Madame Ella steps out from the crowd, her emerald gown as pristine as ever. "I can confirm that the king commissioned dresses for his mistress, Willow Gathin."

All this time, she knew the woman's name and never mentioned it. When our eyes meet across the crowd, she shrugs.

The bearded man turns back to where we wait, his expression giving nothing away. "Do you have anything to verify these claims?"

From his back pocket, Ever withdraws a letter, one bearing the king's wax seal.

I'm not sure what the letter says, but it must be proof enough because the man nods and then collects Ronan's crown from where it lay on the cobbles.

His voice booms across the square, clear and strong. "Let it be known far and wide that King Bandon's son Everett Gathin is now the King of Willowhaven."

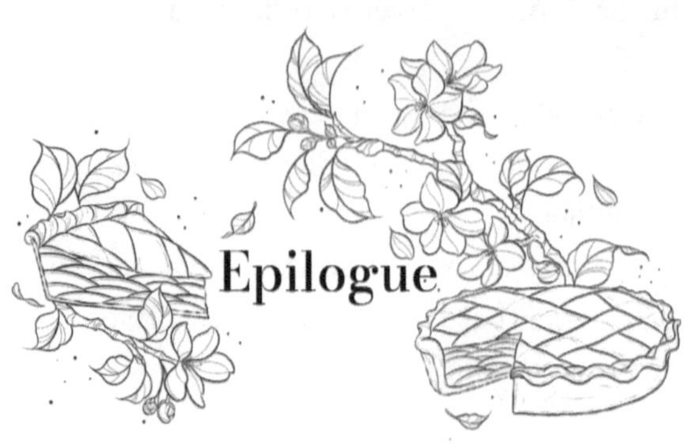

Epilogue

Light seeps through the drawn curtains, marking the beginning of another gorgeous day. Ever's soft breaths tickle my cheek as I count the flowers painted on the ceiling of my husband's barrel-top.

It took a few days, but the Unseelie hunting party found the wolves' den and where they climbed from within the canyon to plunder the countryside. Turned out, the wolves didn't cross the bridge after all. Which was a relief because the people of Rosehill needed to trust the Unseelie fae in order for the council to accept one of them as their new leader.

On the twelfth of June, the Kingdom of Willowhaven appointed their first Unseelie King.

Some of the Seelie fae have yet to acknowledge his rule but most are happy enough to give him a chance, especially seeing as he is half Seelie.

So much has changed.

The well is now open to every fae, no matter the day of the week or which side of The Divide they hail from. The citizens of

Rosehill no longer shutter their windows and lock their doors on Wednesdays.

Ever was expected to move into the castle straightaway, but after two sleepless nights, he decided the rambling towers were too large and open, so he brought his home into the castle gardens.

Every night, we fall asleep tangled in each other's arms, with the sweet scent of spring drifting through the lace curtains.

"We really should get up," I say even as I burrow deeper beneath the covers.

"We really should stay here," Ever murmurs against my collarbone as his fingers trace the fresh teeth marks he left on my hip last night.

"But there is much to do." Treaties to sign. Egos to soothe. Bridges to rebuild.

"Everything else can wait."

Eventually, we make our way out into the bright summer's day. Nyx stomps his hoof in greeting before going back to his feast of grass near the pond. There is so much land for grazing, the unicorn doesn't know what to do with himself. I swear he prances everywhere he goes.

Maddox waves from his own wagon, his pet goat trotting along behind him. When the pair first found each other, I was so distraught that Maddox would eat the little fellow. Turns out, Maddox has never eaten a goat in his life.

"Hello, my queen," he says with a smile as bright as the sun high above. "Tell me, is your cousin by chance visiting the castle today?"

The poor man makes no attempt to hide his affection for Nia. I've tried telling him it's a hopeless endeavor since she and Nolan are trying to rebuild their broken relationship, but he only smiles and says he is a patient male. When I say she'll be arriving after lunch, Maddox practically skips down the marble hallway ahead of us.

Ever stops on the stoop, frowning down at the marble tiles. "Tell me I can do this."

I lace our hands together. "You are a fearsome male. You can do anything."

He turns and takes me into his arms, my favorite place to be. His forehead drops to mine and he whispers, "I love you, Kerris Gathin."

"I love you, Everett Gathin," I whisper back, a smile on my lips and happiness in my heart.

I came to Rosehill for a husband, and to my great fortune, have found one.

Castle Rose
Madame
Salo
The Black Rose
Ronan's Summer
House
Well of Life
Cafe Row
Library
Quill Cottage

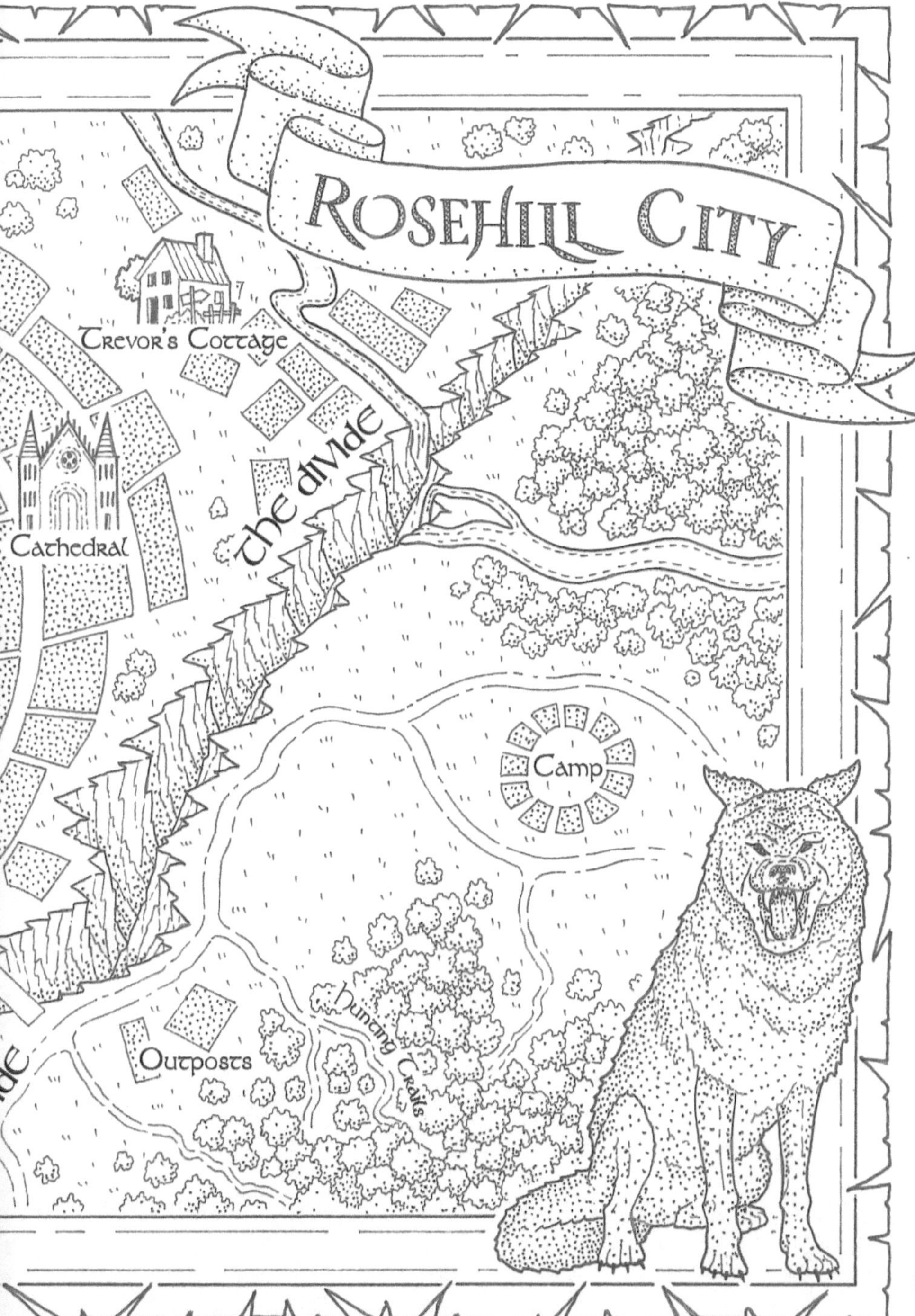

Rosehill City
Trevor's Cottage
the divide
Cathedral
Camp
Outposts
Hunang Trails

Also by Jenny Hickman

BOUND AND FREED

(*Adult Fantasy Romance*)

Bound by Gravity

Freed from Gravity

THE MYTHS OF AIRREN

(*Adult Fantasy Romance*)

A Cursed Kiss

A Cursed Heart

A Cursed Love

Prince of Seduction

Prince of Deception

WILLOWHAVEN ROMANCE

(*Cozy Fantasy Romance*)

For Ever

THE PAN TRILOGY

(*YA Sci-Fi Romance with a Peter Pan Twist*)

The PAN

The HOOK
The CROC

CONTEMPORARY ROMANCE

(Co-written with Natalie Murray)

STILL SPRINGS

Hating the Best Man

Loving the Worst Man

INNER SHORES

Coming Soon